RISE OF THE CAFE RACER
The Realm: Book One

Deano Jones

┌───┐
│  **A gift for you**   │
│   │
│ Merry reading! From Birthgiver   │
└───┘

amazon Gift Receipt

 ## Send a Thank You Note
You can learn more about your gift or start a return here too.

Scan using the Amazon app or visit
https://a.co/d/hmD16Y0

Rise of the Cafe Racer: The Realm - Book One
Order ID: 114-5503116-4970621   Ordered on December 19, 2022

FOREWORD

This book has been created through a series of events, of which a book was the last to arrive.

I never would have imagined that such a detailed world would emerge when I began working on this story, and I have to say that this is easily my proudest creation—combining my music, artwork and storytelling all in one place.

Rise of the Cafe Racer started in Spring 2012, when I was cast in an improvised rock opera at the Hideout Theatre here in Austin, Texas. I was so excited to be a part of the show that I wrote and recorded a theme song for it within days of being cast. Unfortunately though, a few weeks into rehearsals I had so much work come in with my design business that I had to bow out of the musical.

A few months later, after my work had evened out, a friend of mine chatted with me about that theme song. It was Mr. Tom Booker, an owner and teacher at the Institution Theater here in Austin. He just randomly mentioned how much he liked that song I had written and asked if I had ever thought of writing a whole musical. I told him how sad I still was that I didn't get to be in that improvised musical, and that I had always wanted to write a rock musical. Tom's reply: "So why don't you just do it? I bet it would be incredible!"

I guess sometimes we just need to be told that we can do anything we want. It was so empowering to have Tom say that... that I did. I took his advice and I just started writing and recording a rock musical. I didn't have a story fleshed out but knew I wanted something with motorcycles. I had just recently overhauled my old 1980 Honda CB650, had it blacked out and the bars lowered—so Cafe Racers were on my mind.

By the end of the summer I had 12 songs finished and had begun thinking about a staged musical. I was going to use a live rock band in the theater and had decided that I wanted the story to take place in the future with Vampires. I know, Vampires were a bit trendy, but my motivation was mostly what they would look like on stage. I wanted to have the set really dark, with the whole show happening at night with a crazy Victorian era-meets-future-punk wardrobe for the cast. A very gothic, motorcycle rock musical.

As I began outlining the play, I realized I had an incredible amount of information about these characters and their world. I didn't know how I could create a backstory for theatergoers. I thought maybe I would come out and give a few words to the crowd to set the show up but then decided I would probably have to make a pamphlet that would accompany the playbill. I'd give a short history of "The Realm" and that way the audience would be up to speed on all the idiosyncrasies of this world.

Well, after a few pages of scribbling notes, I realized that this was probably going to be several pages, and I began to think that I could make a very small brochure or tiny book to accompany the play. So I started typing. I just outlined the story arcs and improvised dialog, and before long I was ten chapters in. It was clear that I not only had enough material for a book, but that I had enough material for additional books as well. The Rise of the Cafe Racer Trilogy was born!

Because I've been a graphic designer most of my life I figured I might as well create artwork for each chapter and then maybe some posters that might appear in the Realm. Then I thought I might as well make some oil paintings of the past and present KOTUs (you'll find out all about the KOTUs soon). And then I was completely beside myself with joy the day I realized that my book could have MAPS of its world just like the my favorite books of all time, the Lord of the Rings.

And all this happened because Tom Booker told me to do it! A shining example of the power of suggestion. But also having hundreds of improvisers like Tom in this incredible Austin Improv Community to inspire me is truly the reason I was even able to believe I could accomplish this task. Improv has evolved my entire creative process and encouraged me to take mind boggling risks and happily accept failure.

With that, I thank you from the bottom of my heart for taking time to read this book. I poured so much sweat and tears into the music and story and would be honored if anyone loved it half as much as I do. Thanks.

Run for Glory!
- Deano

CONTENTS

MAP OF THE REALM

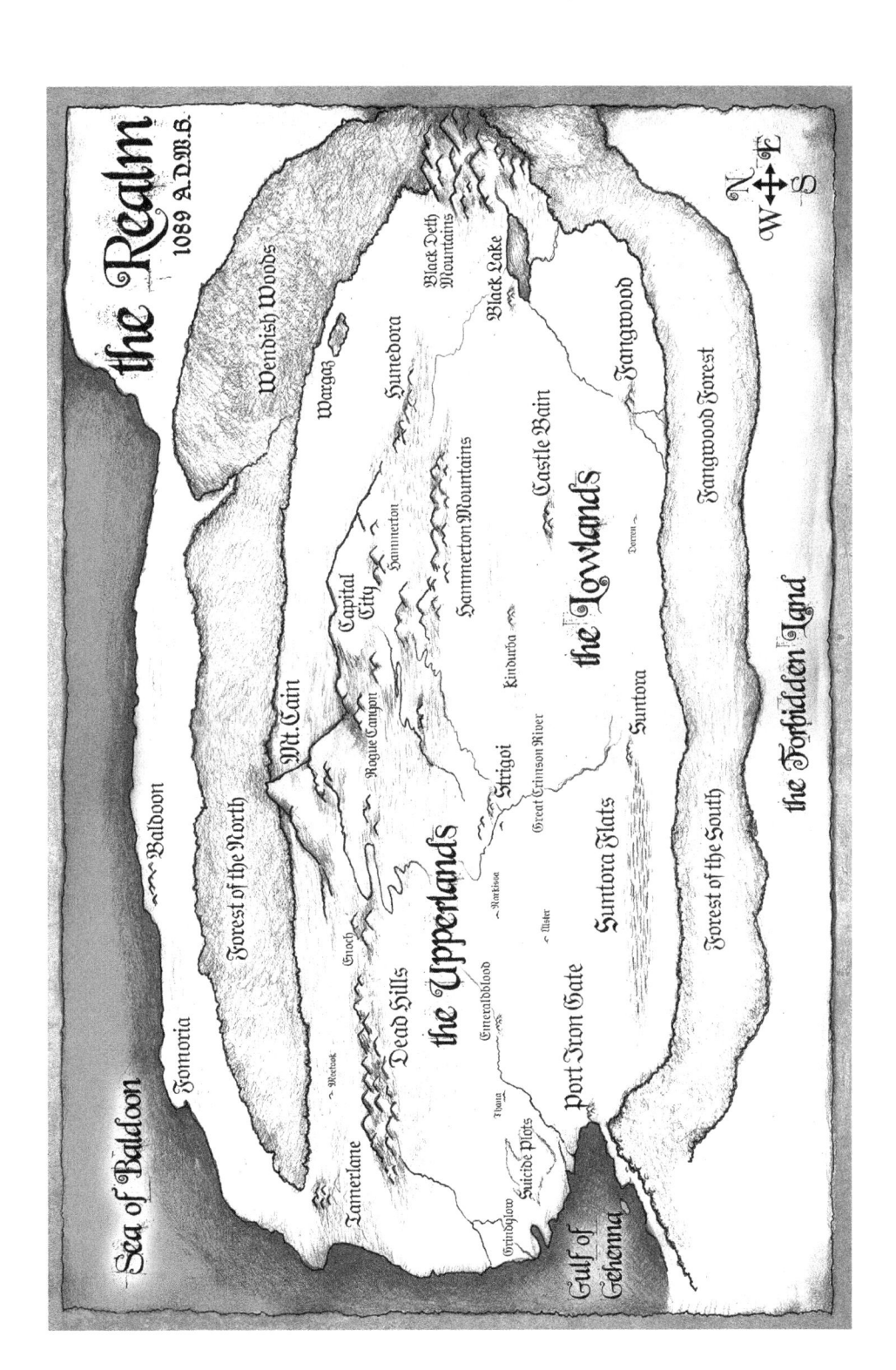

MAP OF CAPITAL CITY

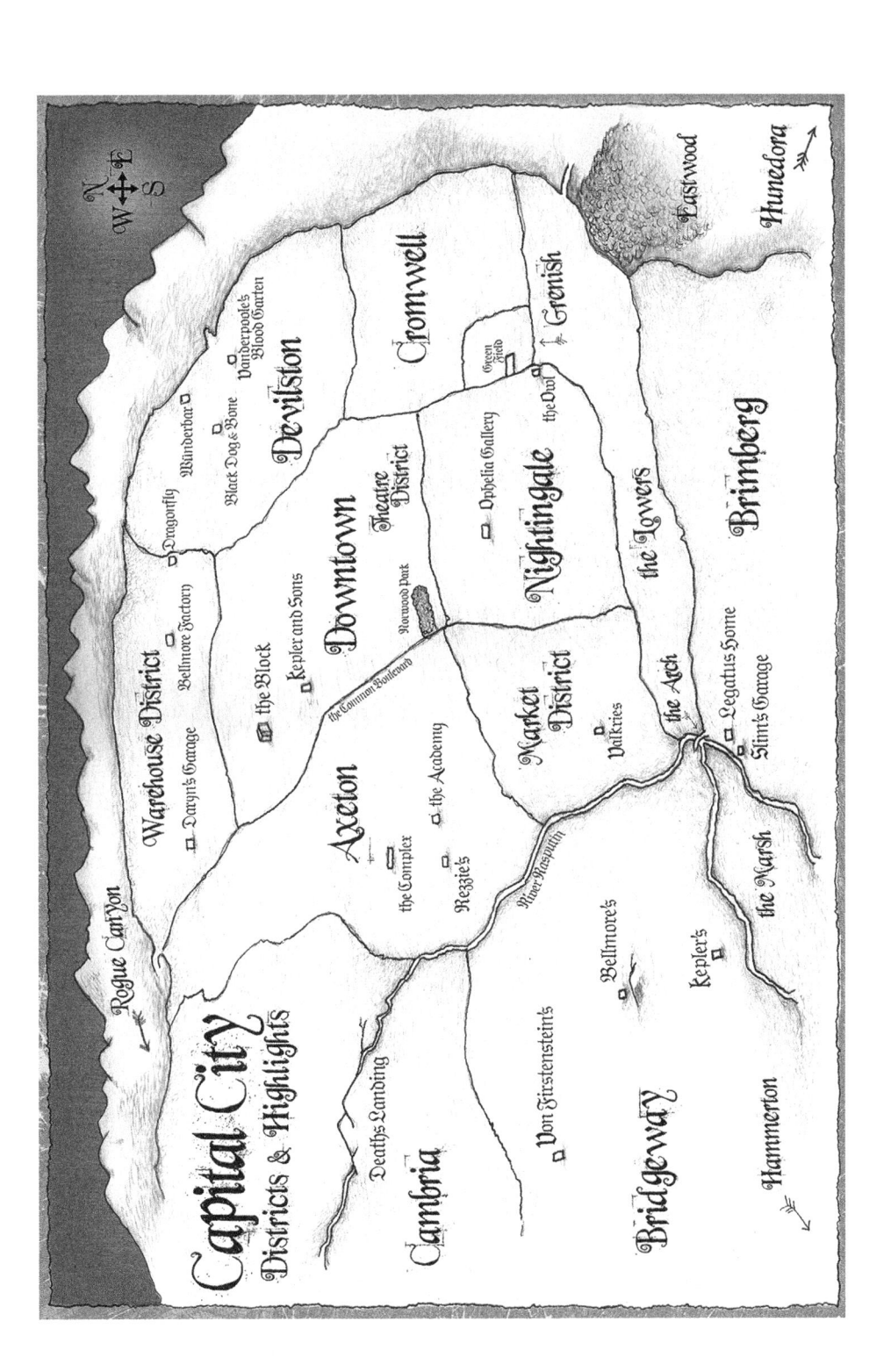

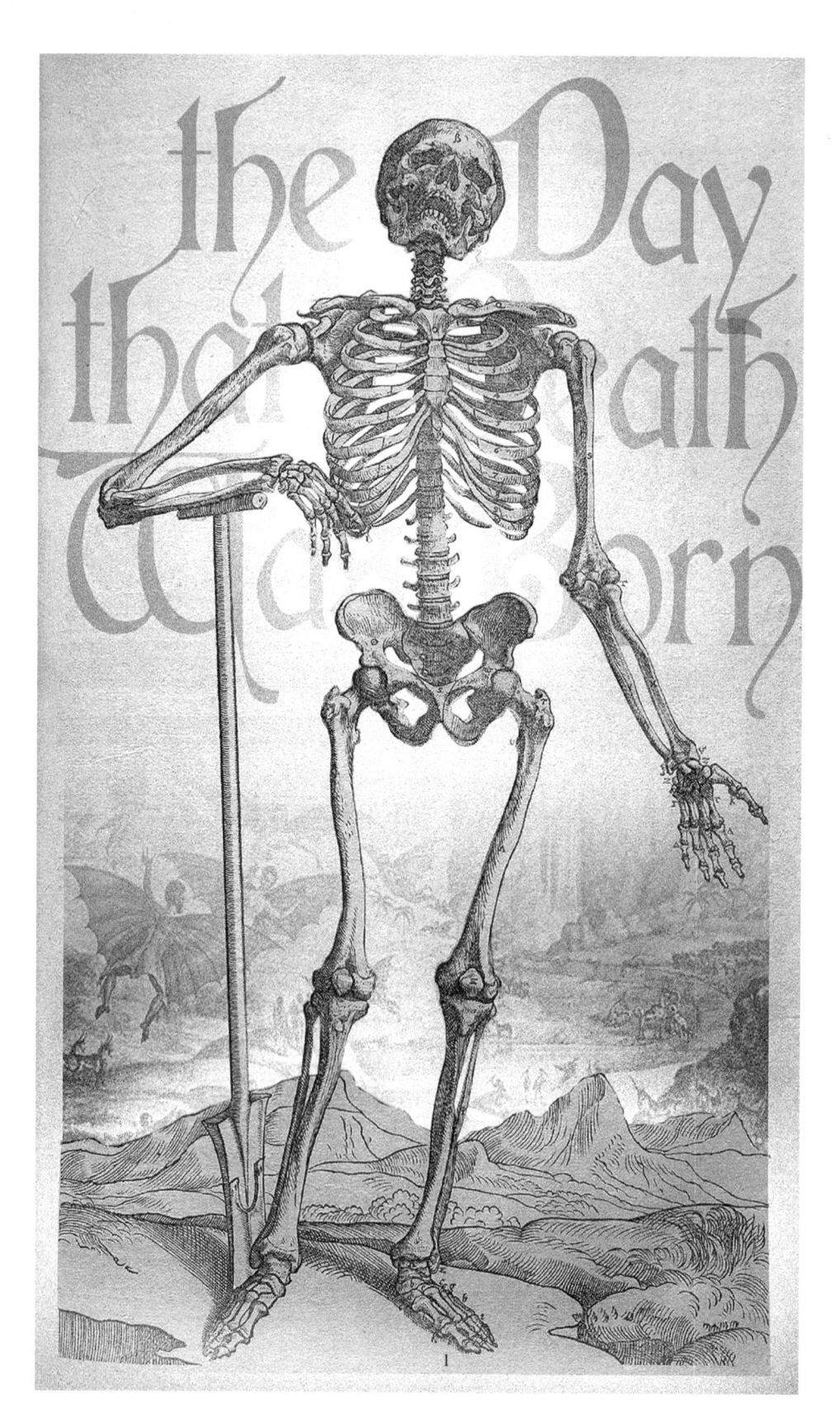

CHAPTER ONE:
THE TUTOR

Sonny was scribbling frantically, trying to get it all on paper before he forgot. He spent so much time in his elaborate daydreams, it wasn't often he bothered to write his ideas down, so he wanted to try to get the complete thought. "What if having an incredible moment could be worth more than a thousand years of life? What if we weren't even supposed to live that long anyway and maybe these sixty years of the Fledge are really the BEST years of our existence?"

Ideas like these were very controversial, especially with older vampires, but were gaining momentum with the younger, increasingly disenfranchised vampires. There was an apathy growing that there was nothing to look forward to after the Fledge, when you found an occupation and settled in for the rest of your days doing the same thing every night. In spite of the countless posters and advertisements encouraging anyone in their Fledge to "Find a mate… Procreate!" and to "Choose a Field of Specialty, the Realm needs all her worker Bees!", there was a reluctance to do either and the beginnings of a movement to do the opposite. Literally, to not work or choose a 'Specialty' but to seek out the 'moments' that would give your existence purpose. It's not that Sonny was a radical and subscribed to all these notions, but it excited him and was a pleasant release from the countless hours spent studying every night.

Andi noticed the sound of manic scratching coming from Sonny's usually quiet side of his room. She moved only her eyes up from the page and watched him write for a full minute before she teased him.

"What's going on over there? You got the Bog or something?"

Sonny was shaking his head and starting to smirk while mouthing the final words he put to paper. He remembered when Andi had contracted Blood Bog Fever many years ago when they were both very young. Her mother would rub a paste made of soot and ash all over Andi's face and arms and she had to stay inside all night. The idea was that even a little amount of moonlight would slow the healing process (moonlight was, after all, sunlight reflecting off the moon). Though most scientists agreed it was harmless, there were still many who were superstitious that moonlight was toxic and should be avoided.

Blood Bog Fever was an infection vampires got from consuming improperly filtered Blood Berries—a hybrid fruit made from synthesizing animal flesh and cranberries and grown in the Lowlands. The Bog made your hands shake during the onset and could last a year. No one was entirely sure, but they thought it came from a by-product of the very tricky process of cultivating these animal plants. And, like many things in the Realm, there was an abundance of folklore attached to any reasonable explanation for anything.

Many of the vampires that worked the mines and farms of the Lowlands took a deeper pride in their vampire heritage than some of the Upperlanders, regularly referring to themselves as "Real Vampires." And, in contrast, could be referred to as "Common Bats" by the snootier of the Upperlanders. Since rarely did anyone in the Lowlands get the Bog, they always insisted it was from forgetting their vampire roots and heritage.

One thing everyone agreed on, though, was that Blood Berries had changed life as they knew it in the Realm, having saved Vampires, literally. When it was discovered some nine hundred years ago that they could actually create a mammal blood-bearing plant that grew from the ground and bore fruit that would satisfy a vampire's blood lust, they all began to thrive. In the years prior, the Realm had been a horrible and painful existence, with nothing to feed on and hundreds of thousands of vampires dying.

When the last human being had been hunted to extinction in the year of Man 2067, the vampires relocated to a fertile and resource rich area, and sealed themselves off from the rest of the World. It was the beginning of the Realm and would become known as the Year That Death Was Born. Now in year 1089 ADWB (After Death Was Born), vampires were completely self-sufficient and in spite of ancient law that contradicts the possibility, were reproducing. There wasn't a huge success rate and it took almost twenty years for the babies to gestate—ten years for the mother to even show. But vampires were having babies. As a result, it was encouraged to the point of enforcement by the Realm's High Council and was one of the most prominent pieces of propaganda in the Realm. In many parts of the countryside you could still see the old tin propaganda signs.

Sonny lifted his upper lip, as if to show his fangs, and in a forced Lowlander accent growled, "Why, no, I only drink Healthy Blood!"

Andi pursed her mouth, feigning anger. One of the only times in

the forty years they had spent as best friends that they had a knock-down, drag-out fight was when Sonny accused Andi's family of exploiting medical information and driving the price of Healthy Blood up for a profit.

Andi was Andromeda Kepler, great granddaughter of Lexmanius Kepler, who was one of the original chemists that developed the process of synthesizing Blood Berries. Her grandfather Raymond Kepler, a scientist and entrepreneur, marketed a triple-filtered, purified version of blood berry juice, known as "Healthy Blood." It'd been wildly successful and revered as medicine in some parts of the Lowlands.

"Oh, really, then why are you gonna fail gymnastics?" Andi giggled and closed her chemistry book.

"Please, I'm not gonna fail," Sonny paused as he recalled what Coach Von Ulritch had said to him a few weeks ago after asking him to his office:

"Legatus, in five hundred seventeen and one half years as head Coach I have never failed a single student in Physical Arts. But if you don't change your attitude, and QUICKLY… you will have the unique distinction of being just that student."

Coach called everyone by their last name and it reminded Sonny of when his mother would huff at him, "Sebastian Legatus, are you listening to me?" He hated being called Sebastian, and hated Legatus even more. Coach almost always started his rants with a vampire's last name, then barked orders and ended saying something about remembering your father being twice as good at whatever it was he was having you do. And that he had a mind to tell your father just how poorly you were doing. The problem was, Sonny didn't have a father. Sonny was an infant when his father left the Realm. It was at the same time that his mother was in an accident and was near passing. She was struck by a speeding motorcar and lay unconscious for a month. It took several operations and was incredibly expensive to rehabilitate her. At one point her employer, Bellmore Industries, as well as her insurance would no longer pay for further treatment. The Realm High Council actually intervened to settle. After that, there was no talk of the accident and no one spoke of his father. When the Council weighed in on non-policy, personal matters, there is little or no public discussion after. His mother, Evanna, couldn't remember anything from before the accident either and until recently Sonny had never thought to ask about any of it.

"Besides, I think they just use Phys Art as a way to beat the Fledge out of us." Sonny added after a long pause.

"Yes," Andi said, "They can't have us walking around too excited." She shrugged. "Did you get your Focus interview dates yet?"

"Not yet," Sonny sighed.

The "Focus on your Future" interviews were conducted on young vampires as they neared the end of their Fledgling years. Usually around fifty-five to sixty years of age. The Realm's governing High Council made it almost illegal to not select a Specialty at that time.

"Well, it'll be no surprise when they recommend research as your Specialty." Sonny noted.

Like all the Keplers before her, Andi was intrigued by science, particularly chemistry. Her Focus interviews would undoubtedly suggest a career in that field. Sonny was less enthusiastic. Although a straight 'A' student, he had no real interest in any field. His mother worked in administrative at Bellmore Industries, and as a teacher before that. It was generally encouraged to follow the career paths of your kin. But he just couldn't imagine a future where he would spend waking hours in an office or in front of a class. He still had no idea what he wanted to do.

"Maybe mine should be bicycling," He smirked.

"Or doodling," Andi poked back.

"Yeah..." Sonny sighed desperately.

"Well, it doesn't last forever. Soon enough we'll change, choose a Specialty and it will all be behind us," Andi said with no emotion.

"Sometimes I think it'd be better to not change." Sonny hated the dismissive attitude older vampires had about this hormonally tumultuous time Fledglings had.

Andi looked at him again for half a minute, waiting for his expression to change. It was then that they heard the kitchen door open. Gentle steps moved about and there was the rustling of paper bags. The steps approached, and then they heard a light tap on the door.

"You in there, Honey?" Evanna Legatus spoke in the sweetest voice. The door opened only enough for a small, slender, middle-aged vampire woman to ease through. Her eyes smiled when she saw both of them.

"Are you kids hungry? I stopped at the market."

"I'm fine," Sonny smiled.

"Me too. But thank you, Ma'am."

"Andromeda, your hair looks beautiful, did your mother take you to Monica?'

"Yes, Ma'am, and thank you."

Evanna paused and smiled at her son.

"I'll be in the other room if you kids need anything."

Andi loved Evanna. She was so graceful and assuring. Not like so many of the women her age who were harder and more forceful. Evanna could float around a room and calm anyone with her voice. She wished her own mother was more like her. Evanna had noticed Andi's hair, and with her easy smile had looked at Sonny to let him know that he too should offer a compliment. Sonny had indeed noticed but ignored his mother's subliminal advice. He had noticed her hair, but felt uncomfortable speaking about any of Andi's new choices of late. The two of them had spent many years together, hanging out, playing in the shed, making fires in trash cans, camping behind their houses and being best friends. Watching Andi take more of an interest in the future and particularly her physical appearance made Sonny feel odd.

Sonny sheepishly grabbed for his notebook and said without looking at Andi, "Yeah, your hair looks nice."

Before Andi could say a word the bedroom door peeked open and Evanna leaned in again.

"I almost forgot to tell you, Honey, I've offered your tutoring service to one of your schoolmates."

"What? Oh Mom, I'm really too busy." Sonny hated tutoring people. He had done it a few years through middle school after being placed in an accelerated program. His mother liked it because she has been pushing for him to choose the teaching Specialty for years.

"I'm sorry, Honey, I know, but I promised Mr. Bellmore you'd help. Brianna's Focus interviews are coming up and he wants her to do well."

Sonny felt flushed. "What?"

"Yes, I'm sorry, but I even said I'd check if you could stop by tonight before light to touch base with her."

His mother was so delicate even when she asked for him to do something he didn't want to. She would hold her gaze, softly lowering her chin until he agreed. In this case it would be unnecessary. Sonny was getting warmer by the second. The mention of Brianna Bellmore made his entire body tense for a second. "Bebe," as everyone called her, had been a crush of Sonny's for years. He had been in several classes with her over the years and he, like every young male vampire, had noticed her transformation from Fledge to young vampire woman. She was a bit of an early bloomer and already looked much older with generous curves etching her Academy uniform's silhouette into the eyes of every young male vampire she encountered.

Sonny pressed his lips together and turned slightly. He was trying to keep his upper lip from curling involuntarily and exposing what would be fangs. He, like everyone, got his fangs filed every month. Although most people were used to young males' lack of control of their top lip and showing of their fangs at the sight of attractive young females, or at the sight of violence for that matter, Sonny didn't want either of them to notice that he had been affected. He pressed hard, and then, after a moment of realization, made a clumsy attempt to pretend that he had something lodged in his teeth.

He finally nodded in agreement and smiled at his mother. "No, I don't mind. I mean, it's the boss' kid, right?"

Evanna's eyes smiled warmly as she moved like a breath of air out of the room.

Sonny's eyes had a soft focus on his book bag across the room on the floor. He was inventorying what he would take to the Bellmores. *To Brianna Bellmore's house!*, he thought, it was unimaginable luck. He pulled at the thick black hair on his head, continuing to search the room with his eyes, as Andi sat across from him, feeling like she should probably go home herself.

"Well, guess that's a tough break," Andi said, "I mean, Bebe will probably be a nightmare to try to teach anything to."

Sonny glanced at his shirt when Andi spoke. He needed to change his clothes, he thought, as he looked back at Andi and smiled.

"Yeah," He nodded as if he were answering an entirely different question.

Andi's face came into focus for him and he repeated himself. "Yeah," Then matter-of-factly added, "It's probably going to be like filing teeth with her."

He quickly stuffed some books in the bag and reached for the door. He stopped short and turned back to Andi.

"Hey, guess I'll just get over there and get it over with." He tried to act apathetic to seem unaffected, but Andi could tell Sonny was excited.

"Sure," Andi said, slowly getting up. "I'll see you tomorrow."

Sonny was already out the door before she finished her sentence. He mumbled to his mother as he passed her in the kitchen and barely touched the ground as he pushed his bicycle that leaned against the back of the house toward the street. He rode that bike everywhere and even as most vamps his age were already learning to use the small motorcars that were popular all over the Realm, Sonny still enjoyed the rush of wind in his face as he pedaled anywhere he needed to go.

It was always a little bumpy until he got out of his neighborhood. The streets were still cobblestone in the Brimberg section that he lived, but his mother had bought a small cottage near the edge of the more affluent Bridgeway district of the Capital City of the Realm. In just a few minutes he would be crossing the Bridgeway Arch and his bicycle would be easing along the smooth concrete roads of the neighborhood where Brianna Bellmore lived. He often raced around the streets of this and many other neighborhoods in the late hours of night, challenging himself to cover great distances before the break of Dawn.

As he flew down the small hill off the Arch, he could hear music coming from the underside of the bridge. As he got closer, though he couldn't see anyone, he heard the distinct melody of "Light of the Moon" being played. He paused and stopped pedaling. Not stopping, but reducing what noise he was generating in an effort to better hear. He knew immediately that familiar chorus—school-age vamps around the Realm were humming this under their breath as a way of protesting long hours spent studying for their Focus interviews.

In the last few years, a group of disenfranchised young Fledges had been getting together on particularly bright nights and playing music. It had started as a relatively innocuous way to merry-make past curfew, but as the Focus interviews approached each year, the meetings became more defiant. Playing music while singing and staring directly at the moon, though not medically dangerous, had become symbolic of rebelling against the Focus interviews. 'Don't Stare at the Moon' was a popular mantra of older vampires to Fledges. It was a way to say to keep on the straight and narrow and to keep your eyes on what was in front of you. It was also a very dismissive answer to any question the younger vamps had about anything they may be thinking or feeling. In some quarters of the Lowlands they actually believed that because moonlight was the sun's reflection off the moon, that it was toxic and could cause a host of ailments. Some of these same people also believed in the ancient stories of flying vampires that were supposedly several times stronger than the weaker descendants that populated the modern day Realm. They also believed that because they weren't feeding on humans, that was why they had lost all of their mystical powers that were once standard for all vampires.

Some of the merrymakers had starting doing impromptu performances in out of the way pubs and cafes under the name "Sweet Death Symphony", the SDS for short. One song of theirs in particular, "Light of the Moon," had become an anthem of the growing movement to reject the concept of focusing on your future and to just live in the moment. It was causing a rippling effect of apathy toward the future with Fledges.

Musical accompaniment for this scene:
"LIGHT OF THE MOON"
FROM THE ALBUM "RISE OF THE CAFE RACER"
DEANO JONES & THE SWEET DEATH SYMPHONY

Many of the older vamps were getting increasingly outspoken against this growing sentiment and some were suggesting the SDS was leading the way in the demise of the Realm. Some older vampires were asking for the High Council to impose stricter curfews past Dawn and to bring the SDS to face charges of conspiracy and blasphemy.

Of course all this attention was helping promote even more fascination with the SDS and its elusive membership. Sonny didn't know anyone who knew any firsthand information about the organization, but it was said you could only be invited to an SDS event.

With the rush of wind in his ear it was difficult to tell if this was a rendition of an SDS song or an actual get-together. He slowed his speed but the level of music seemed to lower in unison. It was unclear now which direction it was coming from. He had been certain it was from under the Arch but now he wasn't sure. Stopped in the middle of the street, with bright light overhead and deep blue reflection of moonlight cast from the River Rasputin that ran under the Arch, the music had stopped. He thought for an instant of walking under and down to the water to investigate. On any other night he most likely would have, but like a dog being called from across a field, he suddenly turned and faced the direction of Brianna's. Remembering that he was en route to spend—who even knew how much time—talking to and answering questions with BeBe, had once again made his neck hot and throat tighten. Sonny's lip rose and quivered. This time he did not restrain himself and let loose a loud wail, rolling his head side to side before pedaling back into the night.

CHAPTER TWO:
BELLMORE MANOR

A small, midnight-blue motorcar rolled to a stop in front of the Bellmores' sprawling Tudor mansion, to the crunch of pebbles underneath the tires. Daryn didn't bother to put the car in park as he glanced over at Brianna Bellmore. Bebe was intentionally taking her time and seemed to be incapable of keeping her hair out of her face as she kept running her fingers through it to pull it behind her ears, only to have her heavy, raven locks tumble back over her face. She continued with this for a minute before looking up and smiling devilishly at Daryn.

"Thank you soooo much for the ride home." She had her bag in her lap but made no move to get out of the motorcar.

"No problem at all," Daryn said, "Take care."

Bebe moved her jaw slowly from side to side while still staring at him. Daryn held the stare for a moment then turned to look in front of him. "I have to go," he scowled.

Bebe tapped her perfect teeth together and said very deliberately, "You should come in and say hi to Father." She smiled, then acted surprised. "Oh wait, they're dining with the Krausses tonight."

Bebe slowly shifted her weight so that her leather skirt and boots rubbed hard against the leather bucket seat and filled the interior of the car with a tight, stretching noise. They had both heard this sound before in Daryn's car, though it had been some time since Bebe had moved around in that passenger seat.

Daryn grimaced. He glanced at her boots, then indulgently let his eyes climb up her until he was looking squarely in her eyes. One corner of his top lip flinched for a second. He bit down and looked back at the street in front of him.

"I have to go home, Bebe." He revved the engine.

"Why are you in such a hurry, Daryn?" She tapped her teeth together. "You don't have to worry about any Focus interviews." She kept twisting in her seat to keep a steady purr of leather grabbing at her while she talked. "Even if you don't make the Pike, you'd hardly need a recommendation for your Specialty."

Daryn turned his torso around to face her and growled, "Make the Pike?! I'm not worried about making the Pike. I will win the Pike!"

Daryn Von Firstenstein was eighth in the line of Von Firstensteins. His father Vladimir Von Firstenstein was the Realm's "King of the Undead." Although it wasn't a ruling position, more of a pageant title really, it came with perks and privileges. As well as being privy to issues of the High Council, King of the Undead could help "suggest" policy and cast decisive votes at any of the Realm's universities and public academies. It was the highest civilian honor any vampire could hold and it was won by winning the "Pike's Run" race.

The Pike's Run happened every one hundred and twenty-one years and was a motorbike race that determined the King of the Undead. It was open to any male vampire between the ages of 50 and 250 years and was encouraged with great vigor by the High Council, the Rule Enforcement Division (R.E.D.), and most of the older vampires. It was the most exciting thing that took place in the entire Realm and was seeped in tradition and honor. There was no greater sense of national pride than the Running of the Pike, as they called it.

There would be qualifying races held all summer during the year of a Run, roughly two weeks apart. They were grueling trials that, although did not follow the actual course of the Pike, covered some of the most unforgiving terrain and took place in six different locations around the Realm. After sixteen weeks of qualifying runs, two Riders would emerge as the finalists. It was so revered to make it even in to the Final Twelve and Final Eight that most all upper-ranking Riders were given positions in the R.E.D. It wasn't uncommon when stopped or questioned by an R.E.D. Agent to see an embroidered patch with a number on their uniform. There was almost no way to become an officer in the R.E.D. without having participated in the Pike.

The Pike's Run would start at First Dark on September 23rd and last all night. The Riders would follow a path that would take them through some familiar terrain of the Realm but ultimately lead them into Forbidden Land, a region unknown to any vampires of the Realm. Nothing was known of what took place in the hours of that portion of the Pike, and the lone Rider who returned would never utter a word of what happened. Yes, only one Rider would ever return from a Pike's Run. And in the eleven centuries, since the Day That Death Was Born, a Von Firstenstein had won every Pike's Run.

Of course Bebe knew all this and was mostly trying to get any reaction out of Daryn.

"Last I heard you still had to make rank," Bebe teased.

"Oh, you can believe I'll rank up!" Daryn yelled back at her.

With both hands Bebe collected all her wild black hair, twisted it into a big bun in the back of her head and leaned toward Daryn, pouting.

Daryn sighed. "Look, I don't have any time for this! I have a lot on my mind, Bebe! My father is giving me such a hard time about the Pike and everything else."

Bebe twisted in her seat. "Maybe you'd feel better if you gave me a hard time." She pouted more and crawled over the center console at Daryn. He quickly pulled her book bag from her lap and held it between them.

"Go," He said as he turned back to look out the front of his immaculately clean windshield.

Bebe screamed and grabbed her bag. She wasn't used to not getting what she wanted, and she wanted Daryn Von Firstenstein. It wasn't just because his father was King of the Undead and Daryn was the favored choice to be next. Or that his family was wealthy and prestigious; her family had wealth and high regard in the Realm as well. Or that he was devilishly handsome—she could have her pick of any young vampire she wanted. It was because he didn't want her. Oh, Daryn liked her physically. They had shared a few spirited times together. But Daryn was a Von Firstenstein, and what Von Firstensteins truly lusted for was power and fame. The pressure had been on him since his birth that he was a legacy to the KOTU title. His father pushed him to be smarter, stronger and better than everyone—by any means necessary. Bebe was needy, time-consuming and also wanted to be the center of attention. Daryn couldn't handle the competition with himself, and as the Pike drew nearer, he was becoming increasingly anxious.

Bebe adjusted her skirt that had crept up her thighs as she stood on the curb staring at Daryn. He looked for a moment, then sped off, fishtailing his quiet sportscar as he pulled away. Bebe was livid.

"I… think I'm…" said the voice behind her.

"Ahh?!" Bebe squealed and spun around, nails pointed and baring her teeth.

It was dangerous to sneak up on even a young vampire. And startling an older vamp would almost certainly result in a fight, just out of pure pride.

Sonny took a step back with his bicycle at his side. He had been there for a full minute but hadn't wanted to interrupt. "Whoa, I'm sorry. I… I'm just here to…"

Bebe dropped her defensive stance.

"What?" She rolled her eyes "Are you *following* me?"

Sonny shook his head with wide eyes. "Oh, no, no, nothing like that." He swallowed hard. "I'm Sonny… I'm supposed to help you… um, study. You know… for the Focus. Your father… he asked my mother if I'd tutor you."

Sonny was incredibly nervous. He had spent many, many long days thinking of Bebe Bellmore. She was a couple years older, but still in his academic group. The Academy would keep all Fledges born in a six-year period together until they chose a Specialty and went on to universities or workforce. Her very name had become synonymous with an ideal Succubus. In the halls of the Academy young male vampires could be heard referring to an attractive female as a 'Total Bebe' or even, (as they would pantomime an hourglass figure), a "Bell-More" (with a particular emphasis on the *more*). As Sonny stood there, within arms-length of *the* Bebe, he could feel his chest expanding and his throat tightening.

"Oh, that figures," Bebe complained, "Daddy is sooo worried about how I'll do at the Focus. Not that it even matters to him what my Specialty would be, he just wants everyone to see that I'm rated for any position in the Realm."

Bebe was already back to being her catlike self. "So, you're a teacher? You seem a little young."

"Um, no. I'm Sonny Legatus. I was actually in your Linguistics class last semester."

Bebe squinted at Sonny and shook her head. "I'm sorry, I think I was asleep in that class anyway." She sighed and slung her bag over her shoulder.

"Well, would you like to come up to the house?"

Sonny stalled in that moment with a foolish grin on his face before nodding 'yes'.

They climbed up the winding stone walkway to the Bellmores' front door. They had hardly touched the top step when the heavy wooden door silently swung open, held by an ancient vampire in a dark grey jumpsuit.

"Hello, Borgo. This is Sonny. Father has asked him to help me with my Focus studies."

Borgo was a statue with perfect black and white streaked hair. He had a chiseled, pale face, and wore the classic attire of the oldest vampires – modest soft-toned one-piece bodysuits, color-coded by their line of work or area of expertise. Borgo Aref was from a long line of valets and handlers, as told by the particular dark grey-green hue of his suit.

For vampires younger than Borgo, 300-500, the tradition of one- and two-piece subtle-toned suits was standard and an obvious distinction from the younger Fledgling vampires. More studious Fledges would be early adopters of two-piece suit fashion in an effort to show acceptance of the inevitable, but lately there was a growing trend with Fledges to ignore these unwritten rules, which was no doubt perpetuated by the momentum of the SDS and their mantra of living for "the moment."

"Of course," Borgo replied and looked knowingly at Sonny as the two

entered Bellmore Manor.

Bebe and Sonny spent a little over an hour in a cozy study before Borgo silently brought two glasses of blood berry juice and a tiny plate with bite-sized venison pieces to the table where they sat. Their time had been mostly Bebe talking about what she was "really good at" or just "pretty good at" in her studies, with Sonny nodding appropriately. This was fine with him. Sitting in that warm, intimate library mere inches from Bebe was almost an artistic rendition of his daydreams. She was very animated as she spoke of herself, her hair falling all over her chest and shoulders, only to be whisked away by her delicate hands and allowed another chance to come back and fall uncontrollably all over her.

She handed Sonny a glass of blood berry and took a breath from what had been a full five minute run-on sentence about her ability to never gain weight no matter how much she ate.

"So… how long were you standing there?" She sipped her drink.

"Where?" Sonny was confused.

"You know, outside."

"Oh," Sonny smiled "I had just only been there a minute." He sipped. "You seemed… you know, involved with something, so I just waited."

Bebe pushed her hair back and focused on the glass in front of her. "Yes, sometimes relationships are soooo difficult."

Sonny nodded in agreement but knew nothing about relationships with female vampires. The closest he had been to a girl was a semester of formal dance with Daciana Rhineland. Coach Von Ulritch had quickly paired up boys and girls to be partnered to work on the traditional dances of the Realm. Daciana was an excellent dancer and by the end of the semester had successfully traded Sonny for Nikolai Von Wallach. Sonny didn't mind since Andi had been Nik's partner.

Sonny hadn't remarked but Bebe continued, "That was my boyfriend, Daryn."

Sonny nodded and smiled.

"Daryn Von Firstenstein. We're going to be wed."

"Oh, congratulations," Sonny said and awkwardly started to raise his glass but rethought and simply brought it to his mouth and sipped.

"I mean, not immediately or anything. There's no rush. Right now he's really concentrating on the Pike." She nodded. "You know, like all of you, I guess." Bebe finished her glass.

Sonny kept nodding, "Yeah."

Bebe kept looking at Sonny. "You're going to try and rank up, right?"

Sonny opened his mouth, then closed it and looked down for a moment. He nodded as if agreeing but said, "I'm not sure yet, you know. What with the Focus interviews and universities and all."

Sonny brought his glass to drink but there was no more juice. He kept nodding at Bebe as he tilted the glass more and more before he realized it was empty. He laughed and pointed at the glass as he set it down.

"Oh don't be silly, Sonny, everyone has to at least try to qualify. I mean it's like... unfaithful to the Realm."

Although it was by far the most important event that happened, and many of the eligible vampires tried to rank, it was true that not all who could did, in fact, try to qualify for the Pike. Statistically, the bulk of the Pike hopefuls came from those with the most and least in the Realm. It seemed like the Pike was populated with the poorer Lowlanders and the more affluent of the Upperlanders. In some ways, for different reasons. The more affluent saw it as a way to flaunt any success and to leverage rankings in future business or politics. For the poorer vamps, there was more of a sense of patriotic duty and the one in a million chance of actually winning and being able to bring your friends and family up in status. It was the middle class that was the less enthusiastic. But not to the sport of it, by any means. In fact, no one in the Realm was immune to the thrill of the Pike—it was inescapable. But the very expensive and time-consuming business of training and qualifying was more than most mid-level vampires cared to engaged in.

It would sometimes be a source of criticism or ridicule if you weren't going to try to run the Pike. Though usually only reserved as fighting words from an accuser, with all of the chest-beating that accompanied such an insult. But to casually mention it could seem offensive.

In a rare moment of self-realization, Bebe paused. "I'm sorry, Sonny, I didn't mean any..."

Sonny cut in, smiling, "No, no Bebe. Couldn't agree with you more." Sonny borrowed a tiny bit of Coach Von Ulritch's bravado and continued. "There's just so much to think about at our age. But... of course, I mean, you have try to rank, right?" He smiled awkwardly.

Bebe's eyes pulsed eagerly at him. "What's your bike like?" But without waiting for an answer, she continued, "Daryn's is incredible. It's gorgeous. It's one of the gold-winged-gargoyle models with, like, an incredible paint job with all these really elegant black lines on the tank. And it's soooooo fast." She stopped and pouted just a little. "But maybe it's not gonna be fast enough!" She reached over and lightly slapped his hand as she playfully smiled and wrinkled her nose at him.

Sonny looked at his hand. In one second it felt like his body temperature had jumped about twenty degrees. The way she was looking at him made him feel like she had just said '*I love you, Sonny.*'

"Ha. Yeah," He stammered. He was incapable of much else.

Bebe kept smiling at him and then suddenly announced, "I think that I had better wash my hair."

Sonny was still nodding and looking directly at her. "Ha. Yeah."

Bebe started to laugh a little. "Are you okay?"

Sonny quickly looked down at his books.

"Yes. Yeah." He smiled and collected the books he had spread out on the table. "Yeah, me too. I mean... I don't need to wash my hair but, you know... I need to be going home."

Sonny stuffed the books into his bag as he hurried to the door.

"Thursnight?" Bebe called after him.

Sonny looked confused then quickly agreed. "Oh, of course. Right after class."

It wasn't until he had descended the long walkway to where his bicycle lay against a tree that he was able to fully exhale. Sonny kept looking around wide-eyed and laughing at the sky. He was tutoring the most beautiful vampire in the Realm.

This was the best night of his entire life, he thought.

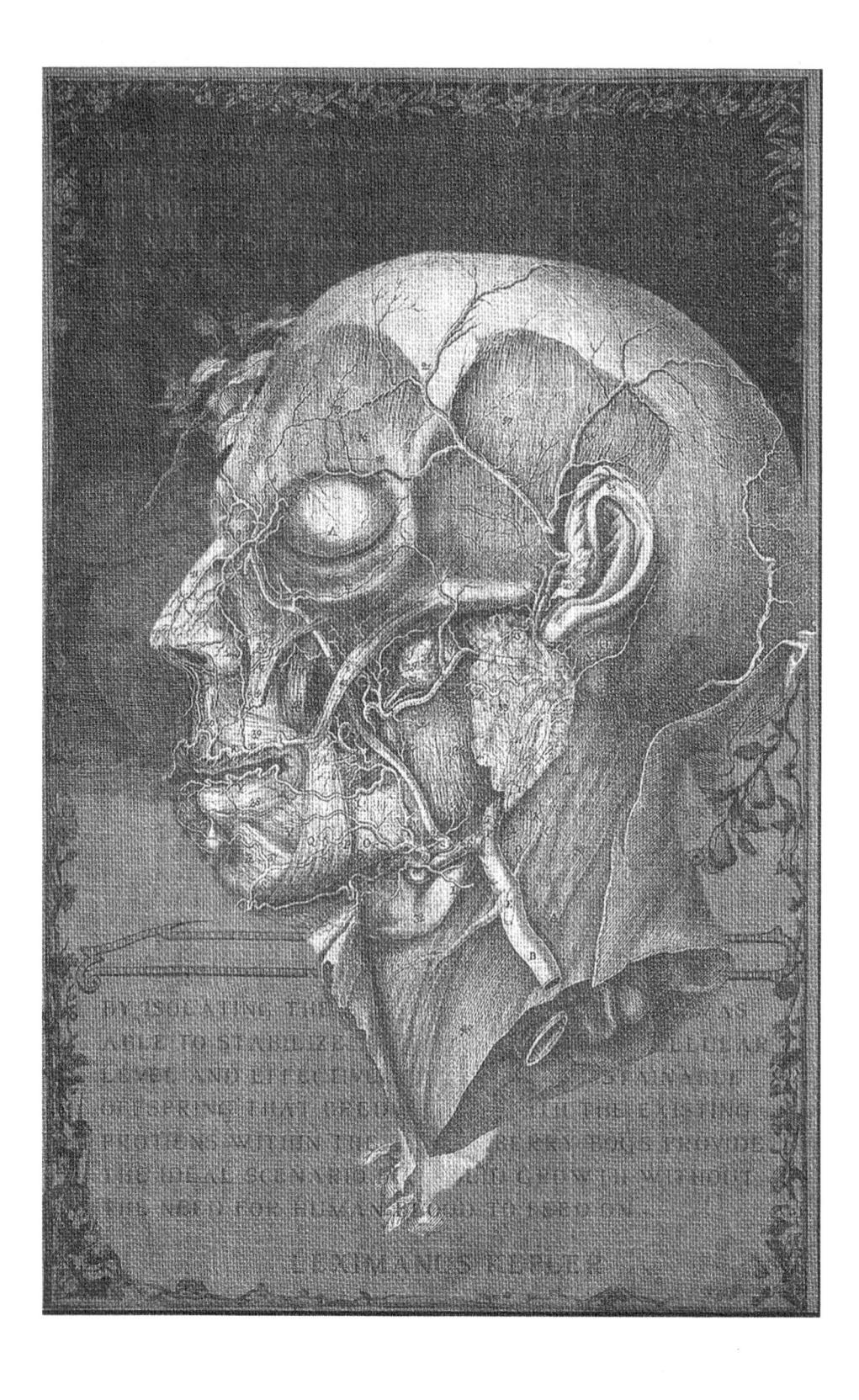

BY ISOLATING THE [...] AN
ABLE TO STABILIZE [...] THEM
LEVEL AND EFFECTIVE [...] REASONABLE
OFFSPRING THAT WOULD [...] THE EXISTING
PROBLEMS WITHIN THE [...] ACRY IONS PROVIDE
THE IDEAL SCENARIO [...] THE GROWTH WITHOUT
THE NEED FOR HUMAN BLOOD TO SUSTAIN

EX HUMANUS SUBLEP

CHAPTER THREE:
KEPLER & SONS

Andi bumped into the kitchen table without looking up from her book. She maneuvered around a chair and opened the door of their incubator. With her nose still inches from her book, she worked her way around the inside of the "Cube," touching and shaking bottles. Finally she let her arm with the book fall to her side, "Mother, we're really out of Healthy Blood?"

The vampire at the table's face was buried in his newspaper, "Lots of fresh swine blood in there."

Andi looked apathetically at her father. "I can't drink that stuff. You know they don't even flash it."

He put down his paper, smiling as he folded it up. "That's because it's poison. Ultraviolet light and vampires don't mix, my dear." He walked past her, kissing her forehead. "And I would love a nice warm glass, thank you."

Andi pulled the bottle with no markings or labels on it from the refrigerator. She and her father, Dr. Toland Kepler, loved to debate nutritional facts, chemical processes, or anything at all for that matter.

"Maybe you should tell that to the people down at your plant. I'm sure they'd like to know how they're poisoning the whole Realm with their delicious Healthy Blood."

Toland grinned. "You know as well as I do that the Agricultural Agenda is very specific about the required use of ultraviolet light as an antiseptic. We don't need the Bog breaking out." He took a long gulp of his swine blood. "And I use the least amount possible to flash HB."

She knew that and they had teased each other over this a thousand times. Andi actually loved that her father, though making a fortune from his own father's invention of Healthy Blood, was always concerned with making a safer product. And that and he donated enormous sums of treasure to the Lowlanders Collective, a group of farmers that chose to grow and market their products adhering to the strictest of Vampire Law. All of which had been written ADWB, after the extinction of humans. Since, after all, humans were pretty much all that was on the menu in ancient times. Andi's father had also always told her that the best part of Healthy Blood's success was the financing it created for his research labs.

"Light or non-light, that just tastes awful," Andi said while making an exaggerated face of disgust.

"Deee-licious!" Toland mocked as he finished of the glass.

Andi started to wander out of the kitchen.

"Hey, have a seat, Honey. How's everything going ?"

Andi had been moping around the house all week, ever since Sonny had been spending most of his time and energy with Bebe.

"Oh, you know, not much," She mumbled.

"I haven't seen Sonny around," Toland said.

Andi frowned. "He has an after school job tutoring."

Toland nodded and smiled.

"Well, you gotta admire him. Good kid that Sonny."

He shot an excited glance at Andi.

"You know, you could always come back and assist at the lab. After school, whenever you want."

Andi had spent lots of summers since she was very young with her father at the lab. At first, just playing quietly as a toddler with beakers and test tubes. But eventually, by her teens, she was assisting on some of the more important projects at Kepler & Sons. K&S had long been a family research enterprise and Toland was delighted when Andi took a natural interest in science and chemistry.

Over the centuries K&S had become a bit of a scientific historical archive as well, with a collection of books that dated back before the Day That Death Was Born. In fact, the High Council had at times convened in Kepler & Sons' library to research judgment during trials. Trials that would affect the entire

Realm. It wasn't just textbooks and essays from some of the great vampire scholars that were stored there, but actual notes and daily logs from some of the greatest experiments and discoveries were on record there.

For instance, the chemical equations that mapped the exact recipe for synthesizing animal tissue to cranberry shrubs were on file here. Handwritten by the scientist who discovered the process as well as founded the labs, Lex Kepler, Toland's grandfather and Andi's great-grandfather.

Andi had loved spending entire nights with these great books. She was fascinated with the ancient world, particularly the stories of their ancestors

KEPLER AND SONS

RESEARCH LABORATORIES
CAPITAL CITY

flying and taking bat shape. Her father would assure her that vampires of old, like those of modern times, enjoyed a healthy imagination and she should not believe everything that she read. And further stressed that she keep most of what she read to herself. Some of what was stored in the great library was considered blasphemous and not to be shown to the public. Most considered the tales of flying vampires foolish daytime stories for children and vampires with child-like minds. Toland would say, 'A serious scientist doesn't give credit to non-scientific speculation.'

During last summer, while she spent endless hours in the library, she had become fascinated with several books ranging from blood purification rituals to vampire folklore. These books were forbidden to be removed from that room. Every night Andi quietly copied by hand the elaborate diagrams and poetic stories that caught her attention. She slowly filled journals with priceless, and sometimes highly illegal ancient knowledge.

Over the last year though, Andi had lost interest in hanging around the lab with her father. Though still obsessed with these historical documents, she was also changing. She was becoming a young vampire woman and was becoming interested in things that had previously never held any importance to her. Things like finding a mate and having a child. She hated that she even thought about it, but it crept into her thoughts more than she liked to admit.

"Some really interesting stuff going on at the lab," Toland said, and leaned toward Andi as if to tell her a secret. "Been working on a lubricant that's showing signs of being able to virtually eliminate friction. Pretty incredible stuff."

Andi squinted for a moment, then shook her head. "Oh Dad, I just don't have any time to come to the lab. I mean, there's my Focus interviews… the Pike…"

"Oh, you're running the Pike?" Andi's mother asked sarcastically as she glided by with rose clippings.

"Of course not, Mother," Andi said matter-of-factly, "But it is kind of a big deal to some people."

Anastasia Kepler was arranging the roses in a black, iron vase. "Really?" She turned to her husband and daughter at the table. "Not to anyone I know."

In spite of rarely agreeing on anything, Andi and her mother were usually quite civil to each other and this was no different.

Ana had always been a little disappointed that Andi didn't share more of

THE
SPECKLED
NORTHERN FOREST
BLOOD BERRY

THE FLAVOR
OF BALDOON!

AVAILABLE WHEN IN SEASON AT
VALKRIES MARKET
420 ENDOVER · MARKET DISTRICT
CAPITAL CITY

her interests, more "girly" pursuits. When Andi was very young, Ana was concerned all of Toland's science and lab time was an effort to have Andi fulfill the "Son" portion of the sign on the side of the K&S building. Lately she had noticed her daughter starting to blossom into a young female vampire and ached to mentor her out of her Fledge with shopping and social events. Ana had always hoped Andi would show an interest in her mother's high-end art gallery, so hearing the two of them talk of Andi going back to the labs made Ana very irritated.

"Oh Ana, the Pike's fun for us all," Toland said. He turned to Andi. "I only wish we had our own Rider to root for."

As innocent as it was, that comment made Ana feel as though her husband was again wishing Andi was a boy. Cheering Riders on the streets of the Realm was something Toland had done with his father and was excited to do with Andi.

"Yes, it's great fun! I can't wait for the drunken lot of Common Bats that loiter on the gallery steps and urinate on the side of the building for the three months of the Pike!"

Ana had been feverishly rearranging the roses and suddenly threw her hands up and walked out of the kitchen.

Andi and her father smiled at each other, not daring to laugh or make any noise at all.

As Ana's last high-heeled shoe stomped on the top step of the second floor she yelled, "It's not funny!"

They both covered their mouths and smothered their giggles. Toland's eyes teared and he eventually coughed and regained his composure.

"You know, Dr. Krauss's boy… Karl. I think he may run the Pike. Let's hope he does well and we'll have ourselves a Rider to cheer for."

The Realm's Second Ever
Pike's Run
Check the schedule with local Council for Qualifying Run times
September 23rd 242 ADWB

CHAPTER FOUR:
THE CAFE RACER

Sonny was kicking a ball around at the far end of his backyard. At the last minute Bebe had canceled that night's studying. She had said, *'There's really more than studying in this world!'* It probably had something to do with the fact that there were countless clearance sales downtown to make way for the saturation of Pike's Run merchandise that was filling every store in the Realm. As Sonny unenthusiastically tapped at the ball, a figure appeared from the garage on the other side of the property fence.

"Sonny boy! How goes the night?" The figure said with a mild Lowlander accent.

"Hey, Slim," Sonny said. He perked up a little and added with a slight Lowlander accent of his own, "At least it's dark."

Slim laughed and added in the thickest Lowla he could muster, "That it is!"

Slim Jim was a middle-aged vampire that lived in the unusual garage type structure nestled between the end of the Legatuses' property and the river. It was a small lot and probably, hundreds of years ago, belonged to the owners of the Legatuses' home. He was probably from the Lowlands originally, but was a lot more traveled and multi-faceted than most of the rural vampires. His Lowla accent wasn't that thick, but it allowed him to travel virtually anywhere in the Realm. This, coupled with an unstoppable vampire charisma, made everyone who met him an instant friend of "Slim Jim."

"Haven't been around much lately," Slim said. "Where've you been hiding?"

"I've been tutoring again, but she had to cancel tonight"

Slim smiled widely. He was a handsome and very muscular vampire. He rested his strong forearms on a fencepost.

"What is 'she's' name?" His Lowla thickened.

Sonny muted a smile and squinted as he looked away at the creek quietly trickling in the background.

"Um... Brianna. Brianna Bellmore."

Slim just kept smiling and staring at him, while Sonny pretended this information was of little consequence. Finally Slim cleared his throat and said casually, "So, this wouldn't be the 'total Bebe' that I've heard about, would it?"

They both laughed. Sonny had known Slim Jim for as long as he could remember and had used that term many times around Slim over the years.

Slim didn't have family or children. He worked primarily as a welder, but was capable of fixing almost anything. He would travel all over the Realm doing odd jobs—sometimes joining large construction outfits as a temporary foreman for large sums of treasure, sometimes welding gate doors on elderly pig farmers' property for a warm meal. He often told Sonny he loved not knowing what he would be doing at that same time next week. It was almost unheard for an older vampire to exist like that, and inconceivable that one would actually like it. But Slim was no ordinary vampire. He had incredible stories from what seemed like ten lives he had lived. Slim had traveled to the Baldoon region, the land beyond the Northern Forest, and worked with mariner vampires. He had fought with the R.E.D. in the Uprising of 767 ADWB. As an iron worker, he had captained crews in the mines of Mount Cain and helped with the construction of the great turbine engines that powered the Realm. Slim Jim had seen and done more than most vampires three times his age. But he still chose to live a modest existence in his live/work shop at the edge of a quiet river in the quaint Brimberg quarter.

"Yes, it's that Bebe," Sonny said, slightly embarrassed.

"Well, just a foot in the door, Sonny boy." Slim smiled devilishly, "That's all ya need."

"Oh, well. No, it's not anything like that. She has a boyfriend and all." Sonny sighed in defeat. "Daryn Von Firstenstein."

Slim nodded. He'd never met this vampire but everyone knew he was Vlad's son. "Well of course she does. And why wouldn't it be a Von Firstenstein. Makes perfect sense."

Slim pointed at Sonny. "All you gotta do is get right down the middle, between the two." He was grinning and chopping with his hand. "Just put yourself right there." Slim winked.

Sonny laughed. Slim was always so optimistic about everything. It was infectious sometimes. "I think I need to do the opposite and just keep my mouth shut. I've already told Bebe that I'm running the Pike."

Slim cocked his head to one side.

"Hmm. Is that what you want to do?"

Sonny looked back nervously. Slim had always had so many exciting tales of bravery and intrigue. Sonny always wished he could be as fearless as Slim. There was something about Slim's tone that seemed not surprised, but almost impressed. Sonny really liked the way that felt. As he hung on Slim's words Sonny felt his head nodding up and down, as to agree, but ultimately he wasn't sure.

"I don't see how I possibly could…"

Although he was only inches from the gate door that joined the field and could have walked through, Slim effortlessly slung his body over the five-foot-tall fence.

"I didn't ask you that, Sonny," He grinned.

Sonny stared ahead, then back at Slim.

"You know, Daryn has a gold-winged-gargoyle, I don't even have a..."

"No, no, no." Slim laughed softly. "I didn't ask you all that. I asked if you *wanted* to."

Slim was inches from him and pointing both index fingers at Sonny's chest.

Sonny imagined how proud he would feel telling vamps at the Academy, and to tell Bebe for real that he was running the Pike. He pictured himself in the full-body leather riding suit. The buckles on the knee high boots and breast plate fasteners always caught moonlight and made a Rider shine—at least in images he'd seen. There were still advertisements that used images of the last Pike's ranking Riders, that's how revered you'd be if you could rank.

Looking at him standing there, wide-eyed and waiting, Sonny could tell that Slim, too, would be proud of him if he chose to run the Pike.

"Yes," Sonny said seriously, shaking his head. "I would love to."

Slim snapped his fingers and spun around on his heels. "Then you should do it!"

Sonny was startled.

Slim gently leaned back against the fence he had just jumped over a minute ago. Shrugging his shoulders he repeated, "Do it."

Sonny fidgeted. "Well, like I said, most of these guys have some pretty impressive bikes."

"Ah," Slim waved his hand. "In my day we ran Cafe Racers, none of these fancy-gadget bikes."

"Of course," Sonny said in amazement. "Why wouldn't I have guessed you had run the Pike!"

"Yup, Number Seven. That was the first time Vlad won."

"Did you rank?" Sonny asked.

Slim smiled and held three fingers up.

"What!" Sonny couldn't believe it. "Holy hell, you were Three!" He shook his head. Slim's modest home was a soft blur behind the lanky vampire. "But, you could've done anything with that kind of ranking. You could just sit back and do product endorsements."

"Nothing's that easy, Sonny boy," Slim laughed.

Sonny was blindsided with this information, and for the umpteenth time he was in total awe of Slim. "So what do you mean, did you have a 'cafe racer'?" Sonny had never heard of this. "Is it better than the Gargoyles or the Hellbirds these guys are talking about?"

Slim seemed to light up with enthusiasm.

"Aw Sonny, you don't need one of those, you need one of these. A cafe is like a stripped down version of a gold-winged. Just bare bones, no extras. The bars are low so you can just ever so gently press into those turns." Slim's eyes shone with excitement. "It's from the old school, sixth century style. You'd take 'em by surprise in something like that!" Slim smiled and motioned over his shoulder. "We could build it right over there in the shop and I bet we could get one up and running in no time."

Musical accompaniment for this scene:
"THE CAFE RACER"
FROM THE ALBUM "RISE OF THE CAFE RACER"
DEANO JONES & THE SWEET DEATH SYMPHONY

Sonny was shocked. Slim was offering to build him a motorbike. This vampire that had ranked Third in Pike Number Seven and was telling Sonny that they could build him a motorbike to run the Pike! Sonny was overwhelmed.

"Slim, I don't know what to say. I don't have any kind of treasure for that."

"We just have to be a little resourceful, is all," he grinned. "I think I can get us a pretty decent block, but we're gonna have to find the rest. Might have to send you out digging around for parts." Slim winked.

Sonny was beaming from ear to ear. He thought about how it would feel to walk into the District Council office tomorrow night and fill out an entrance form.

Slim fished a small cigar from his shirt pocket and clenched it between his teeth as he lit it. With a sweet smelling cloud of blue smoke drifting between them, Slim smiled back, "I'm proud of you, Sonny boy."

CHAPTER FIVE:
THE MIDDLE OF THE NIGHT

The Rezaveche Diner, or "Rezzies" as everybody called it, was conveniently located minutes from the Academy in the Axeton district. For centuries Rezzies had been a mainstay of after-class socializing. Daryn Von Firstenstein and several of his friends were draped over a couple tables in the enormous parking lot that wrapped around the circular glass restaurant.

WELCOME EVERYONE AND ALL

REZAVECHE
DINER

ENJOY THE
YOUTHFUL
ATMOSPHERE
AT AXETON'S
OLDEST DRIVE-IN
RESTAURANT.
"REZZIES"
IS WHERE
THE IN CROWD
GATHERS!

"But if I don't take your money, Erik, how will you ever become a better fencer?"

Daryn was gloating over his Phys Arts class defeat of his schoolmate. All of the friends wagered on their fencing matches and Daryn rarely lost.

Erik dropped his jaw and looked at his schoolmates. "Does it ever end, I ask? Can the great Double Dare Von Foot-inmouth ever be silenced?" He cackled loudly and a chorus of laughter echoed.

Daryn smiled smugly. "To the victor goes the spoils, my friend." He tossed the venison stick and blood gravy he had been playing with onto the table.

"Indeed." Erik motioned as if tipping his hat and quickly flipped a heavy gold piece at Daryn who caught it without moving an inch.

Erik Von Castlekuhn was a handsome, high-cheekboned son of a Council Member who was already chosen for the Specialty of Realm Rule. He loved studying laws and debating and would often perform entertaining "opening statements" worthy of a high court defense, over meaningless quarrels this group, or others, would have. He'd once drawn thunderous cheers from a rowdy bunch of miners in an alehouse after one of these performances. He had overheard vampires complaining about mandatory overtime in the mines and had ad-libbed a rousing plea for shared profits from the management. It was so convincing Daryn had warned him that he may want to choose his comedy routines a little better or they may find themselves working the mines.

Each one of the vamps in the group at Rezzies was from an affluent family, and the collection of expensive motorcars surrounding their tables made it look like an exotic dealership had sprung up at the diner.

"Let's hope your luck continues through the qualifying runs," hissed a light-haired vamp named Millington Brimstone, as he lay on the hood of his car that was pulled up close to the tables.

"Oh, Mills, luck is for the timid and the poor!" Erik laughed as he paced the area. "We make our owwwwwn luck," he howled dramatically.

The group erupted in laughter. There was another voice laughing in the chorus that wasn't theirs and more than a few of them immediately noticed. Simultaneously they shifted their eyes on the uniformed attendant who had taken their order. He was giggling and wore an awkward hat, a size too small, on his head.

Daryn raised his chin and immediately looked irate. "I'm sorry, is part of your job laughing at me and my friends?"

The attendant puckered his lips as if to whistle, then shook his head violently."No, no Sir. I, uh… I just have the bill here." He smiled nervously at Millington, who simply glared back at him loathingly.

"Bring it here." Daryn snapped his fingers.

The attendant flinched. It was unnecessary to be that rude, he thought, and besides, he was seventy years older than this Fledge. He walked the ticket over, to have Daryn quickly pull it from his hand.

"Ah. Hmm." Daryn held it back out. "I'm not paying for the sticks. The blood gravy was disgusting."

The attendant took back the ticket and shook his head in disagreement. "Made that fresh myself this first dark, Sir."

"It was spoiled," Daryn said flatly, slowly blinking his eyes.

The attendant coughed in disbelief, looking around and at the ground, then mumbled, "Reckon it's not the only thing spoiled 'round here."

Daryn leapt up with his chest puffed out."Excuse me?!" He looked at Erik. "Do you believe this ass?"

Erik folded his hands together and approached the attendant like a prosecuting attorney. "I'm wondering if we may need to file an Incident with the R.E.D.? I know that I'm feeling a little squeamish myself." Erik feigned stomach pains.

Through clenched teeth Daryn growled, "Or maybe I should just get KOTU Von Firstenstein down here to lock the doors until we find out if they've got Bog in their batter!"

The attendant was wincing and breathing heavy. He began nodding and looking at the ground. Finally he said, "Maybe I made a mistake, Sir." His eyes darted around the ground in anger.

"What's that, boy?" Daryn asked. Some of his mates laughed.

The attendant bit down on his bottom lip, raised his head up to look Daryn in the eyes. He held his gaze for a few seconds while he brought his breathing down. "I was clearly mistaken about the gravy, Sir. Please allow me to make this a complimentary dining experience tonight."

Daryn smiled and looked at his schoolmates. "Now THAT'S customer service!"

They all broke into loud, hysterical laughter.

"Staying out of trouble, I hope?" Vlad Von Firstenstein said from a large, luxurious motorcar behind Daryn. His driver waited with the engine running as Vlad stepped out and walked over to the boys.

Vladimir Von Firstenstein was tall and stately. He had the classic, slicked back, deep black vampire hairstyle with a thick silver stripe on the left side. He also had a nasty scar near his left eye. He got it during his first Pike. He said it was from some overgrowth down in the forbidden land, but that was all he'd say about it. Vlad truly loved his status as King of the Undead, though most referred to him simply as "KOTU" or "KOTU Council Member." Official duties required hosting many of the traditional affairs, ceremonies, marriages, and even funerals, or "Passing Ceremonies" as they were called.

It didn't happen that often, but vampires could pass. Losing limbs or massive multiple injuries (contrary to the ancient lore) would usually be enough for a vampire to die off from the world of the Realm. There was also at least one or two sunlight/exposure victims per year, usually drunken alehouse patrons caught too close to Dawn, getting incinerated by the light. In spite of the very strict rules of the High Council to never, under any circumstance allow yourself to be near sunlight, some vampires would chance it and would pay the ultimate price.

"What a fine looking bunch of vampires." Vlad had an unmistakably rich speaking voice. And with 222 years of KOTU status, many recognized it as THE voice of the Realm, having grow up hearing that voice officiating every important event that had ever happened in their lives.

"Hello, Father." Daryn's apathy was quickly eclipsed with the other Fledges enthusiasm, with a volley of *'Hello Sir'* and *'Good evening KOTU.'*

"I expect you're all, no doubt, excited about the qualifying trials starting soon?" A strong round of yes's followed.

"Good. Excellent." Vlad put his arm on Daryn's shoulder. "It's important work."

Vlad looked around the group and smiled. "Yes, that's right. I said work. It's hard work maintaining our traditions. Being examples. Vampires like us set a higher standard for ourselves. Upholding the dignity and the order in the Realm." He smiled at Daryn and patted his back. "It's the highest honor."

"Hear, hear!" The boys whooted loudly in the traditional answer of a call to arms.

"Ha," Vlad smiled. "To be finally rid of your juvenile Fledge and to be joining the ranks of vampires. I truly admire you." He waved cheerfully at them and started back to his car. As he opened the door he called, "Oh. Son…"

Daryn left the group. "Yes, Father."

"Do me a favor, will you? Alex and I were talking…"

Daryn scowled as he knew what was coming next.

"He asked if you'd stop by and visit Bebe tomorrow."

Daryn was squinting and trying to open his mouth.

"Look, I've got a pretty important deal I'm in the middle of with Alex." He squeezed Daryn's shoulder and winked. "It's just a small favor for your dear old father." He smiled. "Besides, how bad can it be spending a little time with Bebe?"

Daryn scowled. Between lectures on the virtues of the Pike and having Bebe Bellmore thrown at him by both of their parents, Daryn was sick of his father's gratuitous reasoning. Daryn slowly nodded his head and muttered sarcastically, "Hear, hear."

At that same moment, miles away, Sonny's bicycle glided to a stop in front of Bellmore Manor. He wheeled the bike into the tall shrubbery off the street and turned away from the winding walkway that led to the door. Instead he walked back toward the direction he had come from. After a quick dozen steps

he ducked into the thick trees that separated the Bellmores and their neighbor's equally sprawling estate. Sonny stealthily walked the treeline up until he was alongside the east wing of Bebe's house. Glancing around, he quickly shimmied up the enormous oak that stood twenty feet from the house. Sonny quickly found a comfortable crotch in the tree, thirty feet up. He lowered the brim of his cap and focused on the bay windows that jutted from the house. These provided a clear view of a dark, empty room.

Ninety minutes passed before several wall sconces colored the room with warm yellow light. Sonny opened his eyes to find Bebe pulling her thick black hair into a bun at the back of her head. Even with all the hours they'd spent together studying, his throat still clenched as he watched her. He closed his eyes and smiled, pretending that he got to gently kiss the perfectly pale skin of her neck before she turned out her light.

Musical accompaniment for this scene:

"MIDDLE OF THE NIGHT"

FROM THE ALBUM "RISE OF THE CAFE RACER"

DEANO JONES & THE SWEET DEATH SYMPHONY

CHAPTER SIX:
FALL IN LOVE
WITH ME

"So why would they be using an equation like that?" Andi was confused and talking to herself. "It wouldn't be eliminating elements... it would be... creating." But it couldn't be possible, she thought.

Andi had been waiting in Sonny's room for a little over an hour. He was late, again, from his tutoring with Bebe. Andi had been leafing through one of the many notebooks that she had copied from the great library at K&S. There were several pages from an ancient book on blood purification rituals that she was finding very interesting.

The notes had started with the details of the ceremony to be performed once the blood was finally purified. Things like the exact placement of the goblet on the Alter of Sacrifice—it had to have been cast from pure gold, no metals. So much more pomp with the vampires from several hundred years ago, she thought. As fascinating as the ritual was to her, she knew it seemed unlikely to yield the desired result.

Gradually within her notes there were notes from actual scientific diagrams concerning the chemical process, and this looked promising to Andi.

In the early days before blood berry was synthesized, there was sickness and superstition surrounding the consumption of animals. In the absence of humans to feed on, the vampires were making mistakes in the raising and caring for of animals, and were having what seemed like an allergic reaction to some. Crude rituals would be hastily executed in any attempt the rid the Realm of disease. At the same time, the scholars and scientists of the day were hard at work trying to inoculate or biologically alter blood. Some of the equations in these notes had made sense to her, as they sought to remove the specific elements that defined blood as one genus or another. But there was a particular equation she was looking at now that was like nothing she had seen. It was speculating that, with absolutely no human blood to start with, human blood could actually evolve from the combination of listed elements.

"They were trying to *make* human blood," she spoke out loud again. She flipped ahead and scanned some early results. She rocked her head and mouthed the words she read.

"Well of course not," she pleaded. "There's no surprise that trial failed!" She recognized that there would have undoubtedly been massive contamination with these ancient test subjects. Contaminants her ancestors had not yet discovered. Most of the vampire sickness of that day they would learn was, more often than not, a result of water pollution. The same water that was fed to the livestock that the vampires were learning to consume.

Her mind was racing as she tried to project what some of these similar trials may look like with the benefit of the modern facilities and added knowledge of the day.

"Sorry I'm late," huffed Sonny as he bound into his room, letting his book bag fall to the floor. His excitement overshadowed hers. "It took forever to get over the Arch. The R.E.D. were all over the place. I think they may have been looking for SDS." Sonny raised his eyebrows excitedly.

He had told Andi about hearing some music late at night and she knew he was always trying to find out more about SDS gatherings. Not as much lately, but Sonny had often taken long, late night rides to obscure sections of the city in hopes he may stumble on a group of the merrymakers.

"It's completely fascist the way elders harass the SDS. I mean, do they really need to be having the R.E.D. round up Fledges simply because they're having a little fun?" Sonny was still breathing heavy and peeled off his wet jacket.

"I know," Andi shook her head in disbelief. "Can't we at least enjoy our youth?" Andi was trying to seem more sympathetic than she was actual felt about the merrymakers for Sonny's benefit.

"We have hundreds of years to get sufficiently bored and never look at the moon again." He paused and smiled at his friend, then collapsed into his desk chair.

Andi smiled back. She liked how he looked after one of his long rides—winded and dirty. Sonny was damp to his bones from the rain he passed through. Though his hair was cropped short on the sides, his big mop of dark locks on top had now fallen forward into his eyes. He looked nothing like the vampire boy of their youth that she had spent so many nights playing games and reading books with. She had a sudden, bizarre thought of what a baby vamp of theirs would look like, and it made a tiny laugh squeak out of her.

Sonny laughed back and then winced. "Hey, is it alright if we skip Linguistics tonight? I just spent an hour on that with Bebe."

Andi sunk inside at the mention of Bebe, but did the complete opposite outwardly. "Anything you want to work on is fine," she grinned warmly.

"How 'bout…" he scanned her notebooks, "What's that? Chemistry?"

Andi glanced and remembered the stack of ancient Realm contraband she had brought with her.

"Oh, oh, I forgot to tell you…" She snatched up the journal that had the blood rituals, "This!" Andi froze and pressed her lips together.

Sonny waited, and after a few seconds leaned his neck forward raising his eyebrows, wondering what she was waiting for.

"Okay, here's the thing…" Andi tried to be nonchalant. "During the summers, while I was working at my father's lab, you know, I found all these incredible books in the library. Unbelievable stuff. I mean, things that would completely blow your mind. And, well, of course you can't take them out of there…"

"Because they're classified," Sonny nodded. "Realm security issues."

"Yes," Andi paused. "Well…" she opened the journal and turned to the blood purification equations.

"There are some serious ideas in here."

She didn't bother to show Sonny the actual diagram because he was still at a Fledge academy level with his Chemistry and Biology. And besides that, the 800-year-old notes used ancient symbols that hardly anyone in the Realm, Fledge or Elder, knew anything about interpreting. But Sonny was still intrigued.

"What kind of serious things are we talking about? And by the way… are you completely insane? Even if your father begged the Council for mercy they would probably still leave you out in the light."

"Human blood." Andi smiled and tapped the notebook, completely ignoring the last part of what he just said. "They were working on making real human blood entirely from animals!"

Sonny's face soured in disbelief. "Come on. I would think you'd need a human or two for that."

Andi got more serious.

"Yes, we would think that, ordinarily. But think about what that generation would accomplish. Blood berry synthesis, sterilization, disease-free aqueducts, the HellHound alliance. They had a little bit of a hot streak around the second century, Sonny. And I really think that because these experiments were done before all of those groundbreaking discoveries, their early trials lacked some of the simple ingredients that we now have."

Sonny had been distracted at the mention of HellHounds. He always wished he could see more of them. The powerful canines were once abundant in the Lowlands and anywhere farming and mining took place. There was a powerful alliance in the first century between Vampire and HellHound. Their numbers, too, suffered greatly in the early nights. HellHounds were invaluable to the Realm. As well as being strong, daytime sentinels to oversee livestock, they were highly intelligent creatures capable of a wide array of skilled labor. But with so much farming and daytime necessities being automated, the Hounds were getting scarce. Not so much their numbers; they just populated the outermost regions, the forests of the north and south. Parts of the Realm that most vampires had never gone and never would. Over the centuries Hell-Hounds had shied away from vampires until some people thought the Hounds may hold contempt for vampires. Sonny was reminded of an old Fledgling rhyme:

Vampire and HellHound walked together,
Stars and daylight teamed forever.
But fall from grace, their path's disunion,
One night shall return fate's conclusion.

Sonny focused back on Andi and sighed. "I just think that vampires back then were so ridiculously superstitious. Even if they did invent some great stuff."

"*Supernatural* is more like it. It wouldn't be so well documented if it wasn't true." Andi was starting to talk faster. "Almost every piece of historical record I have ever come across—I'm talking about bedtime stories and court records—will make casual references to vampires flying." She started manically flipping through pages. "There's so much information to suggest that we actually could change shape and fly. So many written accounts, that in a real assembly of a High Council, where vampires acknowledge FACT, the burden of proof would be on the vampire who's saying that we didn't actually do these things." She abruptly closed the notebook and stared hard at Sonny, shaking her head. "It's overwhelming, Sonny!"

Sonny was exhausted and too tired to object. He had stayed slumped in his chair watching her flailing her hands as she worked herself to a boil. It had been very amusing. Andi was not someone who was usually subject to emotional outbursts. Even in Phys Arts she was capable of great focus while engaged in very athletically demanding exercise.

Andi had also always been smarter than him, so part of Sonny was thor-

Vampire and Hell Hound walked together,

Stars and Daylight teamed forever.

But fall from grace, their path's disunion.

One night shall return fates conclusion.

oughly capable of believing every word she had just said. And human blood was, after all, the historical sustenance of vampires. It was definitely enticing to think about human blood and actually getting to taste it.

"Well, if you whip up a batch maybe it'll help me win some of these qualifying runs." Sonny smirked and mockingly polished his fingernails on his wet shirt.

"Qualifying runs?" Andi was startled. "When did this happen? You're really going to do it?" She didn't realize that her jaw had dropped.

"You know, I have been thinking about it for a while. Then I saw Slim the other night and he asked me about it."

"Just like that?" Andi was still surprised.

They had talked about the excitement of the Pike, but she had never heard Sonny mention wanting to actually ride in the Pike.

"What, did Slim talk you into it?" Andi leaned and pointed at Sonny with an eye cocked. "Now, the secret to the Pike, Sonny Boy…"

"Oh come on, give me some credit." Sonny tried to sound offended, but then smiled. "I think it's a great honor and who knows, maybe I can even rank."

A sudden wave of biting emotion pulsed through Andi. The way Sonny had spoken that last sentence made him sound older. He sounded like a "real" vampire. It seemed like anytime she thought of Sonny anymore she would be overwhelmed with ideas of them being together, and not just as friends. She imagined him ranking high in the Pike, then gaining a teaching position at the prestigious Herzog University. They would have a baby and she would have a laboratory built in their brick house in the Cambria Quarter. He would grab her by the shoulders with his powerful arms every morning and kiss her before he rode his bicycle to work.

Andi looked down and blinked her eyes. After a moment she looked back at him. She wanted to just blurt out that she loved him. She was about to open her mouth when a tap on the door stopped her.

Evanna delicately entered the room, keeping both hands on the door.

"Hi, Honey. Hello, Andromeda." She smiled cheerfully. "I don't mean to bother you kids while you're studying, but I wanted to let you know, Sonny, that Mr. Bellmore called." Evanna turned her head to the side and frowned a little. "Apparently you left with Bebe's notebooks and left yours there."

Sonny picked the bag from the floor and after a quick glance sighed. "Yeah, I guess I did."

Evanna reached and touched his wrist, "I told him I would be more than happy to leave a little early and drop…"

"Oh, no Mom," Sonny shook his head. "I'll go back over, I'll take care of it."

"Tonight?" Evanna whispered. "Oh, Sonny, it's still raining."

Sonny had already begun putting a dry jacket on.

"Bebe has a quiz first thing tomorrow night. She's going to need her notes." Sonny was hastily zipping the bag and slung it over his shoulder. "I won't be long, Mom." He kissed his mother on the cheek.

"Guess I'll see you tomorrow, Andi."

"Sure," she piped, as if nothing at all was wrong.

After Sonny eagerly hurried out of the room, Evanna shook her head. "I swear that boy would use any excuse to get on his bike." Evanna made a cute grin that wrinkled her nose. "Would you like something warm to drink, Andromeda?"

Andi was choking on her own tongue. It had made her feel like she was going to throw up when Sonny rushed for his jacket at the mere mention of Bebe needing something. She coughed, cleared her throat and acted like she hadn't a care in the world. "Oh, no ma'am. I'm fine." Andi felt like she may collapse from pure sadness. "Would it be okay if I waited in here until my father comes? I can still get some studying in."

"Well of course, Honey," Evanna grabbed the half dozen or so pieces of Sonny's wardrobe that were strewn around the room. As she walked out she looked back. "If you need anything at all, just let me know."

Once the door shut Andi sat down right down on the floor where she had stood. Her breathing was short and staccato. She wondered why she felt this way. She was physically ill over Sonny. Why didn't Sonny feel the same way about her? How could he possibly not notice her and the way that she looked at him? It was like a dagger had been stuck in her neck. She just wanted it all to stop. How could she make this stop happening? Andi reached for a pen and paper and just started writing:

My soul waits through daylight hours
Till Dark breaks and time is ours
If you would be on time tomorrow I'd make believe it's me
I've asked each star in the sky not once have they replied
Guess it must just be another lie they tell us when we're young
I think I'm hiding in plain sight or could it be I'm not your type
What does it take to catch your eye I'm holding on so tight

Why won't you fall in love with me?
Why won't you take a chance and see?
Was made for you and you for me

Known one another all our lives
Hate all the same things in our time
There's not another that I have told, the things I've told to you
A part of my soul dies each time
You talk of her and I ache inside
Can't you see it's me at your side, I'll never let you down

Why won't you fall in love with me?
Why won't you take a chance and see?
Was made for you and you for me.
Why won't you fall in love with me?
If you'd listen you'd hear me
Not a dream but a destiny.

I'd stand on the cliffs of Mount Cain
There's nothing I wouldn't lose for your name
Would follow you into the Day
Oh, our souls are torn from the pages of lore
An ancient fire that just doesn't burn anymore

And maybe it's my moment in time
But my soul I swear til I die
Why won't you fall in love with me?
If you'd listen, our death song will be
Not a dream, but a destiny
Why won't you fall in love with me?
If you'd listen you'd hear me
Cause I was made for you…
And you for me

Musical accompaniment for this scene:
"FALL IN LOVE WITH ME"
FROM THE ALBUM "RISE OF THE CAFE RACER"
DEANO JONES & THE SWEET DEATH SYMPHONY

CHAPTER SEVEN:
IT'S SONNY,
SONNY LEGATUS

Borgo Aref slowly opened the door to Bellmore Manor. He recognized the young vampire. "Good evening," he groaned, "Brianna will be out momentarily." Borgo swung his arm, offering the gigantic wooden bench in the foyer.

Within a couple minutes Bebe emerged from her upstairs bedroom, stopping at the top of the staircase to smile devilishly at the vamp who sat waiting for her. She pouted and purred like a kitten.

"I hope I haven't kept you waiting long. I just wanted to look extra pretty for you."

Bebe's black anaconda skin pencil skirt looked painted on. She was bursting out of a low-cut, high-collared, iridescent top. Her descent from the second floor took thirty full seconds in her five-inch stiletto heels. Her flawless milky skin seemed it could glow in the dark. After Bebe finally made her way off the staircase she inched across the hallway and pressed her cold cheek against Daryn's, not wanting to smudge her blood red lipstick.

"Everything you see is yours to play with," she whispered in his ear as they embraced.

Daryn was looking straight ahead. He forced a smile. "I was thinking we'd go to Rezzies."

Bebe's eyes twitched for a second. She cleared her throat and stood with her hands on her hips. She smiled seductively. "I may be a bit overdressed for the drive-in, don't you think?"

"Oh, no one will mind," Daryn said casually, turning toward the door.

Fire burned in her eyes. The look she had on her face could have stricken fear in the heart of an R.E.D. Agent. Daryn had walked a couple steps toward the door and then turned back to her. Bebe paused, drew a deep breath then slowly batted her eyes.

"If that's where you want to take me then that's where I will go," she said submissively.

"Alright then," Daryn said with a jump in his step. "Borgo... thank you."

"Yes, Sir," Borgo replied as he pulled the door open for them.

Their decline along the stone walkway was particularly slow with Bebe's heels. She 'oohed' distressfully and held Daryn's arm tightly as they descended. During that time they watched as Sonny arrived on his bicycle down at the street. It still would take Bebe and Daryn another minute before they would be close enough to even speak to him. Sonny didn't mind; he would have bought tickets to this event. He was frozen at Bebe's beauty.

"What's this, a delivery?" Daryn mumbled to Bebe halfway down.

"Oh, that's Sonny." Bebe was having a difficult time with the crevices between the stones on the path.

"You know this vamp?" Daryn asked condescendingly.

Bebe rolled her eyes at Daryn. "He tutors me."

"He looks like a dork. What's with the bicycle?"

"Not everyone has a big sexy motorcar, Daryn," Bebe cooed.

Daryn was fixated on Sonny and had a confrontational look on his face when he and Bebe finally made it to the bottom of the walkway.

"It's a little late for tutoring, isn't it?" Daryn asked rudely.

Bebe was still holding Daryn's arm for support and she lightly slapped his forearm like they were an old married couple.

"Daryn!" She frowned playfully at Daryn and then smiled at Sonny. "You didn't actually bring my notes back, did you? That's sooo sweet of you."

Sonny reached into his bag and fished for the notebooks. "Yeah, I'm so sorry, I don't know how I mixed them up."

On solid ground, Bebe let go of Daryn's arm and fluffed her hair. "There's no reason to apologize for being a gentleman, Sonny." She shot an evil glance at Daryn, and while still looking at Daryn, added, "It's always nice when someone knows how to treat a Lady."

Daryn was pursing his lips and sizing Sonny up.

"You boys have something in common," Bebe said sweetly, enjoying the thought that Daryn might be jealous of Sonny.

"What, we've both given you instruction in the downstairs library?" Daryn said arrogantly.

Sonny turned away, feeling embarrassed for Bebe. He didn't like Daryn. Not just because of how he was acting tonight. Daryn had a reputation as a bully. Though Sonny had never had any problems with him, some of the vamps in Sonny's classes had. Daryn and his friends had dumped a bloodshake on Freddie Mortensen's head in the lunchroom a couple years ago. That in itself wasn't such a big deal, but it had been while Freddie was giving a short lecture to students about what he would do as student council president if elected. Freddie was running against Daryn's friend Erik and they bullied him so much he eventually dropped out of the race. When Freddie's father complained, the Academy said they couldn't do anything about it. Later that year Freddie's father was demoted at his job at the Department of Motorized Transportation.

"No," Bebe said, this time slapping Daryn's arm not so playfully, "Both you and Sonny are running the Pike."

Daryn cocked his head and laughed without opening his mouth. He glanced at the bicycle against the tree. "Is that your ride over there, chief?"

For the first time since he had gotten there, Sonny raised his chin and looked Daryn squarely in the eye. He didn't like him and his bully friends. And he liked less the way he treated Bebe. Trying to muster courage, he imagined how Slim would be holding his body if he were in this situation. With a new-found bravado Sonny laughed. "No, mate. And I'll be running for Glory, you can bet on it."

Both Daryn and Bebe were a little surprised. There was an air of Lowla in Sonny's voice and it changed the tone of this conversation immediately. Sonny suddenly didn't seem like some awkward Fledge. "Running for Glory" was also an old-time saying that referred to the entire contest, but specifically conjured up images of the Rider that wouldn't return. That Rider was immortalized, and in some ways as revered as the winner.

Back in Pike Number Four, Riders were faced with the inexplicable history of only one Rider ever returning from the Pike's Run. When asked if he feared not returning, Rider Wolfgang Snagov said to the crowd gathered in Strigoi's town square, *No matter who wins this race, today we Run for Glory!*' To which he was answered with a deafening "Hear, hear!" from all that were there. "Run for Glory" became the mantra of the 'real' vampire and suggested that you would happily and fearlessly face your demise for the honor of the Pike.

With these words, Sonny had turned this from some schoolboy-type posturing to the proper posturing of vampire men (which of course was always still steeped in juvenile schoolboy theatrics). But nonetheless, if this were a game of chess, Sonny may have well huffed "check" after that move.

In a sort of acknowledgement, Daryn nodded as if addressing one of his fencing partners. He was content at seeking to humiliate this vamp in a more mature way.

"Excellent," Daryn smiled. "I'm running a gold-winged Gargoyle myself. Oh, some slight modifications, but I hope it's enough to rank me."

Daryn smiled broadly then squinted and asked over inquisitively. "What will you be running, Sully?"

Sonny was had been unflinching, but felt a lump in his throat. Again he imagined what Slim would do right now. Calm and cool he thought.

REMEMBER...

RUN FOR GLORY

"NO MATTER WHO WINS THIS RACE, TODAY WE RUN FOR GLORY!"

WOLFGANG SNAGOV

Sonny let a confident smile pull one side of his mouth. "I've got a Cafe Racer."

Daryn dramatically glanced at the sky as if searching the vast memory banks of his mind for a forgotten combination to a lock. Finally looking back. "Strange, I've never heard of one of those. Is that a new model?"

Sonny had still been staring intently at Daryn. He shook his head no and grinned calmly. "It's a traditional bike. Not a lot of fancy gadgets."

"Well I'm excited!" Daryn said gingerly. "We'll get a bit of a history lesson with our Pike." He turned to Bebe. "Shall we go?"

Bebe had thoroughly enjoyed the vampire machismo. Particularly because she thought it was for her benefit.

"Of course!" She offered her hand to be helped off the curb. She then looked at Sonny and smiled. "Would you be a dear and leave my notes with Borgo?"

"Absolutely," Sonny smiled back.

"Thank you," She purred.

Sonny stepped aside as they entered the street and waited as Bebe got in the motorcar. Daryn shut the door behind her and began walking around to his side.

Before Daryn climbed into his side of the motorcar, Sonny called after him, "Hey!" Sonny smiled. "It's Sonny. Sonny Legatus."

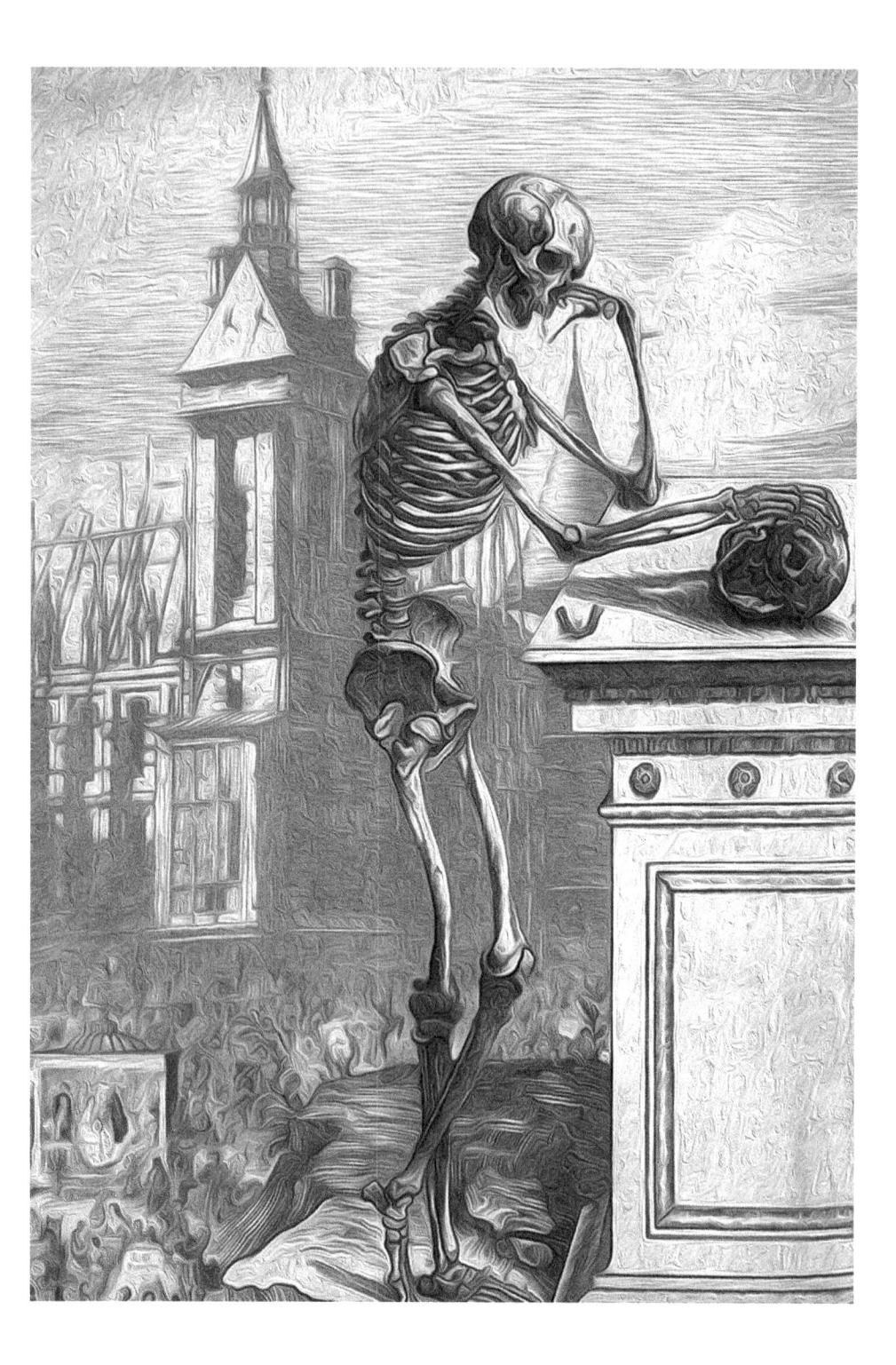

CHAPTER EIGHT:
THE ORGANIZATION GETS ORGANIZED

Slim's truck was piled with iron and tools. It was a beat up rust- and purple-colored industrial style vehicle that had an iron frame welded onto the open-air bed. It made it look more like something used to transport soldiers than scrap metal. He had stopped in front of Sonny's house as Andi was arriving.

"Hey there, Miss Andi," Slim smiled and waved.

"Hi Slim!" Andi hadn't seen Slim Jim is some time but, like Sonny, she had known Slim for many years. In fact, last winter Andi's father had hired Slim to spot weld parts of their iron fence. Slim had done incredible work and was able to fashion the Kepler name across the top of the large swinging doors of the gate to the driveway.

"Sonny told me he's running the Pike! So exciting!"

"It is, isn't it?" He grinned and pointed with his thumb over his shoulder. "I picked up some more parts for his bike tonight."

"You guys are building it yourselves?"

"Oh yeah," Slim nodded. "It's the best way to do it." He winked. "Gotta customize her."

Though Andi wasn't very mechanically inclined, she was fascinated with the way a combustion engine worked. "It sounds like so much fun." She frowned a little. "A lot more fun than studying for the Focus."

Slim was reaching in his back pocket. "You know anything about motorbikes, Andi?" He wiped his fingers with a handkerchief. "We can always use another pair of hands."

"Oh," Andi laughed. "No, I've never even sat on one." She looked at the heaps of black iron in the back of the truck and then intently at Slim.

"But I've always thought it was so interesting the way the expansion of the high-temperature and high-pressures gases in those small cylinders could apply direct force on components of the engine and actually force the component to move its larger body. And, you know, that in the case of motorbikes, with their two-stroke engines... that there's no dedicated intake or exhaust strokes, so..." she smiled wildly. "You know, that it's just the downward motion of the piston that pressurizes a fresh charge in the crankcase."

"Wow," Slim said in astonishment.

"I know," Andi agreed. "Chemical energy manifesting itself into mechanical energy... it's awesome!"

"You, Miss Kepler, just earned the title of Head Scientist on Team Sonny!" He pulled a worn leather cap from his back pocket, punched it into shape and pulled in on his head. "That is, if you want the job." He whispered, "I'm afraid it's not a paying gig, though," and laughed loudly.

Andi would have been happy enough working on a project like this with only Slim. He was so thrilling to be around. He seemed to enjoy every moment in his life. But the idea of working on this with Sonny warmed her to her very soul.

"I accept, kind Sir," she bowed like a Lady, laughing at her poor form.

"Very nice." He motioned at the house. "I need to get Sonny to give me a hand, lemme run in…"

"Oh, he won't be home yet," She cut in. "Unless Bebe has canceled their tutoring session. You know, like if she's getting her hair done or something." Andi paused, resisting the urge to make more fun of Bebe, then perked up. "I just come by early and study before him." She smiled.

Slim heard the spike in her tone regarding Bebe (any vampire within a block would have).

"Well then, maybe you can get your hands dirty tonight!"

While Slim got his truck unloaded back at his shop, Andi went in the Legatuses' home to tell Evanna that Sonny could find her at Slim's. Sonny had already told his mother about his plans to try and qualify for the Pike and Evanna was as excited as Andi. There was something magical about having someone who was going to actually run the Pike. Of course, hundreds of Riders would be eliminated the very first day of qualifying, but there was still a tremendous pride to know anyone who tried.

Evanna wouldn't let Andi leave to cross the field without taking a tin of blood berry pie for herself and Slim. As they ate the delicious pie, Slim got Andi up to speed on the motorbike build.

Slim had secured a used R.E.D. motorbike, which actually only amounted to the frame and engine. The handlebars were missing, the seat was eaten by rats, and the tires were flat. But, as Slim said, it was a start.

Motorbikes, like motorcars, were expensive in the Realm. There were a only a few places that they made them and they took a long time to assemble. All motorized vehicles were assembled by hand. Though there was great iron production and industry in the Realm, there wasn't much in the way of large-scale or automated industry. Even a used motorbike could potentially cost two years pay for someone like Slim Jim. Slim had, however, the advantage of having a vast and varied group of people who called him a friend. For this, he had called on an old friend in the Rules Enforcement Division. Slim had been one of the very few "Regulars" who took arms and fought with the R.E.D. during the uprising of 767 ADWB and they hadn't forgotten him.

Slim had been very young, barely out of his Fledge at the time of the miners' revolt, more commonly referred to as the Uprising of 767 ADWB. Like many at that time, his Specialty had been determined to work mining for iron ores - the minerals needed for iron production. The furnaces within Mount Cain ran twenty-four hours a day producing iron for the Realm. Massive amounts of coal were needed to fuel the great ovens. Though wood had always been abundant in the Lowlands, iron was the material of choice, particularly in the cities. The 700's were the height of expansion in the Realm and the need for iron was greater than what could be produced. Workers were asked to work around the clock and threatened with an even more unsavory reassignment if they complained.

The coal miners could not produce enough coal to satisfy the smelting fires of the iron ore miners. The iron ore mining companies accused the coal miners of deliberately holding out on the coal supply to drive their price up. The much larger iron ore organization, of which Slim was an member, began singling out the coal miner leaders for harassment. Eventually the iron ore mining company had groups of goons raiding entire coal mining camps, marauding indiscriminately. The High Council sent in R.E.D. troops to break it up but they underestimated to size of the iron ore miners' numbers. The 150 R.E.D. vamps were sorely outnumbered by the 1800 iron ore miners. And with winter in Mount Cain setting in, became stuck in the middle of a full-on war, the R.E.D. were facing a massacre. Having seen what his own company was doing, Slim was one of the first Regulars to volunteer alongside the R.E.D. and with what they could recruit from the coal miners, helped successfully hold off the iron ore goons for the long, cold winter of 767 ADWB.

In the Spring, more R.E.D. enforcements arrived and the uprising was put to rest. But because the iron ore mining company was owned, in part, by the sitting KOTU, Dracov Von Firstenstein, there was much political pressure to sweep the incident under the table. The KOTU was lobbying hard to make scapegoats of a handful of iron ore workers who 'were instrumental in soliciting the bulk of the workers to revolt'. Which really meant, everyone that wasn't paid off to keep his mouth shut. Slim's breaking ranks with his Specialty made him a clear choice for persecution. He was labeled an activist leader, and if not for the R.E.D. defending him, may have quite certainly received a 'left out

in the light' judgment from the High Council. As it was, Slim was whitelisted from mining and almost unemployable because of that tarnished record. The R.E.D. tried unsuccessfully to hire him, but it was simply too hot politically to bring Slim into their fold. He also had a metal plate in the back of his head from one of the skirmishes with miners, and the High Council had deemed it a handicap for service in the Rules Enforcement Division. Which, of course, there was no irony lost on the fact that he had been injured volunteering with the R.E.D. It was at this time that Slim Jim embarked on what was now his unique lifestyle within the Realm of not adhering to a Specialty.

Despite of all this, there wasn't an older R.E.D. Agent who wouldn't buy a round at the mention of Slim Jim, and he was able to ask a favor for the used motorbike.

"I recon there's enough time to round up all the little things we need," Slim assured Andi, with blood berry pie dripping from the corner of his mouth.

Andi giggled and motioned at him with her own mouth's corner. "Is this motorbike going to be able to keep up? It looks pretty old."

Slim wiped his face and walked over to the bike. "Oh, she's a beaut, Andi. Don't let a little rust fool you."

"No, it was the cobwebs and flat tires and…"

"Yeah, yeah, yeah," Slim laughed.

He crouched down, closed one eye and framed the bike with his hands. "Sometimes you gotta squint. You gotta just imagine what it can be." He looked hard at the old bike for a minute in silence, before finally lowering his arms and turning to Andi. "Anything in this Realm is possible if you want it bad enough."

Andi was still eating her huge slice of pie. She smiled and chewed, thinking to herself that Slim may very well be from another world.

The door flew open and Sonny was breathing heavy. "I think I broke my own record." He tossed a cloth bag on the floor.

"Braided sleeves?" Slim asked as he picked up the bag.

"Yeah. Made it from downtown to here in thirty-five minutes." Sonny looked at Slim with amazement. "How did you know they would be there?" He turned to Andi. "He told me to check the big debris bins by the Ravensland Medical Center. There were lengths and lengths of this wire braided cable housing."

"Perfect for running our brake and clutch cables in," Slim winked. "They always renovate the medical centers right before the Pike. I knew they'd be running new cabling on the equipment. This is pure gold. Like armor."

"Sorry about being so late," Sonny reached over and snatched a piece of pie filling from Andi's plate. "You want to head back home and study?"

Andi shook her head. She pulled a notebook out and began to write. "Let's start with a list of everything else we're going to need. Right down to oil. You know, not just the obvious—tires, seat, but all the the little things."

She looked up. Both were staring at her dumbfounded.

"Well what's the matter? We have a motorbike to build, guys!"

Slim laughed and emptied the bag of braided cabling on the floor. "Just what this organization needs… some organization!"

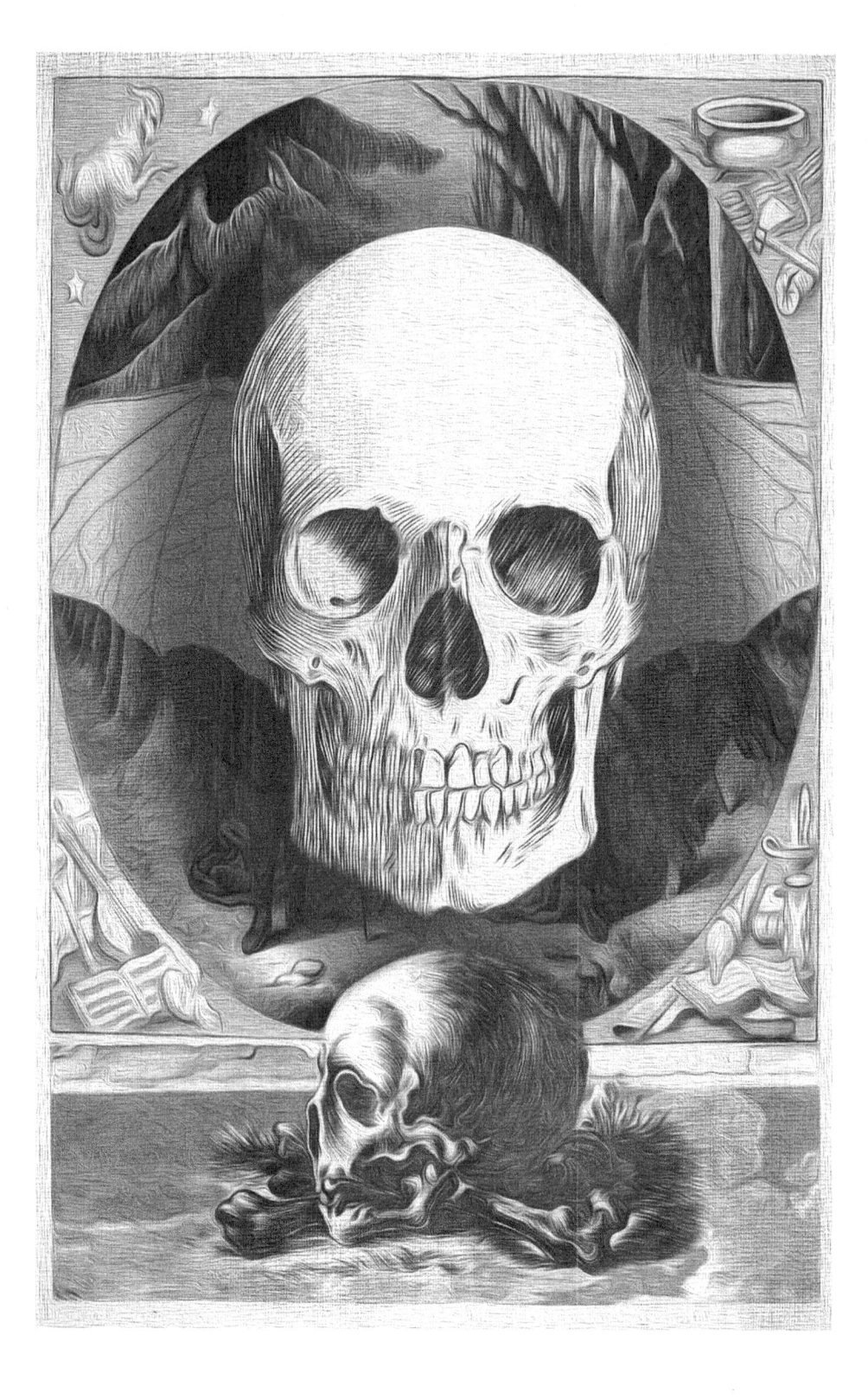

CHAPTER NINE:
THE HELLFIRE INCIDENT

The body was knotted and disfigured beyond recognition. You could almost make out that he may have been wearing a long overcoat, as it seemed there was folded fabric melted to the corpse. This unfortunate vampire had wandered out into the light, or more likely had lost his way home from a night at the alehouse and simply passed out on this bench.

The sun had brought Hellfire to the Earth and consumed this body in flames, shrinking it down to a fraction of its size. Some municipal workers had found this poor soul near first dark on a remote park bench across from a bus stop where they waited for a ride to work.

As required by the High Council, they reported it to the R.E.D. And, as required the Realm, the KOTU Council Member was on hand to make a public record of this 'Hellfire' Incident. The KOTU would help try to identify the body, and traditionally, say a few words asking for safe passage for the soul of the vampire who had passed from the Realm.

"I never can get used to the smell." Vlad coughed and brought a silk handkerchief to his mouth. "How about you, Detective?" He looked at the female R.E.D. Agent on the other side of the corpse.

She was sipping a piping hot cup of goat blood she had bought from a street vendor at an intersection a few blocks away. She had known that the park where the corpse was found was remote and there would be no 'blood wagons' near, so she had wisely grabbed her breakfast.

"No Sir, I never do, either."

She stared at the pile in front of them, turning her head occasionally, then squinting back toward the direction of bustling rush hour traffic, three blocks away.

Vlad was irritated he hadn't thought to grab some warm blood, and was hoping this wouldn't take too long. As KOTU, Vlad would have to stay there until the R.E.D. Agent on-scene made her report. The High Council did not want any conflicting reports sent to other Realm agencies.

"Anything wrong, Detective?"

Vlad had known and dealt with this R.E.D. Agent, Hellamina Muntz, for many years. She was always very thorough in her required duties of investigating Hellfire Incidents. More so, Vlad thought, than she needed to be. She would sometimes delay him for hours while she tried to piece together exactly what had happened.

"Well, I don't think so, Sir," Hellamina cleared her throat. "But I am wondering..." Vlad closed his eyes as he waited for the detective. "Does it seem strange to you that this vampire, even if he may have had a little too much to drink... that he would be walking in the opposite direction of his home?" She sipped her hot drink, still staring at the pile on the bench.

Vlad opened his eyes and smiled condescendingly. "How do we know where he lived, or who he is for that matter?"

Hellamina tapped the small notepad in her uniforms shirt pocket. "Had a missing vamp a few days ago. Stopped by to check with his wife on the way out here. She said he still hasn't come home. And…" before Vlad could interject, "this vamp was missing a couple fingers, from some accident he had at his job at, uh…" She pulled her notepad out with one hand and flipped to the page. "Bellmore Industries. Yeah, and it looks like our vamp here is missing a couple fingers too."

She turned her head sideways, looking at the burnt remains and nodded in confirmation.

Hellamina Muntz was one of the very few female vampires at the R.E.D. In fact, any of the other positions held by women were in administration. She was a lead investigator and was very good at her job. She also had the distinction of being the only female to ever run the Pike. In the running of the Pike of 847ADWB, though highly illegal, Hellamina managed to conceal her gender enough to fool both judges and Riders. She was excellent on a motorbike and made it all the way to the Top Eight before losing a run. Proud of her accomplishment, the night she finally lost a Run she revealed to the crowd at Norwood Park, that she was the first female vampire to run a Pike.

Ordinarily, most vampires would expect a harsh punishment for such a brazen act. But this young girl made such a passionate speech of her love and honor to have served the Realm, that the mob was soon chanting her name as a hero. She was pardoned on the spot by then sitting KOTU, Dracov Von Firstenstein, Vlad's father. That Pike, Number Seven, would also be the first of two Pikes that Vladimir Von Firstenstein would win.

Vladimir casually walked around to the same side of the body that the Detective was on. He stood silent for almost a minute with his head down. When he finally raised his head, he found an imaginary object somewhere in the tree branches, behind the bench and delivered The Begrafen:

"Our fallen Brother has left this World to join the souls of our ancestors, and to begin everlasting life in the Kingdom of the Dead. May the keepers of the Kingdom let this soul pass."

"Hear, hear," Hellamina called after the KOTU, as she finished her cup of blood.

After a long pause she looked at Vlad.

"KOTU Von Firstenstein, because of our lack of any witnesses or any account of the victims whereabouts prior to his demise, I would like to authorize and request the use of a HellHound."

Vlad knew now that he would be here for a good part of the day. He stared at Hellamina for a few moments. He was livid but knew there was absolutely nothing he could say that would change her mind or could force her to do otherwise. He scowled and huffed.

"I shall remain within the scene perimeter in the comfort of my motorcar."

Vladimir stormed from the taped off scene and into the backseat of his chauffeured motorcar where his son Daryn waited.

"Finally," Daryn whined once his father was in the car. "Let's get some warm blood on the way to the Academy."

"We'll be waiting, Cheshko," Vlad spoke to the driver as he took his black leather gloves off. "Looks like the Detective thinks there's something worth sniffing around for."

Disgusted, Daryn whined again. "Of all the days for my damn motorcar to not start." He looked at his father. "Can't we just leave? You are the KOTU."

Vlad had folded the gloves neatly and placed them on his lap.

"Patience, Son. If you mean to be King of the Undead, there is much to be gained from patience." Vlad glanced at the Detective still standing next to the corpse. "Besides, we hardly get to talk. I'd like to hear your thoughts for after the Pike."

Daryn sighed. His father had been using any chance he could to talk about Daryn's future. "I don't know, Father, I try not to think about it."

Vlad grinned with irritation for his son's ignorance. "Ignoring the choices we must make only means someone else will make those choices for us."

Daryn turned to Vlad, angry. "It doesn't matter what I say anyway, you're going to tell me what I *have* to do."

"That's not true, Son," Vlad argued back, "But there is a certain way that things are done. There is an *order* that must be respected."

"You're talking about Bebe, aren't you?" Daryn shook his head defiantly. "I don't want to marry her."

Vlad smiled and exhaled. He looked back at the Detective. "You know, Son, when I married your mother, I think we'd met only once at a cocktail party. She was a shy girl, or so I thought." He let out a soft laugh. "Probably just scared. It didn't matter." He turned to Daryn, "It was what had to be done."

"It's not the Eighth Century anymore!" Daryn cried. "You know, vampires are thinking of choosing their own paths, finding their moments of importance..."

"Stop it right now!" Vlad commanded. "Nonsense. Nothing but idiotic Fledgling nonsense." He looked hard at Daryn. "Do you know what your grandfather would have done to me if I spoke to him the way you speak at me?" He looked down at the gloves in his lap as if recalling unspeakable horror. Gradually Vlad brought his head up. With a pleasant expression now on his face, he spoke calmly. "Yes, indeed it is not the Eighth Century. And be grateful for that!" He looked back at Daryn and waited for his son to look at him. "This obsession with moments, it will pass. Don't you see?" There was genuine concern in Vlad's voice. "Son, it's not who we are. All these feelings you have, they will dry up and pass from your soul the way a snake sheds his skin. You will grow out of the very idea that these, or any one moment matters when you embrace your destiny and the order that exists in this world." Vlad was trying so hard to make his son understand and not lose his temper, but Daryn just stared blankly back at his father. "Someday you will understand perfectly," Vlad promised. "Until then son, please trust in your father."

A large R.E.D. wagon had stopped on the street directly behind their motorcar. The Agents were chatting with the Detective.

"Cheshko, drop Daryn at the Academy and come back here for me." Vlad looked at his son as he opened the door to get out. "I hate these damned dogs."

CHAPTER TEN:
MOLECULAR HYDROCARBON LATENCY LABORATORY

The blade on the miniature windmill at the center of Toland Kepler's workstation table had been spinning for six days from one flip of his index finger. Of course it wasn't a clinical study by any means, it was merely a toy some of the other scientists had set up in the lab. But the fact that it usually rotated for about a week from one hard spin was astounding, and similar to the results they were seeing in other, more controlled tests.

Kepler & Sons always had a handful of products and projects in development. Ninety five percent of them never amounted to much. Their largest discovery to date was still when Toland's father Raymond synthesized animal tissue and cranberries into blood berry, but over the centuries they had still remained one of the most vital research centers in the Realm. There had been many exciting projects over the years at K&S, but nothing as exciting as their recent – the Molecular Hydrocarbon Latency Laboratory they had set up, affectionately referred to as the "Motor Hell" project by the staff scientists.

The Motor Hell project was an attempt to create an industrial lubricant that greatly reduced the friction and chemical breakdown that petroleum based oils succumbed to. The engines that powered huge generators, broke rock in the mines, and transported vampires in their motorcars, all needed oil. And oil was a difficult commodity in the Realm. Currently the only source was from a couple offshore oil rigs, left over from the days of Men. These oil stations were in remote Baldoon region, the uppermost northern section of the Realm. Under harsh conditions mariner vampires worked the rigs and would transport the crude oil on barges along the coast to Port Iron Gate in the Lowlands. Once at Iron Gate, the crude was refined and transported to other parts of the Realm. The process took several months, but there was no other method. A route over land was impossible, with an impenetrable forest and the treacherous backside of Mount Cain between the sea and the population of the mainland.

K&S had started the project many years ago trying to simply improve on the existing method used for refining crude by hydroisomerizing base oil. They soon began blending mineral with plant and animal oils, using highly pressurized hydrogen. There was incredible improvement and little breakdown, particularly under intense heat. It wasn't until recently, when they began reconfiguring the molecular sequence of the hydrocarbon atoms with a model of sequence that mirrored that of vampire blood, that the tests began to change dramatically. Using the ancient notes from theoretical experiments almost a thousand years ago, Toland had altered the actual DNA of the new oil blend and it was virtually indestructible. Motor Hell was so capable at eliminating friction, that in their calculations, it was somewhere around 1400 times more effective than the current oil being used.

"The alloy engines are even cooler today, Teddy," Toland said to one of his lead engineers over the buzz of a small, shiny engine held in place by a table mounted vise.

Dr. Teddy Krauss had goggles and ear protection on, but nodded and yelled back, "They're even cooler today, Sir!"

Toland smiled and made a 'thumbs up' sign, then walked back through the airlocked partition that divided the engine area from the rest of the Motor Hell labs. There were three other scientists quietly working near a large wall of samples. Toland walked directly to their station and folded his arms, watching.

Eventually, a female vampire in a white, two-piece suit raised her head from a microscope and looked at Toland, shaking her head in disbelief. "Even the samples from the kiln are intact. No breakdown whatsoever."

"That's excellent, Dorrenesh. Will you make sure Teddy gets these same ones they're using on the motorcar trial?"

"Of course."

Toland continued across the lab floor and was met halfway by another female vampire. She was dressed in a white, high-necked blouse with a long white skirt and matching white heels.

"Mr. Kepler, Sir, your two o'clock is here."

"Ah, yes. I'd forgotten all about that." Toland focused on the floor and thought for a moment. He looked at his watch and smiled. "Yes, I guess it is."

Toland spent long hours in the windowless offices of K&S and often lost track of time. He was used to his secretary reminding him of little things, but he couldn't remember why Alexander Bellmore had scheduled a meeting with him. The last time he saw Alex was two summers ago during an Archery exhibition at their fledges' Academy. *Maybe there's some sort of function coming up,* he thought. They weren't friends, and Toland found Alex to be rather obnoxious. He thought Alex had an air of self-importance and, like many of the affluent Upperlanders, seemed preoccupied with his business.

Toland still hadn't figured out what the meeting could be about when he reached his office.

"Alex, so sorry to have kept you waiting."

Alexander Bellmore was sitting comfortably in the brown leather chair that faced Toland's desk. He was a stocky, heavy-set vampire in a dark blue-grey suit. Toland had startled him and Alex smiled and placed a small windmill back on the desk in front of him. The windmill was another like the one on the workstation table in the Motor Hell lab and was spinning madly.

"What'll they think of next?" Alex smiled as he stood up. "That blade has spun for ten minutes from one little flick of my finger."

"Ow, for the daylights, you waited ten minutes." Toland shook his hand. "I truly apologize. I get so wrapped up in my work and just…"

Alex waved his hand and squeezed his eyes closed. "Not to worry. I appreciate you seeing me."

"Yes," Toland smiled and paused. "Is there anything at the Academy coming up that I may have forgotten about?" Toland smiled with his teeth clenched together like someone who had made a mistake.

"Oh, no, no," Alex laughed. "Well, nothing I'm aware of."

Both vampires chuckled.

"Well, what exactly is the nature of your visit, Alex?"

Alex cleared his throat, then touched his neck. "You wouldn't have a little something warm to drink would you Toland?"

"Oh, certainly. I'll have Svetlana bring some blood." Toland stepped toward the door.

"Ahhh," Alex smiled and winked. "Maybe something with a little bite."

Toland was caught off guard. He stopped and thought for a second. "You… want," He glanced at his watch to assure himself that it was in fact not too early. "I have some deer wine in the cube?"

Alex let out a hearty laugh. "If it's not any trouble."

"None at all." Toland grinned reassuringly but wondered what in Hell Alex wanted.

Toland crossed the room and opened the doors of the black oak wall unit that consumed an entire wall of his office. There was a small incubator tucked into the corner of a shelf with scientific reference books. In it there were three bottles of Black Lake deer wine from the Tastemaker farm. Johnny Tastemaker's deer wine was grass-fed, aged in applewood casks and was one of the most sought-after inebriants in the Realm. This brand was from a farm in the Black Lake township, in the far west territory of the Realm at the foot of the Black Deth mountains.

Toland brought two glasses to his desk. As he pulled at his desk chair he motioned for Alex to do the same.

"Please."

Both vampires savored a long sip. The apple casks gave a sweet, tangy bite to the fermented blood. After a moment Toland set his glass on the desk and leaned back, folding his hands across his stomach.

"So Alex, to what do I owe this occasion?"

Alex took another sip. "Now that's delicious," he smiled. He rested his glass next to Toland's, leaned back, and cleared his throat again. "Toland, I'm a businessman. Bellmore Industries manufactures seventeen hundred unique parts for over twenty different specialties that affect every vamp, succubus and child vampire in the Realm. Hey, that's the reason at Bellmore we sell more." Alex smiled and paused as if he had always paused at that exact place in his sales pitch. Toland smiled and nodded. "Part of my livelihood requires me to be extra vigilant for anything and everything that could help, or hurt my business. If something is shaking the foundations of manufacturing, I like to be right on top of it." Alex winked. "You know what I mean?"

Toland did not. But he continued smiling and nodding, wondering where exactly Alex was going with this conversation.

"We always use Bellmore parts in the labs," Toland assured him.

"Oh, I know that. And I'm proud of that. K&S is a longtime… a valued client." Alex took a quick sip of his deer wine. "But what I'm saying is… if I said to you, that I have something that may make or *break* your business. Now, you'd want to see if there couldn't be some sort of an agreement, you know, a business agreement, that we could work out. So that everyone can keep their business intact." Alex raised his eyebrows and smiled. He was nodding his head as if to ask if Toland agreed with him.

Toland was shaking his head in bewilderment.

"I'm sorry Alex, I'm not sure what you're getting at." Toland looked at his watch, then back at Alex. "Like I said, we're good with all our Bellmore parts…"

"Toland, it has come to my attention that K&S has a new product that could severely inhibit the need for a wide array of most of the products that we offer at Bellmore."

"What?" Toland leaned forward. "What are you talking about?"

Alex held his hands up reassuringly. "Now, I know, it's not common knowledge, I'm just saying, I think we ought to work together on this, rather than against each other."

Toland stood up. "Just what product are you talking about?"

Alex stood up. "Come on, Toland, I'm talking about the Motor Hell project. I know all about it."

Toland felt a little like the wind was knocked out of him. He looked around the room then rested his hands on his desk before he looked back at Alex.

"Spies? What, you have spies in my company, Alex?!"

"No, no, of course not. But Toland, this is revolutionary stuff we're talking about. You can't expect to keep it a secret forever." Alex smiled and put his hands over his heart. "We're a close community, we need to look out for one another."

Toland was reeling from the idea that his Motor Hell project had been leaked, but quickly focused and looked hard at Alex.

"Look, I don't know what you've heard, Alex, but we aren't going to market with anything soon. And furthermore, K&S will absolutely release an Article of Intent with the High Council whenever we decide to market."

"Toland, Toland, I'm not trying threaten you. Far from it." Alex leaned on the desk. "I want to buy in."

"Alex, I think you've been misled as to what we have here."

"Really!" Alex raised his voice, *"Absolutely no thermal viscosity breakdown, even after two thousand degrees. Friction has been virtually eliminated.* Does this sound familiar?"

"This meeting is over." Toland walked out from behind his desk.

Alex pleaded, "Toland, please, just think about this. This will ruin Bellmore. Let me buy in. Then together we can control what is on the market. There's no need to have it all for yourself, we'll **BOTH** be wealthy beyond anything we can imagine. We can set our price and they'll have to pay it!"

Toland had opened his office door. "Goodnight, Alex."

Alex was directly in Toland's face, begging. "Toland, please, just consider. You'll ruin me."

"I said goodnight!" Toland yelled, focusing on the lobby outside his office.

Alex drew a deep breath and in an instant shed every ounce of humility. He lurched slowly at Toland and hissed, "You are either with me or you are against me in this, Kepler."

Toland remained fixated on the lobby, where a confused Svetlana sat wide-eyed at her desk.

Alex walked into the lobby and turned back, saying through clenched teeth, "I came as a friend."

Toland slammed the door and pressed his back against it. Exhaling heavily, he coughed like he'd been held under water. As quiet slowly returned to his office, he heard the thin sound of air blowing. Looking around the room, his eyes stopped on the miniature windmill that stood on his desk, still spinning as if a powerful wind was blowing it.

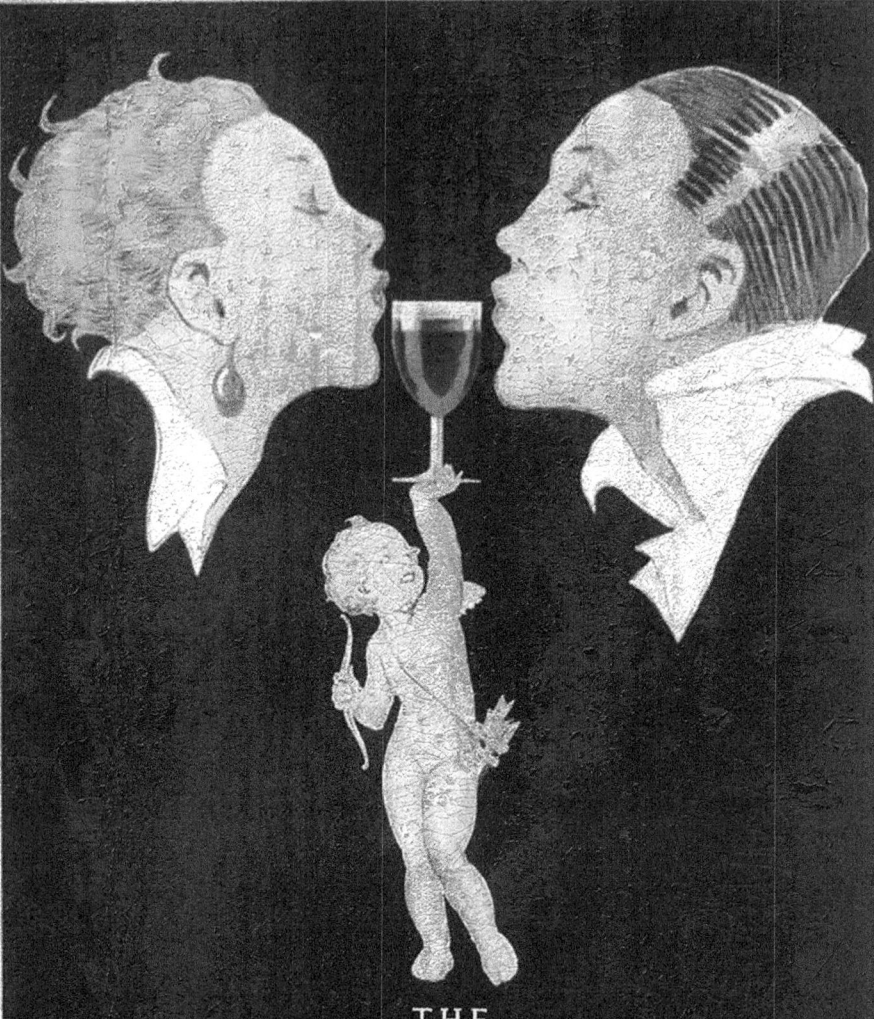

THE

BLACK DOG
AND BONE

DEVILSTON

CHAPTER ELEVEN:
THE RETURN FROM FANGWOOD

"And what about those Common Bats from Fangwood!" Erik screeched.

"Someone needs to tell them it's not 666 ADWB anymore!" Daryn and Millington were laughing hysterically.

"May we please get a shearer at the gate, Sir?" Daryn was crying with laughter.

"I actually thought they had let HellHounds ride," Mills gasped dramatically.

"It was more ridiculous than I ever imagined," Daryn shook his head. "I didn't even have to open my motorbike up."

The three vamps were sharing a corner booth at the Black Dog & Bone Alehouse. Mills topped all of their glasses off with Hell Blood from the pitcher on the table. Hell Blood was fermented Healthy Blood, and another of the most popular inebriants. A little less expensive than deer wine, but more expensive than the sweet and cheap pig ale that most vampires their age chose.

"I swear, I've never seen such hair on a vampire. And the fangs!" Erik made hooks with his index fingers at his mouth

"At first I thought maybe they were doing it to psych out the other Riders," Daryn said as he lifted the mug.

"But their elders!" Mills yelled. "All with the same sideburns and fangs!"

They all laughed.

It had been two nights since the first qualifying runs for the Ninth Pike's Run of the Realm. These initial groups of races were large spectator events and had been held down in Fangwood, a sprawling city on the southern plains of the Lowlands. The qualifying runs would take place in some of the more remote places in the Realm. This was done for a couple reasons. Not just because of the shear volume of Riders (six hundred Riders would be eliminated in the first two weeks of trials), but also because for some vampires, from these remote areas, traveling with their motorbikes just wasn't an option. In fact, it wasn't uncommon for several bikes to not finish (or start) their run. Stalling, mechanical problems, even fires, occurred routinely on the starting line. The more impoverished vamps from the outskirts of the Realm simply lacked the resources to compete effectively past one or two races. However, no one would want to deny any vampire the honor of participating in the Pike. And it would be deemed unfair if large demographics of the Realm couldn't run simply because of economic disparity, particularly when some of the most avid supporters of the Pike were from these same remote territories.

The Fangwood vampires that the Capital boys found so amusing were partial to the 'Real Vampire' way of living that included not filing their teeth and growing traditional side burns. They also had a flavor for some of the traditional vampire attire. Unlike the more modern, older vampires in bigger towns and cities that chose simpler clothes—contemporary suit jackets with slacks and even one-piece jumpsuits—the real vampire enthusiasts were partial to triple-breasted suits, frilly shirts with vests and even top hat and tails—clothing that looked like it was from the ancient days with stories of flying vampires and hunting humans. Oddly, the stylings of the young, urban vampires associated with the Sweet Death Symphony movement mimicked these obscure Lowlanders.

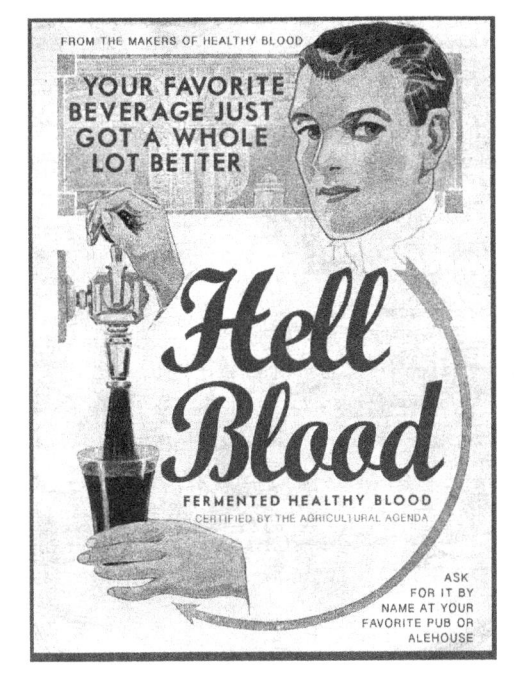

FROM THE MAKERS OF HEALTHY BLOOD

YOUR FAVORITE BEVERAGE JUST GOT A WHOLE LOT BETTER

Hell Blood

FERMENTED HEALTHY BLOOD
CERTIFIED BY THE AGRICULTURAL AGENDA

ASK FOR IT BY NAME AT YOUR FAVORITE PUB OR ALEHOUSE

"Well I'm glad we have almost two weeks until Castle Bain. That'll give me enough time to get all that muck off my Gargoyle," Daryn said, disgusted, "I'm going to have Father's driver polish the chrome 'til it blinds my opponents!" He snickered.

Vladimir was sitting at a table across the room. He was seated with several other dignified vampires, all wearing similar two-piece gray toned suits. The Black Dog & Bone was a favorite alehouse of the wealthier vampires who rarely made it down to the Devilston district. As KOTU, Vlad had officiated the opening event down in Fangwood and was reveling in the pageantry of another opening night of the Pike, back in the comfort of the city. He caught his son's eye at his booth and waved for Daryn to come over.

Daryn nodded in agreement and turned to his mates. "Looks like I've been summoned by the King of the Undead," he rolled his eyes and finished his pint glass of Hell Blood.

"It must be torture to be the son of the KOTU," Erik waved his hand dramatically. "What, with the eyes of every nubile fixated on your vampire ass."

"And worse, he will no doubt insist that you impart the details of your spectacular victory of your opening day Pike to a table of the Realm's most affluent vampires," Mills added.

THE NINTH PIKE'S RUN

Qualifying Runs Schedule

FANGWOOD - JUNE 5. 1089
CASTLE BAIN - JUNE 19. 1089
SUNTORA FLATS - JULY 21. 1089
DEAD HILLS - AUGUST 3. 1089
HUNEDORA - AUGUST 16. 1089
BLACK LAKE - AUGUST 30. 1089
CAPITAL CITY - SEPTEMBER 13. 1089

STRIGOI - FINAL RUN
SEPTEMBER 23. 1089

"Oh, oh, oh, my dear vamps…" Daryn burped and stood up. "If you only knew." Daryn reached over and gulped from Erik's pint. "It's a very small box that our King has me…" Daryn was pantomiming a square shape and searching for the word. He laughed and began winding this imaginary box before yelling, "grinding!"

They exploded with laughter as Daryn added a dance to his organ grinding monkey impersonation.

Across the room Vlad frowned as he watched Daryn. He excused himself from his table and quickly crossed the alehouse floor. Many vampires nodded and lifted their glass as the KOTU walked by.

Vlad softly touched his son's arm, "May I have a word?"

Daryn turned his whole body with his head, as if his neck was solid wood. "You may." Daryn was acting morose and stiff like one of the Von Firstensteins' seven-hundred-year-old valets.

The other two vamps sitting down pressed their lips together and lowered their heads as father and son took a step away from the booth, but still remained in earshot.

"I'm all for having some fun, Son, but we must remember to keep our form, hmmm?" Vlad asked evenly while slowly smiling and nodding at a council member that passed on his way to the washroom. "That seems fairly easy to accomplish, ay?"

Daryn moved his hand in a flat motion while pushing his bottom lip out. "Piece of steak, Sir."

"Excellent. Excellent." Vlad smiled looking around the pub. His eyes flashed as he remembered the other reason he came over to speak with his son. "In a few weeks we'll be having a small cocktail party. Your mother wants it to be a costume party. A lot of the Council will be in attendance, the Bellmores of course." He cleared his throat. "It might be a nice time for an announcement."

Daryn quit his fooling around and stared scornfully at his father. Vlad looked back with a soothing smile. Daryn's nostrils flared a little, and he wavered a bit as he stood inches from his father. The many pints of Hell Blood had him swaying slowly as if he were on the deck of a Baldoon oil barge. He glared into his father's eyes.

"You know," Daryn slurred, "I was having an incredible moment here with my friends. I made the first rounds of my Pike the other night." Daryn thumbed his chest and stepped back. "I want to savor life…" He stumbled. "Find the moment that's worth more than a thousand years of existence…"

"Enough." Vlad said firmly. "That's blasphemy."

"Is it?" Daryn said sadly. His lip curled and he glared hatefully at Vlad. "Down in Fangwood I saw vampires who were living for the moment." Daryn became serious and glanced at his friends, thinking how they had laughed at the Lowlanders wild enthusiasm. He turned back at his father and hissed drunkenly. "And I was ashamed!"

Daryn staggered back to the booth and pulled his riding jacket from the hook above the booth. He clumsily put it on and walked back at his father in the direction of the exit to the street. Daryn stopped in front of his father, zipping up his leather motorbike jacket.

"You're in no condition this close to light!" Vlad whispered angrily.

Daryn abruptly turned up his collar.

"Where are you going, Son?" Vlad said softer, trying to seem reasonable.

"I think I'll go stare into the light of the moon." Daryn snapped a glove over his hand. He jerked the second glove on and smiled. "Don't wait up!"

As Daryn staggered out of the alehouse Erik and Millington sheepishly looked up at the KOTU. They had quietly listened to their quarrel.

After a moment of Vlad looking back and forth between the two Fledges, the KOTU simply pointed with his eyes to the direction that his son had just staggered. Erik and Mills were falling over themselves to quickly get out of the alehouse to find their friend.

CHAPTER TWELVE:
THE BLOCK

Detective Hellamina Muntz rarely found herself at any of these administrative offices in the Realm's Capital City. They were a maze of identical lobbies and hallways, and if you weren't careful, you could get stuck running in circles trying to find your way out.

The cluster of offices and buildings took up an entire city block and was referred to by most in Realm administration as "The Block." The R.E.D. called it the *Chopping* Block, because if you found yourself being asked to come down, it was usually for some sort of reprimand that needed to be officiated in the presence of one or more High Council members.

It was also common to come down to The Block to drop paperwork off, and she figured that must be why the KOTU Council Member had asked her to come down. She had all of her papers in order from their Hellfire Incident the week before, and was hoping to be in and out of the Block as soon as possible.

Most employees were at lunch, so when the Detective reached the KOTU's office there was no receptionist to introduce her. Hellamina tapped lightly on the frosted glass window of The Council Member's office door.

"Yes, come on in," Vlad said from inside.

Hellamina slowly pushed the door open. Vlad was smiling from behind his desk. The chair he was seated in was a sprawling black throne that had a large tree carved into the backrest. His desk was the same dark wood and was an enormous slab of wood that could easily serve as a conference table for ten or more vampires. The walls were filled with paintings of the previous Kings of the Undead, as well as some framed posters of past and present Pike's Run propaganda. Some of the items in this room were as old as the Realm itself, including the Pike's Run trophy that sat on the wall unit encased in glass. It was from the first Pike and was quite an example of traditional vampire imagery.

The trophy itself was a human skull, rumored to be of the last human killed, with a blade plunged into the top of its head. The dagger's handle was a bat with its wings wrapped tight around its body. The skull was fastened to a black rock base that was thirteen inches tall. There was a small, tin tag at the bottom that read "First Prize". The trophy itself had always been referred to as First Prize since Pike Number One.

The very first Pike was only just a motorcycle race. There wasn't a High Council yet in the Realm. Famine and disease were rampant and it was used as a distraction of sorts to boost morale. The last human skull was a fitting First Prize, as it was symbolic of the Day That Death Was Born and the new era that stood before all vampires. It wasn't until after the first Pike was run and won (by Heinrik Von Firstenstein) that the High Council would be assembled.

ATTENTION VAMPIRES OF THE REALM
ANNOUNCING THE FIRST CONTEST OF ITS KIND

THE PIKE'S RUN

A MOTORBIKE RACE
LIKE NO OTHER.

OPEN TO ALL MALE VAMPIRES
FROM AGES 50 - 250 YEARS

FORGET YOUR TROUBLES
AND COME ENJOY AN
EXHILARATING
EXPERIENCE

QUALIFYING TRIALS WILL BEGIN
MAY 23RD IN SELECTED REGIONS
AND WILL CARRY ON THROUGH
OUT THE SUMMER

COURSE TO BE DETERMINED
AT A LATER DATE IN TIME

It was then decided that a King of the Undead title would beholden to the winner and that vampire would also join the ranks of the High Council.

"Thank you for coming, Detective." Vlad stood up.

"No problem, Sir," Hellamina nodded. "I expect this concerns the Hellfire Incident." She held the papers high and leaned forward, placing them on the desk.

"Ah," Vlad squinted. He hadn't thought of the Hellfire Incident since he left the scene last week. He smiled and nodded. "Thank you, Detective."

Vlad walked around the desk toward Hellamina. He tapped his hands together as he moved, with his fingers spread apart, hitting the opposite hand's fingertips with each step. He had something entirely different to discuss with Hellamina but she had reminded him of that case. He stepped around the large desk, looking at her and thinking. She was such a peculiar vampire woman, he thought. Though very attractive, she didn't dress or carry herself much like most females. She wore short, cropped hair and was always in tactical gear even when off duty. True, she was an R.E.D. Agent, and a detective at that, so there was little room for anything else with that Specialty. But there was just something very different about her.

"How did the dog do, Detective?"

Vlad was grinning and being condescending. He knew all too well how much the Detective disliked criticism of the HellHounds. She had started the program within the R.E.D. to work with them. Not everyone in the Rules Enforcement Department shared her enthusiasm for these animals. Hellamina started to scowl. but before she could answer the KOTU added, "I mean HellHound, of course."

Hellamina relaxed. "Actually, it's very interesting. Agent Tarc seems to think that the vamp came from the direction of the warehouse district rather than that of the alehouses."

"Ah, well… yes, *Agent* Tarc, the HellHound." Vlad looked very stern and serious. "Detective, do you think maybe he could be *Tarc*-ing up the wrong tree?" Vlad folded his arms and continued to act completely serious.

Hellamina pursed her lips and looked down in anger. Between clenched teeth she hissed, "Sir?"

Vlad laughed loudly and slapped her lightly on the shoulder. "Oh, come now Detective, we need to keep our sense of humor in the midst of all this Hellfire sadness."

As Hellamina looked up, the KOTU turned his head to the side in an exaggerated show of understanding.

"Interesting, Detective." Vlad lost the previous tone and sounded genuine."You really do care for these beasts, don't you?"

Hellamina stared back assertively. "I'm from Tamerlane, Sir. A very remote quarter of the Realm, out beyond the Dead Hills. I grew up around Hellunds. Many of us who live near the great forests come to owe their very existence to the *Hellunds*." She paused, still staring hard at Vlad. "They are no more beasts than you or I."

Vlad gave a small nod while their eyes were still fixed. He had often forgotten that the Detective was from the desperate and unforgiving region in the west, where they believe in the old stories of HellHound and Vampire alliances. Like much of the talk in the outer regions, Vlad thought it was seeped in foolishness.

"Who knows, maybe someday the great alliance that the ancients wrote about will be reborn between the Vampire and the…" Vlad paused and with no condescension at all, pronounced it with the same affectionate local affectation as the Detective. "…Hellunds."

Hellamina made a very tiny smile and a similar nod to show she pardoned his previously inconsiderate remarks.

"As far as the incident, though, I'm afraid there's not much more the council will pursue in the investigation."

Hellamina was a bit confused. "It seems there are at least a few questions that need answering, Sir."

Vlad broke away from the close range of their conference and began to slowly pace his office. "Ordinarily, maybe I would agree. But I've asked you here to discuss something of the highest importance." He turned from across the room. "It's a matter of Realm national security, Detective." Vlad tucked one arm under the other and put his extended finger to his face, tapping gently. "There is a sickness festering. A growing apathy among some of the youth." He continued tapping the side of his head with his finger and raised his eyebrows. "And I'm not talking about the usual Fledgling theatrics, we're all familiar with that. No…" Vlad made his hand into a fist. "This is different. This is a growing defiance to accept the order of the Realm." Vlad walked toward Hellamina. "Detective, I'm assigning you the task of rooting out and delivering this SDS organization to stand for treason at the High Council court."

"Sir?" Hellamina said blankly.

"The Sweet Death Symphony," He shook his head, surprised. "You've heard of them, yes?"

Hellamina drew a deep breath and moved her head 'no'. "A little, Sir, but not much."

"Oh, not to worry, there's plenty of paperwork on them." Vlad pointed to a leather binder on the chair behind Hellamina. "There's enough to get you started in there."

Hellamina flipped casually through the papers and then put the binder under her arm.

Vlad narrowed his gaze on her. "Detective, I want you to report to me, and me only. At the moment this is not an effort of the R.E.D. or the High Council. We're on a fact-finding mission and it is to be a covert operation. Do I make myself clear?"

"Yes, Sir. Absolutely." Hellamina nodded. "But for the record, Sir, I am an R.E.D. Agent. If I'm involved in an ongoing investigation, having all of the resources…"

"Hellamina," Vlad said gently, "There's more at stake than I can tell you. I need you to believe in your KOTU and do this for Realm and honor."

Hellamina might have liked some answers about the nature of this investigation, particularly about the legality of it. And she still had some serious questions about their Hellfire Incident. But if there was one thing an R.E.D. Agent was capable of, it was doing anything for Realm and honor.

Hellamina smiled confidently at the KOTU and nodded quickly. "Of course, Sir."

"Excellent." He smiled.

"Now, if you will excuse me, Detective, I have to officiate an R.E.D event a few blocks away." Vlad looked at his watch. "I do hope they didn't start without me."

CHAPTER THIRTEEN:
SEARCH & SEIZURE

Almost all of the mice were white. She had six, but she needed to get a few grey ones, and a couple black ones into her basket. Just to make it look good. Her father hadn't been paying that much attention, but he was randomly stopping by with questions.

Andi felt bad about lying to her father, but as a scientist she thought he would undoubtedly understand. Andi was in the animal room at Kepler & Sons, getting some mice for her experiments. Toland was always happy to let her take anything she needed, or even work there at the K&S labs if she chose to. The problem was that he was also very inquisitive to whatever she was working on and usually wanted to help. And even if he didn't have time to help, he could still bombard her with questions and know exactly what was going on from just a small amount of information. He was, after all, kind of a scientific genius of sorts.

Andi had been working on the equations for Human blood from her notes she copied from the ancient books. She had an incredibly well-stocked lab at home, but she was having problems keeping the blood 'alive'. She had done a good job of separating the needed components from the animal blood and adding the newly created human cells. She could also simulate a lot of the same conditions of a living animal host, but ultimately the blood always became unstable outside of a living animal. She had begun using mice as hosts to keep the blood alive during tests, but soon realized that putting her lab-made human blood inside an animal was self-defeating since it was just contaminating any progress she made.

It wasn't until Andi created an actual virus to envelope the blood, that she thought she might actually have a chance at this. Andi developed a virus with a powerful synthetic lipid membrane that was so potent it encapsulated every individual blood cell and effectively housed the blood from any damage. The virus also didn't attack the blood as well as not damage the animal host's cells since it was completely isolated from the animals DNA by the super virus.

Her only problem was that she had ran out of mice and needed to get some more from her father's lab. Of course Toland told her to take whatever she wanted but he was also excited about what she was working on. Andi told him it was a project for her Science Focus interviews. When pressed for details she said that she was working on mice blood elixir and trying to determine if the color of the mouse affected the taste. She immediately wished she had picked a more innocuous excuse. Luckily her father was busy, but he did keep stopping by, asking her very specific questions. She was hoping to scoop up a couple more mice with pigment and get out of there before he came back.

The door swung open at the far end of the room. Teddy was walking quickly with what looked like gigantic oven mitts on his hands. He had a black square box between the two gloves. Toland was right behind him and told Teddy to take it straight to the test shelf cooling rack. Toland stopped and kept calling after Teddy to immediately pull samples. He saw his daughter, smiled and walked over.

"What flavors do we have so far?" He grinned. "But more importantly, who will ever drink mice blood?"

Andi was trying to act preoccupied with catching this fast yellow mouse in the back of the cage. "Hmmm? Oh, I don't know." She grunted as if defeated by the mouse.

"I'm curious," Toland squinted as he recalled. "Didn't you already have a research paper for your Biology Focus?" He paused. "In fact…"

"Got him!" Andi yelled, a bit more excited than she should have been to have a mouse by the tail.

Toland opened the flip-top hatch of the wire basket with her other mice. After she dropped the yellow mouse in with the other half dozen, Toland opened his mouth and looked as if he was about to finish his question.

"Oh, I forgot to tell you," Andi's eyes went wide. "Sonny made his third qualifying run last night!"

Toland leaned back in surprise. "Well, I'll be! Now that is impressive." He thought for a moment, as if adding numbers. "What was it opening day, eleven hundred? Something like that?"

"Twelve hundred Riders!" Andi shook her head. "They cut three hundred the first day at Fangwood. Three hundred there week two. Then at Castle Bain three hundred fifty got cut. Now, it's down to two hundred fifty Riders." Andi had rattled off the statistics at lightning speed.

"Very impressive," Toland repeated. "I mean, he still has a long way to go, but Sonny's out of the meat grinder."

"Yeah." Andi frowned a little. "Next one's Suntora Flats, though."

"Ew." Toland winced like someone pulling a thorn from a finger.

Until then, the qualifying heats of the Pike were mostly about just getting through the muck. There would be a few hundred Riders in a run and the top twenty-five would move on. The terrain was mostly winding, country roads with sections through woods. Not much in the way of high speeds. Most of the entrants weren't accomplished Riders either. In some parts of the Realm it was just a thrill and an honor to grab a bike and try to qualify. Few vampires owned their motorbikes and would simply rent a 'runner' from one of the merchants near the race, a scene that resembled an enormous carnival. Runners were always dilapidated bikes that didn't move fast, or for very long. Sometimes these bikes would catch fire and backfire loudly adding to the spectacle and delight of the crowds. With this portion of qualifying runs done though, the herd had been sufficiently thinned to largely capable Riders with much more able bikes. The next run would be at Suntora Flats and the beginning of serious competition.

The Suntora Flats were about a one hundred and fifty mile stretch of hard, seamless ground in the south western plains of the Lowlands. Excellent for motorbiking, it was actually part of the home stretch of the final Pike Run, that started and ended at Strigoi. Where the previous runs had been about short, maneuverable tracks, Suntora was about speed, and the Riders with the fastest bikes were usually going to prevail.

"Yeah, this is a big hurdle," Andi said the same way she'd heard Slim say a dozen times about Suntora.

The truth was, until last night, Andi had been half expecting that they would have already been beat out of the Pike. Just the sheer numbers of Riders getting cut was staggering. But now, with Suntora dangling over their heads, it seemed like for the first time Sonny's bid for the Pike was real. That they had gotten further than probably any of them ever thought they would go, even if they would never admit it.

To rank at Suntora Flats, they were going to have to get Sonny's bike to move faster than it had ever gone. Maybe faster than it could go. It wasn't that it was a particularly slow bike, but it was built for maneuverability, not speed. The motorbike that Slim had bargained from the R.E.D. was an older and smaller one than some of the others in the fleet. These "Spiders," as they were called, were perfect for the tight cornering in the Capital City, as well as the uneven cobbled stone sections. They climbed stairs, could turn on a gold piece, were light and were virtually indestructible – they just weren't that fast in a dedicated straightaway.

"Well, the bigger the hurdle, the bigger the jump, right?" Toland winked at Andi.

Andi laughed. Her father had always quoted their ancestor Lexmanius

Kepler, who was famous for saying *'The bigger the problem, the bigger the answer'.*

"The problem is, what we need is for his engine to be bigger." Andi looked down. "Of course that would just add weight."

Toland smiled and kissed her on top of the head as he began to walk away. "I'm sure you'll think of something."

He held the door as Dorrenesh trotted through with a hot box between her hands. Toland called after his assistant to quickly get it on the rack then looked back at his daughter and grinned.

"Too bad the motorbike wasn't like an employee, you could just *tell* it to go faster."

Andi stared at her father and thought about what he had just said. It was interesting the way people could seem to muster more power when they really needed it. Her eyes grew wide and she jumped up.

"Yes, that's exactly what I'll do!" She grabbed her basket and ran past the door Toland had still been holding open for Dorrenesh, kissing him on the cheek as she flew by.

"Thanks Dad! See you at home."

Toland smile, a little confused, "Um, okay."

At the same moment Svetlana had approached Dr. Kepler from the reception area of K&S. "Dr. Kepler, there are a few vampires here to see you from the R.E.D." Svetlana was uncharacteristically nervous. "Several." She added.

"Hmm. I guess they sent the samples with the R.E.D."

Toland had been expecting a delivery of blood berry samples to the lab. The High Council was investigating a small outbreak of Bog-like symptoms from the port city of Iron Gate. They had taken various samples and fragments from the sick vampires and wanted Toland to make it the highest priority in determining his diagnosis.

"They wouldn't let you sign for it?"

Toland said it more to himself than his secretary, and he stepped toward the lobby.

"Svetlana, could you please see to it that Lab Three is set up for a contaminant threat. I'll have the Agents transport whatever they've brought with them directly to the cargo lock."

As Toland stepped into his lobby, he froze in wonder. There were no less than ten Agents standing in full tactical gear, many with batons in hand.

Slowly Toland scanned the room carefully.

"Vampires... what may I do for you?"

"Doctor Toland Kepler?"

"Yes, of course."

A massive, muscled Agent stepped forward two steps. He, as all the others, had a visored helmet on his head. The Agent raised his visor and extended the paper in his hand.

"Doctor Kepler, as a sworn Agent of the Rules Enforcement Department, under order of the High Council of the Realm, I am authorized to execute an order of seizure."

"What?" Toland took the paper from the Agent's hand.

"A seizure of what?"

The Agent stared blankly.

"As protocol to the suspicion of the breaking of Rule Seven, Paragraph Three, which forbids the use of classified, or otherwise prohibited literature that resides within the Realm Historical Archives for development, manufacture or sale of contraband created from said historical documents..."

"What is this nonsense?!" Toland yelled.

The Agent continued reading, "...we are authorized to confiscate the listed contraband."

"Contraband?" Toland fumed. "What possible contraband am I being accused of manufacturing? And more importantly, by WHOM?!"

"Doctor. Doctor!" From behind the wall of R.E.D. Agents, Toland heard the instantly recognizable voice of the Realm's KOTU. Vlad waded through the lobby to finally arrive in front of the furious Dr. Kepler. "I apologize for not being here before the Agents. I absolutely regret that this has happened." Vlad was shaking his head and spoke in his sincerest sounding tone. "I tried unsuccessfully to sway the Council, but they insisted that this matter be handled with full enforcement of the Rules." Vlad sighed and raised an eyebrow. "Luckily they have allowed me to conduct this discreetly."

Toland wildly looked around his lobby. "Discreetly? Two dozen Agents outfitted for an uprising is discreet?"

Vlad smiled. "My dear Doctor, if they had their way they would have seized the entire building and arrested everyone in it. As it is, we are only going to confiscate the items in question."

Toland had begun to regain his composure, due largely to the presence of the KOTU, but also from the harsh realization that the R.E.D. did in fact have a history of turning places upside down during search and seizures.

Toland exhaled and asked calmly, "What exactly is the High Council looking for?"

The KOTU nodded in appreciation at Toland's reserve. "I believe the substance in question is being referred to as the 'Motor Hell' project".

Toland sat on the table next to Svetlana's desk as if he'd been punched in the stomach. In the most brutal way, it was being made crystal clear what this was about. Whether the KOTU was directly involved, or whether it was by the order of some other Council Member, it didn't matter. The details of whatever corruption that has allowed this to take place, for the moment, didn't matter. All Toland knew was that his years of work on the Molecular Hydrocarbon Latency Laboratory was about to be compromised by this order from the High Council. And that no matter what was decided, the greed and dishonesty in the souls of vampires would make certain that Motor Hell ended up stolen and reproduced, with knocked off versions of it in use and in the marketplace.

The KOTU bent sympathetically and said quietly, "Doctor Kepler, if you can just tell us the specific lab that the experiments are conducted, I can assure you that these Agents will be as professional as possible. We only need the lab directly involved with that research to satisfy the order."

Toland raised his head and looked at the KOTU wearily. Vlad was being very cordial. Why shouldn't he, Toland thought, there is only one way a search and seizure is going to play out when there is an order from the High Council. Toland glanced at his employees standing against the wall with shock and horror on their faces. He looked at Svetlana and nodded. "They'll show you."

Vlad waved his arm and the entire group of Agents seemed to move in unison behind the receptionist.

Toland stood back up to face Vlad. "This project is not Realm-funded, how could anyone have any valid information as to what it is or isn't? And furthermore, WHAT is the alleged misuse of the Archive charge?"

Vlad nodded in agreement. "Yes, you are correct, Doctor, alleged. These are purely just allegations being brought before the Council. And it won't surprise me that they will find you have conducted yourself safely within all the Rules of the Realm."

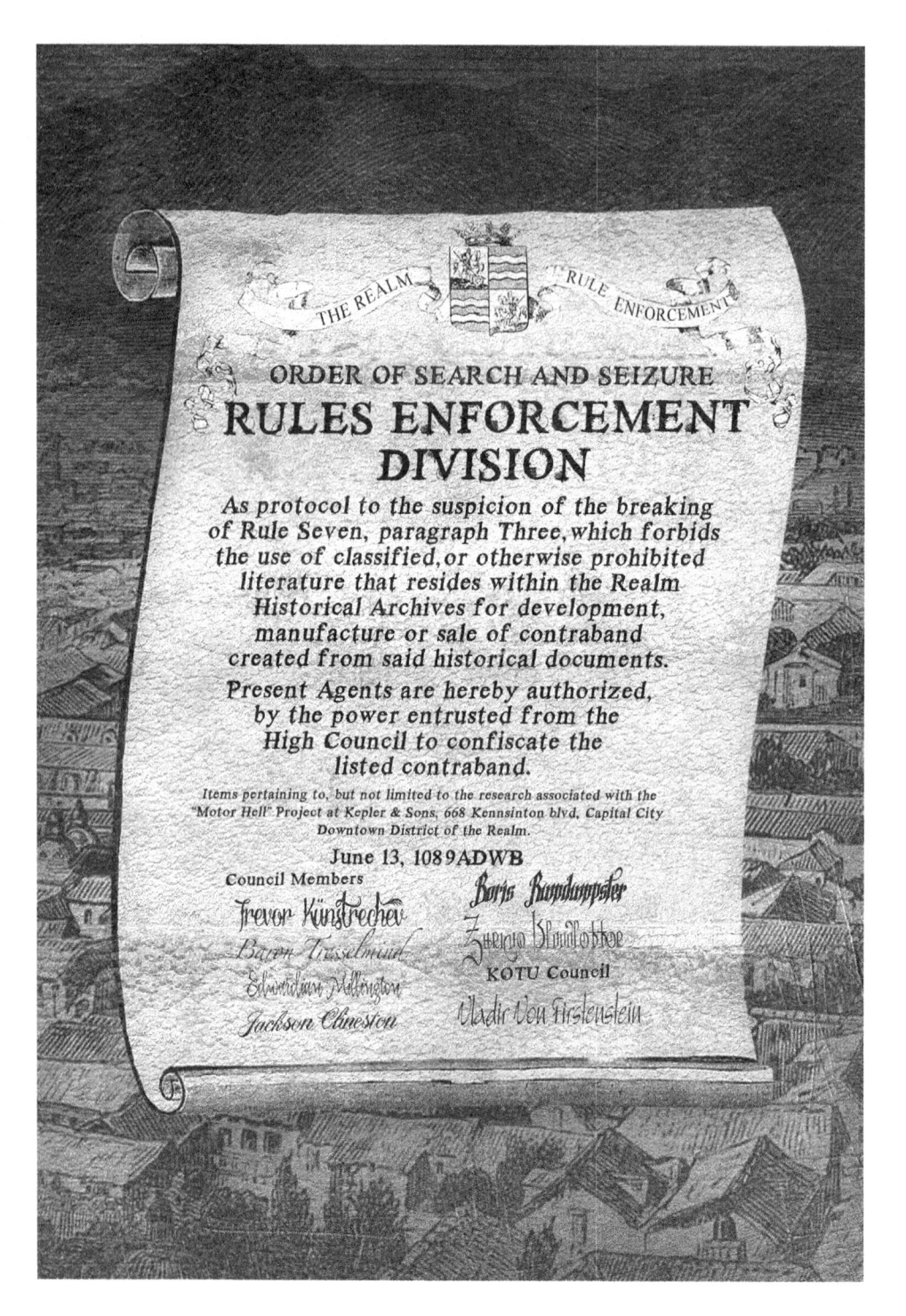

Toland began to find his anger again. "Well if that's the case, maybe the Council could have seen fit to question me first. Maybe face my accuser of these wild and untrue accusations!"

Vlad nodded again, "Yes, I wholeheartedly agree. And as I said, Doctor, I pleaded for that. After all, this is the same Kepler and Sons that has brought the Realm the Blood Berry."

The KOTU cleared his throat and stepped closer to Toland. "But this is different. At the core of the accusation is the charge the very equation used for the creation of the experiment was derived from the ancient scrolls and may even use…" Vlad emphasized with obligatory fright, "Supernatural methods."

"Oh, for the daylights!" Toland yelled. "I can show very explicitly how the compound was made. We have all the notes and logs."

"I know, I know. But you know the Council takes such insinuations quite seriously."

The KOTU was intrigued with the mention of the Doctor's notes. A slow, creeping smile stretched slowly across Vladimir Von Firstenstein's face, the way a pool of blood spreads on a slaughterhouse floor.

"If I may get those lab logs, Doctor, it may help exonerate these charges." Vlad leaned in even closer to Toland and in a breathy whisper said, "Where exactly did you say they were?"

CHAPTER FOURTEEN:
BIRTH OF A DEMON

Sparks were spraying the shop floor. Some even bounced once before they faded out into a speck of burnt iron. Sonny liked using the grinder and would try to hit Slim with sparks as he walked around the bike.

"Don't file yer edge too much, Sonny boy, we need some left to screw to the housing," Slim said solemnly as he looked up from the cables he had been rerouting.

The first few qualifying runs of the Pike had been messy and banged the Cafe Racer up quite a bit. The braided cables had gotten caught on tree limbs at Fangwood and hung loosely from the frame. A couple weeks later at the Castle Bain run Sonny had been stuck in a pileup and had his front brake lever bent beyond use. Luckily, he emerged from the heap and finished the run with only the use of his rear brakes. His headlamp was also smashed and he had only the other Riders and the light of the moon to see what laid in front of him. He had the idea to put a wire mesh cover over the lamp to help keep it from breaking again.

Sonny pressed the iron mesh grill he had in his hand hard against the grinder and made a fountain of sparks fall around Slim's feet.

Slim nodded his head and laughed. "Oh you'll be wishing you had every one of those bits of iron out there if you lose your light again." Slim looked at Sonny for a moment and lightened his mood. "Lets see what you've got."

Sonny brought the grill over to Slim. It fit perfectly on the housing that kept one large headlamp mounted to the front of the motorbike.

"Nicely done." Slim grinned as he hand turned screws to hold the grill in place. "Once we fasten the cables down tight you can take her out and see how the new front brake feels."

Sonny squeezed the new, used lever that Slim had swapped from a wrecked bike at the last run. It felt great and he grinned for a second.

"Don't imagine that I'll be using this too much at Suntora, though." Sonny wrinkled his nose.

Slim stood up shaking his head. "Nope, not likely."

The very real prospect that Suntora Flats would be the run that disqualified the Cafe Racer had just weighed heavy on their minds. After a few moments of morbid speculation Slim piped up, "But hey, you never know what's gonna happen."

Slim crossed the room and pulled two bottles from his incubator. One was a small bottle of Hell Blood, and the other was a slightly larger one of Healthy Blood, that he handed to Sonny.

"I remember when I was at Suntora," he sipped from his Hell Blood, "There were so many pileups I could've walked over the finish line."

"But it's a straightaway, isn't it? There's got to be more than enough room on the track."

Sonny sipped from his bottle, then looked at Slim's.

"Oh yeah, lots a' room out there, Sonny Boy, it's wide open. But it's the dust. Can't hardly see a thing. Vampires running into each other left and right. You'll be smart to take a place on the end of the line, try and stay out of the muck." Slim drank again. "Once you get in it, with any luck we won't be too far in the dust…" Slim looked at the bike, "We'll have to see what she's got."

Andi swung the door of the shop open. Her book bag was over her shoulder and a food tin was in her hands.

"Your Mom had me bring this out," Andi said, as she set the tin on the work desk.

Both Sonny and Slim quickly surrounded the food tin.

"Why haven't you been at the Academy the last couple days, have you been sick?" Sonny said with a mouthful of blood berry pie.

Andi shook her head. "No, I feel fine. But my father has been a pretty upset, so I've been staying close to home."

She sat down on Slim's couch. Though Slim called it the living room couch, it was only fifteen feet from where the motorbike sat in the workshop, and was all in the same large room.

"Hope everything's all right," Slim said, placing his pie on the work desk.

Andi sighed. "There's some sort of investigation down at K&S. The High Council seized some stuff in the labs, the R.E.D. came down. My father wouldn't tell me the details but I guess it's a really big deal. He's been yelling in his office a lot."

Both Sonny and Slim were quiet.

"Sorry to hear that, Andi. Damn Council is always in every vampire's business." Slim said. "Please let Toland know that if there's anything at all I can do to help, to not hesitate to ask."

Slim stood up, finished his bottle Hell Blood and began cleaning up the work desk. Sonny walked to sit on the couch with Andi.

"So, you coming tomorrow?"

"I might." Andi looked to see if Slim was within earshot. He was now on the other side of the shop at the kitchen, bagging up garbage.

"But to be honest, I've been using the time to work on that experiment I told you about." Andi grinned and nodded.

Sonny thought for a second then shook his head.

"Not the bloody bedtime stories!" He made tiny wings with his hands and smiled as if showing his fangs. "I better watch out or you'll turn me into a bat!"

Andi punched him in the arm and Sonny fell over dramatically on the couch.

"Quickly, give me a pint of that delicious Human Blood!"

"Shhh!" Andi looked at Slim who was toweling his hands, then turned back to Sonny who was flailing in mock agony on the couch, and yelled in a whisper, "This is serious!"

"What's serious?" Slim was now in the 'living room'.

Andi smiled dismissively. "Oh, nothing, he's just an idiot."

"Oh, come on," Sonny said, still mocking, "Slim likes a funny story."

Andi was irritated that Sonny didn't take her human blood theory seriously, but equally mad that he would mention it in front of an older vampire, even if it was Slim.

"That I do," Slim agreed and folded his arms in anticipation.

Andi opened her mouth as if searching for the right words. She shook her head no.

"It's really nothing." She glared angrily at Sonny. He sat up and quit acting silly, seeing that she was genuinely mad.

Slim smiled. "Well that's alright, Andi. You do not have to tell me. And don't let this joker make you think you do." He winked at her and leaned in. "And for the record, I would not have laughed at you."

She immediately smiled when Slim said that. It felt like Slim had validated her work and all the ideas she had about the ancient stories and scrolls. She looked again at Sonny as if to say 'see.' Sonny was frowning, having felt a little immature after what Slim had just said.

Andi straightened herself up. "Actually, I've been conducting some experiments with different blood."

Slim was back at the work desk. He nodded. "Oh. Healthy Blood related stuff?"

"No, it's more centered around some old theories I had come across recently." She paused and cleared her throat.

Slim had almost begun fastening the braided cables to the frame, but stopped and looked at Andi.

She sensed a nervousness welling up inside her and quickly continued before she lost her nerve. "It's human blood. The equation that I have was designed to create human blood."

Slim didn't say a word, but it was clear she had his full attention, so she carried on. "Um, from what I've gathered, there is not a requirement that an actual human is needed for this to work. It's quite fascinating. With only a few specific components isolated, and replaced, blood can be altered to have the appearance of *actual* human blood."

Andi grew comfortable and began to talk more quickly.

"Now, of course, whether or not the chemical makeup is the only determining factor in what would constitute human blood, I don't know. But can you imagine if it was. And furthermore, if all the ancient stories of human blood being the secret to unlocking the supernatural powers of vampires, including flight, shape-shifting..."

Slim raised a hand. "Now, let me ask you something." He scratched his chin as he looked at her. "Where exactly did you get a recipe for human blood? It's been awhile, but I don't recall having any classes like that when I was at the Academy..."

Andi closed her eyes and rocked her head for a moment. "It's true. It's not exactly common knowledge."

Slim's eyebrows were raised as he waited. She drew a large breath.

"As a Kepler—I mean, my father owns the building that holds some, well, *many* historical books. I found very specific notes left by scientists detailing the process."

Slim was not entirely sure what to think. He nodded and thought hard before speaking. "I'm not a scientist, so whether or not something like this could even be vampirely possible, I don't know." He cleared his throat. "And as far as the stories we've heard of ancient flying vampires and the power that human blood supposedly gave us, well, I have no desire to leave the ground... even if I could." He paused. "I guess I would ask, why, given all the other scientific minds that the Realm has seen over the years, would this be so obvious to you but not any other scientist with access to the Archives?"

Andi paused. She had not said that she was referring to specifically using information obtained from the Historical Archives. That mere fact would take this conversation from being inconsequential scientific speculation, to a Rule infraction worthy of serious High Council action. Even possible treason charges.

"Well. As a very young Fledge, I spent many nights wandering the halls of K&S. I was left alone to play in the Archives, or anywhere else I wanted. I would look through all the old books in the Archive and even before I had learned proper Realm script, I was reading ancient books that used dead dialects and the symbols of Man. I would guess that there aren't many who would even possess the ability to decipher such work. Particularly since some notes, such as the ones with the human blood equations, were hand-written and open for interpretation."

Slim nodded as if satisfied with her explanation. "So… what are you gonna do with human blood, even if you can make it?"

Andi lowered her head and searched for the right words. She felt very self-conscious because there weren't eloquent words to describe her intentions. She wasn't trying to isolate human blood so that she could write a paper on it and lecture to academics about it. After a moment she raised her head and said with total conviction, "I would drink it. And I would hope that it unleashed the supernatural powers of our ancestors." She let her head fall and immediately felt as if her words sounded like that of a child.

Even though Slim was unconventional, to say the least, Andi was bracing for a lecture on the irresponsibleness of such actions. Or at least for Slim to tell her that she should confess and solicit her father to oversee the experiments. Or just simply that it was nonsense.

Slim looked back and forth between Andi and Sonny, nodding his head and smiling. Eventually he laughed with his lips still pressed hard together. Sonny joined in with a chuckle, with what he guessed was the sensible response to assertions of Andi's being able to unleash supernatural powers in vampires with her concoction.

Slim waited for Andi to bring her head back up, and said firmly, "It sounds beautiful, Andi." He slapped his hand on the work desk. "Vampires need dreams. Without dreams we're just dead inside, passing our time like living corpses." Slim kept nodding. "And if anyone can do it, Andi, it will surely be you. I hope you prove 'em all wrong, honey, and change us all back to bloodsucking bats." He laughed loudly and winked. "Your secret's safe with me."

Both Andi and Sonny were awestruck, shocked at what they had just heard. Sure, they had known Slim all their lives, he was their friend. But he was also a vampire over three hundred years old. Older vampires just didn't *say* things like that. With a few quick words Slim had just promoted dissent, supported blasphemy and collaborated to conceal Rule infraction, and was now back working at the bike.

The Fledges stood dumbfounded as the light noise from Slim's screwdriver touching the bike frame echoed in the shop.

Slim looked over at them and laughed. "Now if you only had an equation for making the cafe racer supernatural."

Sonny was pulled back from his stupor. "Yeah," he agreed.

As Sonny watched Andi, he could see her almost glow from the words Slim had spoken to her. He wished he had been a little kinder and more supportive with her blood experiments, and joined Slim at the bike.

"But I'd settle for just faster!" Slim laughed

Andi cleared from her haze at the word *'faster.'*

"Oh," she squeaked, and began digging around in her book bag. "I almost forgot!" She pulled a folded paper from the bag and went to the desk.

"I have an idea about just that thing." She pressed the paper to her chest as if giving a book report to a classroom.

Slim stopped working and smirked as he prepared for another interesting observation from her.

"Okay... I was thinking about this and it was driving me crazy. I was thinking that, like all of us are, that a bigger engine would probably make the bike go faster. But of course, we can't afford one and it would no doubt add weight with the bigger block as well as structural reinforcement. Then I thought, there ought to be a way to get our existing engine to just simply work a little *harder*. Like when my dad tells an employee to 'move faster' or 'lift more'. They don't go out and get a bigger person to do it, they simply tap into energy that is already there...within them..." Andi smiled like she was getting to the good part.

Both Sonny and Slim were sitting with their arms crossed nodding along with her.

"So, if we had to find more strength on a motorbike... it'd probably be in the pistons, right? You know, because of the downward stroke of the piston on the bike, not all the air that is capable of getting into the engine actually does. There is still a measurable difference between what is in the engine and what *could* be forced into the engine. And as we know, the more air, and fuel, we can get into the engine, the bigger the explosion is that occurs, and the more power is generated."

Andi flattened her sketch out on the table.

"So what I've done is sketch this idea I have for an extra part. A device that I think will help that engine get more of that energy. I think that you can weld this together, Slim." She spun it around to face them properly. "With this simple device, I think we could harness the energy of the exhaust to propel a fan that would push air through a compressor that would force more air into the engine." With her index finger she traced the path of the air.

Sonny and Slim's heads moved in unison, like two cats following a length of string.

"Now if we just increased the amount of fuel being sprayed in, we would be creating a denser, more powerful explosion at each turn of the pistons."

Proud of herself, she placed both hands on her hips.

"Guys, we would be generating more power, with the same exact engine!"

Slim frantically looked at the diagram as if he was a couple of sentences behind what she was saying. As he traced the path and reached the part about a more powerful explosion he nodded. He raised his head and looked at her with total bewilderment and buried his face back in her diagram.

"Probably gonna need to bore out the exhaust to help get rid of the extra exhaust energy, but…" Slim was shocked. "I think that this… could actually work!"

Andi smiled and jumped a little. "Yeah, my calculations were anywhere from twenty-five to a forty percent increase in performance."

Sonny and Slim were looking at each other in complete amazement. Slim rubbed his head hard and gave a howl. He jumped up and kissed the top of Andi's head on the way to the cube.

"When do you have all the time for these incredible ideas?"

Slim flung the cube door open and grabbed a bottle. He took a gulp from a small bottle of Hell Blood and shook his head again in disbelief at Andi.

"So, am I gonna find out this was in some holy scrolls in the Archives?" He swigged again from the bottle and laughed loudly.

"No, you know what… I don't even wanna know!"

CHAPTER FIFTEEN:
THE VERY MOMENT

In the wee hours of the night, two young female vampires quietly made their way down the cobblestone street and past the entrance to the Dragonfly Tavern. Two older male vampires on barstools inside looked surprised as the girls walked by. Not because they didn't come into the tavern, but because they were even out on the streets of this deserted part of the city at this hour.

The Dragonfly Tavern was a working-vamps watering hole on the edge of the warehouse district. It wasn't a particularly interesting tavern, and even most vamps who worked near it opted for one of the more modern alehouses a few blocks away, in the Devilston neighborhood that was home to a dozen or more taverns.

When the girls reached the alley behind the tavern, they walked into the dark and lightly tapped on the iron door that lead to the basement of the Dragonfly. After a moment, the iron plate at eye-level slid open and a Fledge-aged vampire with scruffy sideburns looked back at the girls. Without a word the girls each handed two cards through the window of the door.

Each card was grey, stiff and playing card-sized. There was only an image of a black top hat on it, nothing else. The iron plate slid back in place. After a few seconds the door opened wide enough for them to enter and quickly shut behind them.

Across the street, Detective Hellamina Muntz rolled to a stop on her motorbike. It wasn't an R.E.D.-issued bike, but a beat up old Gargoyle she had ridden for years. She was dressed very much civilian with black dungarees and a traditional riding jacket. She had a leather skullcap-type helmet that she left on, after moving her eye goggles to rest on top of it.

She walked directly to the iron door, hidden in the shadow of the tavern, and tapped once. The same vampire looked through the window. For a couple

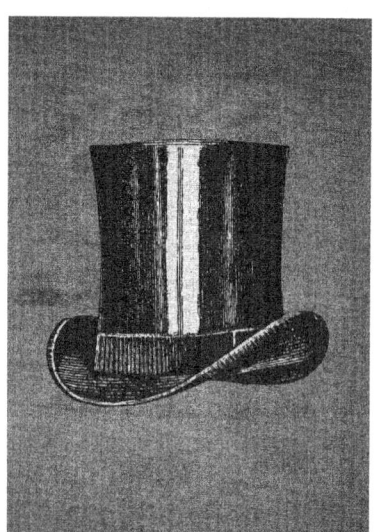

seconds they stood staring at each other until Hellamina reached to her chest pocket and produced the top hat voucher. The iron window closed and the door opened.

The other side of the door was a small, dank landing at the top of a stairway that led down a poorly lit staircase. The walls were solid stone and had no doubt been carved by hand in the first century. During that time hundreds of thousands of vampires were starving and many worked digging through the rock, building what was now the Realm's most modern, and only true city.

At the bottom of the stairs was a set of swinging doors that led through a room that housed dozens of kegs and cases of fermented blood. It was at the other end of that room that Hellamina could see groups of vampires at tables.

When she stepped into the room, a few vamps at a table in front of her smiled and nodded. They had frilly shirts with vests on. Looking across the room there were several similarly dressed male vamps, some with long overcoats and triple-breasted jackets. Some had canes lying against their tables and pipes clenched in their teeth. There were female vamps in short-sleeved dresses with low necklines. Their dresses were very tight in the torso, some wore corsets on the outside. The bottom halves of their dresses were frilly and puffed out behind them. Many wore boots and leggings under their dresses, and some had gloves that reached to their elbows.

Most of this clothing was made by the wearer and pulled from the stories of the ancient vampires. There was certainly nowhere to buy entire outfits like these anywhere in the Realm. Even some of the 'real vampires' in the Lowlands, though fancying traditional clothing, had nothing this ornate. There was an attention to detail that was breathtaking.

At the far end of this room was a makeshift stage. Mostly wooden palettes that had once held cases of blood, they were now laid together to raise the performers a few inches above the heads of the crowd. A crowd which was now at standing room-only capacity.

As Hellamina took the first sip from her pint of Pig Ale, a tall and lean Fledge walked onto the stage. He had a black top hat on his head and his sideburns went almost to his chin. He wore a vest over a grey and black striped shirt with suspenders and when he smiled, he displayed large fangs.

"Welcome, Vampires, one and all," he yelled. The room clapped and cheered.

"It is the hour and the time to forget about this Realm. Forget about our specialties, and…" He rolled his 'r' dramatically, "…responsibilities!" The room cheered wildly. "It's time to lift our glasses and live in the moment!" He held a pint high as the room howled. "Time to clap our hands and welcome the Sweet… Death… Symphony!"

As the crowd clapped and yelled, several vampires, both male and female, stood up from tables around the room and made their way to the stage. Once there, they began picking up instruments that had already been lying against the far wall. Some looked to be Fledgling-aged, but some even looked in their two- and early three-hundreds.

A male vampire with a bowler hat walked to the front of the stage. He had a shirt and vest on with a large gold chain attached to a pocket watch in his vest. He looked around the room and nodded. He paused as he gazed at Hellamina across the room, leaning against the bar. She was staring directly back at him. Without turning away from her he yelled, "Let the merrymaking begin!"

One of the three drummers began pounding the timpani drums to the bass guitar. The vamp in the bolero stomped his foot to the beat and began singing.

This very moment in time,
Looking for the dead.
There's a girl in disguise,
It's all inside your head.
To the Fledglings they lie,
Oh, for the Realm they bled.
And when the Midnight eye is mine,
These words inside my head…
We all see the the World,
Through different eyes in spite of ourselves,
We are all the same.
The very moment I tried to stay beneath the waves.

When the World comes crashing down,

I can't escape the pain.

It is a lonely life tonight,

Just make it go away.

Living to fulfill your dreams and die.

We all see the the World,

Through different eyes in spite of ourselves

We are all the same.

We must cast our fears aside.

Never give up and never give in to the other side.

This very moment in time,

Looking for the dead.

There's a girl in disguise,

It's all inside your head.

Through the window I cried,

And turn into a R.E.D.

And when the Midnight eye is mine...

Musical accompaniment for this scene:
"THE VERY MOMENT"
FROM THE ALBUM "RISE OF THE CAFE RACER"
DEANO JONES & THE SWEET DEATH SYMPHONY

The Sweet Death Symphony played many more songs through the rest of the night. As the first light of Dawn broke the horizon outside, the vamp who worked at the top of the stairway bolted and locked the iron door. The SDS and their merrymaker friends would stay in the cellar all day singing, laughing, and ignoring the Realm.

The Ninth Pike's Run

SUNTORA FLATS

QUALIFYING RUNS
7·21·1089ADWB

CHAPTER SIXTEEN:
READY, STEADY, GO

It was a hot summer night on the Lowland Plains of the Realm. The usually sparse trading town of Suntora was now electric with energy and to capacity with Pike Riders and spectators. Like many towns in the Realm, Suntora had enormous iron warehouses that served as public places during the daylight hours. Many "Dayhouses" had freestanding shops and smaller structures under their massive domes. In more remote locations there were even vamps who had homes and lived within these massive structures.

Suntora was truly unique because it was in the middle of the lowlying plains and was a mega trading outpost positioned midway between the eastern vamps of the Lowlands and the western vamps from the Port Iron Gate and the Dead Hills area. It was also more than a mere dayhouse at Suntora, it was colossal, over a mile long, fifty feet high and housed taverns, markets, restaurants and residents. Even a brothel or two during a Pike year.

Sonny and Slim had driven down with the cafe racer in Slim's truck the night before. They had parked at the west end of Suntora near the Flats, where most of the other Riders were camped. A small sub-city had popped up with two hundred fifty Riders getting ready to run plus a few thousand Pike spectators, many of who were eager to talk to Riders and find a favorite.

Many of the vamps at Suntora City seemed to know Slim; he'd had dozens stopping to look at the cafe racer and wish them luck. And with day ending, many were packing up to make their way onto the Flats.

"Tell you what, Sonny Boy," Slim said jumping off the back of the truck, "I'll go check in with the judges. You take it easy." He slapped Sonny on the shoulder. They had just fastened the bike down for the short drive to the Flats, where the race would begin shortly after first dark.

Sonny nodded, "Thanks." He *had* been a little nervous but didn't know that Slim could tell. For some reason the first few runs hadn't bothered him, probably because he didn't have any expectations. It was so messy and disorganized in those early runs, it had been like herding cattle to slaughter. But now even the crowd seemed different. There was a serious tone. Vamps had stopped by their truck all day asking about the bike, and about Sonny too. Where he was from, where he went to school. He had felt strange. Not just because of the attention but also the questions about whether his father had run the Pike. More than a few vamps had asked if Slim was his dad. Slim always had a quick reply, like he 'wished he'd had a son doing this well in the Pike,' or 'I'm just the pit crew,' and would then ramble on about something funny that served to change the subject. More than a few times Sonny had wished that he had a father there with him. He had even looked at Slim a few times and wished Slim could be his father. He imagined how great it would be to be able to tell these spectators that he had a father who had ranked Three in the Pike in his day.

As it was, Sonny was feeling unsure of himself and also worried that Andi's little invention wouldn't work properly. They had been calling Andi's device the Little Demon since it seemed to have a mind of its own. When it worked properly, it made the bike screaming fast. But it had been stalling sometimes and been difficult dialing in the perfect combination of air and fuel. Sonny had been riding the bike around back home with the Demon engaged and was itching to get out in the night and warm it up.

"Well, well, well, if it isn't the tutor and his… what did you call it, casket racer?" Daryn Von Firstenstein said through clenched teeth.

Erik Von Castlehuhn and Millington Brimstone were snickering beside him. All three vampires were in full-body leather jumpsuits. They were very modern and similar, with accent panels of deep blues and greys. Small buckles and family crests adorned each vampire's suit and Daryn had a cape hanging from clips on his shoulder.

Erik pointed at Sonny's bike, "Is that the same runner you rented at Fang-wood?" They all laughed.

"Look, it's held together by a thread!" Millington howled and reached toward the small black ribbon tied to the handlebar. Sonny's mother Evanna had put it there for luck before they had left for Suntora.

"Keep your hands off my bike!" Sonny hissed and stepped toward the three vamps.

"Or what?" Mills yelled back.

Daryn held his arms out between Mills and Sonny.

"Now boys, touching another Rider's bike could disqualify you," Daryn smirked, "And besides, you may have to buy him a new one if you broke it." Daryn eyed the bike in disgust. "Where in the Realm did you say you got this… uh…" he feigned he was searching for his name.

"Sonny," Sonny said with a blank stare.

"Yes, that's right, I remember. Sonny Legatus." Daryn tapped the side of his forehead. "Now, I forget, this is a…"

"It's a cafe racer, and I built it myself." Sonny slammed the tailgate up on Slim's truck.

"He's a liar," Mills huffed from behind Daryn.

"No, No," Daryn waved his finger in the air, "Bebe tells me Legatus here is *very* smart. He's a regular brianiac." Daryn nodded and stared at Sonny. He thought for a moment, as he looked hard at Sonny. "Yeah, he's so smart he probably thinks he's actually got a shot with my girl too," Daryn frowned angrily.

"What?!" Sonny shook his head and tried to walk past them.

Daryn, Erik and Mills all surrounded him and made an imposing wall, with Slim's truck behind Sonny.

Daryn leaned in and with a hateful whisper said, "You listen to me cafe boy, you're just a common bat on a junk bike. And after today you'll be just another loser."

Sonny tightened his fists and glared back at Daryn. He hated Daryn beyond words but knew beating him on the track would be so much more satisfying than any couple punches he may land right there.

"When you're done signing autographs, Sonny boy, we got a race to run." Slim had a big piece of jerky in the side of his mouth. He walked through the middle of the group, forcing the three vamps to step back from Sonny. As he walked by he handed Sonny a slab of jerky. He opened the door of the truck and looked back at the vamps.

"Eat up, kid, gonna be a long night." He bit a chunk off and looked at the three vamps in their expensive, customized racing suits. He glanced at their midsections and made a slightly agonized face.

"It's not painful with all that tight fabric down there?" Slim made a circular motion with his hand over his own midsection and then shook his head, shuddering quickly as if trying to erase the image from his mind, turned, and got in his truck.

Mills and Erik had already backed off and turned away. Daryn and Sonny stared bitterly at each other as Daryn slowly stepped away. They held on for a few more moments, neither one wanting to turn first, until Slim called, "Let's get a move on," from inside the cab.

As they edged the truck from the cover of the dayhouse, Slim smiled and winked at Sonny. "All that means is you got 'em scared, Sonny Boy." Slim broke another piece of jerky off in his teeth. "There are two hundred fifty Riders running today, and those three came to mess with your head." He laughed loudly as they entered the edge of the Flats. "Just means you're scaring 'em!"

A trumpeter played the Seven Notes of the Pike and Riders began assembling on the line. The Seven Notes were just a short, easily recognizable battle cry of sorts that could be heard at a great distance and let everyone know that Riders could take their marks.

Musical accompaniment for this scene:
"THE SEVEN NOTES OF THE PIKE"
FROM THE ALBUM "RISE OF THE CAFE RACER"
DEANO JONES & THE SWEET DEATH SYMPHONY

The first of four runs would start shortly. There would be two runs with one hundred twenty five Riders in each. After the ninety-mile sprint to the finish, the top sixty Riders from each run would all race back to Suntora. From that one hundred twenty Riders, the top sixty would go on to the next qualifying run, a week later near the Dead Hills. Roughly three out of four Riders were done after that day.

Sonny found a place near the left hand side on the line. Judges were walking down the line, inspecting bikes for ancient symbols and additives as well as checking for qualifying paperwork. The bike inspection portion was just a formality that started in the sixth century, when a trend to summon the powers of the supernatural emerged. During that time Riders were placing symbols on their bikes and making superstitious gestures, like adding HellHound blood in the tank or mounting jackalope horns to the front of their bike. The High Council responded by outlawing any ancient folklore artifacts from inclusion of the Pike. But they used the opportunity to leverage further restrictions on even mentioning of ancient powers of vampires publicly, driving the ancient folklore further into obscurity and making it the talk of only the commonest bats of the outer reaches of the Realm. At that time several slogans and Realm propaganda also emerged as a way to ridicule such thinking. Things like 'You've got Bats in your belfry if you think your ancestors flew' and 'Mining: The Super-natural Specialty'.

The judges would still dunk a thin stick in each gas tank and crank case to taste for additives, though. There was even a handful of creaky old vampires who were official "tasters." They had been tasting tanks for centuries and could tell if there were any foreign additives in the mix. Everyone called them the "Geezers" and it was another sign that you had arrived at the Pike, since they didn't come out for the first three runs. In remote towns of the Lowlands

You've got Bats in your belfry,
if you think your ancestors flew.

Superstitions can lead to
further misconceptions.
Stop the spread!

REALM PUBLIC SERVICE MESSAGE

it was very prestigious to simply make it to Suntora Flats and "Git yer bike Geezered!"

The KOTU was on hand, talking and soaking in the pageantry, with all three vamps that had harassed Sonny lined up near him, directly in the center of the line. Within a few minutes the first run was ready to begin and the KOTU was entering the podium that elevated him high enough for all to see. The crowd was lined up on either side of the line and there were two large light boxes on each side that would serve to start the race.

"Looking good, Sonny boy." Slim called from his close spot at the edge of the line. Sonny was remembering everything he had just told him, *'Now remember, Sonny, flip the Demon on high after about ten minutes, once you've separated from the muck and have a little room.'* Sonny gave a thumbs-up. He, like all Riders, was on his bike, goggled and ready to go.

"Run for Glory, Sonny boy!" Slim howled.

"Welcome, everyone and all!" The KOTU yelled from the podium. "The fourth qualifying night of the Ninth Pike Run is ready to begin." The crowd

cheered wildly. "The judges have determined that Riders are within the Rules. The lights on the sides will shine bright blue when it's time to run. And of course the crowd will lead us in the count!" Everyone cheered and clapped until finally the KOTU yelled, "Vampires, start your engines!"

The sound was deafening, with one hundred and twenty five motorbikes revving their engines. The crowd grew quiet and waited until the KOTU raised his arms and conducted them to start the race. Then all at once the spectators screamed at the top of their lungs, rising over the volume of engines.

"Ready... Steady... GO!"

The spectators all dropped their arms in unison with the KOTU. The light boxes shined a soft blue light that cut through the grey of first dark and the motorbikes screamed from the line.

Sonny was low and tight to his bike and only looked straight ahead. He had a nice start and already had lurched in front of the handful of Riders next to him. There were Riders several yards to the right that seemed to have pulled ahead of where he was but so far he had escaped the dust that he had heard so much about.

It continued this way for several minutes and Sonny was able to lean more toward the center of the line. The ground beneath him was so smooth, except for the rushing wind and noise of the Riders, it could seem like he was standing still. It looked like a handful of Riders were ahead of his bike, and after a quick check to both sides he decided it was a good time to kick in the Demon. Slim had placed a small switch next to the right hand grip. Sonny tightened up to the bike as he flipped the Demon's switch with his thumb.

There was a quick bark from the bike and it lurched forward. Sonny grinned and narrowed his gaze, but almost immediately the bike coughed like an old vamp catching his breath. Sonny revved the throttle quickly to punch through it but he started losing speed and was joining the ranks of Riders who had been several yards behind him. He continued revving, but the bike kept coughing. Soon two Riders had made it past him closely on each side. Dust started filling up his view of the track. He panicked and flipped the Demon's switch back to Off. He was frantically trying to remember how many Riders were in front of him before he flipped the switch and wondering how many had crept up. He leaned left to roll back on the outside and tucked it in tighter than he had all night. His chin was touching the gas tank as he ever so slowly felt himself inching by one of the Riders who had passed him. There was a slight bump underneath the bike as the perfect track was showing cracks that raised its surface. It was worse in the center, where deep cracks from the hot summer days left two-inch gaps in the track. From the corner of his eye he saw a Rider's front tire rattle and send him flying into a group of bikes. Dust billowed from the center of the track and Sonny squeezed his handlebars ferociously. His bike was bouncing on the track and he let off of his throttle slightly to regain control. In the distance he saw the faint blue light of the finish. The wind had switched directions and was blowing dust across the track. Within seconds there were several Riders within arms' length of him. There was dust from ahead of them and it appeared Riders were crossing the finish line. He tucked in and looked at the switch. He wanted desperately to try to use the Demon but couldn't chance it slowing him down. He managed to pull ahead of the small group of bikes he was in as he crossed the line but wondered how many had made it over the line before him.

He coasted to a stop before trying to pry himself from the bike. When he finally moved he was surprised how cramped he was. This had been an intense run. As soon as he could move he frantically made his way to the judges' table. He handed a Geezer his run card with his number and tried to stand fully erect while he waited. The old vampire looked at it, confided with the judge next to him and them handed Sonny a new card for the race back.

"Congratulations Rider, you ranked Twenty-One in that run."

Sonny howled and kissed the card. "Thank you, Sir!"

As he walked back to his bike he almost immediately forgot of the run he had just made and began to wonder how he could rank in the run back to Suntora. Andi's Demon had never failed so miserably before.

There was a dayhouse with fuel and drink for Riders. Most Riders were scrambling to ready their bikes for the run back that would start in thirty minutes. The second race from Suntora would be arriving within minutes and Pike officials were reminding ranked Riders to get their bikes fueled. Sonny could see Daryn and a group of other similarly dressed Riders in the ale tent getting drinks while uniformed vamps fueled their bikes for them. Daryn caught Sonny from the corner of his eye. He stood and yelled from the tent.

"Hey Legatus, if you're not doing anything, we need an extra boy to fuel bikes!"

Sonny stared back with no expression and kept walking. Slowly he held up his card that qualified him for the run back.

"Ah," Daryn howled. "Touché!"

Sonny pushed his bike to the fuel tent and pulled at his hair trying to figure why the Demon wouldn't run. Trucks pulled into the pit with bent bikes from the wreck. Dirty faced Riders with sad expressions piled out of the flatbeds. Some went straight to the ale tent but most began helping other qualifying Riders with refueling. A scruffy vamp with a large rip down the sleeve of his jacket approached Sonny as he refueled.

"That's a sharp bike, friend," He said cheerfully, "I remember seeing you at Fangwood."

Sonny thought for a moment. "That seems like a long time ago, huh?" Sonny shook his head.

"It does." He nodded at Sonny's bike. "My bike is pretty broken up, but if you need anything I'd let you have it."

"Aw, thanks, but I'm well out of treasure." Sonny topped off the gas tank.

The vamp smiled, "Come on, this cafe racer. Everybody's rooting for you."

"Really?" Sonny stopped. "What do you mean?"

The vamp shrugged. "I mean, older vamps, I think. My dad knows Slim. He says this looks like the bike Slim ran."

Sonny gave this vamp a gentler and longer look, then smiled and held out his hand. "Sonny Legatus."

"Viktor Blackheart," he said grabbing Sonny's hand.

"Where you from, Viktor?"

"Port Iron Gate."

"You gonna go Mariner as your Specialty?" Sonny eyes were wide as he pushed the bike out of the fuel tent. He was always interested in meeting mariner vamps.

"Ha," Viktor laughed. "You been talking to my parents?" He shook his head. "If I had my way I'd just ride my motorbike all over the Realm for about a century."

Sonny nodded. He knew exactly what Viktor was feeling.

"Yeah, my mother wants me to teach at the Academy."

"Oh, hey, you're in the Capital, huh?" Now Viktor was wide eyed. "That's gotta be great."

"Eh, you know. It's alright." Sonny pulled his bike backwards onto its center stand.

"What? Oh, I'd love to go there. Lots of girls, things to do." He looked around and leaned in. "You ever seen the SDS?"

Sonny stopped and looked at Viktor with a slight grin. He slowly shook his head no. "I wish. Guess they gotta invite you or something." Sonny pulled his tools from a small tin fastened near the back of the seat. He looked sideways at Viktor.

"You've heard of them all the way down at Iron Gate?"

Viktor was shaking his head violently, "Everybody's heard of the SDS."

Sonny was kind of shocked, "Small Realm, huh?"

"The whole Specialty thing is just crap." Viktor shook his head in disgust. "I know a lot of Fledges that don't care one bit about anything that the High Council says."

They both nodded and grinned at each other. "But hey, you have a run to make back to Suntora brother!" Viktor clapped.

"Yes, yes I do," Sonny smiled.

"Is there anything I can do to help?" Viktor pointed at the cafe racer.

Sonny winced, "Well, I just have this little... uh, booster here that was messing up on me."

"How's that," Viktor squatted down next to Sonny as they looked at the carburetor.

Sonny tapped the Demon with a screwdriver. "This little Demon pushes air into the engine. Makes it go faster. Worked great back home, but it was stalling here."

Viktor squinted, not entirely understanding. "Hmm." Eventually he just rubbed at his head and said, "I know my dad says the air's different up there in the Capital. That you vamps got less of it there. So I'd bet you got a whole lot more down here than you were planning on."

Sonny looked at Viktor wondering what that meant exactly. "We have more air?"

Viktor shrugged and both vamps stared at the Demon for a few moments. Finally Sonny tapped at the engine with the screwdriver and smiled at Viktor.

"I bet I need to let a little more fuel flow in to offset all the extra air down here." He glanced around the pit at all the Riders tooling with their bikes. "I mean, at this point I better try something, I was near the end of that last run."

Viktor still didn't know for sure what the Demon did but he liked that Sonny liked his suggestion so he agreed. "It sounds like a plan Sonny."

As Sonny made the small adjustment to allow a tiny bit more fuel to feed into the engine, he heard the Seven Notes of the Pike.

"Aw, bloody Hell." Sonny threw the tool down. "I wanted to give her a test."

Viktor reared his head, "Sorry, Sonny, I completely distracted you."

"No, no worries Viktor," Sonny gave his hand. "I was nice to meet you."

As they shook hands Daryn's bike was being wheeled to him at the line. Both vamps watched.

"I just want to beat him back to Suntora." Sonny growled and nodded at Daryn.

"Who's that?"

"It's the KOTU's son and he's a bat turd."

Viktor smiled. "Of course he is, that's why he'll be the next KOTU!" They both laughed.

Within a few minutes all Riders were at the line. The KOTU gave his regular address to the spectators, though this group was a fraction of the crowd at Suntora and was mostly the other Riders who didn't rank and crew. Sonny found a spot on the right side of the line so he could ride essentially the same track that he had ran out there. He wanted to make sure he avoided the deep cracks in the center of the track. Other Riders felt the same way and there was an empty patch in the middle of the line that the KOTU had decided to stand in to officiate from.

The engines were all roaring and the KOTU had raised his hand. Sonny was hoping that he got it right and the Demon would kick in. More than anything he wanted to rank high. He even wondered if he might be able to just run the cafe racer straight, with no Demon and still rank. Before he could answer himself the blue light popped on and the entire line jerked forward.

The moon was bright and the Suntora Flats were gleaming with a frosty blue-grey phosphorescence. In spite of the noise of the motorbikes there was a calm to the way the bikes moved in unison over the glassy clay ground. A handful of Riders had pulled ahead of Sonny on his left, reminding him that he needed to beat half of these one-hundred-twenty Riders. The thought of waiting too much longer to find out if he had use of the high setting was killing him. He knew Slim warned of running too hot if he engaged too early, but he felt like he needed to make the move, so he flipped the Demon's switch up.

At first there was no difference. In fact, he glanced at the switch to make sure it was up. Then the cafe racer coughed as it had on the first run of the night and Sonny cursed loudly. But before he could decide if he should toggle the switch back down the bike pulled forward. It was as if a tow-rope was yanking him from a dead stop and the cafe racer began a steady crawl toward the handful of bikes in the lead.

It took a few minutes, but Sonny could soon make out the Riders ahead and to his left. There were several expensive looking bikes at the very front. He recognized Daryn garish, shiny Gargoyle at the lead. Sonny dug in tight and stared hard at the back of Daryn's bike. With every second, he was gaining on him.

Soon Sonny was alongside Riders at the rear of this group and only a few arms' lengths away. It was then that he noticed that the normally blue light on the mile marker was red. The whole course had been lined on either side with small lights, with a mile between them. They had always shown blue, same as the opening light. Now he had passed another red light. He turned to look at the Rider next to him. The Rider stared back, no doubt wondering the same thing and shrugged his shoulders.

Before the next marker, ahead maybe a quarter mile, there were shadows moving over the track. At their speed there were few seconds before the group of Riders were at that spot. Sonny noticed Vamps at the side of the track waving lanterns and their hands in a motion to slow down. Before anyone could react shadows emerged onto the track mere yards ahead. Sonny instantly recognized the silhouettes running across their paths. These were tiny Lowland deer, and within a second the Rider next to him, that only moments ago had shrugged, was broadsided by a deer running full speed. Riders let off their throttles as a dozen deer entered the track ahead. More and more vamps were along the sidelines waving them to slow down. The Riders were frantically looking in every direction. Not just for deer, but they all wondered if every other Rider was slowing down as well. Suddenly dozens of deer were running over the track. The vague shadows and sounds of Riders hitting deer and each other all around Sonny was shocking. He slowed and weaved around deer darting in front of him. Sonny quickly shot a look over his shoulder to see dusty pileups with deer and Riders lying on the track.

By now the Riders were crawling through what was a herd of deer ahead. Daryn and his friends were laughing at each other, careening around the obstacle course. Ahead the deer were thinning out but large shadows ran up and down the sidelines. Some of the large shadows were running out and snatching the small deer shadows. Sonny tensed up with excitement, he knew these shadows had to be HellHounds. It made sense, they weren't far from the Forest to the South that supposedly had incredible numbers of the beasts.

Within a few more moments the bikes drew almost to a stop as two Hell-Hounds hunted a handful of the last deer off the track. Dozens of Hounds lined the sidelines, along with farmers, creating an impenetrable wall. Riders were stopping. Some were circling, looking for a break in the wild hunt that was going on. There was something about the way the other Hounds on the side were looking though, that suggested they wanted the Riders to let them do their job and clear the track. Not only that—the rural vamps who had come out to watch were waving and clapping for the Riders, so Sonny and many others waved back while the Hounds finished up.

The crowd cheered as a massive Hound crushed down on the last spotted deer in front of the Riders. This last Hound was a monster of a Hound and dwarfed the tiny deer in his jaws. The Hound realized he had effectively cleared the track and made a small victory prance in a circle while the crowd and Riders clapped. As the Hound pranced proudly off the track the country vamps seized the opportunity to "officially" re-start a Pike Run and all cheered "Ready… Steady… Go!!"

Riders exploded from a dead stop and into the last stretch of the Run. Sonny imagined there couldn't be more than thirty miles left. He wasn't as worried about ranking since the deer had taken out a third of the Riders. He just wanted to beat Daryn.

Sonny had left the Demon on its high setting and the cafe racer had already screamed back near the front. There were only two other bikes between Daryn and Sonny. The wind blew hard and Sonny's bike slid to the left and elbow's length from the number two slot. He stared hard at that Rider as the cafe racer inched its way ahead of him. Sonny was opened up as far as he could and the finish line of Suntora Flats was coming into focus in the distance. Daryn was still to the left of where Sonny was. He didn't know if he'd have enough time to slowly gain on Daryn. He leaned slightly to let his bike creep up next to Daryn. Eventually, though a half a length back, Sonny would creep to only inches from Daryn's gold-winged gargoyle. Sonny stretched his neck out and leaned forward. His chin was on the center of the handlebars. Daryn glanced over and almost impulsively lifted his boot from his foot peg. As if kicking at the Rider next to him was an obvious response.

Probably because they were in view of the crowd and he was solidly ranked to go forward, Daryn dropped his boot back on the peg and grimaced at the finish line. Sonny was gaining tiny increments alongside Daryn. It was like they were standing still and both pushing bikes made of solid stone across the line. Hands and teeth clenched in death grips as they roared over the line. It would take them until halfway to Suntora City before their bikes slowed and turned back to the crowds at the line.

Sonny knew Daryn was the first one over the line but didn't care. He was proud that he took the very, very close second spot. As they idled their bikes back the short distance to the line they stared at each other. There were no words. No taunting. This was a hard day and an exhausting run back. Sonny was glowing with the pride that he knew he could have beaten Daryn with some more track. And Daryn was furious at the reality that this common bat was even that close.

Back at the line the crowds were thundering with applause. Word had already trickled back that Hounds had cleared the track. Locals thought that was a powerful omen. The HellHounds of the South were nothing like the hounds of the Northern Forest. Down there near the southern border HellHounds were reclusive and dangerous. It's true that some still helped keep livestock safe, like their northern cousins. But they were wilder and very openly hostile to some vamps. They made it very clear they were not kept by vampires. For Hounds to assist with the Pike, something that would seem to have no importance to them whatsoever, was very unusual.

Slim ran from the side as they pulled up. He was hollering like a madman. Amid all the cheering, as Sonny peeled his dusty half helmet and goggles from his head, he heard the distinct sound of a secondary chant coming from the crowd. It was probably only a few dozen very loud vamps chanting, but it was clear to anyone standing that part of the crowd was chanting *'Sonny, Sonny!'*

Sonny pulled his gloves off and rubbed his ears with his index fingers. He stared at Slim with eyebrows raised. Slim just nodded and smiled.

"That doesn't usually happen till the Final Eight, Sonny boy!" Slim was beaming.

That was true. There were still four more qualifying runs and still sixty other Riders in the Pike. To have the crowd chanting for one Rider already was very strange.

Daryn had dismounted, his bike immediately taken by a handler. He pulled his helmet off and adjusted his hair with an arrogant smile. He waved at the crowd cheering but soon cocked his head. As he listened the smile faded from his dirty face. His eyes grew wide as he heard the thundering sub chorus in the crowd chanting Sonny's name. He threw his helmet hard at the ground and stormed to the ale tent.

Sonny and Slim had watched the entire scene from ten yards away. Sonny grinned. That was almost as good as beating him, he thought.

"Gonna be a Hell of a Pike this year!" Slim howled and threw his arm around Sonny's shoulder.

CHAPTER SEVENTEEN:
THE RANGE

The fletching of the expensive arrows was brushing against Vladimir's cheek. He held the string taut with an eye closed, then released. The arrow instantly crossed the length of the range and struck within the second ring of the target.

"Still an excellent shot, Vlad" Alex's voice echoed in the empty, indoor archery range at the Complex in the Axeton district of the Capital.

The KOTU frowned slightly and arched his head while looking at his target. There were several other arrows within the first two rings of the bullseye.

"There was a time when I could sink one arrow through the heart of another on my target." He looked at his hand as it held the bow. "But I was a much younger vampire then." He smiled at Alex and pointed to the bow and quiver he had the range lay out for Alex.

"Oh, for the daylights, Vlad, I haven't pulled a bow in a century." He shook his head, "I may embarrass myself."

The KOTU looked around the empty range gratuitously, "Well, your secret's safe with me." He let loose another arrow that split down the middle of the last one he fired. "I'll put it in the crypt with all the skeletons." He laughed.

Alex smiled but only to agree with the KOTU. He had known Vlad for many years and for many years had yearned to find a path to the High Council. Alex Bellmore was a wealthy, successful businessman, but that wasn't nearly enough to get a seat on the Council. He had spent years doing favors and donating to all the 'charities' of the Council, but it was only when his daughter Bebe and Vlad's son Daryn had started being romantic that Alex truly felt he may have a chance at a seat. In addition, marrying into the Von Firstensteins could also open up countless business opportunities.

Vlad had, on occasion, asked for Alex's unquestioning assistance. Things like access to the Bellmore factory after hours, sensitive information about Bellmore's clients, and even once a Bellmore vehicle was used to deliver an unknown cargo down to the Gulf of Gehenna. In return, the KOTU had been able to deflect unannounced inspections of Bellmore Industries factory, as well as award some lucrative Realm manufacturing contracts to Alex. So when Vlad asked Alex to the range, Alex wasn't sure what the KOTU wanted, though he had hoped it was to discuss the matter of the K&S seizure and the Motor Hell project.

Alex reluctantly held a bow and unenthusiastically searched the quiver for a suitable missile.

"Speaking of which," Alex fumbled with an arrow, "I'm wondering if the Council's ongoing investigation of that horrible contraband situation might be a long and time consuming event?"

He let his arrow fly. It missed the target entirely and struck the padded wall at the far end of the range.

"Holy Hell, old vamp!" The KOTU acted horrified then chuckled. "Let's hope we never have to go 'Able-All' in an uprising".

Able-All was an old saying that meant all able-bodied vampires were needed. Vlad had remembered his father Dracov yelling it on occasion during the uprising of 767. His father had needed to secretly encourage the ironworkers to war with the coal miners, who were, of course, being defended by R.E.D. at the High Councils order. As a secret stockholder of the iron ore mining company stationed on Mount Cain, Dracov would scream at his Captains 'I need Able-All to crush these pathetic coal miners into submission', all the while talking publicly as the KOTU of the atrocious feuding in the Realm's mountain industry that was 'tearing at the core of our values'.

Vlad had actually asked his father why he seemed to support dual positions on the Uprising. Dracov would say then, and many times after, *'Vladimir, one day when you're King of the Undead, you will learn that the more distractions you can provide the vampires of our Realm, the better they are likely to be.'*

Dracov had similar words earlier, during a rash of Hellfire Incidents in the winter of 666. During that time some vampires were citing ancient folklore and drawing associations to their Realm and the devilry of Man. So many Hellfire Incidents were happening that the High Council ordered lockdowns during daylight hours, closed Dayhouses and expanded on forbidden writings and spoken words. Dracov would tell his son, *'As KOTU you will find that simply shifting the publics attention can do all the work of the Realm for you.'*

Vladimir fit another arrow to his bow's string. "Yes, I'm afraid it could be a very long and tiresome process investigating the Kepler charge." He smiled and let loose his arrow.

This made Alex extremely happy. "Oh, that's too bad. You'll undoubtedly have to sift through years of K&S's paperwork and lab reports. Probably even a few samples in there." Alex let loose with another arrow that was so poorly aimed it hit the ceiling of the range and bounced down along the stone floor past the target.

Both Vlad and Alex froze as if to enunciate the silent question mark that was the response to that shot.

"You're plucking, Alex, you know that." Vlad offered sympathetically.

"I know, I know. I told you, Vlad, it's been awhile." Alex was irritated and breathed heavily. "I'm just wondering when I can..."

Vlad brought his index finger to his lips and softly smirked.

"Easy, old friend. I told you. We need to be gentle." He rested against the short wall between them and the length of the range.

"I have made arrangements to have some samples of *your* new... product," Vlad offered a congratulatory nod, "...discreetly shopped around to some of the Realm's industrial complexes. We will release it slowly into the market. Creating a dependency for this magical lubricant. A dependency that will allow us to essentially charge whatever we want." Vlad smiled.

"Of course, It's important that no one will connect myself to this product of yours, as the similarities to the seized product currently under investigation are shocking." Vlad nodded.

"Of course." Alex was back to being extremely happy with the way their conversation was going.

"So the details of our partnership can just remain between us." Vlad smiled again.

Alex was relieved to hear he was going to be getting the Motor Hell project to knock off and go to market with, but the businessman in him wanted to hash out the details of the split. "What exactly are you thinking as far as those details, Vlad?"

"Oh, there's lot's of time for that," Vlad waved his hand dismissively. "Besides, we will undoubtedly be family by then." The KOTU smiled broadly.

Alex beamed at the mention of the family's merging. That certainly would create a fair amount of security in their business dealings. But he was concerned with the status of that little business deal as well. "Yes, we will, won't we," Alex livened up. "How is Daryn?" He took a deep breath. "You know, we all know how dramatic young girls can be but Bebe seems to think Daryn may not be that happy with their..."

Vlad was waving his hand and shaking his head. "Not a thing to worry about, old boy. Daryn's just got a lot on his mind with the Pike and the Focus and all. You remember how it was in the Fledge, always some distraction." Vlad pushed a button on the wall that sent the target moving back towards them on a pulley.

The KOTU had raised his chin and looked at the ceiling of the range after he spoke of his son. After a moment he grinned without showing his teeth and looked back to Alex. As if he had needed a minute to actually assure himself that Daryn was perfectly synchronized in the plans they were making.

"Yes, Alex, Daryn is just fine." Vlad pulled his paper target from the pulley. "It's just like at the range. If our arrows aren't landing where we want them to," He put a hand on his chest, "We simply hold them very, very close and point them in the direction that we want them to go."

Vladimir wadded up his target and threw it in the garbage can.

CHAPTER EIGHTEEN:
GALLERY OPHELIA

The light from Gallery Ophelia was spilling out into the street, as were her guests. Anastasia Kepler's boutique art gallery was having a show opening that included a handful of local artists' work. Most of the show was pretty standard upscale pieces. Pottery, some oil paintings—vampires *loved* oil paintings— and various sculptures. But Anastasia had also decided to include a few pieces from some of the local artists in the neighborhood, some of the much edgier art from the residents of this changing district. That decision was less about supporting the newer artists and more about trying to see how much attention she could garner.

For many years, this Nightingale section of Capital City was where residents shopped for more high-end or exotic art and Houses of the Holy Union (wedding) gifts. There were cozy cafes, restaurants, and expensive apartments for wealthy vamps. It was near many parks as well as the theatre district, so it was also very suitable for walking and window-shopping.

It always had a portion of local residents who called themselves artists. Local artisans were just vamps with craftsmen specialties who had honed the skill of presenting their art in a more upscale way, in an effort to sell more. These denizens played the part well, dressing and acting more lavishly. Truthfully, most of the art on the walls of these galleries differed only in price from work found in small towns in remote parts of the Realm. There was simply just a great effort to promote the district as exotic.

In recent years though, the Nightingale area had been attracting different vamps entirely. The cheap neighboring Grenish neighborhood was attracting some vamps who were staving off their inevitable choosing of a Specialty. They were choosing instead to move into the abandoned dayhouses near the huge Green Fields of Grenish. Fields left largely unused after the construction of a large competition complex across town in the Axeton district.

These new residents were artists and musicians, and though not interested in the ecosystem of the nightingale art district scene, they were not impervious to the lure of easy treasure. Some of the district gallery owners, like Ana, saw the marketing value of these bohemians and their art and had courted individuals to show their work at her gallery.

Which meant that on this night at Gallery Ophelia, there was a crowd of chic, modern-dressed vamps with disposable treasure mixed with a few handfuls of more dandy, traditionally-dressed artist vamps.

Toland had brought Andi and Sonny to the opening. He had asked Andi to invite Sonny to come. Toland hadn't seen Sonny in a long time and wanted to see this vamp who had now just come out of the Dead Hills run in the Top Twelve and would go next onto Hunedora.

Toland had promised Anastasia that there would be no talk of K&S or the R.E.D. search and seizures, that tonight it was just about her opening. He was more than ready to ignore the High Council's investigation too. It had consumed him and been making him insane at times. The fact that the Council could basically do anything they wanted anytime they wanted to whomever they want was now a glaringly obvious truth to Toland.

"That's just incredible, Sonny," Toland said as they all stepped out of his small motorcar, "You realize you are already a minor celebrity."

On the drive down, at Toland's request, Sonny had just recounted every step of the run at Dead Hills, right down to his rear tire bursting as he rolled over the finish line.

"Thank you, Sir," Sonny said modestly. "I'm as surprised as anyone. I keep thinking it's just a dream and I'm going to wake up and have to start at Fangwood." He smiled.

Toland beamed back at Sonny. He had known him since Sonny was a small vampire. He and Andi had been inseparable as kids. There were years where Sonny came home with Andi after school and Evanna would pick her son up at the Kepler's house when she got off work. Toland was hardly around back then, he was almost always at K&S working on some new idea or equation. So even though Sonny had spent so much time in his home and felt like family, Toland didn't know Sonny nearly as well as he should.

As Toland watched this polite, handsome young vampire shut the door of the motorcar, he realized that in all this time, all these years, he had missed this opportunity, right in front of him, to have a son. That he had chosen to obsess over his work, shunning all else. *And for what?* To have it all taken from him anyhow.

Toland walked to the back of the motorcar. "Come over here, Sonny, I want to show you something." He unlocked the trunk but held his hands on top of the motorcars rear hood. Toland waited until Andi had joined them as well. He gratuitously cleared his throat. "In support of the Realm's rising superstar, Kepler and Sons would like to be a proud sponsor of team Sonny Legatus." Toland opened the trunk to show two brand new motorbike tires. Sonny and Andi both screamed.

"Dad, that's so great!" Andi hugged her father.

Sonny shook his head and stared at the tires. "I don't know what to say, Sir."

"The funny thing is, I had ordered these before you even had your blowout." Toland smiled. "Guess it was perfect timing."

Sonny was speechless. He and Slim were wondering how they could ever scrape enough money for tires. Any tires. Used tires were expensive enough, but new tires were only for the very wealthy. "Thank you, Sir," Sonny shook

Toland's hand.

"You're very welcome, Sonny." Toland closed the trunk. "We can't have our vamp running on retreads now, can we?" He smiled then made a serious gesture toward the gallery across the street. "Now lets get to this party before your mother drives a stake in me."

They stepped of the curb. Before they had even made it across the street, an older looking vampire in the crowd outside the gallery waved at Toland. Their suits were similarly toned reflecting a scientific specialty.

Toland turned to his daughter. "I need to speak to this vampire. I'll see you kids inside." He touched Andi's arm and looked at Sonny and winked. Toland walked ahead and joined the older vamp and they laughed into the lobby of the gallery while Sonny and Andi stood outside.

"I cannot believe your father got me tires." Sonny closed his eyes. "I had no idea where I would get some."

"Yeah, I think he's really into the fact that you're doing so well in the Pike." She took a deep breath and smiled. "We all are."

Sonny smiled and pulled at his sleeves. The suit he had on was a little too tight. His mother insisted that he needed to dress in a proper two-piece for this event. No dungarees. *'Soon the Fledge will be over. You need to get used to being in a proper suit,'* she would say. It had been a long time since he had a suit on, and he had filled out a little bit. Andi had noticed Sonny fidgeting with his snug suit and giggled.

"You're already looking like an old professor," She laughed and put her hand over her mouth. Not as a fashion statement. On the contrary, they simply had gotten older and put on weight and not bothered to update their wardrobe.

"Very funny," Sonny moaned. He looked at Andi's attire. "Looks like you've been shopping, though?" He intentionally did not attach any condescension to his tone so as not to hurt her feelings. She was dressed wildly and had wore what looked like a modern lab technician's dress, that would be in keeping with her presumed specialty, but she had made some unusual additions. Andi wore gloves that fit almost to her elbows, a small funeral headpiece with tiny dangling dark stones and archery boots that laced over her calves. It was similar to what some of the more unusual attire that the Grenish residents were wearing. She was happy he noticed, but acted nonchalant. "Yeah, I've been seeing a lot of styles like this down here on the weekends." She shrugged, "I'm just trying it out."

Sonny remembered a conversation he and his mother had recently where she told him that it was important to compliment female vampires on their appearance. To smile and tell them they looked lovely even if you had absolutely no idea why they had made the fashion choices that they did.

"It looks really nice," Sonny said smiling.

Andi was caught off guard and raised her eyebrows, "Really?"

Sonny continued nodding, "Yeah, you look... lovely."

Andi immediately put her hands on her hips, sensing that Sonny was being sarcastic. He had instantly regretted using his mother's word and raised his hands in defense.

"No, I really mean it. You do." He paused and put his hands down. "It's kind of a neat mix of modern with some of the traditional looks I've been seeing on these real vamps down in the Lowlands."

Andi smiled and looked at her gloves bashfully. "Thanks, Sonny."

Through the large glass windows of the gallery they could see the huge crowd, including Ana Kepler laughing as she talked to groups of vamps about different pieces in her gallery. The street in front was just as crowded with dozens of vamps, mostly the more oddly dressed locals, talking and drinking. Sonny looked at them and then at his own suit.

"I feel a little overdressed," He furrowed his brow.

Andi pursed her lips and seized the chance to copy Sonny. "Well I think you look... lovely." She grinned.

Sonny couldn't help but laugh even though he tried not to. "Maybe I just need some gloves," he said smartly. He pushed up the sleeves of his suit jacket and mimicked a dramatic conversation two outrageously dressed artist vamps were having a few feet away.

Andi widened her eyes and whispered, "Sonny, stop."

At that moment a server for the party walked by with a tray of drinks. Andi pulled two glasses from him as he glided by with a nod.

"No, *this* is what you need," She sang, "Father brought a barrel of the most delicious deer wine for the party. Black Lake Farms," she nodded as they both drew large sips from their wine glasses.

"Andromeda." Anastasia Kepler walked to them on the sidewalk in front of her gallery. She shook her head arrogantly at her daughter. "Why are you standing in the street, dear? There are some vampires I'd like you to meet inside." Ana completely changed her tone when she looked at Sonny and smiled. "Hello, Sebastian. How are you tonight?"

"Oh, very well, Ma'am." He lightly raised his glass. "This is a wonderful party, thank you for having me."

"Why, thank you, Sebastian." She glanced at his suit. "Look at you, so handsome. Now this is what a young vampire should look like, wouldn't you say, Andromeda?" she turned to her daughter and pursed her lips.

"Mother." Andi's face was solemn.

Ana seemed to become more animated at Andi's embarrassment. "I'm just saying, you're such a fetching young vamp, Sebastian. I would think that a girl would be foolish not to jump at the chan…"

"Mother, PLEASE!" Andi hissed.

Ana stared at Andi, who was scowling. After a long pause Ana looked back at Sonny and smiled. "It's nice to see you. We are all so very proud that you're doing so well in the Pike. If you'll excuse us, I need to take Andromeda inside."

Sonny nodded. "Thank you, Ma'am."

Ana turned to go back in the gallery holding Andi's hand. Andi rolled her eyes and finished her glass of wine, setting it on a passing server's tray and grabbing another in a fluid motion. Sonny chuckled and made a tiny wave to his friend.

Sonny adjusted his sleeves and turned his head, making it obvious to anyone he was uncomfortable in his suit. Within a minute of Andi's absence he wondered how much longer he would have to stand around, not knowing a single vamp there. With a hand in his pocket and glass in the other, he casually paced the sidewalk, quietly watching the partygoers on the street. He found himself wandering and ended up sitting on the stoop of the antique furniture store directly next door to Gallery Ophelia.

Sonny sipped his wine and thought

about how crazy it was that he had made it all the way to the Top Twelve in the Pike. It was unbelievable, really. He never would have even considered it if it hadn't been for Slim. Well, he thought, he wouldn't have gotten anywhere without Slim, but Bebe had been most of the reason. He had really entered to impress her. He had not seen Bebe in over a week. The Pike had kept him traveling quite a bit, but with the next two runs closer to home he could resume their tutoring sessions. Most vamps were already in the midst of their Focus interviews but Bebe had applied for and received an extension for her interviews. Nobody ever got an extension, not without a funeral or some other tragic event. But somehow Bebe had gotten one, and she acted like it was perfectly normal. That was fine with Sonny, he was dreading not having an excuse to see her anymore. They had actually become pretty friendly with each other and would often talk as much as they would study.

She would tell him about wanting to have a fashion boutique or an expensive spa, as well as a big family with Daryn. Sonny would ignore every mention of Daryn, and Bebe would sometimes joke that she was spending more time with her husband-to-be's competition than with Daryn himself.

The worst part of it, Sonny thought, was that Daryn didn't even deserve her. Sure, most vamps would say that they probably deserve each other. But underneath Bebe's sometimes overbearing, rich girl exterior was a really fun and interesting person. But Sonny knew that there would never, ever be a chance for him with her. Not just because she was from a wealthy, powerful family. But because Sonny knew Bebe was genuinely infatuated with Daryn.

"A vampire shouldn't drink alone."

A scruffy looking vamp in traditional attire and a bowler hat on top his head said with a wink. Sonny pointed his glass toward him and finished the old saying in a thick Lowla accent.

"Make sure you see your barmates home!" Sonny answered.

They both chuckled and sipped their drinks. The scruffy vamp wrinkled one side of his face suspiciously.

"Aren't you running the Pike?"

Sonny nodded and sipped again.

"I thought so. I've seen you rolling around Cromwell and Devilston late at night." The scruffy vamp pointed at Sonny.

"Yeah, I like it at that time. Nobody's out, I can open her up out there."

Sonny confessed.

"The names Vanian," he held out his hand. "Vanian Von Schlieben."

Sonny stood and shook his hand.

"Sonny Legatus."

"So I've heard." Vanian smiled from the side of his face again.

Sonny's eyes widened a little. "You've heard of me?"

"Indeed. You're not just running the Pike, you're shoving it right in the face of that Von Firsten-shit!"

Sonny laughed loud and Vanian joined in.

"Yeah, well, I'm doing my best to beat that vamp." Sonny sipped from his glass.

Vanian was thinking of what Sonny had just said. He nodded but made a sort of puckered frown as if he were chewing on those words. Eventually he brought his glass near his mouth."If it was me I think I'd probably be coming in last in one of the next runs. I sure as Hell wouldn't wanna get stuck in the final run." Vanian sipped from his glass.

Sonny was uncertain what he meant by that. He cocked his head. "You wouldn't want to win?"

"Is that what you're gonna do, Sonny? You're meaning to actually win the Pike?" Vanian was casual and smiling. It was completely confusing Sonny.

A VAMPIRE SHOULDN'T DRINK ALONE
MAKE SURE YOU SEE YOUR BARMATES HOME.

"I don't get your meaning. I mean, isn't that the whole reason?" Sonny was squinting and waiting for this scruffy vamp to say he was just fooling around or something.

Vanian put a foot on a step so that he could lean in toward Sonny. "Me, I think it's a charade." He winked and sipped his wine without turning his eyes from Sonny. "Just a big fancy way for the Von Firstensteins to hand control down to their next of kin."

Sonny pressed his lips together and

narrowed his gaze on this unusual vamp. The Pike was the most honored tradition in the Realm and there were some very specific Rules about what could and couldn't be spoken about it. "That's a pretty, well… that's sacrilege at the least," Sonny noted, but the comment had been more of a knee-jerk reaction. He was pretty comfortable from his glass of deer wine and a little curious where Vanian was going with this.

"All I'm saying is, don't you ever wonder what happens to the second Rider? And that it's always a Von Firstenstein that takes First Prize?" Vanian was inches from Sonny as he spoke but quickly popped up and laughed. "I'm just saying. That's all. I just think about these things."

Sonny was still very skeptical about the natural of this conversation but laughed. He liked this scruffy little vampire's style. Vanian seemed like he'd be an excellent storyteller. Sonny shrugged, he didn't have an answer for him.

Vanian looked at his empty glass and back at Sonny. "You should come join me in a daytavern some time." He reached to his vest pocket. "A little drink, a little music." He handed Sonny a firm, grey little card with a top hat on it, "A little merrymaking."

Sonny's eyes grew wide and a weary smile crept over his face. He took the card and began to hold it with both hands. Vanian signaled with his fingers to put the card away. Sonny shook his head seriously and tucked it in the inside pocket of his jacket. He leaned in toward Vanian. After darting his eyes to either side of him whispered, "Are you a member of the SDS?"

"It's just some merrymaking." He winked and nodded. Sonny smiled and nodded back.

Vanian walked back toward the gallery. Before he stepped into the lobby he turned back at Sonny, who was still staring at him. "Good luck in Hunedora, it's my hometown!"

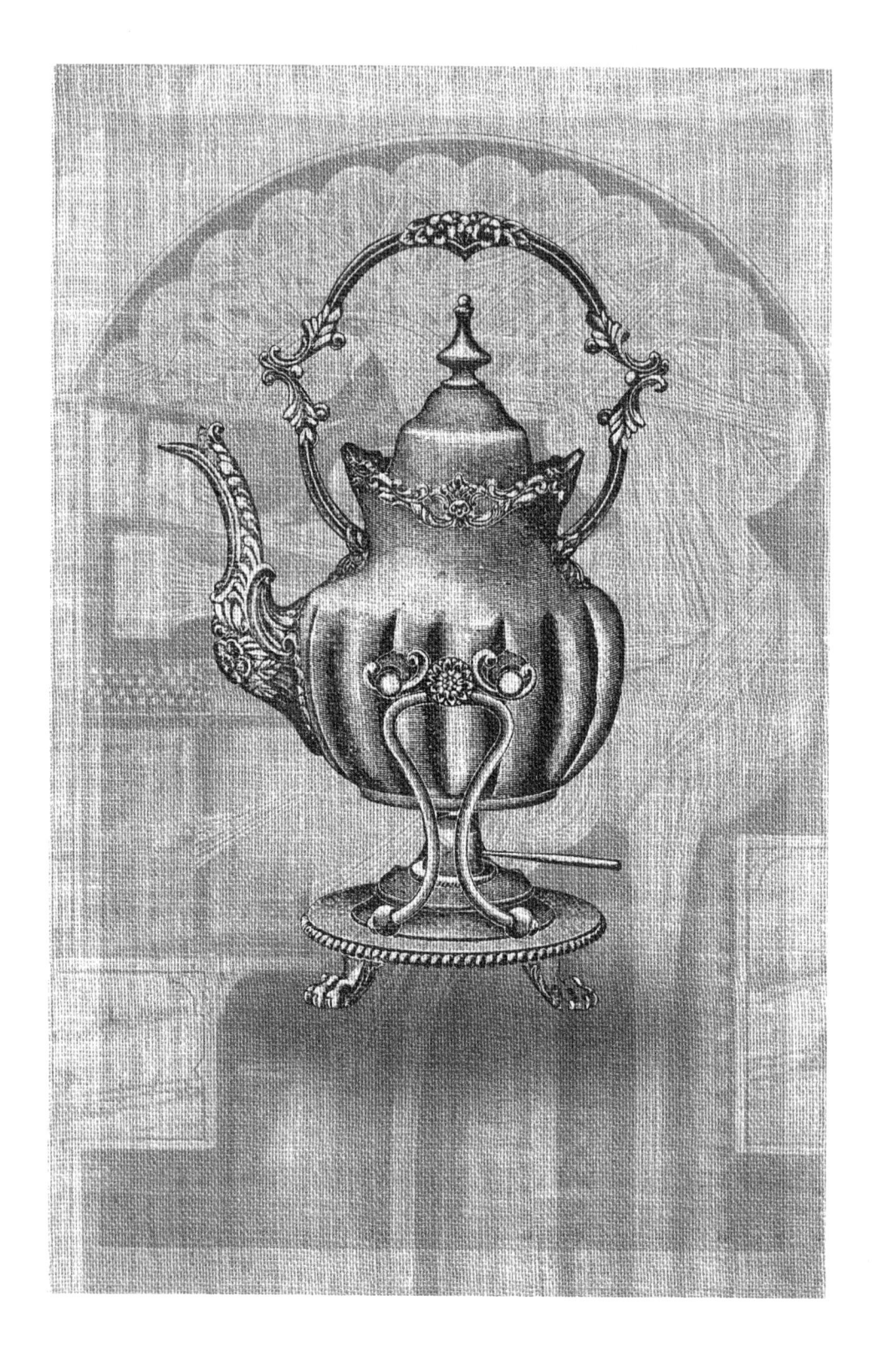

CHAPTER NINETEEN: HOUSE CALL

Slim raised his middle knuckle to knock, but paused. He could see Evanna sitting at her kitchen table. She was smiling to herself and holding a newspaper. Slim looked at her, expressionless, for several moments. He finally drew a breath, smiled broadly, and tapped at the glass on the back door. Evanna turned and raised her brows, smiling back when she recognized him.

"Hello, Jim," she said gently, opening the door. "I'm afraid Sonny's left for the market."

"That's why I'm here," he smiled, slightly raising the toolbox in his hand. "Thought I'd take a look at the Cube."

Evanna turned her head to the side and shook her head thoughtfully. "Oh, aren't you a darling."

She held the door as he walked in, wiping his boots on the black bristled doormat.

"I've just put some blood on the stove," Evanna opened the cupboard. "Would you like a cup?"

"No, thank you, I've already had a cup this morning." He inhaled slowly and looked at her. "You still put a few rose petals in there, don't you?"

"Mmm-hmm," she smirked and filled a cup for him.

Slim set his toolbox next to the incubator and took the hot cup with both hands. "Thank you, Evanna," he took the tiniest sip and rested the cup on the small kitchen table. Evanna sat down with her cup.

"Sonny's run to Valkries," she shook her head. "He was worried everything had spoiled in the cube. I think it's only been broken a day or so."

Slim rested his hand on the top of the tall incubator. "Most of the time it's the regulator's blower fan. It goes out and then the first set of base coils short out."

Evanna lowered her gaze and pursed her lips. "You may as well be speaking Hündesh."

Slim laughed, "It wouldn't be the first time." Evanna smirked and shook her head.

Hündesh was what vampires called the language of the HellHounds. Almost no vampires understood it and it sounded similar to the barking that regular dogs made—but with a lot of 'kha' and 'esh' noises. The expression 'Speaking Hündesh' mostly meant that you didn't understand what someone meant, but was also commonly used to describe being very, very intoxicated.

Slim had turned the cube around and begun taking the back panel off the machine, peeling the manufacturer sticker that covered the first screw.

"I must say, it's really something that Sonny's gone so far in these qualifying runs." Evanna watched Slim nod from beside the cube. He still had his hands inside the back of it as he looked back, agreeing.

"You know, I think it's all the years he's been pedaling around on that bicycle. It made him a natural for the Pike," Slim said as his eyes rolled up and he leaned into the cube.

"Now he's the same way with that motorbike. Any reason at all to get on it," Evanna waved her delicate hands toward the door, "and he's gone." She smiled and then looked concerned at Slim who was grunting and grinding his shoulder into the back of the incubator. "Is there anything I can do to help?"

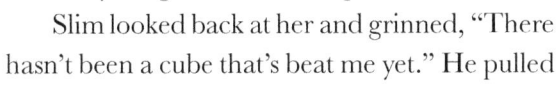
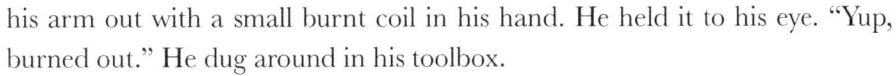

Slim looked back at her and grinned, "There hasn't been a cube that's beat me yet." He pulled his arm out with a small burnt coil in his hand. He held it to his eye. "Yup, burned out." He dug around in his toolbox.

"I just hope when this is all over he gets back on track with his Focus interviews and getting his Specialty." Evanna sighed.

Slim nodded as he was searching in his bag.

"I'm hoping he decides to follow teaching." Evanna was lowering her chin and smiling softly at Slim.

He kept nodding, but as she continued quietly staring he looked back. His eyes focused on her hands as she lightly caressed her cup of blood. Looking back to her eyes, Slim watched her lower her gaze. He shrugged.

"Um. That's probably a nice thing." He said awkwardly.

Evanna calmly brought her cup to her mouth. "I would bet that if he heard you say that, he may take it more seriously."

Slim furrowed his brow and opened his mouth to speak but rethought his words. He took a deep breath and smiled. "Well, I'm sure he'll choose what's best for himself."

Evanna took a drink and looked at her cup. "I'm sorry.'"

"Oh, that's fine," Slim laughed as he pulled a new coil from his bag. "He's lucky to have a mother that worries about him."

"I know." Evanna kept staring at her cup, "It's just that right now I wish he had a father to tell him what to do."

Slim shook his head and looked down. "Never heard a word from him, huh?"

Evanna shook her head and focused on the folded-up newspaper across the table. "I always thought that one day some vampire would show up on our doorstep, saying he's sorry." She smiled faintly.

Slim continued replacing the coil but made a quiet 'hmmm' sound so she'd know he was paying attention.

"The thing is, I wouldn't recognize him no matter who came to the door. I can't remember a single thing that happened before the accident."

Slim stopped and looked at her, gravely shaking his head.

Evanna made a gratuitous smile. "I guess he thought I wasn't going to survive. Nobody did, really."

"No." Slim squinted and looked at the incubator angrily. "I hope you don't mind me saying that you're better off without a coward like that. Any vamp that would leave his family…" He paused and went then back to repairing the cube, feeling like maybe he shouldn't have said anything.

"Well," Evanna opened her eyes wide and cheerfully turned to Slim, "It's ancient history." She stood and took her cup to the sink, slowly rinsing it out and trying to forget about the last part of their conversation.

Slim stood also and slowly edged the incubator back in place. He looked at the soot on his hands and began to wipe them on his shirt but stopped. He quickly returned his tools to the box and stepped over to stand next to Evanna at the sink.

"Should be fine now." Slim smiled.

"Hmm?"

"The cube… it should be running fine. Maybe an hour or so to warm up."

"Oh," Evanna laughed lightly. "Of course." She reached to turn the water off.

"You can leave it on." Slim held his hands up like a surgeon only with black dirt on his fingertips.

Evanna took a small step and opened a drawer to bring a hand towel out. As Slim washed his hands she looked at the towel.

"I shouldn't have brought that up, about Sonny. You've already done so much for him. I just… " She handed him the towel. "I just worry about him is all."

"You don't have to apologize for a single thing." Slim dried his hands. "And

Sonny's gonna be just fine." He paused. "He's a heck of a lot smarter than most vamps his age. Smarter than me, that's for sure."

Evanna watched Slim cross the room back to his tool box. He was in perfect shape and had arms that looked like they were carved from wood. Though he had grey hair on the side he looked younger and more fit than most vamps half his age.

"Why didn't you ever marry?" Evanna spoke gently and her tone sounded less like she was asking Slim and more as if she were asking the world.

Slim's back was to her. He slowed as he picked up the toolbox, then straightened up and faced her. He grinned and shook his head. "I made a lot of poor choices when I was young."

At that moment the door swung open and Sonny ran in with a paper sack in one hand.

"Hey!" Sonny smiled as he saw Slim. He kissed his mother's cheek and set the bag on the counter next to Slims hand towel. He looked at Slim's toolbox and laughed.

"The whole way to Valkries market I was thinking 'I bet Slim's gonna fix that cube'."

"Oh yeah, as if I had to be a mind reader or something." Slim laughed too, "You might as well have taped a work order to my shirt, *'I dunno what's wrong with the cube, Slim wha wha wha'.*"

"Sonny!" Evanna scowled playfully.

Sonny played along like he was being interrogated. "Oh come on, the last time I tried to fix the cube I almost burned the house down."

Both Slim and Evanna looked at each other and agreed, then laughed.

Slim clapped his hands. "So how are those new tires?"

Sonny's eye widened and jaw dropped. "Un-be-lievable." He shook his head side to side. "It's like I have suction cups for wheels!"

"That was one heck of a nice thing for Toland to do." Slim exhaled hard.

"It certainly was," Evanna agreed.

"We need more vampires like that Toland Kepler," Slim added loudly.

"You've got to come and see them, they're top of the line tires!" Sonny said as he grabbed Slim's toolbox.

Slim put his hand on Sonny's shoulder as they stepped toward the door.

"Yeah that Toland is one of the best vamps I know." As Slim opened the backdoor he asked, "You know he was a teacher before he took over K&S, don't you?"

"Really?" Sonny said while he stepped outside.

As Slim shut the door behind himself, he looked over his shoulder and winked at Evanna. She fought back laughing and instead lowered her chin and stared gratefully.

CHAPTER TWENTY:
THE OWL

Hellamina lifted a dirty mug filled with lukewarm blood, then decided otherwise. She figured she could wait it out for a place that didn't scream of blood bog fever. Looking around the dilapidated lobby it was hard to believe that this was once one of the swankiest hotels in Capital City.

This was, of course, a few hundred years ago when the Green Fields of Grenish were the epicenter for any competitive sport, and the Howlston, just a few blocks away, was fit for a king. At that time red velvet curtains with gold clasps hung on all the walls from the ceiling to the black tiled marble floors. The lobby bar was a magnificent work of carpentry with a black oak argyle inlay, gold-trimmed edge and shaped like an 'H'. The lobby bar slowly rotated and was surrounded by matching tables for two, with coves of banquet seats against the walls. The booths were covered with supple blood red leather. The backing was quilted with gold button accents. The cathedral ceiling was entirely consumed by a gigantic chandelier that was a weeping willow tree made of iron. Its trunk was eight feet across and grew from the center of the bar. At the end of every one of the two hundred twisting limbs was a light bulb.

This great willow frame was all that remained of the once magnificent Howlston. The business abandoned, the hotel stripped by vandals, even most of the sign on the façade had fallen. The only remaining letters that hung high above the hotel entrance were 'the owl'.

Hellamina was leaning back in the banquet seat, staring at the gorgeous metalwork sprawling above her. The booth she sat in was now just a hard, bare wooden bench with years of graffiti and names carved into every inch. She smiled as she looked up.

"Boo," Vanian Von Schlieben whispered from the other side of her booth.

Hellamina calmly lowered her head to look at Vanian. Her arms were still extended and resting on the back of the booth.

He grinned. "Hope I didn't startle you." He bounced his eyebrows up and down and eased his bowler hat back with an index finger.

Hellamina shook her head and pushed her bottom lip out slightly. "No, not at all." She pulled her arms in to rest on the table. On top of each of her fists was a four-inch blade that looked like a giant eagle talon. She looked at them and quickly flicked her fists downward. Each blade snapped back into the sleeve of her leather jacket. She looked sideways at Vanian and smirked.

"If you'd have scared me I may have removed your head."

Vanian leaned back, a little shocked. He immediately grinned with intrigue. He brought his index finger to his mouth, then shook it at her. "I knew you were mad when I met you."

"A girl's got to take care of herself," she smirked.

His eyes pulsed wide, "Indeed they do! Even in this modern Realm we live in." He slapped his palms on the table. "I need a drink, what're you having?" Vanian looked at her mug and screamed.

"Oh bloody Hell!" He turned at the skinny, ghoulish vampire behind the bar. "Holy Hellfire, Knuckles, are you *trying* to destroy the loveliest lady that has ever agreed to see me publicly?"

Knuckles shrugged apathetically.

"May I please have two Hell Bloods over here? Thank you, Sir." He looked back at Hellamina, but then as if remembering something very important, called out, "Oh, and bottles Knuckles! We definitely need *bottles*." Vanian smiled sweetly across the table. "I apologize, they don't get a lot of... um, non-regulars around here."

"Really? I can't imagine why," Hellamina looked around and back at Vanian. "It's so tantalizing."

Vanian closed his eyes, nodding his head. "Yes, it is a bit off the beaten path, but quite cozy I think."

Knuckles quietly placed two bottles on the table and left the filthy mug that had been sitting directly between them. He had already walked away before they noticed. Reluctantly Vanian picked up the mug, handling the glass as if it were animal feces, and placed it in the booth behind him.

"You didn't actually drink any, did you?"

Hellamina shook her head no, smirking.

"Good, good." He crossed his legs under the table. "Don't get me wrong, I'd have waited for you in the medical center... just outside."

Hellamina laughed and shook her head. "Afraid of needles?"

"No." They clinked their bottle's necks together. "No, I just like to steer clear of any of our Realm's official buildings."

"Why?" Hellamina leaned in and whispered playfully. "Are you a wanted vampire?"

Vanian looked up thoughtfully. "No, I don't think so." He sipped. " But that doesn't seem to matter to these R.E.D. thugs."

Hellamina took a slow drink. "You having trouble with the R.E.D.?"

"Not if I don't see them." He winked.

"Because of merrymaking?" Hellamina scoffed.

Vanian sighed and smiled at her playful condescension. "Oddly, the Council seems less tolerant of such matters here in the big city rather than out in the wilderness that you motor about in." He waved outward as he drank from the bottle.

The night that they met at the Dragonfly, Hellamina had told Vanian and his bandmates that she was from Tammerlane in the West and that she traveled the Realm on her motorbike. Which of course wasn't a lie. She just omitted that she was an undercover R.E.D. Agent sent to infiltrate the Sweet Death Symphony.

"I think the High Council is roundly intolerant. They just choose their battles." She sipped. "What a radical fledge in the abandoned section of the Capital *thinks*, is as monitored as what a blood berry farmer in the marshes of Fangwood *does* with his surplus crop. If those Lowlanders want to pretend that they're 'real vampires', it's of no consequence to the Realm so long as they don't get any supernatural ideas about supply and demand."

Vanian's eyes pulsed and he smiled hypnotically at Hellamina. "You are as brilliant as you are lovely." He raised his glass. "However, I don't think blood farmers are worried about being taken in for questioning and winding up in a crispy little pile in the middle of the day somewhere."

Hellamina acted as if what he was saying was the rantings of a madman and returned with more intentionally slight sarcasm. "Do you mean to say that the Realm is assassinating the SDS? Oh come on." She finished her bottle and jiggled it at Knuckles.

Vanian was a bit irked by her dismissiveness but didn't want to show it. "My dear, let me tell you, the SDS poses a VERY real threat to the perpetuation of the mindless order of these old vampires." He tapped his finger on the table as he spoke. "We challenge their very notions of what an existence should be. We're telling young vampires that there's more to this world than eight or nine hundred years of the same boring crap, night in and night out, until your frail bones can no longer sustain themselves and you collapse. That there can be as much joy and…" he searched, "and love and passion in a moment, in a single moment, than in a lifetime of their fearful perseverance. With all their caution and repression." He waved his hands angrily.

Hellamina was admiring his conviction but also smirking at his very animated behavior. He caught himself and laughed with her.

"You know, what we're doing is not all just merrymaking and fornicating." Vanian raised his bottle at Knuckles and leaned in toward Hellamina, "Though that is the fun part."

They sat looking at each other until after Knuckles had shuffled unenthusiastically from behind the bar to refresh their drinks. Hellamina drew a breath very slowly.

"Have you ever thought that maybe you ought to travel out there into the Realm singing your songs of dissent and salvation?" She asked it still with an ounce of playfulness, but Vanian could tell she was not making fun. He could see that she completely understood the meaning of what he'd said. This was no ordinary vampire woman trying to bed some exotic, non-conformist Fledge to break the numbing monotony of her existence. This was a mysterious, well-rounded, and, from the looks, quite dangerous vampire. He exhaled and shook his head.

"Of course. But it's one thing to sing songs about living in the moment to a group of disaffected intellectuals in the basements of the City's alehouses. And quite another thing to arrogantly parade these notions around the countryside to the coffee shops of the frontier, with their Hellhounds and their traditional superstitions." He drank and shook his head, shuddering.

"Oh, so you're afraid," Hellamina said flatly.

Vanian thought for a moment, looking from the corner of his eyes at the ceiling gratuitously, "Yes, most definitely. I would imagine a very dark end for me and my colleagues. Probably with my head impaled on a pole. Do they still do that in Tamerlane?" He smirked.

Hellamina laughed. "No, that's only for pig thieves. They'd only tar and feather you." Vanian laughed as well.

Hellamina drank, then said seriously, "But don't be so arrogant to think that you're the only vamps with an original thought, or that your message would fall on deaf ears on the countryside. Because I've seen in the eyes and the souls of a thousand vamps around the Realm, a hunger, just like yours… to dream." She looked hard at Vanian and with total sincerity added. "Vampires need dreams. Without dreams we're dead inside, just passing our time like living corpses."

She drank slowly from her bottle and continued staring at Vanian. "And sometimes we need to be told that we can dream,"

Vanian raised his brows and leaned back against the booth. He squinted at

Hellamina skeptically. He had hardly imagined that this Midnight rendezvous would have such soul searching conversation. He thought carefully as he stared at her beautiful eyes and searched for his words. He finally spoke calmly.

"Well you can't simply set out on the road. Just stop at any one Hound town that pops up."

Hellamina tilted her head. "You could."

"We can't just be reckless, you know, we have to plan our affairs. They need to be secret, sometimes under the cover of day."

"But why?" Hellamina spoke firmly, then continued as he searched for an answer. "Yes, in the Capital maybe it's more effective to be cautious. But there's more R.E.D. and High Council scrutiny here. Not to mention a few hundred thousand vampires. But not out there. Out there you would be just a band of musicians, whose songs are lighthearted and merry. Only the vampires who want to hear your message would truly hear it"

Vanian thought about that as he looked at her. It seemed impossible to him. It also seemed brazen, rebellious and like the most exciting adventure he had ever thought of doing.

"It would be quite an undertaking to say the least and I doubt any of us would know our way around well enough to accomplish anything. We'd likely end up in some HellHound-infested forest."

"Well, I doubt you'd go that far South. Those southern Hounds are the only ones you'd need to worry about. The ones up North are quite friendly." She paused as she looked at him. "Yeah, you'd probably need some help out there."

"It sounds to me like you may have just signed on for the Director of Realm Affairs position at the SDS." Vanian lightly clinked his bottle to hers.

"Hmmm, what's the pay?"

"Well, we're in a bit of an economic recession now… but… there are fringe benefits." He winked.

Hellamina leaned back. "No, we'll have none of that if we're to be working together."

Vanian frowned. "Where's the fun in that?"

Hellamina paused and returned to her serious tone. "If you really want to do this properly we would want to maximize our effort." She nodded as she thought. "Why not go to where you'd have the ear of vampires from every corner of the Realm."

Vanian thought then snapped his fingers. "The newspapers. Brilliant."

"No," Hellamina was smiling widely. "We go to Strigoi."

"Strigoi?" Vanian stopped. "When? They're about to be overrun with Pike spectators."

Hellamina nodded her head yes. She leaned back soaking the thought in.

"I'm not sure I follow you. The Pike Run starts and ends at Town Square in Strigoi. Do you mean to find some dayhouse and throw a party?"

Hellamina closed her eyes and smiled to herself muttering "Perfect." She looked back at Vanian and cleared her throat. "No, I mean to have you play at the commencement ceremony of the Ninth Pike's Run."

Hellamina looked devilishly at Vanian. She raised her bottle and sipped it slowly, licking some blood that had snuck to the side of her mouth.

Vanian watched her with complete astonishment. He thought that the wild Tamerlanian female was either the best or worse thing that had ever happened to him. Eventually he breathed deeply and laughed.

"I suppose if I'm going to spend my time screaming, I may as well stand up and scream while the whole Realm is listening."

CHAPTER TWENTY ONE: I CAN KEEP A SECRET

Ordinarily Bebe would have been long gone from any appointment if someone was even two minutes late. She was by no means happy about this, but was too excited to be anything but cheerful when Sonny finally showed up at Rezzies a full ten minutes late.

Everyone in Capital City was already talking about the final four Riders of the Pike. At the previous week's qualifying run, many from the city had made the trek down to Hunedora and watched eight Riders emerge from the dozen who began that race. The qualifying run at Hunedora was filled with hills and ramps and required one hundred laps around its grueling five-mile track. It was an exciting and exhausting run with a few spills and some incredible jumps.

Because the following qualifying run was in Black Lake a few days later, many Riders went directly to that small town near the foot of the Black Deth Mountains rather than return to the Capital, which was in the other direction. Black Lake was a favorite destination for many of the affluent vampires of the Capital since it was a lush, lakefront town, free from the trappings of many of the Lowland villages. There were specialty farms and most of the high-quality fermented blood in the Realm came from this area.

Bebe hadn't seen Daryn, or Sonny, since they both left for Hunedora ten days prior. She was curious to hear about the run at Black Lake that left Daryn, Sonny and two other Riders in the Top Four. The other two were a Rider named Valentino Vossen and a Rider named Marius Mockba.

Val was from Enoch, near the Dead Hills and was a fierce competitor. Rumors had already made it as far as Tamerlane that in the home stretch of the Black Lake run, Val had summoned the spirit of the HellHounds and screamed off his competition, edging in at fourth place.

Marius was from the Capital and his father was a Council Member. He knew Daryn and they were relatively friendly as they ran in the same circles of wealthy Capital City vampires.

"I truly apologize, Bebe, I've only been back a few hours and had to attend to some things with my bike," Sonny said as he laid his book bag on the outdoor table at Rezzies. Bebe had suggested they meet at Rezzies to study so they could grab a snack, but she also wanted to flaunt the Top Four Rider as her tutor.

"Oh Sonny, you're too sweet," she purred and kissed him on the mouth, then sat down across from him at the table. "Daryn's not back until tomorrow night so I want to hear all about the runs!"

Sonny paused. Bebe had never greeted him with a kiss. He was tired from traveling and racing but still realized that if that had happened a month ago he still may have passed out. But in the time since all the qualifying runs it seemed like a lot had changed. Not only was he different, but vampires were treating him differently too. Everywhere he went, vampires knew his name. Female vampires were following him and other Riders around as well. Some were very young females, too shy to do anything more than scream their names from the ropes at the winners circle. But some were anything but shy, pawing at them and pulling them to secluded—and sometimes not so secluded—places to show their appreciation for the Realm's finest Riders. In fact, only three nights prior, after a post-run party at the Black Lake Country Club, Sonny and Slim returned to their suite that the Club had provided Riders, to find their room full of the most beautiful vampire women Sonny had ever seen. The ladies roared when they both walked in, handing them glasses of fifty-year-old deer wine. Sonny had looked at Slim questioningly and Slim had said simply, "I think this is one of those moments you're always talking about, Sonny boy." Then he shut the door to their suite.

So it wasn't that Sonny still didn't appreciate the fact that Bebe Bellmore had just kissed him squarely on the mouth at Rezzie's drive-in, it was just that it almost felt like a natural occurrence.

"Okay," He smiled back at Bebe and sat down, facing her. He cleared his throat. "Well, um… Hunedora was pretty tough. We had a hundred laps, and boy was that track was all over the place… there were a lot of Riders falling in and out of the lead spot. We all knew nothing was certain, and you could lose a lot of ground quickly."

"How did Daryn do?" Bebe was playing with her hair.

Sonny shook his head and thought for a moment. He couldn't really tell Bebe the truth, that Daryn was a rotten bastard who seized every chance he could to further himself in the runs. That Daryn would take the inside on hard turns and deliberately spray dirt into the faces of other Riders. That Daryn still would try to intimidate Riders before every run, and scream and throw his helmet if he didn't rank first. And that he had made it his life's mission to defeat Daryn in this race.

"Oh, he's a great competitor," Sonny smiled. "He ranked First at Hunedora and First at Black Lake."

Bebe clapped and squealed. But then she smiled cutely."How did my teacher do?"

Sonny grinned and held up two fingers.

Bebe grinned and tapped her teeth together, wrinkling her nose like a crazy kitten. "Well you better watch out, Daryn Von Firstenstein, 'cause Sonny Legatus is running for First Prize!"

Sonny liked that Bebe was always conscious of his stake in the Pike, even if it was an afterthought. She was so incredibly sexy that in just five minutes she had reminded him that he had not wasted all those years dreaming about her. Because as beautiful as some of those female vampires were that he'd seen out in the Realm, there was indeed no other like Bebe Bellmore.

"Oh," Bebe became quieter and folded her arms tightly, like a little girl ready for a scary story, "What happened with Val Vossen at Black Lake? I mean, they're saying he used some sort of sorcery to turn into a HellHound or something." Bebe's eyes were wide.

Sonny laughed and shook his head no.

"Val is just a tough vamp, that's all." He laughed again. So did Bebe, she knew she had embellished the rumor and deliberately jiggled as she shuddered for effect.

"I mean, he did get really aggressive in that last stretch. He was neck-and-neck with some vamp from Dorren. And in the last few seconds Val turns at this vamp and just lets out a scream." Sonny made a manic, teeth baring face. "I mean, like a Banshee! They were saying that vamps in the stands jumped back in their seats. Slim told me that it was something else. And then this other Rider that Val screamed at, he just backed off I guess. Enough to cost him his ranking."

Bebe was still listening intently.

"But no, there's none of that sort of thing. That's just stuff from the pages of lore." He smiled and Bebe smiled back.

A Rezzie's attendant appeared out of nowhere and placed two bottles of Healthy Blood in front of them.

"The vamps inside over there have bought you these drinks." He smiled and winked, "Run for Glory, Sonny."

On the other side of Rezzie's huge front windows they could see a group of Fledge-aged vamps with their arms in the air, chanting 'Sonny, Sonny, Sonny!' Sonny smiled, then waved back as he sipped the bottle.

"So how does it feel to be a famous vampire, Sonny?" Bebe drank slowly from her bottle.

"Honestly, it's a little strange. I don't really know what to do." He sipped again, "Guess you just smile and wave."

"Yeah, you look like you've gotten the hang of it." She smirked.

"What?" He smiled and posed dramatically, rubbing his chin. "What is that supposed to mean?"

Bebe was looking Sonny up and down and tapping her teeth together lightly.

"Oh, you've definitely got a little swagger now, Sonny." She was looking at him but began focusing on something behind him. "Looks like you have another fan, Mister Swagger."

Before he could turn around he heard a familiar voice.

"Hey Sonny!"

"Hey," Sonny spun around to Andi's voice. He squinted for a second, then hugged her. "I almost didn't recognize you."

Andi looked up and smiled. She was wearing tight black work pants, rolled up to the knees with knee high lace up boots and a leather corset over a deep necked, long sleeved knit shirt. She also had her hair up, separated and shaped into what looked like two bat ears.

"I know, Mother threatens to throw all these new clothes out every time I see her."

"You look great." Sonny stepped to the side so Andi could see Bebe.

"Hey, Andi, this is Bebe Bellmore." He turned to Bebe. "This is my friend Andi Kepler."

"Oh my gosh, it's so nice to finally meet you, Andi," Bebe grabbed her hand. "Sonny has told me about how smart you are, helping with the motor-bike and all."

Andi smiled, "Oh thanks, Bebe, it's nice to meet you too."

"Your outfit is adorable," Bebe said to Andi then looked at Sonny. "You're such a goof, Sonny." Bebe turned back to Andi. "The way he talked I pictured you in overalls and frogs in your pockets." Bebe smiled. "Really, a 'tom-boy' Sonny?" Bebe smiled again. "But I love this old fashioned corset. Where did you get it?"

Andi was still digesting the tomboy remark, trying to picture how it had come up in Sonny and Bebe's conversation. But Bebe was already touching the bottom of Andi's corset.

Lux LaRoux's

Corsets

1313 PITCH STREET
GRENISH

"Um, I found it at a small shop on Pitch Street, near the Fair in Grenish." Andi looked at Bebe, confused. "You… like this?"

Bebe flipped her hair and nodded her head. "It's soooo beautiful. And totally perfect for this costume party I'm going to next weekend."

Andi was now convinced Bebe was either really kooky or making backhanded compliments. Or both. So she smiled and turned directly at Sonny and slapped at his arm.

"Hey, I can't believe you're in the Top Four!" She hugged him again.

"I know, I know, it's pretty insane. I was just telling Bebe how Hunedora was really hard but Black Lake was actually not as bad. I mean, still a fairly long run—all the way around the Lake. But early on it was me, Erik and Daryn out front, so I felt pretty confident by even halfway."

"I'm so proud you made it this far." Andi smiled and shook her head at him.

"Well, it's not over, and I intend to make it all the way." He smiled but then felt a little awkward. He had never talked competitively around Bebe. After all, he was running against her boyfriend. Quick to change the subject, he asked Andi, "So what have you been up to the last ten days?" He reached down and grabbed his bottle of Healthy Blood.

"Oh!" Andi's eyes lit up. "Oh, yeah. That's what I came to tell you." She rolled her eyes, "I mean, of course, I wanted to congratulate you on the win, but Sonny," She swallowed hard. "My project I've been working on, it's ready to test." Her eyes were wide and she nodded her head as if to remind him.

Sonny thought for a moment then rolled backwards. "Ahh, the blood experiments."

Andi furrowed her brow. "We don't need to discus the exact details of it now, but yes…" Andi was staring hard at Sonny, "Those experiments."

Sonny glanced at Bebe and back at Andi. He felt confused and wondered why Andi had brought it up if she didn't want him to talk about it in front of Bebe.

"Well, um… that's great then. What's next?"

"Vampire trials," Andi said in an eerily serious tone that made Sonny do a double take.

"Oh my gosh," Bebe squealed. "That's where I recognized it. Kepler, of course. You're Doctor Kepler's daughter, right?"

Andi nodded and smiled.

"Yes, I think our fathers do business together. I'm certain I heard my Father talking about K&S recently. That's your family's business right?"

Andi nodded again and smiled. She looked back at Sonny.

"I really want to do the trials tonight. Can you come by when you're done?"

Sonny was exhausted and having a hard time remembering what he was and wasn't supposed to talk about. He sighed and was about to beg that she do it tomorrow. But he could tell the way she was almost bouncing up and down that she wouldn't be able to wait.

"Sure, I'll be over later." He smiled.

Andi jumped and squealed. "This is gonna be big, Sonny!" She turned to Bebe. "It was nice to meet you, Bebe. I guess I'll probably see you at Norwood Park."

The next, and final qualifying run would take place in their Capital City. It would begin and end at the north west corner of Norwood Park, running the side streets of the entire city as its course.

"I'm sure you will. It was very nice to meet you as well."

Andi made off quickly. Sonny and Bebe sat back at their small table. Andi was barely out of earshot when Bebe leaned toward him and whispered intently, "What in the daylights was Andi so secretive about?"

Sonny smiled. "Oh, it's just an experiment she's working on. I think it's for her Focus interviews." He lied, then looked at Bebe, "You know, she's going into a research Specialty."

There might be some things that you could sneak by Bebe, but a hot, juicy secret was not one of those things. She knew with absolute certainty the way Andi shot that look of death at Sonny that this was no extra credit for Andi's Focus. Bebe knew that whatever it was she was talking about was either very important, illegal, immoral or embarrassing. Or at best, all of the above.

"Well, what's the experiment about?" Bebe purred.

"It's a…" Sonny paused. "You know, she's very sensitive about it, so I think

I shouldn't talk about it." As Bebe held her stare, Sonny added, "It's really no big deal though."

Bebe made an ardent '*hmmmm*' and reached across the table. She grabbed his hands, pulling him in playfully.

"Oh come on Sonny, I have to know now." She tugged at his hands until he was leaning in, too. "You can't get me all worked up about a secret experiment and not tell me. You are my teacher, after all!" She was giggling and not letting go of his hands, pulling him in closer and closer.

"Andi would be mad at me if I told anyone," he said as solemnly as he could.

Sonny was making a very, very poor effort to take his hands back. The truth was that his throat was getting a lump in it, and as much as he was trying to act otherwise, this was an incredibly delightful experience.

Bebe had no intention of not finding out all the details. She blew her hair out of her face and growled like a pouty cat.

"Well what do you think I'm gonna do if you don't tell me!" She laughed as she refreshed her grip, moving up to his forearms. "Don't you think I can keep a secret, Sonny?" She batted her eyes and laughed. "Oh, I can."

"No, no, I trust you. I just…" Sonny laughed as she pulled him forcefully to the middle of the table. She turned her neck to him and pressed her mouth to his ear.

"Just tell me, Sonny. Just whisper it in my ear. Nobody will hear."

She held him there firmly, breathing quick, excited breaths into his ear while she waited. Sonny felt his upper lip pull and he fought the urge to bare his teeth. Her hair smelled like jasmine and he could almost taste her skin in his mouth. He closed his eyes and just wanted to stay clenched with her.

"I'm not going to let you go until you tell me, Sonny." She had pressed her lips to his ear as she hissed those words.

Sonny was almost frozen at the sensation of Bebe's lips lightly pressed at his ear. His mouth opened, baring his teeth. He casually tried to move as though he had only opened his mouth to speak, but Bebe giggled as his mouth tried to form words, knowing exactly what had happened.

"She's working on…" He swallowed hard and tightened his lips as if to try and control himself.

Bebe growled quietly and yanked him closer over the tiny table that separated them. She laughed and pressed into his neck whispering "Tell me, tell me..."

"She's trying to make blood. Human blood." Sonny was breathing heavy and started to loosen his grip.

Bebe loosened hers as well but slowly. When her face was back to where Sonny could see her she still whispered."Is that it?"

"Well, pretty much." Sonny sighed as they let go of each other's hands.

Bebe was looking at him skeptically. "There's got to be more than that. What's the big deal? I mean, aside from it being gross."

"Well, there is a theory that, with human blood, we vampires are very... different than we are now. That is can give us supernatural powers." Sonny raised his eyebrows.

"Ok, I get all that. And I'm sure there's Rules against that sort of thing too, but that's with older vampires. Scientists and stuff." Bebe was trying to see the importance of this. "I mean, Andi's just a Fledge, isn't she being a little dramatic? Does she really think she's going to make human blood?" She shook her head. "That's impossible."

"If it was anybody else, I would agree with you," Sonny smiled. "But you don't know Andi. She takes this very serious."

"It kind of gives me the creeps." Bebe shuddered, then smiled back. "I guess I'm just a Blood Berry kind of girl." She looked at their empty bottles and back at him.

Sonny pointed at the bottles and Bebe batted her eyes and nodded.

"Two more coming up!" Sonny grinned widely and grabbed the empty bottles.

As Sonny walked toward the outside counter at Rezzies he was a little faint from having Bebe all over him. Being a Top Four Rider in the Pike was incredible, but having Bebe Bellmore whisper in his ear and crawling at him was definitely not what he thought was going to be happening tonight. In his wildest dreams he would have never thought these two events would happen to him, and certainly not at the same time!

Who knows, he thought, *maybe Andi might just turn into a bat after all.*

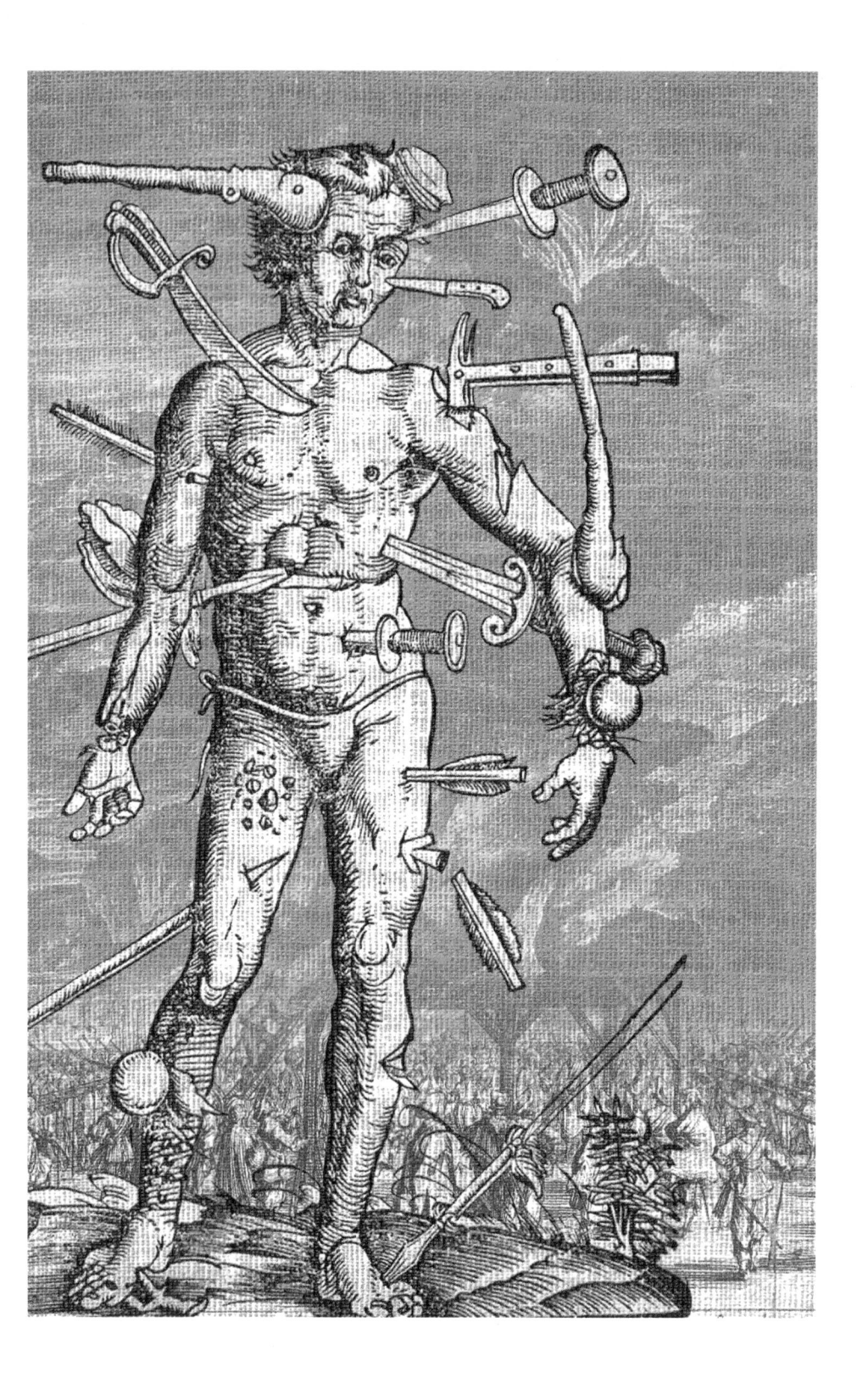

CHAPTER TWENTY TWO: MY GREATEST MOMENT

Ever since the run at Black Lake, Daryn's father had been constantly lecturing him about improving his chances at the Pike and criticizing him that he wasn't taking the qualifiers seriously enough.

During all the qualifying runs, Vlad had pushed Daryn to be more intimidating to the other Riders, particularly now that the 'cafe boy' was gathering a lot of public support.

"All I'm saying is you have to make absolutely certain that we get you to the final Pike Run," The KOTU huffed as he cut his steak. "After that, I'm not as worried. In a two-vamp race you're sure to win." He chewed violently. "Besides, a Von Firstenstein has always won."

Daryn was looking at his food and nodding. He could feel his father glaring at him. He eventually looked up, chewing, and said angrily, "You have told me this so many times, how do you think I could possibly not know all this?"

Daryn was exhausted from the past two weeks of travel. Hunedora, the Black Lake, and then his father had led them back to the city through the Hammerton mountains so that they could stop at Hammerton and do a little 'publicity'.

"Oh, Vlad, let Daryn eat. He'll be no good on his motorbike if he doesn't get some nourishment," Tessa Von Firstenstein said coldly from the other end of the dining table.

Daryn's mother Tessa was adamant about Daryn winning the Pike too. On occasion, though, she would defend Daryn from Vlad's relentless critiques.

Tessa was a cunning and sophisticated vampire and the perfect 'Queen' to the King of the Undead. Officially referred to as "Lady KOTU", Tessa took an active role in the public relations arena concerning the Realm's push for young females to wed and conceive. She created programs that traveled the Realm teaching etiquette in schools and academies and made celebrities out of females that successfully birthed more than one child. She also was the first Lady KOTU to ever have a portrait of herself commissioned and hung in the official KOTU office downtown. The Realm had never seen a female this publicly aggressive with her position. She was also lobbying to allow herself to be on the High Council, like Vlad, after his term as KOTU ended.

"My Lady," Vlad cleared his throat and smiled. "Of course I share your interest for our son's well-being. But we are at the Final Four now." He was trying hard to remain calm. "I'm particularly concerned about this cafe racer vamp that everyone seems to favor." Vlad stared hard at Daryn. "You know, if Dracov was here, he'd say..."

"For the daylights, I know!" Daryn yelled, standing up from the table. *'Win*

the mob to win the Pike'—is that what you were going to say? Or was it *'Never forget that for us it's a birthright'*—was that it?" Daryn leaned with both fists on the dining room table of the Von Firstenstein estate and said with a quieter, but very deliberate tone, "I have been drinking lots of Healthy Blood, sleeping through the day. I'm training like I'm in a marathon, I have changed my evil ways, Father." Daryn looked at the enormous chandelier above his head. "Believe me, I'm sick and tired of hearing that this new guy, Sonny Legatus, is so popular with the crowds, but I am doing everything I know how to do." He looked back down and laughed. "I mean, he built his own motorbike, and he actually thinks he has a chance at winning the Pike's Run!"

"And that is my point exactly, Daryn. This cafe boy has been running neck and neck with you these last few runs!" Vlad lowered his tone. "We cannot underestimate any vampire. We have too much at stake, we *have* to win. I think we need to take measures to *guarantee* that we succeed."

"I will bring this to the family!" Daryn yelled. "I will keep the line in place. But this is MY moment, Father!" He pounded his chest. "This will be my greatest moment in time and I will not be treated like a child by you!"

Daryn walked to the closet and grabbed his riding jacket. As he stormed out of the house he stopped and looked hatefully at his father. "I will beat them with style and grace. I do not need your interference!" Daryn slammed the door as he left.

Vlad looked at the door. He and Tessa said nothing for about a minute. Vlad would bite his lip, then smile. He shook his head, then frowned with ferocious anger. He scanned the room with his eyes, stopping at his wife who sat silently sipping her wine. He opened his mouth and drew a large breath. He looked at his wife and exhaled. A calm set in on his face.

"I've been playing this game fair and square. I've made little noise." He shook his head and thought more, looking at the door his son had just ran out.

"But I think it's time that I reached into my little bag of tricks."

Musical accompaniment for this scene:

"MY GREATEST MOMENT"

FROM THE ALBUM "RISE OF THE CAFE RACER"
DEANO JONES & THE SWEET DEATH SYMPHONY

CHAPTER TWENTY THREE: HUMAN BLOOD TRIAL

"Hi, Leshka," Sonny waved from the other side of the screen door.

"Eh," She laughed, "You almost scared me, Sonny."

"I'm sorry." He tiptoed through the kitchen door and hugged the Keplers' housekeeper.

Sonny had known Leshka ever since he was a very young vamp and she felt almost like a grandmother of sorts to him. Sonny had always come around back and used the kitchen entrance when he visited the Keplers, mostly because he was always on his bicycle and he would lean it against the short iron fence that ran the length of the Keplers' west wing.

"How come I don't see you around here, Sonny?" She held him at arms length and looked him up and down. "I swear, you've grown three inches." She smiled.

Leshka was a solid and hearty older female vampire. She was originally from the Baldoon region, and like many from that part of the Realm, she had wider features and a Northern brogue. The tricky thing about the way the Northerners spoke was their peculiar way of using relatively ambiguous gestures for widely different responses. "Dooners" might respond *Ah'* if asked if they'd like a drink. Or *'Hmm'* if asked if they enjoyed themselves at an event. It was slight variations in their intonation that would indicate how they felt. Most of the Dooners living in the Upperlands had shed that obscure language affectation, but if you walked into a neighborhood Dooner tavern, it sounded like vampires grunting to each other. Hence *'doon, doon, doon'* was a popular phrase to describe the sound of the Northerners talking.

"I've been too busy motorbiking for anything else," he grinned.

"Eh, so I hear." Leshka nodded. "Everybody's talking about you, Sonny." She smiled proudly. "Our Sonny is in the Pike's Run!"

"Well, not yet, I'm not. I still have one more qualifying run." Sonny looked over her shoulder at the pot on the stove. "Do we need any testers, Leshka?" He joked.

Leshka had seemed to hang on her own words and was still looking at this boy she had watched grow up into this strong young vampire.

"Eh," She used both hands and removed a pin from her uniform's collar. She grabbed his hand and placed the small pin in his palm.

"Wear this when you ride, Sonny, eh." She nodded. "It's black schörl and it brings good luck to the wearer." She folded his fingers over the pin.

Sonny looked at Leshka gratefully and kissed her cheek. "Thank you," he whispered as he hugged her.

"I knew I heard something going on out here," Toland said, as he walked into the kitchen. He had a pipe in one hand as he held out his other. "How are we tonight, Mister Top Four Rider?" Toland laughed.

Sonny quickly shoved Leshka's pin into his pocket and grabbed Toland's hand. "Just great, Sir." He shook Toland's hand hard. "I still can't thank you enough for the tires."

"Oh, my pleasure. Hopefully they will bring us more success this weekend."

Toland smiled as he clenched his pipe in his teeth.

Sonny nodded confidently. "You know, Sir, I feel really good about the coming run."

"I should hope so, son, you've only been riding these streets of the Capital on your bicycle for forty years now." He grinned and puffed from his pipe. "Smart treasure's betting on you, Sonny boy."

Sonny smiled and looked down graciously. "Well, I appreciate that, Sir."

Sonny sure wasn't getting tired of this feeling. The entire Realm was different since he was running the Pike. It wasn't just the random vampires on the street and in the market who called out his name, though that was nice too. It was the way that vampires around him, the ones he'd known all his life, were acting that was such a bolster to his spirit. Their eyes would light up and they'd tell him they were proud of what he was doing. They would say 'we' are gonna win this week. 'We' made it to the Top Four. This wasn't just his race, it was theirs too. On the last few runs he had felt like he had a thousand hands at his back. It was incredible and unlike any feeling he had ever experienced.

"I don't want to seem rude, but would you both excuse me, I promised Andi I'd get over here as quickly as I could."

Toland stepped out of the doorway and closer to the stove, eyeing Leshka's pot.

"She's out in her lab, Sonny. We'll set you a plate for dinner." Toland turned to Leshka, and through pipe clenching teeth said, "Did you say you needed some testers in here?"

Leshka laughed and stirred her pot. "You boys. Out!"

Sonny walked past the living room and down the long corridor to the library. The Keplers' home was styled like a castle, with a garden courtyard separating the east and west wings. He passed a washroom and a couple sitting rooms before he reached the end of the hall, where pushed open one of the double doors to the library. As he crossed the floor of the huge room, he lightly ran his hand along the top of the twelve foot long headmaster desk that had always sat in the middle of the enormous library. At the end he stopped, as he always did, to play with the five iron balls suspended from an iron frame on top of the five hundred-year-old desk. The gadget was just a toy Toland had made for Andi when she was young and he called it "Andi's Cradle." If you lifted one ball and dropped it, the ball on the opposite side would pop up, then fall back down making the first ball pop back up and the process would repeat. Sonny loved watching the iron balls swinging back and forth, never stopping. He was always fascinated with this little toy.

"Oh, for the daylights," Andi huffed from the doorway that joined the library to the courtyard. "How long have you been in here?" She folded her arms, feigning anger.

Sonny stopped the balls with his hands and smiled. "Oh, I just got here. I was talking to your father and Leshka." He looked down at the metal balls. "I don't know why I love these balls so much!" He laughed. "Why your father never make a million of them is beyond me." Sonny raised one ball and let it drop, starting the infinite swinging motion again.

"Because they serve no purpose." Andi rolled her eyes as she stopped them with her hands. "Do you want to assist in my vampire blood trials or not?"

Sonny grabbed her hand and sat on the edge of the huge desk. "Andi, let me ask you something." He shook his head upward then returned to focus on her intently. "Tell me again, why it is exactly that you want to try this on yourself?" He touched his chest and squinted. "Me, I would be worried that I could get really sick from some bad blood. I mean, remember when you had the Bog?"

"It's not like that. Not at all." She pulled her hand from his and took a step back. "First of all, my lab is cleaner than a Healthy Blood factory. Also, I've spent months troubleshooting the equation, testing and re-testing small samples. And since I've started using mice as hosts, the blood has been completely stable." She looked hard at Sonny. "I have already bred some mice with human blood, and the blood is showing that it is completely stable. It's still reading chemically that it's human blood."

Sonny was intrigued and folded his arms. He looked at Andi and thought about what she just said. "I can't believe that you haven't drunk some already."

Andi smiled slightly, appreciating that Sonny wasn't questioning her chemistry any further. "Believe me, I have considered it." She glanced around at the books on the shelves of her family's library. "But this has to be documented, Sonny. I need you to take notes. And..." She changed to a very serious expression. "I have no idea what might happen when I introduce human blood into my body." She closed her eyes for a moment and got tight lipped at the thought of the words she was about to say, and how they may sound, then looked directly at her best friend. "I could very well turn into... I don't know, a bat." She paused. "Or it may jump-start my heart!"

Sonny was absolutely unflinching and nodded his head as if agreeing. He drew a large breath and pressed his lips together with resolve. "Alright then." He continued nodding slowly.

Andi waited. She wondered if there was going to be anything else that he may add to that, like a tiny bit of sarcasm or a "bat" comment. But when he said nothing and just kept staring back at her, she wanted to scream with joy. She hadn't been able to tell anyone about these experiments and Sonny had been gone the last ten or so days, not to mention consumed by all of his Pike business. It was a relief to have her friend back and that he believed she was on to something. Or, she thought, at least he was willing to help.

"Thank you." She hugged him tightly and then sprung into action.

"Okay," she cleared her throat. and they walked into the courtyard. "I have prepared a double-needled syringe for my injection, and will be delivering it into my neck similar to the way a vampire would bite a human." She held the door to her laboratory for Sonny, and didn't wait for him to ask why she would be using a double needle and injecting it in her neck.

"I know, I know. But it's not because I'm superstitious. It's that there's a large, primary artery right there in the neck that goes directly to the heart, so it's really the best place for the injection." She smiled. "Okay, the double-pronged needle is kind of for effect..."

Andi laughed and so did Sonny, shaking his head.

"What about the virus you created to protect the blood from contamination within the mice?" Sonny asked calmly.

Andi stopped in her tracks, eyes wide. "Oh my gosh, Sonny, you remembered." She had imagined that he was just humoring her most of the time that she talked about the specifics of the blood experiments. At that moment she felt like he was the only person in the world who understood her. "Yes, I had used a simple virus to keep the human blood intact in the hosts." She smiled wildly. "But Sonny, it's incredible, I've now bred three generations of mice that are actually *born* with human blood in their veins. There's really no doubt that this is one hundred percent human blood!"

Sonny had been in Andi's lab hundreds of times over the years, but now it looked completely different than he'd ever seen it. There were half a dozen glass tanks with mice in them. Three industrial incubators, microscopes, and against the wall was a heavy, over-sized, wooden chair. Andi pulled several worn leather belts from a drawer in a tin cabinet and sat down in the chair.

"I'm going to give a status report every five seconds." She sat in the gigantic chair and began wrapping her ankles with belts and fastened the buckles. "You'll see there is a chart on that clipboard with spaces for notes." She looked at Sonny. "I just use 'NC' for no change."

Sonny nodded. He began to realize Andi had undoubtedly been chomping at the bit, ready for days to start this trial. In spite of her manic pace, without a word, he wrapped her remaining wrist tightly to the chair with a belt and just tried to listen carefully to what she wanted him to do.

"The cube marked 'Two' has the syringe in it, and there's a sanitizing swab on the sink."

Sonny went to Incubator Two and removed the double-needled syringe. The mice were playing in their tanks and oddly most all of them stood on their hind legs with paws on the glass as Sonny walked by, on his way back to the chair where Andi sat. He thought for a moment that in their own way, they were like crowds at the qualifying runs, tiny fans cheering on their human blood doctor. As he started to laugh, he looked ahead at Andi seated seriously in her chair, breathing deeply. He knew he would be wiser to save this little comedic metaphor to share with her later.

Sonny slowly rubbed the iodine swab on Andi's neck. He raised the syringe and gently rested the needles on the red spot that the iodine had left.

"Are you ready, Andi?" Sonny said calmly.

Andi closed her eyes and exhaled.

"I'm ready."

"Ok." Sonny swallowed. "I am going to inject you with human blood that you have created in a laboratory."

Sonny gently pushed the needles into her neck. Andi winced, but quickly relaxed her expression. Sonny slowly pressed his thumb until all the blood had emptied from both sides of the syringe. Andi gasped and Sonny quickly pulled the empty syringes from her neck.

"Are you ok?" He jumped in front of her and knelt down.

She nodded yes, still with her eyes closed. Sonny stood up, grabbed the clipboard and pulled up a stool in front of her. Seconds passed and she had not made any status reports. He decided that he wasn't going to ask her anything, that he would wait for her to speak about whatever she was experiencing.

Eventually Andi opened her eyes, but continued to look forward silently. A minute passed without Andi saying a word. Sonny placed his hand on her wrist and checked for a pulse. *Not that he even knew what a pulse felt like,* he thought, but he just wanted to feel useful. Andi began glancing at Sonny, still not saying anything, but there seemed to be a look of acknowledgement. Sonny thought this was a good sign, looked at his watch and made a note on the chart, *'seventy nine seconds - subject shows signs of awareness.'*

Andi began looking at Sonny. She took turns looking alternately at each of his eyes. Sonny was wondering if it was something he should be writing down and stayed poised to scribble any new reaction on Andi's part.

Another minute passed and she sighed. Andi looked down and frowned. When she pulled her head up her lips were quivering. She shook her head side to side. Sonny began mirroring her in confusion, still not know what was going on with her. Finally she whispered, "Unwrap me, please."

Sonny placed the clipboard on the table and quickly unwrapped all the belts, holding his hands out to help her out of the chair. Andi pushed his hands away.

"Oh, Sonny, I'm fine," She mumbled and rubbed her wrists.

Sonny was still shaking his head. "What does it feel like?"

Andi looked directly at him, her lips trembling.

"It feels like I'm an idiot who believes she can bring an extinct animal back to life with my chemistry set." She swatted the clipboard off the table.

Sonny sighed and looked over at the mice. They were all still on hind legs watching them. He turned back to Andi and grabbed her hands.

"Hey, this doesn't mean anything, Andi. It's just another scientific trial. All you've done is find something that doesn't work, that's all." He smiled and shook her hands gently.

Andi was limp with sadness. She turned her head from Sonny even as he still pulled at her arms, now more playfully.

"Andi Kepler, you are not going to sulk over an experiment." He let go of her hands and spread his arms wide open.

"Look around here! I've never seen your lab like this. You've isolated an ancient equation of blood and placed it in a stable host. There are grown vampire scientists who wouldn't be able to do that! You're a genius, for daylights sake!" He laughed as he tapped at the mice clawing at the glass. "How can you be sad about that?"

"I wanted it to work, Sonny!" Andi cried.

"It will. I know it will." He stepped to her and squeezed her hand.

"You don't understand, I want it to work *now*." She turned to the chair and yelled, "I want to change NOW."

"What? Why?" Sonny waved his hands at the lab. "Isn't it more important that the work is ready first?"

"I'm sick of being plain, Sonny," Andi tore at her chest, "I want to be special to someone." Her chest heaved and she stared back to him.

"I want to be special to *you*, Sonny," She said quietly and tilted her head to the side, looking angrily at the lab floor.

Sonny opened his mouth in confusion. He searched for the words and was unsure what to say. He stepped to her side, and put himself in her view.

"You would *have* to know how important you are to me. You're like my family, Andi." He took both her hands in his. "I mean, I know with the Pike and all maybe I've been a little… I don't know, self-centered…"

Andi brought her head up to look directly at him, "I want to be special to you the way Bebe is special to you."

Andi sighed heavily and continued staring at Sonny. She felt like she would choke if she tried to speak more. It felt like madness was inside her. To her it seemed like with every second that passed, a powerful new emotion would dominate her mind and body, making it impossible to act on any one. She tried to just stand still.

Sonny looked back warmly at Andi. He understood what she meant. Oddly, she hadn't frightened him, or shocked him by saying this. He had never considered her that way, but right now he knew that was irrelevant. As she trembled at the end of his hands he knew that all he needed to do was stand still and be there, in this moment for her. Somehow he sensed every one of the emotions that were coursing through her body, and he just stood still and held her hands tightly. As the seconds passed, Andi stopped trembling and tried to smile. She opened her mouth and considered her words. Sonny lightly shook his head no and smiled back. He pulled her to him and hugged her with all his might, resting his chin on top of her head. He pet the small of her neck softly and pulled her closer with every stroke.

With every second that passed, Andi felt better. With her eyes closed, hugging

Sonny, nothing in the Realm mattered. She would happily trade everything—her experiments, the Pike, even hundreds of years as a scientist to stay right there, like that, forever. She drew her biggest, deepest breaths and savored the greatest moment she had ever known.

Leshka tapped on the outside of the laboratory door, 'ta, ta, ta... ta'. She knocked with three quick hits with her knuckles, a pause, then a single knock with her palm. The same way she had thousands of times over the years.

Sonny and Andi stayed hugging in the middle of the lab but looked at each other and laughed.

When they were small vamps, Leshka would play hide-and-seek with them in the castle. When she was done counting, Leshka would announce simply 'Ready or... not' to the beat of that signature knock on the wall.

Sonny released Andi from their hug and squinted dramatically.

"Ready or not?"

Andi smirked and nodded her head enthusiastically.

"Ready."

CHAPTER TWENTY FOUR:
MOTOR HELL

"So let me make sure I get this straight. I'm *not* going to charge him for this, and I can't mention that you are involved in any way?"

"Yes, I think you've finally got it." The KOTU rolled his eyes and looked at his watch.

"I apologize, Sir, I'm just trying to make sure I do this exactly the way you want."

Vladimir smiled wearily at the vampire sitting at the other end of the back-seat in the motorcar. Isaac "Ike" Bludworth was a low-level card hustler and thug. He had done some work for Vlad in the past and was usually reliable enough, but for some reason Ike kept asking a lot of questions about this particular job.

"The only thing you have to worry about is that this goes in the bike." Vlad laid his hand on the flask-shaped cans between himself and Ike. "And that this is a brand new product and *I have nothing to do with it.*"

Ike nodded, but still had a bit of skepticism on his face. He was used to doing less theatrical work for the KOTU like driving trucks to dump cargo in the Gulf of Gehenna or stealing wagons with a crop of blood berry. Acting like a salesman for a new engine lubricant was not exactly his forte.

Ike flipped opened the briefcase on his lap and put the three cans of oil inside. When the lid wouldn't shut he tried rearranging them, then looked at the KOTU nervously. Vlad quietly watched Ike. The KOTU's eye twitched and he looked out the window, trying to remain calm. He reached down between his legs and handed Ike the cloth bag that he had carried them in.

"You don't need a damn briefcase, you're not presenting a case to the High Council," Vlad snapped.

The motorcar stopped across the street from the garage where Daryn kept his motorbike. Vlad turned to face Ike.

"Convince him that he needs this. That you favor him and that's why you're doing this. That *he* is making this decision for himself." Vlad looked at the garage, then at his watch. "Then get back to Bellmore Industries before first light. We've got some work to do."

Ike stepped out of the KOTU's motorcar. Vlad held the bag for him. Ike grabbed it, but the KOTU held tight.

"If you mess this up, Bludworth, I will have you left out in the light." Vlad let go of the bag.

Ike stared at the KOTU and then nodded before shutting the door.

The lights were still on in the garage, though it was late enough that Vlad had said all, or most all, of the mechanics would be gone. Daryn had stayed down at the garage the past few nights.

Ike crossed the street and noticed Daryn's vehicle parked on the side of the building. He walked to the office door and knocked. After a few moments he pressed his ear to the door. Ike could hear talking, and it seemed like it may be coming from the back of the shop. He knocked much harder. A minute later someone opened the door.

"Yes?" A large, mechanic looking vamp asked apathetically with a bottle of Hell Blood in his hand. There was the sound of several voices in the background.

"Hello, I'd like to speak to Mister Von Firstenstein, please," Ike said with a tight-lipped smile.

"Would you?" The mechanic burped and took a drink. "What's it all about?"

"Well," Ike drew a breath, "I'd rather speak to Mr. Von Firstenstein directly."

The mechanic stared blankly at Ike and raised his hand to the door as if to close it.

"It's about the Pike's Run, specifically," Ike said, narrowing his gaze.

The mechanic sighed. He continued looking at Ike, then at his bag. Finally he turned his head toward the noisy shop.

"Daryn!" He yelled, "Some vamp here to see you!"

The noise quieted. Behind the office, down a short hallway, was an opening into the shop floor. Daryn stepped into the light of the hall and looked down at Ike and the mechanic.

"Yes?" He asked comically with a hand on his hip and a drink in his hand.

"Hello, Sir," Ike cleared his throat, "I'd like to speak with you about the Pike, if I may."

Daryn pulled his head back a little bit and stared at Ike. He drank long from the bottle, finishing it. The room to his left had become silent. Daryn wiped his mouth with his sleeve and tossed the empty bottle in the trash. He smiled broadly.

"Piss off!" He stepped back into the shop, which erupted with laughter.

The mechanic smiled and slammed the door.

Ike stood there for a full minute, wondering what he would do. He raised his hand to knock, but let his arm fall to his side. He turned back toward the street. He had worked with the KOTU long enough to know that if he said he would leave you out in the light, that you would have to take a slow boat to Baldoon to escape that wrath. And even then, there would most likely be an

R.E.D. Agent waiting for you there.

Ike looked at the bag and pulled a can out. There was not much on it; it was just a shiny yellow tin can that had the hand-painted words "Motor Hell." He put the can back and looked at the building. The garage continued down the block with light pouring out of an archway halfway down the block. Ike slowly walked toward that light. As he drew closer he could hear the voices of vampires laughing and talking. When he stood in front of the arch he discovered it was in fact the vehicle entrance to the garage. The rolling garage door was only open a quarter of the way, about knee level. Standing in front of the door he could hear Daryn and other vamps talking on the other side, no more than fifteen feet away. Ike looked up at the sky and thought about what the KOTU had said. He looked back at the garage door and rolled his head, stretching for a moment.

"I've got this idea!" He yelled. "A premonition... of sorts!"

Ike paced around in front of the garage door, waiting for whoever had shushed the vamps in the shop to get their full attention.

"I mean, we really can't think of *everything*, can we?!"

He paused, tapping his head thoughtfully as the vamps all stood on the other side of the rolling door, still unable to see where this voice was coming from.

"Of course there's always room for improvement!"

The rolling door opened. Daryn and five vamps stared at Ike on the street.

"It's just this idea I had of what it might be like to be a Pike Rider!"

The large mechanic shook his head angrily and started to move toward Ike. "I'll handle this!" The mechanic clenched his fists.

Daryn raised his hand and smiled devilishly. He looked at Ike and waved his hand. "Proceed."

Ike nodded a *'thank you'* and continued.

"Well, you've spend your life preparing, the race is on your mind. Every details been considered and now you have your time." He smiled then quickly raised his index finger.

"Oh, then why…" Ike tapped at his heart, "Are you second-guessing that you might not win tonight?"

The mechanics stepped toward Ike and again Daryn raised his hand to let him proceed.

"It's true, you've bleeded out all hesitation, but the odds you just can't deny. There's still the possibility of failure." Ike smiled and grabbed the bag.

"But here's some free advice. Don't lose your mind!" He shook his head. "Put a little extra something in your ride. You need to see this for yourself…" Ike pulled a can out of the bag.

"You need Motor Hell."

He tossed the can to Daryn, who had no choice but to catch it. Ike took a couple steps closer.

"One little bottle in your engine and friction can't survive." He pulled another can out of the bag and held it up.

"It is a classified, top secret substance I provide." He shook it at the vamps.

"And when you ride, you will move like a Mother Truckin' Demon in the night!"

A couple of the vamps began looking at the can Daryn held in his hand.

"Don't be found out or ever tell." Ike tossed a can to each of them. "Use Motor Hell."

All the vamps were looking at the cans.

"Is this some sort of Lowland superstition?" One of the other mechanics asked.

"It's science, friend. Pure and simple. This product eliminates friction. It's absolutely guaranteed to make your bike move faster." Ike nodded and held his hands out, palms up.

Daryn stared skeptically at Ike and walked towards him. "Who sent you here?" Daryn squinted.

"My employers are just some research scientists who have been working on this lubricant for years. The truth is, this hasn't been approved by the Council yet." He smiled at the other vamps. "But they're loyal to the Realm and they favor you in the Pike." He bowed his head. "Just trying to help any way that we can, Sir."

Daryn grinned. He was still very suspicious, but the thought of anything that would make his bike go faster was intriguing.

The large mechanic who had met Ike at the door stepped to Ike.

"What if he's trying to sabotage the bike?!" He put his hand inside his vest and gripped the handle of a blade.

"Ah," Daryn nodded, "Lucius is always thinking of the worst in vampires."

He smiled and looked at the can. "Whereas I'm an optimist. I tell you what we're going to do..." He tossed his can to a vamp behind him and walked to Ike. "Put a can in the Gargoyle. I'll take it out for a ride." Daryn laughed. "If my supporters are correct then I should notice right away. Move like a Demon, you say?"

Ike smiled and attempted to widen the margin for error. "That's what I was told. At the very least there should be an increase in output."

"At the very least..." Daryn interrupted and pushed Ike at Lucius. "The least does not concern me. If this product of yours... Motor Hell? If it does what you say I will send my warmest gratitude and be indebted to my supporters." Daryn turned and pulled on leather gloves as his gold winged Gargoyle motorbike was wheeled over to him. "If it does not do what you say, Lucius will cut your hands off."

He kick-started his motorbike, revved the engine and laughed. "Let's hope we shake hands at the end of this night."

Daryn's bike shot out of the archway of the garage and down the street. He made his way down the side streets of the warehouse district and toward the Realm Roadway, the wide, commercial trucking route that ran along the hills in Cambria. He would be able to open up the bike and see if there was any difference. He was thinking that it already felt a little odd. Just the way the motorbike was responding to the throttle. It seemed to jump at the slightest touch.

He leaned in to turn onto the ramp of the service road. He was already moving pretty fast, but when he gunned the throttle the front tire rose up from the ground and he almost lost control. He knew at that moment that his bike was moving faster than it ever had before. As the hot summer air rushed over him he laughed at the idea of a Demon. That would be crawling. This felt like Satan's stallion was his horse and he was burning past the gates of Hell. He thought of all the times he had wished for something that would propel his Gargoyle like this and thought of how this gift would lead him to the glory of his name. It was the final, missing link for what would undoubtedly be his victory. He was certain that fate had spoken, and he would use this to destroy that ridiculous cafe boy and his homemade motorbike.

Daryn howled triumphantly, as if he had been crowned King of the Undead at that very moment. Nothing could possibly stop him now.

Musical accompaniment for this scene:
"MOTOR HELL"
FROM THE ALBUM "RISE OF THE CAFE RACER"
DEANO JONES & THE SWEET DEATH SYMPHONY

CHAPTER TWENTY FIVE:
THE LIGHT OF THE MOON

Sonny stood on the corner of Edmont and Gant, wondering what to do. From where he stood on the street he could see everything inside of Vanderpooles Blood Gärten, but that wasn't saying much. There were a handful of middle-aged vamps quietly having drinks. He rolled his head back and looked straight up, trying to think if he may have missed something on the poster.

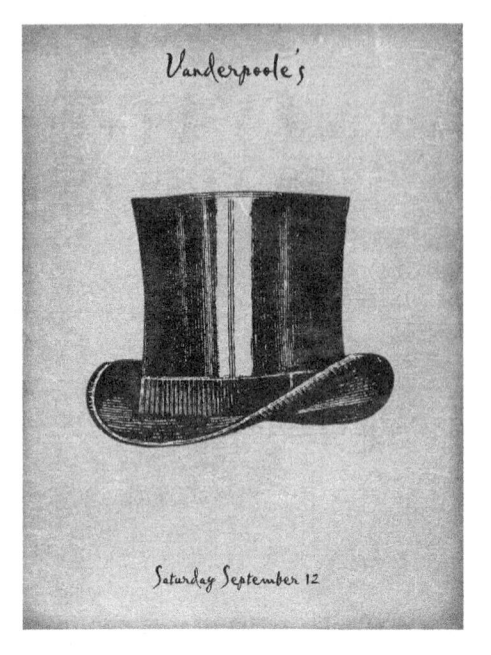

Vanderpoole's

Saturday September 12

A few days before that, Sonny had seen a poster with a simple top hat, exactly like the one on the card Vanian Von Schlieben had given him. There was a date at the bottom and the name 'Vanderpooles' in small type near the top. Small enough where you might never give the random image of a top hat another thought if you didn't have a reason to think otherwise. He nodded that he was sure of the date and the name and looked around at the deserted intersection of the Devilston district. It was late on a weeknight, and his Top Four qualifying run was at first dark tomorrow. *Maybe I ought to just leave,* he thought. Figuring that he must have confused the date, he buckled the chinstrap on his leather riding helmet and swung a leg over the seat of the cafe racer. Before he could kick the engine to a start he watched a small figure turn the corner at the entrance of Vanderpooles. The vamp walked past the front door and along the sidewalk. Near the middle of the block the figure stepped down a small stairway along the side of the building. A moment later, yellow light leaked from complete blackness and the figure was swallowed up into the shadows.

Sonny grinned and hopped off the bike. He laughed that the top hat was *under* the word Vanderpooles on the poster. "Very clever," he said out loud as he hopped down the few stairs. It wasn't entirely clear where the door was, but almost immediately the door cracked open slightly. A massive vamp was peeking at him from the other side and said nothing. Sonny smiled and nodded, eventually raising his eyebrows at the awkwardness of the silence.

The massive, older doorkeeper stared intently and finally groaned, "Card."

"Ah," Sonny smiled and fished for the card, not remembering where he had put it or if he had even brought it.

As Sonny checked his jacket pockets, the doorkeeper leaned a little closer. "You're a Rider, aren't you?"

Normally being recognized made things easier, but Sonny could see the doorkeeper's face becoming more skeptical. Sonny drew a deep breath.

"Yes, as a matter of fact, I am. The name's Legatus. Sonny Legatus."

The massive vamp shifted his weight. "I know who you are. Still need the card."

Sonny tapped at his many pockets on his jacket and smiled. "Well, I understand that now. Wish that vamp Vanian had told me I would need it to get in." Sonny smiled and stepped back. "Thanks anyway, friend."

The large vampire kept looking as Sonny pulled his leather riding gloves out of his back pocket.

"Vanian gave you a card? Is that asshole your friend?" The doorkeeper had opened the door a little more.

Sonny smiled and stopped climbing the stairs. "Uh, I... I met him a while ago at an art show."

The doorkeeper folded his arms and walked out from behind the doorway. "He try to steal your girlfriend?"

Sonny looked up at the street then back at the gigantic vampire. It was an unusual situation to begin with, but the way that this doorkeeper was acting made Sonny think that maybe this was a really bad idea coming down there.

"You know, I don't have a girlfriend so... " Sonny smiled, "Nobody's stealing anything." He laughed half-heartedly and pointed his thumb to the street. "I guess I'll just..."

"Come on, a Pike Rider like you, you gonna tell me that you don't have a bunch of females?" The doorkeep stepped to almost the bottom of the stairs.

At this point Sonny realized that it would be impossible for him to turn and run the rest of the way up the stairs. This massive vamp was hardly more than a couple arms-length away. He had no idea why, but this vamp clearly had some problem with him. It didn't really matter anyway. Maybe he had a big problem with Vanian, maybe he didn't like that Sonny was a Pike Rider, or maybe this massive vamp was just bored. But it was increasingly obvious to Sonny that this was about to turn into something unfortunate for him.

Sonny remembered a few years ago when Slim was telling him a story about tangling with the miners in the uprising. Slim said that in one of the many skirmishes, he had to fight four vamps at once. Sonny was awestruck and asked Slim how he could do such a thing, and wasn't he scared. Slim had gotten very serious and said *'You know, when you have to fight a bunch of vamps, or even just a vamp bigger than you – you gotta do two things to succeed:*

First, you do the exact opposite of how your opponent thinks you'll act. They're expecting you'll be intimidated and scared of a fight that you're sure to lose. They'll wanna see you try to talk your way out, or even run. That's what you DON'T want to do. No, you put on your meanest, most insane cold stare and sit tight. Stretch your fingers a little, move your shoulders. You act like you're EXCITED for this to happen. You need to convince them that even if you know you can't win, that you will hurt them sons of bitches good before you lose.

And the second thing is, you never take the first shot. Never. No matter where you think the confrontation is going, don't swing first. That way, you didn't bring it on yourself.'

At the time he heard that story, it seemed like perfectly sound advice. It made for one hell of a story too, that's for sure. Right now, though, with the prospect of this gigantic vampire pummeling him, Sonny wished Slim had also listed *'Run for your life'* as one of his options.

There was little time to consider anything, and before he even knew it, Sonny had continued pulling his gloves on. He smiled and stepped down from the stairs and closer to the doorkeeper. He stared up at this massive vampire's eyes and imagined Daryn Von Firstenstein's face. Sonny clenched his teeth and slowly growled, "I didn't say I don't have females. I said that nobody's stealing anything from me."

The air and night were deadly still. Sonny slowly opened his clenched fists and extended his fingers so the leather would creak. He glared as hatefully as he could at the doorkeeper and waited, occasionally shifting his weight from foot to foot.

"Is that so," the doorkeeper grunted.

"Yeah," Sonny nodded and stared harder.

The door vamp was so huge that even when he opened his mouth it sounded like a leg being pulled from a turkey carcass. The door vamp coughed with his mouth closed. It was just a short breath but his head and chest jerked violently. He coughed two more times and opened his mouth. Then a rapid succession of coughs that morphed into a roaring, full bellied laugh. He smiled and shook his head at Sonny, who had still held his ground, expecting a surprise punch in the middle of this giant's self-indulgent chuckling. The more evil Sonny tried to look, the more the giant laughed, until he finally raised his hands as if surrendering to Sonny.

"Ha, ha, ha! If you ride half as tough as this, I may have just tried to pick a fight with the future KOTU!" He laughed loudly and stepped back through the doorway. He looked at Sonny and nodded toward the inside. "Come on in, Sonny Legatus."

Sonny waited for a second. With this massive vamp back on the other side of the door, Sonny knew he could easily be up the stairs and gone before that vamp even stuck his head out. He also knew that prior to all this Pike Run business, he had been more excited about the Sweet Death Symphony than anything else in the Realm. The very idea of meeting vampires who were not just thinking about living in the moment, but were acting on it and truly questioning the Rules of the Council was inspiring to him.

Sonny took his leather gloves off and shoved them into his back pocket. He smiled as he walked through the doorway, and not only because he had successfully made it past the door vamp into an SDS event, but because he was handing the grey card with a top hat on it to the giant vamp, who was now back on his stool behind the door. Apparently, the card had been under the gloves in his back pocket.

The door vamp laughed some more as Sonny handed him the card.

"Hang on to it," the door vamp said, holding his hand up. He motioned with his thumb toward the doors at the other side of the room.

"And Run for Glory, Sonny Legatus!" the vamp called after him.

Sonny smiled affirmatively and crossed the basement of Vanderpooles Blood Gärten. The noise of a crowd grew as he walked the narrow path between cases of empty bottles. The two doors at the end of the walkway opened next to the bar in a noisy and smoky room. Sonny immediately noticed how lavishly everyone was dressed. It was as he had always imagined—suits with tails, frilly shirts and vests. Some female vampires had big bustles blooming from under their corsets and long gloves that went up their arms. Sonny immediately thought of Andi and how much she would love this clothing.

A vamp behind the bar looked at Sonny and raised a brow as he mixed a drink, as if to ask if he wanted anything.

"A Hell Blood, if you please," Sonny said loudly so the barkeep would hear over the busy room.

"Me as well, and two snorts of Penny Whistle!" Vanian yelled from behind him to the barkeep.

"Hey Vanian, how are you?" Sonny grabbed his hand.

"Lovely, lovely my friend. Nice to see you here," Vanian yelled, "Glad you made it!"

"I almost didn't." Sonny shook his head. "You never mentioned that I needed that card."

"Oh, yes." Vanian looked surprised. "So how'd you get by Stürmer?"

"Ha," Sonny's eyes were wide. "I don't know. Is that vamp psychotic or what?"

"No," Vanian laughed. "My brother is just an asshole!"

Sonny looked at Vanian apologetically but Vanian slapped him on the arm as the barkeep laid their drinks down.

"No worries," Vanian winked as he raised his glass of Penny Whistle.

Sonny grabbed the other glass and exhaled quickly in anticipation. He had a race tomorrow and hadn't planned on starting the night with rot-gut pig liquor.

"To the continued success of our Vamp from Brimberg, Sonny Legatus and his Cafe Racer!" Vanian yelled loudly.

At least a dozen vamps in their immediate vicinity quickly raised their glasses and answered, "Hear, hear!"

They downed their shots and slammed them on the bar. Sonny grabbed the edge of the bar with one hand and grimaced. Vanian smiled and wiped his lips.

"I suppose it is a bit early for the Penny," Vanian breathed deeply, flaring his nostrils. "But she really does have a way of improving a vamp's disposition, wouldn't you say?"

Sonny's eyes were still closed but he nodded and made a thumbs up. He opened his eyes and strained to focus, then drank long from his Hell Blood bottle.

Vanian leaned in and grabbed an elbow on the bar smiling. He looked Sonny up and down. "You've become

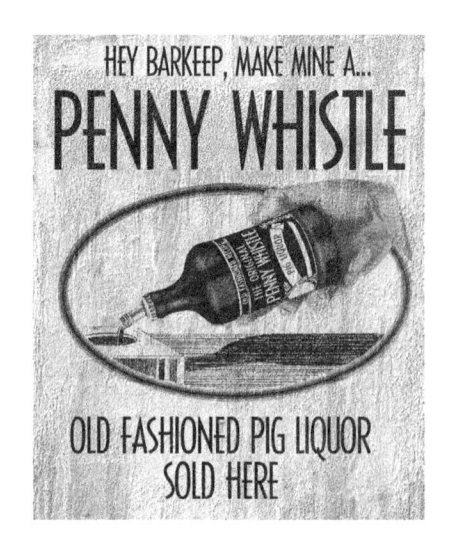

a bit of a famous vamp since I'd seen you last."

Sonny shrugged, "All I'm doing is riding my motorbike."

"Well, if you don't rank this week you'll have a nice job as a poster vamp for the Council." Vanian drank from his bottle. "Ra-Ra Realm, and all that." He set his bottle on the bar. "But if you rank, then hey," Vanian squinted, "Now you're onto something."

"That would indeed be something," Sonny agreed and lifted his brow.

"Yes. You'll either be at the bottom of the Gulf of Gehenna or our my new KOTU." Vanian wrinkled his nose as he smiled.

Sonny smiled and looked down at his drink. He hadn't given that much thought. It was true that in the last eight Pike's Runs a Von Firstenstein had won. It was widely speculated, though never spoken, that the other Rider wound up in the Gulf since no one ever heard from him once the Riders headed South from Iron Gate into the Forbidden Land portion of the race.

Until then Sonny always imagined that the better, faster, more skilled Rider would prevail, and that if he was, in fact, good enough to rank all the way to the final, that he may actually have a shot at First Prize and being the KOTU. Something about Vanian's frankness and the fact that they were in a secret basement event to hide from the sight of the Realm's powers that be made that idea seem naïve.

Sonny looked back at Vanian with a tight-lipped grin. He thought for a moment longer and nodded resolutely.

"I should be so lucky," he smiled.

Vanian squinted at his drinking buddy with a confused look.

Sonny took a long drink.

"There is a Realm full of vampires that will never, ever have the chance to do what I'm doing. Who will carry on night after night dreaming of the moments where they could be a ranked Rider? If I have to meet my end, then why not as a Rider of the Pike? It would be my greatest moment in time!" He yelled at Vanian but several vamps around them were nodding as he spoke.

A smile crept over Vanian's face and he grabbed the two more short glasses of Penny Whistle he had motioned the barkeep for. Handing Sonny his glass, he said, "If that's not living for the moment, then I don't know what is, my friend." Vanian raised the glass. Sonny rolled his eyes and smiled, raising the other glass.

Sonny didn't have to hold the bar to steady himself this time, but still needed a minute to focus after the shot. Vanian's nostrils flared for a moment but he continued with his thought.

"It makes me wonder, though. Whether you rank out or go onto the finals, why not use your standing to promote the message? You'll have the ear of the Realm, Sonny, you could speak for all of us." Vanian signaled for two more bottles of Hell Blood. He leaned in close to Sonny and accented his words with his hands.

"A Pike Rider is more revered than any vamp in the Realm. Certainly more than some High Council fool that only serves his own interests." Vanian pointed at Sonny. "What if *you* stood up and told them they don't have to take it? That vampires can dream, that we can choose our own way. No one has ever done it, Sonny."

Sonny stared at Vanian and took several deep breaths. He laughed quietly with his tight-lipped grin. Eventually he shook his head. "I'm no hero, Vanian. That's something for these vamps." Sonny waved his hand at the handful of vampires walking onto the stage and casually tuning their instruments. "Yeah," Sonny nodded, "The singer for the SDS would be the vamp for that job."

Vanian shook his head dismissively. "No, he's a wanker. Besides, no one outside these speakeasies would ever listen to that obnoxious vamp."

"You know him?" Sonny blinked, surprised. "Aw, the SDS are brilliant. How much of a wanker could he possibly be?" He took a long drink to that and realized he was a little intoxicated.

Vanian smiled and grabbed Sonny by the shoulder. "You're a good vamp, Sonny Legatus." He shook him as Sonny laughed.

"You'll have to excuse me for a little bit. Gotta go earn my keep." He winked.

Vanian crossed the floor and stepped onto the stage. Sonny's expression went from total confusion to total shock. Sonny slowly shook his head in disbelief as Vanian began addressing the crowd.

"Welcome everyone and all!" He yelled.

The crowd cheered and stomped wildly.

"Tonight we will forget our misery and leave our troubles at the door! No worries of our Specialties or our races!" Vanian winked at Sonny. "Tonight we will speak our dreams, savor the moment, and scream at the light of the moon!"

The band immediately launched into the song "Light of the Moon." Vanian waved his arms like a mad conductor, pacing the stage and encouraging all to join in the chorus. The entire room shook as a two hundred vampires sang the words with him.

Musical accompaniment for this scene:
"LIGHT OF THE MOON"
FROM THE ALBUM "RISE OF THE CAFE RACER"
DEANO JONES & THE SWEET DEATH SYMPHONY

It sounded so beautiful, Sonny thought. He wished Andi could be there to hear it with him. As he looked around the room at the vamps singing along, Sonny felt a lump in his throat. It was an incredible feeling of oneness in this dank cavern. It didn't matter who you were, what color suit you wore or what Specialty you belonged to. It was just vampires in this room. Vampires who were pretending that the whole Realm didn't even exist, that all that mattered was right here and now in this moment.

Sonny threw his arm around a dandy dressed vamp who had handed him a drink. They continued singing along with the band. Eventually all the vamps in the room had locked arms as they sang along.

Back near the bar, at a table in a dark corner of the room, Hellamina Muntz sat quietly sipping a glass. She slowly rocked her head with a subtle smile as she watched Sonny.

A Rider of the Pike, a darling of the Realm, she thought, *at a speakeasy singing protest songs on the eve of the Top Four run.* She lit a hand-rolled cigarette and crossed her legs. *Very interesting.*

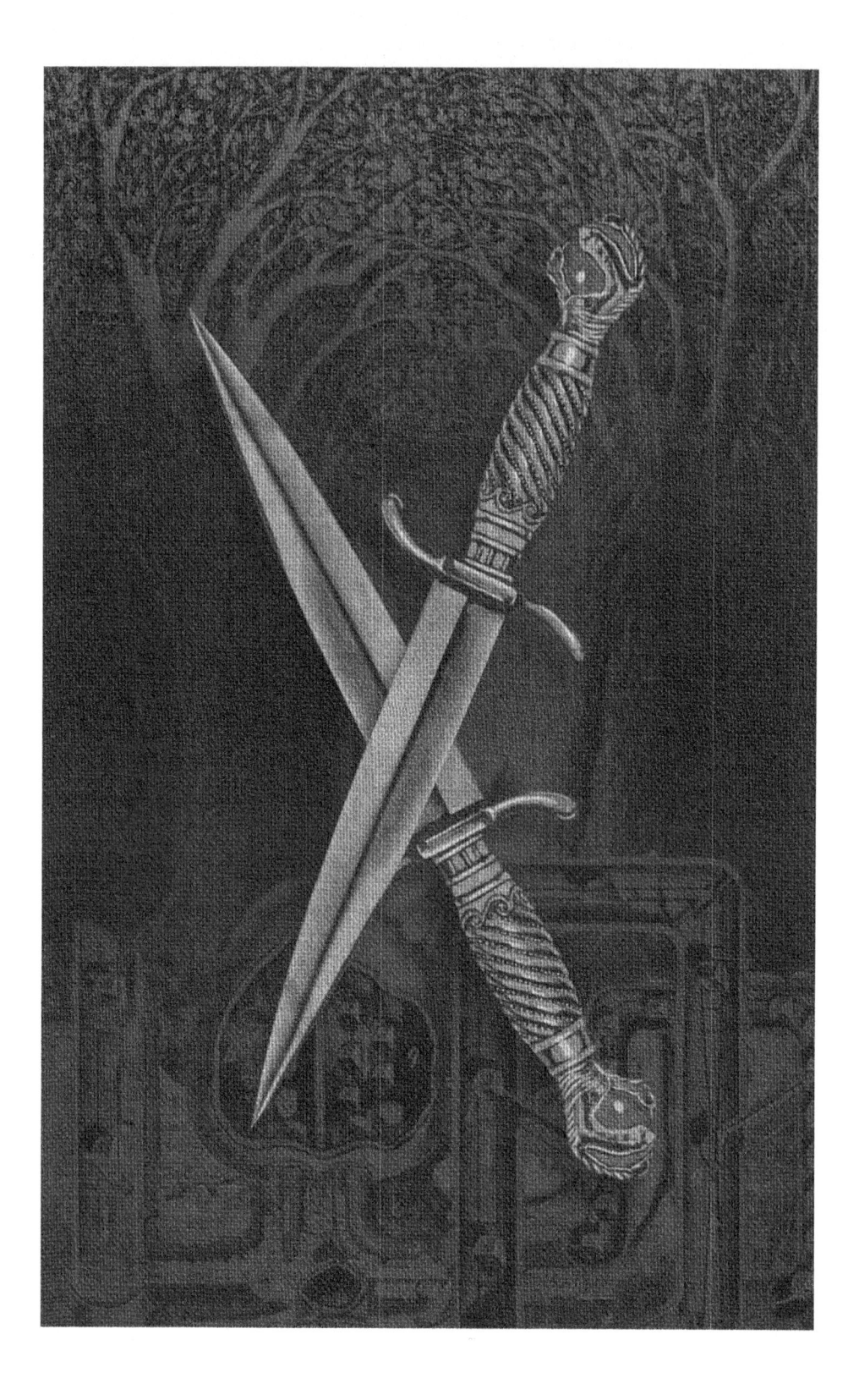

CHAPTER TWENTY SIX:
NORWOOD PARK

Sonny slowly rolled his head in a circular motion, groaning as he stretched. When he stopped, Andi was standing in front of him. She had a flat expression on her face and moved her head deliberately from side to side.

"What were you thinking, the night before a run?" She held out a cup of piping hot blood.

Sonny made a painful smile and looked at the cup. "I think I'm going to just leave my stomach alone for awhile."

Andi continued staring, more worried than angry.

"Hey, buck up, Kepler," Sonny smiled, "I could run these streets with my eyes closed."

There was a sizeable crowd already assembled there at Norwood Park. From there, the remaining four Riders would run for the Top Two slots of the Pike. The path of the race was closed off to traffic and would wind through every district of the Capital's city streets. This race was less about speed and more about agility. There would be a couple opportunities to open up along the commercial route that wrapped around the city, but most of this race would be spent weaving through the side streets of the Capital.

"Where's Slim?" Andi looked around the Riders' pit and didn't see him anywhere.

"Oh, he's not gonna make the start." Sonny closed his eyes, inserted an index finger in his ear and rattled the side of his head.

Andi looked at him strangely. "What are you doing?"

"Oh, I'm just..." he opened his mouth, "Just trying to get this ear unclogged."

"So, why?" Andi raised her eyebrows.

"I dunno, I guess it's that Penny Whistle stuff... I never..."

"No, you dork, why isn't Slim coming?"

"Oh," Sonny smiled. "I saw him before I went out last night and he said he got a last-minute emergency job. Something about a day shift welding a broken water main for the city. I guess there's a *lot* of treasure involved. He said it was just too much to pass up."

"That's kind of sad," Andi frowned, "You know, just that he couldn't be here."

"Well, he said he'll come straight over. Thinks he might miss the start but will definitely make the finish." Sonny perked up, not liking the somber mood. "Besides, if I can't beat these clowns in my own streets I'm no kind of Rider."

"And even if you don't, that's fine too," Andi said quickly. "What I mean is, there's no shame in that, you know..." She looked down. "If you don't go on to the final run."

After the failed human blood experiment their dynamic had been slightly skewed. At first Sonny thought it was sweet that Andi had revealed that she had feelings for him. But in even the short few days since then, she had been on his mind more. It was as if she had given him permission to think of her as a female vampire instead of a little girl. Even now, he couldn't look at her as a kid sister that he could dismiss with a joke about not returning from a final Pike Run. Sonny reached down and gently took the warm cup from Andi. He sipped it and drew a deep breath.

"Hey, when I started this, I had no idea what to expect." He paused. "I thought it would be an exciting distraction from the Focus." He sipped more and smiled, looking at the crowds lining the street. "But these past couple months, running these trials and traveling the Realm has changed me, Andi. Changed the way I look at everything."

Andi raised her head and Sonny stared directly at her.

"I knew the history of the Pike when I began this. It's true, only one Rider has ever returned from a Pike's Run. And you know what, whether my place in history ends today or in the final run of the Pike, so be it. I will savor my time and know that I lived in the moment, no matter when my days end."

Andi was startled. She looked at him with a skeptical eye. *He looks like Sonny, but who is this vamp?*, she thought. These weren't the words of the fifty-three-year-old Fledgling vampire she had grown up with who was shy and bookish, tutoring students to please his mother.

Andi looked at his shoulders in his tight riding jacket and his square jaw that hadn't been shaved tonight. Sonny was no longer an unsure Fledge from Brimberg—he was a Rider of the Realm. As she looked up at him her eyes grew wide and she gently held his hand. Sonny smiled warmly and kissed her forehead.

"I'm going to be fine, Andi."

"Oh, isn't that sweet," Daryn Von Firstenstein yelled from his corner of the pit, "Does your little sister tuck you in at night too, Legatus?"

Sonny became instantly enraged.

"That's it," Sonny said to Andi, throwing his cup on the ground.

Andi immediately grabbed both his hands and pleaded, "No, Sonny please, just ignore him!"

Andi was holding tight and Sonny had started to pull her. Several vamps in the crowd were already cheering for Sonny to get him. Andi kept begging, even as Sonny had dragged her halfway to Daryn's corner.

"This is all he's trying to do Sonny, to get you disqualified. He's afraid of you, Sonny!"

Daryn and a couple of his crew casually walked toward Sonny.

"Yes, I'm afraid of you, Sonny," Daryn mocked.

The other two Riders, Val and Marius, were watching now from their corners. Sonny held up a fist and bit his lip. He gradually relaxed the fist and pointed at Daryn. He opened his mouth but reconsidered. Andi was only barely holding onto one of his hands now.

"Yes? Is there something you want to say, Legatus?" Daryn asked smugly, tightening the scarf around his neck and rubbing his hands together.

"Not only," Sonny growled hatefully, "Will I rank today..." Sonny shook Andi's hand free and took three steps to be eye to eye with Daryn. "I will beat you in the Pike." Sonny hissed with such conviction several vamps on the sidelines 'ooooo'd' quietly.

Daryn's expression became hardened and he leaned in even closer.

"Bring it on, Cafe Boy." Daryn snarled back at him.

"Vampires!" The KOTU yelled as he entered the Riders' pit, "Try to control yourselves!"

Vladamir walked squarely between the two and separated them with his hands, pushing them away from each other.

"You're representing the Realm right now. Show some damned respect." The KOTU looked around at the crowd lining the streets behind the barriers. He smiled and waved to some youngsters. "This is a family event!"

"I'm sorry, Sir," Sonny said quietly.

Daryn simply huffed and walked back to his pit corner. Sonny looked at the KOTU and nodded apologetically before returning with Andi to his bike.

Sonny began angrily fueling up his bike. Andi didn't say anything. She looked over at the other two Riders Val Vossen and Marius Mockba.

"I wonder why Daryn only starts trouble with you." She turned her thumb at the other Riders. "Those other vamps could win as well, couldn't they?"

Sonny made a sour grunt as he stared at the fuel tank. "Val's the only one to worry about. Mockba's father is on the High Council, I guarantee you Marius has no desire to try and win this. He'll be in his cushy Specialty by the end of the week." Sonny topped off the tank and screwed the cap back on.

"Val, on the other hand..." Sonny looked over at Val fueling his bike. "He's from Enoch, out near the Dead Hills." He raised his eyebrows and looked at

Andi. "Not a whole lot to go back to."

A hundred and twenty years before, Enoch had been hit hard with Blood Bog fever. More than half of the vamps in that area perished and they were still reeling from it. That coupled with the already barren land surrounding them in the Dead Hills, made for a difficult existence in that part of the Realm.

The Seven notes of the Pike sounded, calling Riders to the starting line. Sonny huffed as he pulled his gloves on and buckled his chinstrap.

Musical accompaniment for this scene:
"THE SEVEN NOTES OF THE PIKE"
FROM THE ALBUM "RISE OF THE CAFE RACER"
DEANO JONES & THE SWEET DEATH SYMPHONY

"Wish me luck," Sonny smiled.

Andi hugged him tight and whispered "Run for Glory" in his ear.

"Thanks." Sonny winked at her as he pushed his bike to the line.

The KOTU was already addressing the crowd when Sonny reached the line. As soon as the Riders rested their bikes on their kickstands for the Geezer to inspect, the KOTU quickly stepped off his podium. He moved like a snake between the Geezer and the line of motorbikes.

"Do me the honor of being the official tester in my home city, Sir." Vlad smiled and gently pulled the four sticks from the old vampire's hand.

"What?!" The Geezer wailed.

The old vampire tasked with judging these motorbikes' fitness was easily in his eight hundredth year and showing it. Soon he would be confirmed to retirement to spend the remainder of his time under the care of the Realm at Rogue Canyon. In spite of the folklore about enduring forever, vampires generally lived around nine hundred years. It was then that their bones gave out. By the time vampires reached that age bones would shatter beyond repair very easily. The Realm saw to it that the aged received complimentary retirement at one of their two massive complexes, in Rogue Canyon or Kindurba.

"That's right, Sir, I would ask for the honor today." Vlad smiled and nodded.

The Geezer's confusion erased and he became angry. "I have tested motorbikes for the Pike for five hundred years, dear KOTU, and I won't be retiring today, Sir." The Geezer gently grabbed Vlad's wrist with the tester sticks in them.

Vlad smiled and looked around. He made a small chuckle, as if he were having a casual conversation with the official. He placed his hand on the Geezer's wrist and leaned in close.

"If you make me execute my executive authority, I will see to it that you're banned from Kindurba and the Canyon." Vlad smiled broadly as if they were old friends. "I'll also see to it that you're Specialty is reassigned so that you spend your golden years checking stool samples for the Bog in Baldoon."

Vlad leaned back and chuckled as if they had shared a joke. "And you have my word on that, Sir," Vlad said loud enough for Riders to hear.

The Geezer released his hold and scowled. He muttered to himself angrily as he stomped to the ale tent.

The KOTU worked his way down the line, with all the appropriately serious gestures associated with tasting motor oil for impurities.

Although Daryn had no idea that Vlad was behind the Motor Hell that was given to him, he was curious why his father had insisted on testing. And when his bike passed for impurities it made him wonder if his father may have been involved. But there was little time to speculate since after deeming all motorbikes legal to run, Vlad was back on his podium and the Riders were ready to begin.

The KOTU ordered the Riders to start their engines and the crowd roared. In spite of their great excitement Sonny thought how quiet it had become compared to the deafening chaos of the earlier runs with hundreds of bikes.

The enormous crowd helped the KOTU countdown to the blue light. The streets around Norwood Park echoed with mad energy, *'Ready... Steady... GO!'* and the four Riders shot from the starting line.

Sonny immediately jumped to the front with Daryn right next to him. The beginning of this run had the Riders weaving in the tight and narrow alleys in the downtown area. Vampires cheered from the sides as well as from the office windows high above the street.

Sonny's smaller bike and familiarity with every stone of these streets was making it easy for him to carve away at a lead very quickly. By the first five miles he had already put himself a block ahead of the others. Daryn and Val were neck and neck with Marius several blocks back. Marius had overshot a corner and struck the curb, bringing him to a full stop.

By the time they were into the Market district, Sonny was keeping a solid lead. The streets of the Market district had been largely goat paths before proper roads and were even more winding than the Downtown district.

Once out of the Market, that qualifying run had Riders taking the wide Realm Roadway that circled the city. They would spend sixteen miles on this and take it all the way around to the Warehouse district.

When Sonny leaned into the first turn of the Roadway, he glanced over his shoulder and didn't see anyone. He howled loudly, convinced the cobblestone roads in the last section had effectively slowed his rivals and any chance of him not winning this race. He was elated at the idea of not just beating Daryn in their hometown, but beating him good. With his generous lead he had left the Demon disengaged to keep his bike cool.

It wasn't until he was several miles down the roadway that he noticed the sound of Daryn's bike coming up behind him in the distance. And he was coming up fast! Sonny tucked it in tighter and flipped on the Demon with his thumb. That seemed to keep the distance between them for a few more moments but soon Daryn was moving past Sonny at an alarming speed. For a minute Sonny thought something must have happened to his cafe racer. He toggled the Demon on and off with his thumb, but it seemed to be working fine. Sonny was dumbfounded. *How could he have just blown past me like that?* he thought.

In the few more miles of the Roadway portion Daryn had put a mile or more between them. He was already rolling into Cambria before Sonny and the other Riders were even off the Roadway. Once back on the side streets of Axeton, though, the Gargoyle's increased speed, brought on by the Motor Hell, wasn't as useful. It's true—the bike would jump forward a little quicker, but too much speed could actually ruin him here if he were to dump his bike on the many sharp turns. Daryn played it safe, reduced his speed and carefully navigated the third quarter of this race, having regained a sizable lead on the Roadway.

Within a few more minutes Daryn was leaning onto The Commons Boulevard, which would allow a relatively straight shot for the last couple miles of the run. This would be the most heavily populated portion of the race, and since he was already ahead he decided to gloat, taking his goggles off and waving as he cruised down toward the finish. The crowd was smiling and clapping, but Daryn was still irritated with their lack of enthusiasm. He wanted the same wild enthusiasm he'd seen the crowds giving Sonny. He had been going mad trying to figure why the crowds favored Sonny so much. *They should show their KOTU a bit more affection,* he thought angrily to himself.

As he made his way on the last city block of this run, Daryn slowed down and revved the bike. He revved it loudly several times more and then popped the clutch, riding a wheelie over the finish line. By the time he dropped back on two wheels, the applause had almost stopped as everyone in the crowd was trying to see Sonny and Val battling it out for second place a few blocks back.

Sonny had flipped on the Demon as he leaned into Commons Boulevard and was many lengths ahead of Val. But at that speed, as they roared down the boulevard, it was still any vampire's race. The smallest hesitation or stall would make all the difference.

The crowds on the street were going completely crazy as the Riders flew past, leaving dust and debris in their wake. As they tucked in on the final city block Val wildly threw his helmet off and let out his signature bloodcurdling shriek. Sonny thought about how much that vampire from Enoch must want this. The honor was undeniable anywhere in the Realm, but when a Rider was from a small, remote town like Enoch, every vampire in their village felt like they were in the Pike with him. 'No greater honor than running the Pike' was a phrase Sonny had heard a thousand times and now he was suddenly overwhelmed with the reality that he was in fact, one of the two Riders in the Pike's Run.

And as he soared over the finish line ahead of Val Vossen, Sonny was met with deafening applause. He let his bike roll far into the pit. He knew within moments he would have to return to the line and receive the crowd, but first he wanted to catch his breath. Until now Sonny had just glossed over the idea of making it all the way. In spite of the fact that he really wanted to, he was never really sure if he actually would make it to the actual Pike's Run. Sonny looked around for Slim but didn't see him anywhere. He could see Andi, though—she was running through the pit area toward him. When she was twenty feet away she just stopped and stared at him, smiling, her arms folded. This moment was just as emotional for her, but she knew it was not hers. As she smiled at Sonny her lips began to quiver. In spite of all the happiness in this moment, she realized that any dreams she may have had of her and Sonny together had just been erased.

Sonny was still on his motorbike. He had started to get off to see Andi but the crowd was chanting his name. Andi shook her head and nodded at the finish line.

"No," She whispered to herself as he rode past her and back to the line, "You belong to the Realm now."

CHAPTER TWENTY SEVEN: NIGHTSHADE

While the last qualifying race had been running, Hellamina Muntz waited a couple miles away in front of a Devilston tavern called Wünderbar. She was responding to a Hellfire Incident and knew the KOTU would be late since he was needed to start the race downtown at Norwood Park.

There was a badly burned body crumpled against a street lamp and Detective Muntz had roped off the area. It was probably just another vamp who drank too much and passed out before he could make it home, she thought and shook her head. 'A Vampire shouldn't drink alone… Make sure you see your barmates home' was a common expression with signs practically everywhere in Devilston. How could anyone forget this?, she thought.

As she waited for the KOTU, Hellamina remembered how she had felt on her qualifying run back in 847 ADWB. She had made it to the Top Eight before losing at Black Lake. She had been so proud, and so drunk, at the party afterwards that she revealed to everyone that she was in fact a female. She laughed out loud remembering how some of those Lowlander girls who had chased her around all night didn't even stop after they found that out. Everyone just wanted to be near the Riders.

"I always knew you enjoyed this detail, Detective," Vlad said as he walked up.

"It beats working in an office." Hellamina looked around, "Where'd you come from Sir? I mean, you didn't walk over from Norwood, did you?"

"With all this traffic I probably would've gotten here quicker if I'd have walked the entire way. But no, I just had Cheshko drop me off a block over." He groaned and gave the Detective a dry look. "I told him to wait, that I wouldn't be too long."

Hellamina tossed her half-finished cup of blood into the trash can she had been leaning against and wiped her hands.

"Well, lets get started then."

They both ducked under the R.E.D. incident tape she had placed around the site. Normally they didn't always bother taping off these sites, but with all the spectators on foot out for the final qualifying run, Hellamina wanted to keep vamps out of the scene. Even though the bulk of the crowds were on some of the more scenic parts of the route, the Realm Roadway was actually only two blocks away and the Riders would be passing by them within the hour.

Hellamina took out a small metal baton and knelt near the corpse. She wrinkled her nose as she looked closely at the burnt vampire. She looked at Wünderbar across the street and back at the KOTU.

"I'm wondering where this vamp came from," Hellamina said flatly to

Vlad.

The KOTU made an obligatory glance at his surroundings then back to her. "I'd say he was likely at the tavern over there and, well… " Vlad had his hands together and flared his fingers outward, "Poof!"

Hellamina grimaced lightly. "That's what I thought." She nodded. "But… I checked with the barkeep at Wünderbar, they said that all their patrons are accounted for. Every single one."

"So," Vlad sighed, "He was probably at another tavern in Devilston."

"Yes, probably." Hellamina stood up. "But why is he over here? This is the outskirts, there's nothing over here. I mean, there's only the roadway over there. There's not even parking." She squinted at the corpse and back at the KOTU. "It doesn't make any sense."

"Well, Detective, you know how these incidents go. I'm sure we'll get a report of a missing vamp." Vlad looked at his watch. "Maybe a Pike reveler who strayed off in the big city."

Hellamina half-heartedly sighed. "Maybe, but still, there's no sign of anything over here."

Vlad was already growing impatient, he could see the impending request for a Hellhound mounting in the Detective's eyes. He looked over her shoulder and pointed.

"Look, there's a motorcar right over there," He smiled at the Detective. "That's probably how he got here."

Hellamina spun around. She looked around for a few seconds, then held her hands out. She shook her head, not seeing anything.

"Over there, away from the street lights, in the shadow of the building." Vlad pointed again, this time leaning over to show Hellamina where he was looking.

She cocked her head, surprised. "You have excellent vision, Sir. I completely missed that."

"Well, I'd say that clears a bit of the fog. I'd say this vamp was on his way to his motorcar from the tavern and, poof." The KOTU wiped his hands ceremoniously as to signal they were concluding the investigation.

"Yes, Sir, but as I said, the barkeep at Wünderbar said all heads are accounted for."

She dipped under the tape and was halfway to the truck before the KOTU could even voice an objection.

"Detective, can we at least make a ruling and sign off?!" He yelled behind her.

The truck was a rusty work vehicle with scraps of iron and a huge welding machine in the truck bed. Thick cables attached to the welder hung out of the truck and down into the manhole almost directly under the truck. Hellamina recognized the truck even before she saw "Slim Jim's Ironworks" painted on the drivers side door. She knelt to the hole in the street and looked in. It wasn't a tunnel to the sewers, it was only a small crawlspace that housed a water main junction. She knelt down and peered in and could see that there was no one in the tight space. She could also see that there were fresh welds on the two large wheels at the center of the junction box.

She stood back up and thought how great it would be if Slim had been there late and had maybe seen something. She hadn't run into him in quite a while and was excited at the thought. Looking around though, she wondered where Slim would have gone that he would have left his tools out like this.

The KOTU had slowly, begrudgingly walked over to where Hellamina was at the truck. She had been quickly running scenarios in her mind, cocking her head and pointing. There was nowhere to walk to to get food or drink, and he wasn't in the Wünderbar. The Detective looked at the corpse and thought No. As the KOTU finally reached her, tapping his fingers together and drawing a breath to no doubt ask if she was satisfied, Hellamina's eyes widened and she bolted away, back to the incident scene.

The KOTU rolled his eyes and threw his hands to his side.

"Detective, please!"

Hellamina ran across the street, slipped back under the incident tape and dropped to a knee next to the burnt Hellfire victim. She pulled the thin baton she kept in the inside pocket of her uniform out and used it to lightly move parts of the corpse. It was always only a stroke of luck if some portion of a Hellfire Incident victim was left unscathed, but it happened on occasion. In this case, though, this poor soul was burnt beyond any recognition. She shook her head and continued slowly examining the body.

Vlad joined her at the scene and the Detective stood up. She was racing through possible explanations in her mind as she looked at Vlad. Now all Slim's truck was doing was creating more unanswered questions.

"Detective, I have a splitting headache," The KOTU growled. "And it has been made worse by slamming my toes into that damn metal plate that was left in the street!"

"OH!" Hellamina looked at the KOTU with wide eyes.

She instantly remembered that Slim Jim had a metal plate put on the back of his head after an injury fighting in the uprising. Hellamina dropped the baton and used her hands to examine the corpse. The head was hard as rock. The hair and flesh had melted onto the skull and it was all soot black. Running her fingers over it she couldn't tell if any of it was metal or bone. She grabbed her baton and tapped on it. The top of the skull sounded hollow like wood. When she struck the back… it made a metallic sound. She looked at Vlad, wide-eyed. She took the skull in her hand and smashed it on the pavement. The burnt skull in her hand broke into a dozen pieces, with black dust pillowing out. A metal plate landed on the pavement.

"Alright, Detective, I've had enough!" Vlad stepped under the tape and away from the mess that the Detective was making of the incident scene.

Hellamina stood with the plate in her hands. She couldn't believe what she was seeing. She looked at the KOTU.

"Vladimir, do you know who this is?" She breathed heavily.

"How could I know who that is?" He huffed. "Why? Do you know this vampire?" The KOTU was completely apathetic.

"Sir." Hellamina stepped to him, holding the plate out. "This is Slim Jim."

The KOTU took the plate from the Detective and examined it. After a moment he looked back at Hellamina with a confused look.

"Sir." Hellamina looked at Vlad with an expression that suggested he couldn't possibly not remember Slim having a metal plate in his head.

During the uprising of 767 ADWB, doctors had placed this plate on Slim after intense fighting at Mount Cain. The iron ore mining company thugs—who had the support of Vlad's father, the sitting KOTU Dracov Von Firsten-stein—had waged war on a smaller number of coal miners. Even though Slim's Specialty was with an iron ore mining company, he broke ranks and volunteered to fight alongside coal miners and the outnumbered R.E.D. Agents sent in to protect the coal miners at Mount Cain. Slim was so influential he actually led others to break rank and volunteer to defend the coal miners.

After the uprising, the R.E.D. wanted to make a hero out of Slim and have him permanently join their ranks. Changing Specialties would need the approval of the High Council, and Dracov was furious with Slim. Not publicly, of course, because officially the R.E.D. had been sent to defend the coal miners who were being terrorized by the iron ore miners. But behind the scenes, Dracov was an owner of the iron ore mining company and wanted to control coal production in order to drive up the price of iron. Slim had been instrumental in foiling that objective.

When Dracov handed down the refusal to allow Slim to join the R.E.D. it was "officially" on the basis that the metal plate in his head rendered him 'not pure' and unfit to serve. Dracov would later try and use the same argument to keep Slim out of the next Pike's Run eighty years later in 847 ADWB. It would be the overwhelming public opinion that swayed the remaining Council members to convince Dracov to vote with them, and allow Slim to run. Vlad, Slim and Hellamina would all ride in that Pike's Run Number Seven. Slim had ranked Three in the same race that was happening on that very day.

Vlad was still acting like he was drawing a blank, and Hellamina had become visibly irritated. She took the plate back from him. Vlad raised his brows at that and took a handkerchief from his suit pocket to clean his hands.

"I'm sorry Detective, but I am the KOTU, I haven't kept a scrapbook of the Class of 847."

Hellamina turned and faced Slim's truck so as to not let the KOTU see that she was affected by this.

Vlad kept cleaning his hands.

"Look, Detective, it's always a terrible loss to have any vampire perish in a Hellfire. It is made worse by the fact that we know this vamp. I'm sorry if this has been emotional for you."

Hellamina turned and glared at him. He folded his kerchief and continued apathetically, "I, however, do not have that luxury. I will mourn when it's the time, tonight I need to serve the Realm and greet Riders. So, if you please?" Vlad waved with his hand for the Detective to join him.

Hellamina walked back over and stood with the KOTU over the burnt body of Slim Jim. Vlad cleared his throat and sighed loudly.

"Our fallen Brother has left this world to join the souls of our ancestors, and begin everlasting life in the Kingdom of the Dead. May the keepers of the Kingdom let this soul pass."

The sound of motorbikes sprung up in the distance. Within seconds they were screaming by, only a few blocks away on the Realm Roadway.

As the smaller crowd out there on the edge of the city cheered their Riders on, Hellamina shook and nearly choked on her response to the Begrafen and whispered softly, "Hear, hear."

CHAPTER TWENTY EIGHT:
COME ON, COME ON

The pot of blood on the stove had reached a boil. The rose petals Evanna had put in it were filling the kitchen with a warm smell that reminded Sonny of being a very young vamp. She had been straightening his collar when the pot whistled quietly across the room.

"Oooo, let me grab that quick," Evanna whispered and stepped to the stove to turn the heat off.

She turned back at Sonny and smiled warmly. "You do look so handsome in that suit, honey."

"Thanks," Sonny said, quietly trying to mirror his mother's lighter spirit.

It had been two nights since Sonny had ranked Second and won a spot in the Realm's Ninth Pike's Run. And two days since R.E.D. Agents had come to their house to tell them that the vampire who lived in the garage near their property had been found under a streetlight in Devilston, apparently having been out in the daylight.

After winning, Sonny had ridden around town looking for Slim after he hadn't shown up for the celebrating. It just wouldn't have felt like he had really won until he could see Slim, so Sonny had stopped at a few places hoping to find Slim before returning home. When he finally pulled up to his house, Evanna, Andi and Toland were all in the front yard talking to the three R.E.D. Agents.

Sonny could not believe what he was hearing. It seemed impossible, there had to be a mistake. Slim? The same Slim that fought in the uprising, traveled the far reaches of the Realm, sailed with mariner vampires, and could fix or do anything. That Slim had been found in the *daylight?* As the Agents, family and friends tried to console one another, Sonny had simply gotten back on his motorbike and rode the rest of the night.

The next night, as friends and supporters sent their condolences, it finally begun to set in that Slim really was gone. It just seemed impossible for Sonny to believe. The KOTU came by and offered his sympathies. He also told Sonny that the High Council would grant him a pardon from running the Pike, if he so chose to do so, and they would offer his slot to the Number Three-ranked Rider, Val Vossen.

At the time Sonny didn't know what he thought of the idea, he was so consumed with grief that he simply nodded and thanked the KOTU for taking time to come by. There were still a few more days until the Pike's Run and the more he thought of it, the more he couldn't imagine traveling down into the valley, to Strigoi, without Slim. Sonny thought about the past couple months working on the bike and traveling all over the Realm with Slim. It had been the best of all his time. He felt nauseous thinking about trying to go to Strigoi without Slim. It felt self-indulgent to even consider such a thing on the night of Slim's Passing Ceremony.

Sonny and Evanna were dressed in their best clothes and in just a few hours would join what would undoubtedly be a large gathering to honor the passing of Slim. Because it was a Hellfire Incident there would only be a small iron box with the remains at the ceremony. The box would be committed to the ground at a later date. This was just the formal matter of the Passing.

Evanna brought Sonny a cup of the warm rose petal blood. She rubbed her son's shoulder as he looked out the front window. Because Slim's house was so secluded from the street and everyone knew that he and Sonny were teamed for these qualifying runs, dozens of roses and cards were laid on the Legatuses' front yard. It seemed every ten minutes or so someone would stop and add something to the pile.

Sonny sighed and looked at the clock on the dining room wall. He couldn't imagine standing around for hours in this suit. He sipped the cup and handed it back to his mother.

"I need to get some air." He tried to offer a genuine smile but failed miserably, wrinkling his lips dismally.

Evanna moved her head gently that she understood and brought his cup to the kitchen. With another group of vampires showing up in the yard to leave gifts, Sonny opted to leave through the back door. Once outside, he swung his arms and drew hard breaths of the chilly air. Autumn had crept in early and the cooler air seemed to be perfectly cued with the events of the last two days.

Sonny loosened the tie around his neck and paced in his back yard. He knelt to grab a few rocks to throw and his hands felt something. He brought it from the grass and stood examining it in the moonlight. *Ha, it's those needle nose pliers of Slim's*, he thought. Before the last Run they had been looking everywhere for them. He smiled and impulsively stepped toward Slim's garage, eager to show him. His eyes grew wide and he felt like he would gag once he realized what just happened. He coughed and tried to shake off the feeling. Slowly, he turned his eyes toward Slim's house. There were no lights on and at this distance it was just a shadowy form near the riverbank. Once the best place in the world for Sonny to be, now it seemed morbid to look at it.

Sonny threw the pliers on the ground and began walking toward Slim's garage. He crossed the same field he had his whole life, but now with a lump in his

throat. When he reached the fence where he and Slim had had so many long talks, he could see Slim's old rusty truck in the driveway. The R.E.D. Agents had driven it back there and it still had R.E.D. incident ribbon on it. The house, too, had R.E.D. incident tape on the door and windows. Sonny stood at the door looking at the tape wondering what they would actually do to you if you crossed it. He cocked his head and thought that he could probably step through the space between the ribbons criss-crossing the doorway. He reached out and wiggled the doorknob but it was locked. He could hardly remember that door ever being locked. He thought for a second, then looked up. He stepped up on the tips of his toes and reached for the jackalope skull that hung above the doorway. Slim had told Sonny that he had shot this horned hare in the farthest Southern woods of the Lowlands and that there were herds of these animals down there. Sonny gently unscrewed the right antler from the head. Slim had bored out the skull and threaded the horn. At the end of the antler Slim had carved the bone to match his house key. It fit perfectly in the lock and the door pushed open. Sonny looked at the ribbons again, wondering if he might be able to squeeze in but finally just walked through the R.E.D. tape, wadding it up.

"I guess they'll have to find me first," Sonny said out loud. Slim had always said that when he did something questionable. Sonny cracked a genuine smile for the first time since he came home two days ago and immediately bumped his head on the tool cupboard in Slim's hall.

The light was in the middle of the room and Sonny had always bumped his head on that cupboard each time he walked in to that room in the dark. He pulled the light on and looked around Slim's garage, slowly rubbing his head. He sighed. It was such an incredibly eerie feeling to look at the big workshop-house without the company of Slim. Sure, Sonny had been there alone before, but now this place that had felt like more of a home than his own, seemed like a building that had been abandoned for a century. It was musty and dead as if been pulled from the bottom of the sea. Just a garage full of meaningless clutter, each heap having a distant memory attached to it. Everywhere he looked in the room he would picture Slim working on the bike or telling a story. He wanted so badly for Slim to just walk out of the washroom, saying *'Sonny boy! Where the hell ya been!'* .

That thought made his knees weak and Sonny sat down at the worktable, grabbing its edges. At once his jaw and his hands shook. It felt like his chest was being crushed. Sitting there he felt so alone in the world. Slim had always made any problem seem easy. Nothing frightened Slim. There had been so many times over the years that Sonny thought he wouldn't have the courage or know how to do something, and without even knowing, Slim had shown him everything he needed to do. Slim had taught him how to face his fears.

"Why did you have to leave now?" Sonny's voice echoed in the room.

He suddenly felt like he was suffocating. The Pike's Run that he had been so certain about, that he was ready to end his days over, was now a frightening prospect with every eye in the Realm on him. Sonny wished he hadn't any part of the Pike, that he could just quietly disappear and not be a vamp that anybody watched or cheered for. He slid from the chair and onto his knees at the worktable. He dug his fingers into the wood and opened his mouth. He was so terrified he couldn't even scream, he just rocked his head and stared at the ceiling.

"Save my soul just one more time." He coughed and hit his fists on the table.

"Come on!" He pleaded to the empty house. "Come on!"

Musical accompaniment for this scene:
"Come On, Come On"
FROM THE ALBUM "RISE OF THE CAFE RACER"
DEANO JONES & THE SWEET DEATH SYMPHONY

He waited and stared at the walls, praying that Slim could somehow come back, or tell him what to do. But it felt like a mausoleum.

After a few minutes, he sighed and stood up. It didn't make any sense to him, but oddly he felt as if a small weight had been lifted. It was as if coming there had allowed him to fully accept Slim's passing and he was grateful he had gone to the garage. Going first to Slim's home was at least much more personal than what he was expecting later at the very public Passing ceremony.

The tiniest of smiles formed in the side of his mouth and he was grateful he had come to the workshop. He looked around the room again before leaving. He was nearly startled out of his skin to see an R.E.D. Agent standing in the doorway.

"Oh!' He yelled.

Sonny looked completely confused and wondered if the Agent had come about the tape at the door.

"Sorry, kid, I didn't mean to startle you." Hellamina raised her hand apologetically.

The Detective held onto the doorframe with one hand and calmly looked over the whole room. She would stop and stare at an object, then move on slowly. Sonny stood silent next to the worktable wondering what was going to happen. When Hellamina's gaze returned to Sonny he swallowed hard.

"I guess this is about the… " Sonny pointed at her.

Hellamina looked curiously at Sonny, not knowing what he was talking about. He straightened his posture and cleared his throat. "What I mean to say is, yes, I did. I removed that tape." He looked down at the shiny black shoes that matched his suit. "I just, uh, really wanted to come in here, Agent. I…"

"Relax, that's not why I'm here." She looked at the wadded-up R.E.D. tape and laughed gently.

"I'm Detective Hellamina Muntz." she walked to the worktable and extended her hand. "I'm the Agent assigned to Slim's Hellfire Incident."

Sonny was visibly relieved finding out that the Agent wasn't there to charge him for removing the tape. When she laughed he realized it was probably a bit absurd to think they could have known and responded so soon anyway. Sonny recognized her name.

"You ran in the Pike with Slim, didn't you?"

"Yes, I did," she nodded.

Sonny had heard stories from Slim about the wild female vamp from Tamerlane dressed like a male that made it all the way to the Top Eight.

"Were you friends with Slim?" Sonny asked quietly.

Hellamina looked thoughtfully around the garage with all Slim's belongings. She turned back to Sonny and rocked her head slowly. "I hadn't seen Slim in a very long time." She sighed warmly. "But we were good friends."

Sonny nodded and looked at her uniform. The Detective had snapped her leather riding gloves to the epaulet on her jackets right shoulder. Agents of the motorbike division of the R.E.D. wore heavy black jackets that zipped up the left side. They also wore heavy, waxed black denim trousers tucked into their knee high, lace-less boots. Hellimina had on the same uniform except the trousers. Instead she wore heavy-duty knit leggings with leather panel accents on the knees and outer thighs. All Agents had batons secured on the back of their jackets. It was a sign of impending doom when an Agent reached to the back of his or her neck to reign down a baton strike in one fell swoop.

As he studied her uniform, it struck Sonny odd that the R.E.D. would be "investigating" the incident. As unbelievable as it sounded, it seemed clear to the three Agents that delivered the news that Slim had simply wandered into the daylight.

"There's an investigation?" Sonny asked humbly. "I mean, is there any suspicion surrounding this?"

Hellamina stared rigidly at Sonny as if deciding whether she would answer this as the Detective or as Slim's friend. Gradually she relaxed her shoulders and leaned her head to the side.

"I'm always suspicious at every Hellfire Incident. Not necessarily for foul play, but simply how any vampire can find themselves caught in the light in this day and age." She shook her head in disbelief. "Even if you've drunk more than you should, how could this still be happening?"

She became lost in her own thoughts for a moment as she recalled the countless hours she had spent on and around Incident scenes, tracing the steps of the victims to find ridiculously preventable circumstances that led to the demise of a vampire. She quickly came back from her fog and shot a pessimistic eye at Sonny.

"But when I find Slim Jim at a Hellfire, I'm more than suspicious. He was the most resilient vampire I have ever met."

She faded back to her thoughts recalling a time about a hundred and eighty years before. She Slim had been drinking past Dawn at a dayhouse in

Formoria, on the northern coast. Slim had gambled all the treasure from the mariners they were merrymaking with. When the room ran out of wine Slim knew that wouldn't help these ornery Dooners feel too well about this stranger taking them for all their treasure. It wasn't uncommon for a traveler to be accused of a petty crime and end up leaving town with a few less digits than he came in with. So, long before that would happen, Slim fashioned a portable dayhouse from a child's wagon, curtain rods and a black tarp. He crossed the road to another dayhouse and purchased a case of deer wine and returned a hero. He also started what is now a popular practice in the north of using covered wagons, or a "day tortoise," to move goods in the daytime. Only in the north though; most Lowlanders wouldn't be anywhere near the daylight and considered the vamps in the north insane to do so.

Before Slim would walk his day tortoise that morning in Formoria, Hellamina would beg him not to go, asking him why he would risk getting exposed to daylight for some wine. Slim had simply told her *'There's nothing wrong with a calculated risk.'* Slim had then looked at the drunk mariners, who by that time were arguing amongst themselves and out of liquor, and smiled at Hellamina, *'Before the day is over, these vamps would likely take my hands, my treasure and my girl.'* He winked and ventured into the day.

Recalling these memories brought on incredible sadness to the R.E.D. Agent. It seemed so long ago now. She thought of all the misfortune and injustice that had followed Slim, and thought of her own loss of not ending up with him. Slim was the only vampire Hellamina had ever loved. She had thought that they were made to be together, but there was a dark cloud that followed Slim and he needed to keep moving so as not to get stuck under it. As a result, she only spent a short time traveling with Slim.

Hellamina looked again at Sonny. She recalled him from the SDS event last week at Vanderpooles. She had watched at how even the disaffected souls of the city's underbelly were electrified by him and had locked arms in song at his lead. The Pike is what had shone the light on Sonny, but he had something that drew you to him. It reminded her of Slim. As he stood there in his suit, looking far more handsome and mature than she remembered, her throat choked with emotion. Hellamina turned and walked to the entryway as if she was leaving, but only gently pushed the front door closed. She stepped back to the worktable as Sonny looked at her wide eyed.

"Sonny, I want to tell you a story." She suggested with her hand that he sit at the table.

Hellamina walked to the incubator knowing that there would be a couple bottles of Hell Blood and returned, opening them on the table.

"Fifty-six years ago, when you were just an infant, your mother had a horrible accident. Well…" Hellamina sipped lightly from her bottle to wet her lips, "She was the victim of a horrible accident. Marcus Von Firstenstein left an alehouse inebriated and ran over Evanna in the street with his motorcar. Marcus is the former KOTU Trevor Von Firstenstein's son, and is Dracov's nephew." Hellamina drew a deep breath.

"While your mother lay in an unconscious state, doctors not knowing if she could be saved, our KOTU Vladimir Von Firstenstein was hard at work doing damage control. Marcus hadn't even stopped after hitting your mother and even tried to deny being there. It was a huge embarrassment for the KOTU as well as the entire High Council."

Hellamina sat down across from Sonny, she had his complete and undivided attention. Sonny had always wondered about the details of this event that no one ever seemed to want to speak about.

"Doctors were saying that they would need all the Realm's medical resources to save her. It would be incredibly expensive and even then, they didn't know if she would make it. Evanna had little or no treasure to speak of. Her husband was an unconventional vampire who had shunned the Specialty and had no profession, no savings, and little income."

Sonny became alert with anticipation of mention of his mother's husband but didn't dare interrupt the Agent.

"The KOTU publicly announced that the Von Firstensteins would provide for these medical charges, which would help with the initial recovery. But Evanna would also need a few years of staffed care. Not wanting to risk public outcry against the shameful Marcus Von Firstenstein's behavior, the KOTU went on to add the the Von Firstensteins would provide that extra care and even more—a home, free of charge for Evanna. During this time, former KOTU Dracov Von Firstenstein, Vlad's father, had intervened and pushed the High Council to resolve that in exchange for the generosity of the Von Firstensteins, providing what Evanna's husband could not—that this shameful vampire would be required to forego his name and family. That Evanna's husband could no longer use his own name in the Realm and would no longer have the right to his wife and child, that they too would forego their name and revert to Evanna's maiden name of Legatus. He would have to agree to a Blood Oath."

Sonny had heard of Blood Oaths in ancient stories and knew that breaking one would bring physical destruction to a vampire. You swore with your soul to uphold a Blood Oath.

"There were some who disapproved," Hellamina drank from her bottle, "But the Von Firstensteins are cunning and Dracov knows his Rules. There is an ancient Rule that is mostly used for disputes with property and bloodstock, but states very clearly that if a vampire cannot provide for his debt, public or private, then the payer of this debt may dictate the terms of said debt. Once agreed upon, the terms will be Rule and upheld by the sword of the Realm."

"Evanna's husband..." She paused. "Your *father* had no choice. He had no means to provide for her medical care. Without that care she would have certainly expired and died from this world. It was a difficult thing to do, I'm sure, but he did it to provide for you both."

Sonny was filled with emotion. He had resisted speaking so that he may absorb every detail of what the Agent was saying. But so many questions were running through his mind now. So many that would question the authority of the Von Firstensteins to request such a thing, and also why would they demand such a horrible term to someone that had been wronged by their kin. But more than anything he just wanted to know who this vampire was who had sacrificed his name and right to his family— who was his father?

Sonny simply stared at Hellamina. He knew that he did not need to tell a detective what question was burning on his mind. It was the question that had burned on his mind and weighed heavy on his heart for as long as he could remember. In an instant he realized that this R.E.D. Agent was going to tell him who his father was and he suddenly became nervous. He drank long from the bottle of Hell Blood and clenched his fists to prevent his hands from shaking.

Hellamina's eyes were fixed on Sonny's and she drew a heavy breath.

"I'm telling you this because that vampire, your father, was named James Nightshade." She paused and swallowed hard. "And until two days ago, he lived in this house and was known only as Slim Jim from the day of the Blood Oath."

Sonny furrowed his brow and shook his head no. He felt at once like both freezing and boiling blood was coursing through his veins. He couldn't tell what he thought about from one moment to the next. *This can't be possible,* he thought. There were feelings from years of suffering without a father, crashing against the elation that finding out the vampire whom he had admired most in the world was his father. It was bittersweet and horrific, relieving and enraging, plus painfully sad, all at the same time.

The two of them just looked at each other for a couple minutes. Sonny calmly allowed each emotion to rear up and posses him until they all had taken their turn. Slowly, as each demon fought its way through his consciousness, a resolve washed over him. *'Those are just things that have already happened'* Slim had said a thousand times. And once again, Sonny thought, Slim was right. All the other questions Sonny thought were so important didn't matter anymore. Or at least not at this moment. This was all history now. It was done.

Then, as if a tiny light was shining in the far distance, guiding him to find the path to the good in this news, the beautiful notion appeared in his mind that at the least Sonny had been given the opportunity to love his father… even if he hadn't known it at the time. An odd peacefulness crept over Sonny's spirit as he realized the tragedy that would have been if he had found out his father passed without ever knowing him.

"You know, at Suntora I had wished so much that Slim could be my father," Sonny smiled painfully, "I guess my wish was granted."

Telling this story, Hellamina thought about all the stories she had ever heard of Slim. The uprising, with Dracov denying Slim admission to the R.E.D. The Pike, that Dracov again tried to thwart Slim from entering. The accident, with Slim's wife being stuck by a car driven by a Von Firstenstein. Someone might wonder if the Von Firstensteins wouldn't be happy to hear that Slim Jim Nightshade had been found out in the day.

Sonny looked at Hellamina and thought about the words he was about to say. In spite of her uniform and imposing nature, Sonny couldn't see her as an R.E.D. Agent right now. He didn't ask Hellamina, but simply stated, "You think that the Von Firstensteins destroyed Slim."

Hellamina didn't pause to wonder if she would reply as an **R.E.D.** Agent or as a friend of James Nightshade to his son. The Detective replied calmly, "Yes. Yes, I do."

CHAPTER TWENTY NINE: FUNERAL FOR A VAMPIRE

It was almost High Midnight and several hundred vampires were already assembled at Death's Landing for the Passing ceremony by the time Sonny and Evanna arrived. The Legatuses had ridden with Andi, Toland and Anastasia Kepler, and then walked the footpath that led the short distance up to the Landing. Soon they would all stand together at the Alter as the KOTU spoke over the remains.

Death's Landing was a clearing on a set of foothills in Cambria that overlooked the Capital City. In the early years of the Realm, shortly After Death Was Born, a small group of vampires had traveled up through the Hammerton Mountains and stood on that landing looking onto the valley, deciding it would be an ideal location for a settlement. From that day forward, Death's Landing would be the site for the most important ceremonies within the Capital. When vampires wed, their "Houses of the Holy Union" would take place at the Landing, as well as the "Passing" funerals. Even the King Of The Undead inauguration was held there.

In this case, the R.E.D. had provided an urn for Slim's remains. Normally a vampire's urn or coffin would reflect his Specialty in the Realm; the R.E.D. had provided an official Agent urn and there had already been internal squabbling within the High Council about this. The R.E.D. insisted that Slim's service in the uprising provided for such an urn, while Vlad argued his father's ruling—that the metal plate had rendered Slim 'impure' for the Rules Enforcement Division. The R.E.D. was unyielding, and the KOTU, in the interest of keeping the argument from going public, conceded to the use of an Agent urn.

The crowd was becoming enormous. Vampires had come from far and wide to pay respect for Slim, and there was also the added spectacle of the Pike, now only days away. Vampires who ordinarily would have never come out that night were filling the surrounding field near the Alter and even lining the streets on the hill. The incident itself had become an extension of the last run, with wild rumors that Slim had sacrificed himself in an effort to provide a spirit guardian to his Rider and help him take First Prize from the Von Firstensteins. As ridiculous as that sounded, gossip and speculation of devilry were fueling the mania of this Pike and reaching all corners of the Realm.

Sonny held Andi's hand tightly as they stood near the Alter with the large, black urn placed in the middle of the platform. The R.E.D. urn was a sort of miniature coffin intricately decorated with a carving of a sleeping vampire, sword in one hand, rose in another. There were HellHounds and Gargoyles carved on all corners, woven together with more swords and axes. It was a magnificent work of sculpture and clearly a warrior's burial urn.

After everyone had assembled, seven vampires carrying various horns stood and took the Alter. The already respectfully quiet crowd became entirely silent. Almost nine hundred vampires crowded around an urn, and hundreds more trailing down the hills, and you could hear a pin drop. In part because of the timeliness of this event to the Pike, there was an underlying association to it and sense of Realm pride, but also because the Funeral March of a Vampire was quite possibly the saddest piece of music ever created. Vampires didn't die off that often and when they did, the Funeral March was always performed at the Passing ceremony. When you heard the heavy-hearted moaning of a horn section play that song, you couldn't help but be filled with bereavement. Even humming it in a crowded alehouse could have the same effect. It simply spoke to every vampire.

It was no different on this night. As the clock struck Midnight, miles away near Norwood Park, the horns wailed slowly from the Alter.

Sonny stood firmly at attention, mirroring the dozens of R.E.D. Agents to his right. The High Council members and Von Firstenstein clan were standing on the opposite side of the Alter. Daryn and Bebe were almost directly across from Sonny. Bebe held Daryn's arm and looked like a sitting Queen. Her eyes met Sonny's and Bebe wrinkled her forehead for him with genuine grief. Sonny pressed his lips together tightly as a 'thank you'.

Vladimir sat stoically with his wife Tessa. Normally both former KOTUs Dracov and Trevor Von Firstenstein would attend a Passing of this significance, despite whatever their personal opinions were of the vampire who passed. But as both ex-KOTUs were currently caretakers of the retirement communities in Kindurba and Rogue Canyon respectively, they were instead en route to Strigoi for the Pike's Run.

Sonny looked around the crowd as the horns played and couldn't help but think of everything Hellamina had told him. He imagined what it must have been like for Slim all these years, living like a dog behind his family's home. Never able to speak his name or tell Sonny and Evanna that he was their kin, or tell Sonny that he was his blood. The forces of the Realm had tried so hard to shame and break Slim but he had remained strong, almost defiantly the opposite of what most would think a vampire would do in similar circumstances.

When the Funeral March of the Vampire finished, the KOTU approached the Alter to read the required words of a Passing. Sonny became agitated. He felt a sense of pride and purpose unlike anything he had every felt. He knew who he was now. *I am the son of James Nightshade*, he thought. It almost made Sonny laugh out loud at the obviousness of what was happening. Like anvil weights rolling off his shoulders, Slim's passing suddenly freed Sonny from the chains of uncertainty. The knowledge of who he was had not only guaranteed that Slim would live on, but it also made it abundantly clear that Sonny had only one duty. He would carry on in his father's name and restore the honor that the Von Firstensteins had worked so tirelessly to destroy.

Sonny stared at the KOTU. He watched as Vladimir's lips moved, reciting the passages that spoke of permitting the recently expired vampires soul into the Kingdom of the Dead. Sonny couldn't even hear the words, he just glared at the KOTU feeling an overwhelming sense of purpose. Sonny tilted his head back and drew a deep breath as he heard the KOTU ask if there were any vampires who would like to say any words on Slim's behalf. Most in attendance, at least within proximity of the Alter, had assumed that Sonny would be saying something, but none were prepared for what he spoke.

Sonny stepped forward, not on the Alter, but enough to separate himself from the crowd. His words rang like a defiant song with a voice so loud and powerful it carried down the hillside:

There's no time left to tell you.
No words could ever make it right.
Like smoke that drifts away in time,
You have risen to the other side.
You don't need us to tell you,
You've gone beyond the Realm and sight.
This life was just a passing spell,
Now you're walking through the Gates of Hell.
I found my strength besides you.
I'll keep our dream awake in spite of the dying souls,
Death and demise.
Running while my bones are still alive.
They may have tried to kill you,
But you still walk among us.
I bet the Underworld will know it well,
When you're walking through the Gates of Hell.

Gone are the days, your life has passed.

I'll see you again when the days are end.

I will avenge you, Death won't pass.

Into the darkness, life everlast at last.

I'll follow long and slowly, their Houses of the Holy die.

Your life they couldn't steal or sell,

As you're walking through the Gates of Hell.

Fear has left me screaming. The life I had is leaving now.

Like a son who loved his Father well, I will follow to the Gates of Hell.

Musical accompaniment for this scene:
"Funeral March of the Vampire/Gates of Hell"
FROM THE ALBUM "RISE OF THE CAFE RACER"
DEANO JONES & THE SWEET DEATH SYMPHONY

As Sonny finished his words he looked intently at the KOTU. Vladimir's nostrils flared as he drew air and stared back at his son's challenger to the title of King of the Undead. Other Council members sat with similar expressions of surprise at Sonny. Passings were not the place for such words or the confrontational way he was behaving.

Daryn was staring at Sonny as well, but with a peculiar eye. As much as Daryn had always singled Sonny out for ribbing before their qualifying runs, it had been mostly at the request of his father to intimidate the competition. That, and the fact that Sonny tutored Bebe, had made it easy for Daryn to justify hating him. But something about the way Sonny had just spoken struck a chord with Daryn. It was as if he had just now seen Sonny as something more than a concept to hate, or a generic common bat. Sonny suddenly appeared much more complex. And if the way that the KOTU was staring at Sonny was any indication, there was a lot more to this cafe racing Rider's story than met the eye. One thing was for certain, Sonny had a look of determination that Dayrn had never seen before, in any vampire. It was as if Sonny had just declared war on the Realm for what happened to Slim.

Maybe for the first time in his life, Daryn had a genuine sense of admiration for another vampire. Not the fear, or obligatory reverence for elders and family that his father had demanded, but genuine respect. It was exhilarating to witness and for a moment Daryn felt a kinship to Sonny—kinship that was beyond explanation. Daryn felt like he could take arms and follow this vampire into battle. To claim their world, their moments in time. It was indescribable, and Daryn's upper lip curled slightly in awe of what he was witnessing. Daryn stared at his father who was still locked on Sonny. His father breathed heavy and looked at him. Daryn went cold. He had never, ever, seen fear in his Father's eyes... until this moment. Daryn knew in an instant that the KOTU saw the same transformation in Sonny and saw a real threat that Sonny could win the Pike and take the title from the Von Firstensteins.

Four R.E.D. Agents had taken the Alter and began walking the urn with Slim's remains down the hill. The Legatus's and Keplers had filed in directly behind. The KOTU and group of High Council members had followed and were still visibly affected by Sonny's words, staring unbelieving at the Rider as he walked by.

At the bottom of the hill the KOTU held the door to his large motorcar as the Lady KOTU, Daryn and Bebe stepped in. Before getting in himself he glared at Sonny and shut his door.

As they held the doors of the Kepler's motorcar for the Ladies, Toland looked across the hood at Sonny. Toland squinted until Sonny looked at him.

"I don't know exactly what happened up there," Toland said calmly, "But I do know that I've never seen Vladimir Von Firstenstein look scared until today."

Sonny looked back with no expression. Toland closed the door and leaned onto the roof of the motorcar.

"If you have decided to go to Strigoi, you'll need help." Toland sighed and lightened the mood, "At least let me drive that old rusty truck of Slim's for you."

An easy smile finally broke on Sonny's face for the first time that day and he nodded gratefully. Toland acknowledged their 'deal' with a light-hearted tap on the car roof. But as they both moved to get in the motorcar he added sternly.

"There's never been a Pike's Run like this one. You might just make history, Sonny boy."

CHAPTER THIRTY:
COSTUME PARTY

"You haven't even touched your drink," Bebe pouted at Daryn from behind her mask.

Daryn sighed and took the musketeer hat he was wearing from his head. "I'm sorry, I'm just not in much of a party mood."

Bebe quietly raised her floor-length, bustled skirt to one side, exposing her gartered leg. She wore a corset around her waist and above that, a deep-cut blouse that displayed her abundant cleavage. Her hair was in huge curls pinned up into a massive mound on top of her head, with long, loose pieces flowing on either side.

The Von Firstensteins were hosting a costume ball before the mass exodus down to Strigoi for the Ninth Pike's Run. Largely all of the High Council families as well as the Capital's most affluent vampires were in attendance. Most guests wore similarly ancient costumes of vintage fencers, musketeers, harlots, Ladies, and everything in between. As usual for functions the KOTU hosted, it was well attended, made even more exciting by the fact that the Pike was only three nights away.

"What kind of party would you rather have?" Bebe purred, touching Daryn's leg with her foot.

Daryn stared blankly at Bebe. She acted like a cat behind her mask, pawing at him. He looked at her outfit and gently smiled. She was truly beautiful and had tried very hard to make that whole costume party tolerable for him. Over the past weeks of the qualifying runs Bebe had been going out of her way to be accommodating, probably because of the pressure she knew Daryn was under with the trials, but no doubt trying to be on her best behavior for the impending wedding proposal that both of their families were expecting before the final Pike Run.

To any vampire in the Realm, marrying Bebe and carrying his father's torch would seem like an absolute dream. Who wouldn't want all that? But now more than ever, Daryn was unsure of everything in his world. He felt completely helpless to determine any of his own destiny, especially after hearing Sonny's transformative words at the Passing the night before.

The way Sonny had stood defiantly in front of the KOTU and the whole Realm made Daryn realize he had never done anything of his own. Every single event in his life was already predestined and predetermined. The only thing he could claim his own was the immature bullying he had become known for... hated for. Even this race, and the Pike's Run, it was commonly expected by most that he would win and carry on the tradition of the Von Firstensteins as reigning KOTUs. It was now actually exciting to him that this unknown vamp had come up and rattled the chains of everyone with his ambition to win the Pike. Daryn imagined not winning, not coming back to marry Bebe and do his father's bidding. He imagined just walking away from the next seven or eight hundred years of what was planned for him. Of course one problem with those fantasies was that there was the nasty business of only one Rider ever returning from a Pike. But there was so much secrecy surrounding that portion of the Pike, it was hard to think of it realistically.

"Thanks, but I'm just…" Daryn shook his head. "I guess I'm just thinking about the Pike again."

Bebe frowned and stepped close to him, putting her arms around his neck. She swayed gently as if dancing and whispered, "Maybe what you should be thinking of is AFTER the Pike." She batted her eyes. "We will have nothing but time to do whatever we want. My father said he would send us on a holiday anywhere we choose." She lightly tapped her perfect, white teeth together as she pressed herself against him. "You know, if we were… thinking about our future that way." Bebe lowered her chin and looked adorably at him.

Daryn sighed and felt irritated. As if it weren't bad enough that his father was constantly insinuating that they should wed, now Bebe had started.

"Now that's a lovely picture!" Vladimir bellowed at Alex Bellmore from behind Daryn.

"It certainly is," Alex agreed loudly, "Makes me wonder what their little ones would look like."

The KOTU pulled Bebe's hand from Daryn and kissed it. "You look absolutely stunning as always, Brianna."

"Thank you, Sir," Bebe curtsied for effect back at the KOTU and kissed her Father's cheek.

"Good evening, Sir," Daryn held out his hand for Alex.

"Nice to see you, Son," Alex nodded as he grabbed Daryn's hand. "What a wonderful night. There's not much that could happen that would make a night like this any better."

"Oh I can think of one thing," the KOTU said with feigned shyness and then broke out laughing. Alex chuckled back at him and Bebe clutched Daryn's hand.

After a second of uncomfortable silence Alex piped up at Daryn. "So you must be getting excited about Strigoi, eh, Son?"

Daryn was nauseated by this entire exchange, particularly that Alex Bellmore had called him "Son" twice, and he immediately seized this moment. "You know, I really am, Sir. In fact…" he turned to Bebe. "If you would all excuse me, I'm leaving at first dark tomorrow and am truly exhausted."

Bebe's jaw dropped and Alex looked dumbfounded as Daryn started to pull away. The KOTU narrowed his eyes at his son. "Before you go anywhere,

Son, I have something for you. Come into the study, would you?"

Vladimir smiled a warm fake smile and waited for his son to walk in front of him. Daryn made an even larger fake smile back at his Father and walked to the study. Once inside, the KOTU shut the door behind him and drew a deep breath. He continued with a sense of fabricated excitement and went to his desk drawer. He drew a long skeleton key from his vest pocket and opened the top drawer of his gigantic four-hundred-year-old desk.

"I found something that is perfect for the occasion. It took a little while," He chuckled. "I had almost forgotten where I had put it, it's been so long. This belonged to your great-great-grandmother, Eva Von Firstenstein, Lady KOTU to Lazarus."

Vladimir handed a small black velvet box to Daryn who froze with suspicion. As Daryn opened it up he grimaced in anger. There was a large, oval, black diamond ring inside. It was a mesmerizing stone on a platinum setting of tiny eagle talons.

"I even had it sized for Brianna," The KOTU smiled.

Daryn slammed the ring on the desk. "I will NOT be forced to do this! I told you if I decide to wed, you will be the first to know!"

The KOTU tapped his fingertips together in front of his chest patiently.

"Daryn," He spoke gently, "In four nights' time you will be the sitting King of the Undead in the Realm, and you will be your own vampire. You'll be free to do whatever you fancy." He exhaled nonchalantly and sat on the edge of his desk.

"But Son, a KOTU needs a Lady KOTU." Vlad hardened his gaze. "The Realm needs a Lady KOTU."

Daryn stared bitterly at his father, breathing heavy. He began shaking his head in disbelief.

"Free?" Daryn coughed. "I'll be free after the Pike? Ha, that's a laugh! The only way I'll be free is if I don't win that race."

For an instant the KOTU's eyes flared with ferocity, but he refrained from speaking. Vlad stared at the small box on the desk. After a few moments he slid it slowly into the desk drawe from which it had come. Gradually a grim smile appeared across his face.

"I believe I've neglected my duties as a father," Vlad shook his head as if he was having a realization of how difficult a time Daryn was having. "This is a troublesome time right now. I understand." Vlad smiled genuinely at Daryn. "I won't ask you again, Son, you have my word."

Daryn was a bit stunned. He kept waiting for the catch or his father's conditions, but the KOTU just watched his son silently. Daryn managed to simply nod back at his father and mutter, "Thank you," as he started toward the door.

"Oh, just one thing, Son. If you could just stay and stand with your family while I toast our guests, I would appreciate it deeply." He smiled. "Then you're done."

Daryn paused, deciding that he wouldn't have a problem with that.

"Of course."

"Wonderful." Vlad moved from the desk and the two quickly made their way back to the main room of the social.

As he crossed the ballroom The KOTU signaled staff for deer wine and asked Bebe to join them at the front of the room. Vlad waved to his wife Tessa and she walked to the front of the room as well.

There were a couple hundred of the capital's most affluent socialites in attendance. The room quickly quieted when Vlad lightly tapped his wine glass with a dinner fork.

"I would first like to thank all our lovely guests for joining us tonight. The Lady KOTU rarely needs an excuse to throw one of our costumed balls, but we thought it long overdue and what better time than days before the Ninth Pike's Run."

Polite clapping spread across the room.

"But we are also celebrating our son Daryn's heroic rise through the ranks to be one of the Final Two Riders!"

The clapping continued, gaining volume with some cheering as well. After a moment the room returned to only a few whispers.

"And lastly, but certainly not least. We would like to raise our glasses…" Vlad paused until every glass in the room was in the air.

"I am proud and pleased to announce the Houses of the Holy Union that will take place between Brianna Bellmore and my son, Daryn Von Firstenstein."

Daryn's entire body jerked stiff like he had been electrically shocked. He glared at his father. Bebe's mouth opened wide screaming with joy. She hugged Daryn wildly as the KOTU led the room in three 'Hip, hip…hooray!'s. Bebe instantly saw the look on Daryn's face and knew that something was wrong and that the KOTU may have forced this. She felt Daryn's chest gathering deep breaths as if he were planning to howl at the top of his lungs painfully at the end of the partygoers chanting.

Bebe pressed her mouth to his ear as the room cheered. "I am truly sorry if this was not your doing, Daryn. I truly am. But please, please, I beg of you, do not humiliate me right now. This was not my doing." She pulled her head from his ear and stared earnestly at him.

Daryn stared back at Bebe, enraged. His anger was tunneling his vision and everything around her face had gone black. Time slowed down the way it had when he'd wrecked his motorcar two summers ago. The only thing keeping him in that moment was Bebe's look of desperation. Her eyes were begging for mercy and she clutched him tightly. Something about the way she was looking at him was unsettling. She was so raw and vulnerable, as if offering her entire soul to him. Daryn swallowed hard as the crowd died down. As angry as he was at his father for this, he knew how devastating it would be to refute the announcement right now. It would shame both entire families, and most of all Bebe.

The room grew still as the crowd waited for Daryn's words. The KOTU held his glass high like a stone statue and smiled intently at his son. Daryn slowly looked around the room at familiar faces and friends. He reached out to the waitstaff vampire who stood with a bottle of deer wine, wrapped in a towel, waiting to refill glasses. Daryn snatched the entire bottle from the waiter and held it out.

"What can I say, I'm the luckiest vampire in the Realm!"

As the entire room erupted with cheering, Daryn finished the half bottle of wine and pushed it aggressively at his father when he finished. The KOTU laughed for display, elbowing Alex and muttering something like 'that's my boy'.

Daryn turned back to Bebe, who pulled him close.

"That is the nicest thing anyone has ever done for me. I thank you from the bottom of my heart."

Daryn made a weary smile and tried to forget what had just happened. He began pulling from her grip but she held tight and continued whispering, "I know that I may not be your first choice, or maybe you just don't even want to wed." Bebe winced and looked seriously at Daryn. "I just want you to know that I would be a loyal and dignified wife and Lady to the Realm. I would always honor you, Daryn."

She quivered as she spoke and Daryn was caught off guard by her emotion. "I have loved you since the very day I laid eyes on you, Daryn. And no matter what happens after this day between us… " Bebe squeezed Daryn tightly and pulled closer. "This is my greatest moment in time. Right here. With you."

She kissed him slowly as several partygoers clapped and 'aww'd at their young love. Daryn gently pulled his head back and smiled at Bebe. In spite of how angry he was at his father for doing this to him, Bebe was actually very comforting right now. Daryn realized that although Bebe had the capacity to be a spoiled brat sometimes, she truly hadn't been difficult in quite a while. In fact, as he held her there, he started to see her in a different light. He had known Bebe for so many years and she was shaping up into a rather mature female vampire very quickly. As Daryn stood looking into the eyes of the girl who had just professed her undying love, he suddenly realized there were far worse things that could have happened to him that night.

"Hmm," Daryn laughed as Bebe smile back at him.

"You know, you just might be the only real friend I have, Bebe."

CHAPTER THIRTY ONE:
GOOD LUCK CHARM

Andi was sneaking looks at Sonny through the gaps between the engine and the motorbike's frame. He had the Cafe Racer up on the worktable at Slim's and had hardly said two words to her since she had gotten there.

Sonny had mentioned earlier that he needed to check the air intake Demon to make sure it was working properly. He told Andi that Daryn had passed him like he was standing still back on the Realm Roadway in the last run and before they packed up for the trip to Strigoi, he wanted to flesh it out at the shop.

Andi had left him alone once she arrived, since Sonny seemed so preoccupied with the last minute tuneup, so she just walked around the shop touching objects and thinking about Slim.

Andi had discovered some rolled-up posters in Slim's bedroom closet and had brought them out to the worktable. Sonny had the bike running on its stand and sipped a Hell Blood while making final twists at the small Demon mechanism. Once he seemed satisfied, he cut the engine and looked back at Andi through the openings in the bike's assembly.

"It seems like it's working perfectly, I don't know what could've happened out there."

Sonny looked tired and Andi suspected he was obsessing about the Cafe Racer in an attempt to not think about Slim. Which, of course, was a little ironic since they were working in the house they had always known Slim to live in. They had discussed it on the ride from the Passing and agreed that it would be easiest to continue to use the shop since it was set up with all the tools and sufficient room. Still, they both knew it was very odd feeling to be working on the bike there now that Slim had passed.

"Maybe Daryn has some sort of Demon of his own," Andi shrugged.

"Whatever he has, he'd better hope it's working properly," Sonny said coldly as he stared at the engine.

Andi hadn't known what to say to him since the night before. Sonny had told them all on the way home everything he had found out from Detective Muntz. He hadn't mentioned who had told him about his identity, only that it was an R.E.D. Agent. It seemed so surreal to Andi and she couldn't imagine how Sonny must have felt to find out only after Slim had passed that he was his father.

Toland reminded them that it was still Rule of Law in the Realm that the name Nightshade continued to be stricken from use. Technically, anyone could be imprisoned for uttering it publicly. *'How could that be allowed to happen?'* Sonny had asked. Toland told him that the KOTU would often go unchallenged by the Council, that it had always been that way. For some reason the King of the Undead always held considerable power when he weighed in on matters. It had given Sonny pause and he remembered that Toland was in the middle of having the Council all but close the doors to K&S over some matter of a Rule infraction. *They just did whatever they wanted whenever they wanted,* Sonny thought.

Andi had untied the strings around the rolled paper and held up a poster for Sonny to see. He looked at it, puzzled.

"Where'd you get that?"

"It was in the bedroom closet. Are these actually from the Uprising?"

They both studied what looked like the propaganda style posters that could still be seen around the Realm. However, these had quite different messaging. One read *"Iron and Coal work better together... than torn apart"* with a working vamp style illustration. Another read simply *"Resist the Uprising! Don't be fooled into fighting!"*

"I guess Slim was probably pretty active in trying to stop the uprising," Andi sighed.

Sonny held the poster close and studied the ink. He hadn't told his mother or the Keplers that the R.E.D. Agent suspected the Von Firstensteins of trying to destroy Slim. If Slim had also been an activist, it would add even more fuel to the suspicion.

Sonny let the poster fall to the table. He looked at Andi and said deliberately, "I must win this Pike." He slowly moved his head side to side. "Think of what a commoner could do with that power."

Andi smiled sadly at Sonny as he stared wildly at her. She had no idea what to say. It broke her heart to think that he would leave Strigoi as one of the two Riders. That hours later, only one one Rider would return. She knew that the new-found knowledge of his father had given him a drive and determination like nothing she had ever seen. But she had also witnessed how the KOTU was breaking her own father in two, smashing the Doctors life's work unchallenged. The Realm took what it wanted and it seemed a fantasy to think that Sonny could take something as enormous as the King of the Undead title from these vampires. She thought that they would destroy anyone or thing in their path to maintain power.

RESIST THE UPRISING

DON'T BE FOOLED INTO FIGHTING

Sonny looked back at the bike. "Well, the Demon's working, I guess we just need lots of luck."

Oh!" Andi squealed and dug into her coat pocket. "I forgot, I have my good luck charm for my Rider!"

She pulled her hand from the large, outside pocket of her long tailed overcoat and produced two fat mice. She gently spilled them onto the table and made a magician type of 'Ta-Da' gesture with her hands.

Sonny pressed his lips together hard and stared skeptically at Andi. He almost laughed, but quickly regained composure. *Surely she can't be serious*, he thought. It was definitely a time-honored tradition for Riders to accept tokens from female vampires for good luck in the runs. And it was actually considered bad luck to not accept if offered. Sonny eventually exhaled hard and cocked his head.

"These are the... human blood mice, yes?" He pointed at the two very docile, well-behaved little mice now standing on hind legs looking at Sonny.

Andi nodded with a big grin.

"According to all my tests, all my mice have 100% pure human blood coursing through their veins. And they are so intelligent. I've been testing their memory skills and social behavior. They are truly different. Regular mice are afraid of the human versions and are almost treated like pets by these little men."

She smiled and put her hand out. Both mice very politely stepped back onto her hand and almost seemed to smile back at her, sitting quietly staring at the two vampires.

"I've done several more injections on myself. So far, no unusual effects. But I have to say, I really feel great." Andi shot a self-conscious glance at Sonny.

"I mean, you know... considering everything."

Sonny reached and put his hand on Andi's shoulder.

"I truly appreciate this thought. I do." He drew a large breath of air. "I just… don't… know about being able to take live animals. I mean, maybe… a lock of hair?"

They both laughed for a moment and Andi leaned in to Sonny, sliding her arm around his waist.

"I just know that you're supposed to give something that's near and dear to you for your Rider." She whispered.

Andi was excited that Sonny had kept his hand on her shoulder as she moved closer to him.

"There's just something really special about them to me. And I want so badly for you to have any advantage you can." She looked up sadly at Sonny and wrapped her other arm around him.

Sonny smiled warmly and leaned down to kiss her. Andi softly closed her eyes and melted a little bit in anticipation of his lips.

Sonny kissed her quickly on the forehead and released her.

"You're the best, Andi. I will have to check if there's anything mentioned about having a live animal, though. You know, I don't want to be disqualified at the starting line."

Sonny looked at his watch and raised his eyebrows. "I told your father we'd be there in thirty minutes. Guess we better get this bike in the truck."

Andi was still standing where she thought she would be getting the first kiss of her life from the vampire of her dreams. She could not understand why, in the last two times they were alone together, he had kissed her on the forehead like a child. She had heard stories of Riders being chased by girls all over the Realm, and she could tell that Sonny was interested in that sort of thing. Just the way he had been acting in the last few weeks, the way he was carrying himself, she knew that he had undoubtedly been with female vampires. *So what is wrong with me?* she thought. *Why does he not see me?*

Sonny lowered the hydraulics on the worktable and had begun pushing the bike out toward the living room. The far living room wall had a rolling garage door and Slim's rusty purple truck was already backed up to the building.

Sonny called behind to Andi as he pushed the motorbike on the truck.

"Would you roll those posters up and bring them?"

"You want to take them to Strigoi?"

Sonny looked back and bit his bottom lip for a moment. He began to nod as if deciding it was a great idea.

"Yeah, there's someone I want to show them to."

Andi shrugged and began rolling the posters back up into one secure roll. Sonny watched her as she bundled them, and before he turned back to fasten the bike down called out.

"Hey."

Andi looked up wide-eyed and ready to help.

"You need a hand?" She tucked the posters under her arm as she looked at him.

"No, no," He smiled. "I just want you to know, that whether or not I can take your mice with me on the Pike… that you've always been my good luck charm." Andi's face went blank. "I couldn't have done this without you, Andi."

She became self-conscious for a few moments, looking down and fidgeting with her hands, but quickly looked back and made a tiny smirk before saying shyly, "Thank you."

They softly grinned at each other from across the room. Just as Sonny was about to turn and attend to the Cafe Racer, Andi's chest heaved slightly as she quickly drew air.

"I love you, Sonny."

His cheeks smiled warmly, making his eyes squint.

"I love you, too."

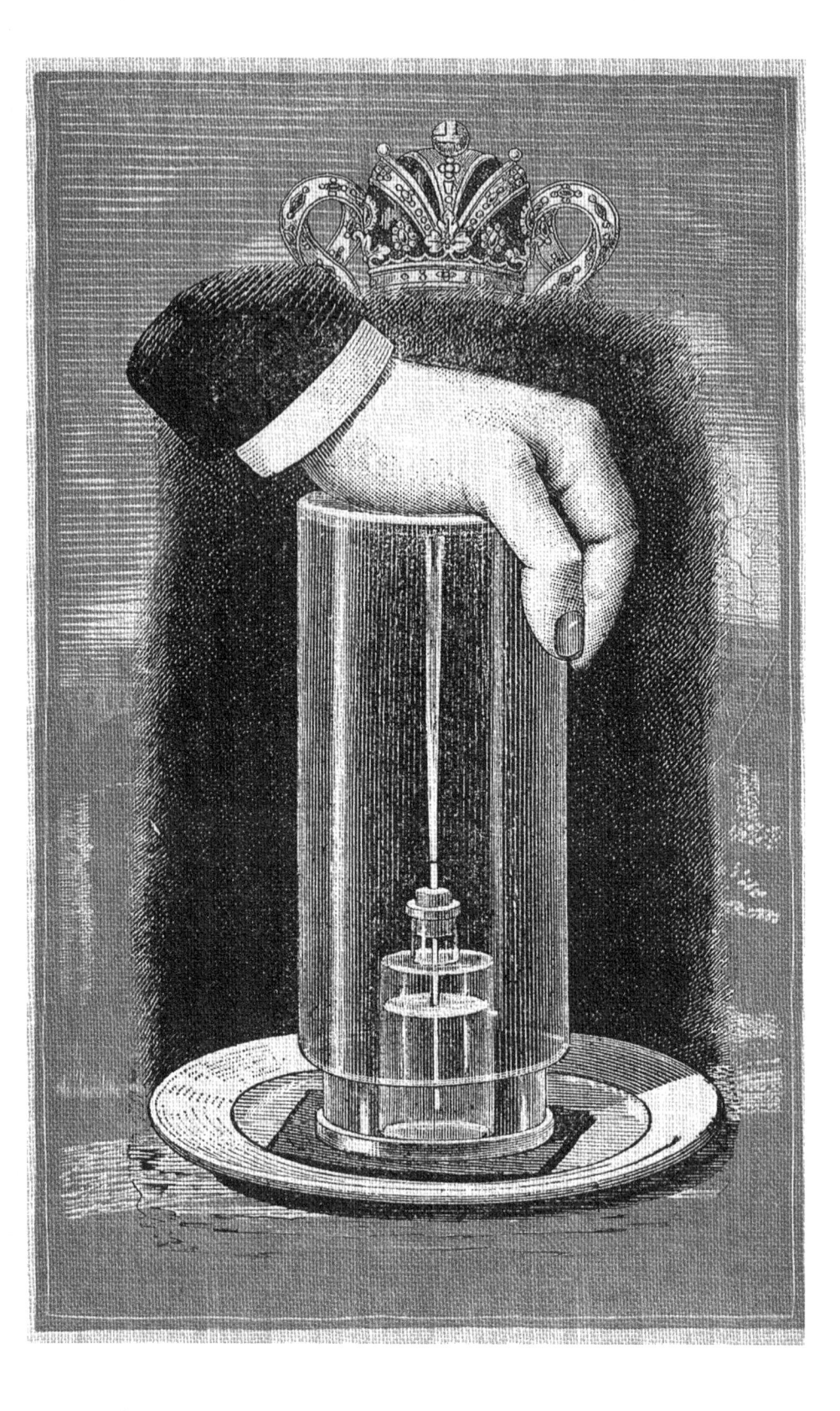

CHAPTER THIRTY TWO:
LEAD WITH A FIRM GRIP

Vladimir Von Firstenstein was collecting scrolls and shuffling paperwork in his official KOTU office. He was doing some last minute double-checking before he and his family would leave for Strigoi. As he closed his briefcase on a stack of papers, he paused and looked around the room. He had been King of the Undead for two terms—two hundred forty-two years. Upon his return from the valley and the Ninth Pike's Run, this would no longer be his office or title.

He would undoubtedly join the ranks of the High Council after a short nomination process—a formality, really—but being the KOTU and sitting on the Council were entirely different. The High Council was a relatively anonymous position, behind the scenes. The KOTU was the spokesperson for the Council and the Realm.

He sighed quietly to himself at the thought of simply blending into the fabric of the Capital aristocracy. In some ways it would be a relief to be out of the driver's seat, but he knew that Daryn would, as he did, need tireless guidance in his first years of KOTU.

As he unhurriedly soaked in the room, Vlad's eyes paused on each oil painting that hung on the walls. Since the Day that Death was Born, every single KOTU had a portrait in oil created of himself that hung in this office. Vlad looked at his own portrait. Next to his own was his father Dracov's portrait. Dracov's brother, Trevor, hung next to that. His grandfather Lazarus hung next, proudly wearing a coat made from the massive bear he had killed at the edge of Wendish Woods. And next to Lazarus was Vlad's great-grandfather and first KOTU to the Realm, Heinrik Von Firstenstein. He smiled at Tessa's "Lady KOTU" portrait on the opposite wall and thought how she will undoubtedly miss this as much as he.

Vlad was proud of the lineage his family had with the King of Undead title. Studying the oils, he was reminded of how troubling it was that Daryn seemed indifferent at times about claiming this throne. There was no way he could convey to Daryn just how important the KOTU position was until after Daryn had won the race, until he took First Prize.

Vlad turned and looked at the First Prize statue in its glass case. He thought how he would hand this to his son after Daryn rode back into the town square at Strigoi. The skull of the last Human with a dagger through its center. A bat with wings folded onto itself was the dagger's handle and seemed fitting. Quiet and contently the vampire on the knife had crushed the Human—morbid symbolism to remind them who they are. What they were.

As Vlad packed the First Prize into a leather traveling suitcase, his mind drifted about all the imagery of their Realm, and about how important it had always been for the KOTU to uphold and reinforce their history and truths. He prayed that the drive down to Strigoi would be an opportunity to reach out to Daryn and convince him how important it was that he heed his calling as

DRACOV
726 - 847

TREVOR
605·726

HEINRIK
121-363

King of the Undead.

A powerful knock on his office door startled him from his thoughts. His secretary was gone tonight. It was, after all, the greatest occasion of an age. Even if vampires couldn't attend the race in Strigoi, it was an event everywhere in the Realm, with large feasts and celebrations. The day of the race their would be gatherings in dayhouses all around the Realm waiting on updates from Strigoi as well as points along the path of the Run.

With most of downtown deserted, Vlad knew who was at the door, he had asked Detective Muntz to stop by and wasn't surprised that she arrived exactly when he had requested.

"Come in," He replied loudly to the knock.

Hellamina walked in and walked directly to his desk. The KOTU was finishing buckling the suitcase and didn't look up before speaking.

"How are we tonight, Detective?"

"I'm fine, Sir. And yourself?" Hellamina stood with her hands behind her back.

In spite of all the time they spend together on Hellfire Incidents in the street, where it was much more casual, she would always make a point to respect the protocol of R.E.D. and KOTU while in the office. She would often stand at a relaxed attention upon entering this office, addressing the KOTU as a superior officer. Hellamina knew that the KOTU enjoyed her attention to that detail and had assumed in part that was why he had asked her to come downtown tonight, rather than pick a location closer to both their homes to meet before Strigoi—one last formal briefing in his official office.

"Excellent," He tapped the suitcase and looked at her. "Everything here is set to go," He glanced at his watch. "The motorcade should be leaving precisely on schedule." Vlad breathed out and turned his head sideways at Hellamina.

The R.E.D. motorbike division would shadow the KOTU's motorcar to Strigoi. They were the personal security to the KOTU, the First Prize and really anything associated with the Pike's Run at this final event.

"I realize we will be in close contact until the completion of the Pike's Run, but I wanted to just take the last opportunity to see you here in the office as KOTU." Vlad smiled gently at Hellamina. "I know we haven't always seen eye to eye on everything, Detective, but I respect your loyalty to the Realm... and the professional way that you've always conducted yourself."

Hellamina was a little touched by his words. In spite of knowing that the KOTU was a conniving, self-serving, and probably murderous vamp who was wholly capable of spewing pseudo-heartfelt compliments if it could help his objective, Hellamina had seen a glint of honesty in his eyes.

"Thank you," she cleared her throat. "I've always taken great pride in the way I serve," She continued nodding, "And I appreciate you mentioning that, Sir."

"Well, the next KOTU will need Agents like yourself." Vlad began lightly tapping his fingers together.

"There's always the threat of troublesome vampires who would seem to revel in any unrest they could create for the Council. It's good to have such trusted and valued servants of the Realm."

He looked at Hellamina for a few moments before wrinkling his brow. "Which reminds me, I found it a bit odd at the Passing last night with what that Legatus vamp had to say for his final words."

Hellamina nodded and tightened her lips.

"It was almost as if he had been polluted with heresy or something. I mean, it is a shame what happened to his family, but that matter was not only ruled on by the Council, it was Ruled as an Unspeakable... that would amount to treason if any vampire was to break that ruling and tell that poor boy of his father's misspent youth."

Hellamina simply continued nodding, waiting for the KOTU to finish, not wanting to speak about this. Vlad, however, sat gently on the edge of his desk and folded his hands together.

"What does your gut tell you, Detective? I mean, surely you noticed the rather peculiar choice of words the Legatus boy chose to speak of his... mechanic?"

Vlad turned his head sideways again and waited for an answer. Hellamina opened her mouth and blinked slowly.

"Well, I would tend to think that he may have been under a bit of stress, Sir. With the pressures of the Pike compounded with losing his mentor of sorts. Probably just some over-emotional words on his part." Hellamina shrugged a little. "Honestly, I can't even remember what he said."

"He ended with, 'Like a Son who loved his Father well, I will follow to the Gates of Hell.' That struck me as quite out of the ordinary fashion for a

Passing." Vlad replied quickly. "Particularly because he did not know Slim Jim to be his Father. But the 'Gates of Hell' portion raised eyebrows as well. Me, I'm no scholar of ancient lore, but a few members of the Council reminded me that in the old, nonsensical stories of lore, it was the murdered vampires who go straight through to the Gates of Hell, rather than into the Kingdom of the Dead. In fact, many saw that as an omen. Council members told me they hadn't heard vampires talk of that since back in the summer of 666 ADWB."

Hellamina only looked back expressionless at Vlad as he stared aggressively into her eyes.

"I'd like you to keep a close eye on Legatus down there. Make sure he's running a clean race. None of this hocus-pocus talk has any place in the Pike. That's all we need is to rile up the Realm with superstitious nonsense."

Vlad stood up from the corner of the desk and brushed at his suit jacket sleeve. Again he spoke without looking at her.

"How's this business with the radicals going? The undercover SDS investigation."

"Good, Sir."

Vlad had moved to tapping lint from his lapel and dramatically raised his head when the Detective added nothing further.

"Good? That's it?"

"Well, yes, Sir. I've been to a couple events that have occurred. Talked with several vampires associated with organizing and whatnot." Hellamina squinted at the KOTU. "So far it seems like pretty innocuous Fledgling merrymaking, Sir."

The KOTU glared at Hellamina and said sarcastically, "Really? Just some harmless fun, huh?"

Hellamina opened her mouth as if to clarify but the KOTU raised his index finger toward her, shaking his head 'no'.

"I am not interested in whether or not you believe these reprobates are in violation of the Rules of the Realm. I have scholars for that, Detective! Your job is to infiltrate and make record of the vampires and establishments that are involved with these activists. I will need a detailed list in this office upon our return from the Pike." Vlad stared at Hellamina as a small amount of anger rose in his tone. "We'll start a new administration by rounding up some enemies of the Realm." Vlad liked his idea and smiled broadly at himself. "Yes, 'lead with

RISE OF THE CAFE RACER

a firm grip' as Father always said."

The KOTU nodded to himself and looked at Hellamina. She would stay here until he released her. Vlad would savor these last few moments in his office. Though he looked directly at her, Hellamina knew he was deep in thought, smiling and looking at her.

"I know, I know. I can only imagine what you must think of me sometimes." Vlad muttered eventually.

"Sir?"

Vlad gently raised one hand as if to allow her to disregard what he had just said, or at least not to worry about answering him. He was still dancing in and out of his own thoughts. He almost laughed for a moment and then just shook his head.

"If the Realm only knew what it is to be the KOTU. A burden… made no lesser by the inevitable necessity of a firm rule."

Hellamina had no idea what he was talking about, other than Vlad's general inflection of a couple hundred years of doing anything he wanted, to anyone he wanted, coming to an end. It was only now, with a side-by-side comparison in her mind of having a young Daryn Von Firstenstein as KOTU, that she appreciated some of Vlad's qualities. Like him or not she thought, he knew the Realm and its Vampires. He was charismatic and could captivate a crowd. He fought tirelessly to promote the ethos of the Realm, (as well as his own personal gain.) Daryn had none of his father's charm. Or if he did, it was as of yet unrealized.

Eventually Vlad sighed and dismissed his own introspection.

"I will see you at the motorcade in an hour, Detective."

"Yes, I'll see you then, Sir." Hellamina turned and walked to the door.

"Detective, leave the door open, will you? I'm expecting a business associate shortly."

Hellamina bent her head slightly in assent and left.

She walked out and back down the long hallway that emptied into the enormous lobby of the city building. As she pushed through the revolving glass door that emptied into the street, a vampire stepped into the opposite section of the door from the street side. They looked at each other as he continued into the lobby.

On the street Hellamina paused, trying to recollect where she had seen

283

that vampire before, he seemed very familiar. She looked back at the lobby for a minute but was unable to place him. Slightly irritated, she continued on her way.

Once through the revolving door, that vampire followed the long hall to the KOTU's office. He tapped lightly on the open door and stuck his head in.

"Come on in, Ike, and shut the door."

Ike Bludworth stepped silently to the KOTU's desk, hands in his pocket and toothpick in the side of his mouth. Vlad looked at him coldly.

"I'm going to need you to go down to Strigoi. There's just one more job before the Pike."

CHAPTER THIRTY THREE: RUN FOR GLORY

The road to Strigoi started with a long and winding trek down mountain terrain. It was approximately two hundred miles as the raven flies, but with the added congestion of travelers to the Pike's Run, it took the vampires from the Capital most of the night to get to the lush valley city. Spectators from all corners of the Realm had been arriving for days and with only one night before the Run, dayhouses and inns were filled to capacity.

Every city in the Realm had a Township Castle that let rooms out. The Pike Riders, their families and the High Council were all provided rooms at Castle Strigoi, which stood magnificently in the heart of the city and at the center of all the excitement. There was an absolute non-stop festival atmosphere throughout the city, with street performers and merchants clamoring for spectators' attention. There were even puppet shows with a mock Pike's Run for the small Fledglings.

The KOTU had been furious that Daryn had departed the Capital ahead of his family, deciding to travel to the race with Erik, Mills and his mechanic Lucius instead. Vlad had been counting on that time to work at Daryn's attitude and once in Strigoi he couldn't seem to find his son anywhere.

Sonny had traveled with his mother and the Keplers to the valley, getting in close to Dawn last night. After a large Midnight meal with the group, Sonny wanted to relax and get some air, but the crowds had made that difficult. Getting spotted on the street meant engaging with a constant flow of well-wishers, and was exhausting.

The valet at Castle Strigoi had suggested they grab a pint at a secluded alehouse near the docks of the Great Crimson River, in the opposite direction of Town Square and all the commotion. The house was called The Lumper's

Head after the old mariner vamp from Iron Gate who owned it. The story went that he took his life's savings from working the docks and moved inland. Not wanting to be far from water, he found an old boathouse near Strigoi's docks and made a cozy alehouse for the vamps working there. While fixing it up with locals he joked that it had been a dream of his for many years as he lumped the docks down at the Port. "Lumpers" were vampires who did the tedious work of off-loading cargo from ships as they arrived from the North. He had told his helpers that the idea for a pub inland had 'been in this Lumper's head for an age.' A helper had laughed and said the mariner ought to just call the bar that. So he did.

Andi had been with Sonny when the valet told them about the secret spot, and she asked that they go there together later that night. Sonny had agreed and Andi had run off saying she would meet him in the castle lobby in a couple hours.

Sonny had spent that time with Evanna. When Sonny had explained what the R.E.D. Agent had told him, he didn't bother mentioning Slim's activist past, he just focused on the sacrifice Slim had made to provide for them. At first, Evanna had seemed to handle the news very well, realizing that there was nothing that could change what had already been done—probably in part because she had no memory of being married to Slim. But now that they were actually in Strigoi, she was faced with the very real prospect that her son would most likely not return from the race the next night. Her spirits had sunk to their lowest ever. She would tell Sonny that until then it had been like feeling sad at a story someone tells, that it hadn't felt like her life because there was no recollection of any of it. But the idea of losing Sonny had made her wish he had never started the Pike. She had, of course, apologized and pretended that she was fine before Sonny had excused himself to meet Andi, but seeing his mother so shaken had weighed heavy on him. Now more than ever, Sonny was intent on winning the Pike. He stepped angrily down the gigantic spiral staircase and into the castle's lobby. He stood near the entrance and paced, waiting for Andi. All the hatred and resentment he had for the Von Firstensteins was now pulsing through him. He breathed deeply and looked at his watch. *Where was she*, he thought. He glanced around the lobby and didn't see her anywhere—just the bustle of wealthy and formally-dressed vampires arriving and stepping out for a night on the town.

As he moved his eyes quickly back around the spacious lobby he caught a glance from an attractive female vampire at the lobby bar. She was perched seductively on a tall stool at the magnificent glass bar and pursed her lips at him as he continued scanning the room. He was used to females in the Run cities being aggressive, and ignored her, looking back at his watch. After a moment he raised his head as if completely surprised; something was very peculiar. Sonny carefully looked back at the lovely young succubus at the bar. She was slowly sipping her drink as she tried to hide behind it. Sonny crossed the lobby floor, dodging bellhops and keeping his sights on her until he was

standing directly in front of her. His eyes immediately widened as she set her empty drink on the bar.

"I was starting to think I'd been stood up," Andi pouted a little as she smiled.

Sonny shook his head slowly with his mouth wide open. Andi was completely unrecognizable. She was dressed in ultra modern, extremely form-fitting clothing and had an entirely new hairstyle with similarly new, bold make-up. She looked stunningly gorgeous.

"I… um. I, honestly did not recognize you over here," He continued moving his head from side to side in disbelief. "When did you…" he stammered as he looked at her outfit, finally bringing his eyes back to hers, stating boldly, "You… look… so… beautiful."

"Why, thank you," Andi purred playfully, "But you haven't even seen my skirt."

She stood from the barstool and tugged to straighten her short, tight skirt. It was a black, clinging knit with leather panel accents on the outer hips. The leather caught light and helped outline her hourglass figure. Her legs were long and lean, balancing perfectly on five-inch stiletto shoes with criss-crossing leather straps that wrapped around her ankles. With five-inch heels on her feet she was almost looking Sonny in the eye. She wore an asymmetrical chainmail top that draped from one shoulder and plunged down to fasten under her opposite arm. The mail links were tiny polished iron hoops and shined iridescently as they clung desperately to her breasts. Andi's hair had been straightened and pulled back, with dramatic white streaks on both sides. A swirling raven-feathered bun held the hair at the back of her head and from that poured heavy black hair extensions, arching out six inches from the back of her head and flowing down past her shoulders. She had powdered her face and her lips were covered in wet, blood red lipstick. The heavy black makeup she wore on her eyes was pulled out to points at her temples and made her look like a tall, sexy cat.

She placed her hands confidently on her hips and slowly turned sideways, then completely with her back to him. She intentionally adjusted her skirt again and smiled over her shoulder at Sonny.

"Do you like it?" She gently swayed her hips, with hands still at her waist.

Sonny was shocked and immediately covered his mouth. He began rubbing his lips as he looked at her. She changed her expression playfully and pouted.

"It's not too small, is it?" She said in a loud whisper.

Sonny shook his head wildly. "Absolutely not. It's perfect. In fact, I had no idea that it was so…" He searched for the words and looked at Andi. His lip curled slightly for a second. "Full."

Andi gave him a confused look and turned around.

"But… I bought this skirt today. This was the only size they had."

She continued looking at Sonny sideways and he suddenly went wide-eyed with embarrassment. He leaned back and then coughed gratuitously, realizing she had been asking him about her skirt—not exactly what he had critiqued. Slowly Andi pursed her lips and smiled when she figured it out.

"Well, I'm glad you finally noticed."

Sonny laughed at his sudden clumsiness around her, and at how wonderfully she was playing into being this dolled up. It had taken him a minute to remember that this was also his best friend and he should loosen up. He looked back at her, smiling warmly.

"This is a very, very… pleasant surprise. I must say, Andromeda, you are breathtakingly beautiful."

Sonny's words gave Andi a lump in her throat and she couldn't say anything. She simply lowered her chin and beamed back at him. Sonny offered his elbow.

"It would be my honor to go show you off around Strigoi, Miss Kepler."

Andi almost screamed with excitement but managed to just wrinkle her nose and grin. She took his arm and they stepped to the street.

The castle valet recognized Sonny and immediately snapped his fingers at a vampire in the street. A three-wheeled bicycle with a small bench built into the frame at the rear rolled in front of the lobby doors. The valet helped Andi on and shook Sonny's hand. He told the driver to take them to the Lumper's Head and winked at Sonny.

Strigoi was beautiful and quaint. Tea lights and candles lined the shops and even at that hour the streets were alive with revelers. It became less noisy as the bicycle made its way down to the docks. The cool air off the Great Crimson gave Andi a shiver and she cuddled into Sonny. She laid her cheek on his shoulder and dreamt of living with Sonny down here in the valley. She imagined they would have one of these wonderful tiny shops on a picturesque side street where she could do research and he could do anything he chose.

The Lumper's Head was a short brick house with lanterns hung from iron hooks on the outside of its walls. There was a large sign on the side of the building with the name and a picture of a lumper on it.

The inside was like a cozy lodge, with a large roaring fire at the far end of the room and cozy booths around the walls. Most of the few dozen vampires in the room smiled when they saw the Rider and his date take a booth. Sonny went to the bar to order drinks, but before he could say a word the bartender extended his hand across the bar.

"Julian Evermore at your service."

"Thank you. Sonny Legatus."

"Oh, I know," The bartender smiled. "We're honored with both of the Riders tonight!"

Sonny turned to search the room. Sure enough, across the floor in a big circular booth was Daryn, Bebe, Erik, Mills and Lucius, as well as a couple other female vampires. Daryn had watched Sonny come in and was already looking at him. The two Riders stared at each other expressionlessly for almost a full minute. Sonny eventually turned back to the bartender thinking he may decide to leave the Lumper's Head now that Daryn and his entourage were there. Julian had already placed a pint of Hell Blood and a fancy red drink on the bar in front of Sonny.

"Oh, I'm not sure if we're…" Sonny tried to be polite but Julian cut him off.

"Now, I could be wrong, but I figure you for a Hell Blood type." Julian was smiling and leaning on the bar.

"And I've never met a lady yet who doesn't love a Red Crimson. Blood berry with fifty-year- old fermented Valley Hare Blood. Deee-licious." He winked. "And a real leg-spreader too."

"Excuse me!" Sonny pulled his head back, startled.

"A real go getter, Sir," Julian snapped back without missing a beat.

Sonny looked at the bartender suspiciously, who had begun pouring a patron a Hell Blood draught from the taps. Sonny finally chuckled and Julian laughed out loud. Sonny reached for the velvet pouch in his coat for coin but Julian held up a hand.

"All your drinks will be on the Lumper tonight, Sir." He winked again and sped off.

As he walked his drinks back to Andi, several of the patrons winked and tipped their glasses at him. It had quickly made him feel comfortable in spite of the surprise of having Daryn at the other end of the room. Andi sat cross-legged at the edge of the booth, smiling sweetly when he arrived. He was once again truly taken aback at how lovely she looked.

"Apparently, you're going to *really* like this." He gently placed her glass down and sat across from her.

Andi raised her eyebrows, then giggled.

"Um, you ordered me a Red Crimson?"

Sonny was shocked and then laughed at her reaction.

"No, no. I have no idea what they are. I've never even heard of them." He smiled. "Really. The bartender just gave them to me. What am I missing here?"

Andi repeated her expression as if it seemed unimaginable that he couldn't know. But this time she was even more dramatic and quite pleased with the direction of their conversation.

"Come on... Rabbits? You brought me a glass of sweet, fermented rabbit blood?" She giggled again. "Is there something on your mind?"

"Is that even true? I mean, that's just a rumor. Right?"

Andi carefully raised the glass and sipped slowly. She purred a breathy '*mmm hmmm*' as she drank. After she set her glass down, she smiled. "There are only two things that rabbits do, Sonny. Eat... and make more rabbits!"

Sonny let out a hearty laugh. Andi tried to stay demure but burst into laughter as well.

"You are too much tonight, Andi." Sonny grabbed his pint and they touched glasses, laughing hysterically.

Across the room, Daryn set an empty glass on the table. He was in a fog. He'd had a few pints and his crew had been rambling on about smashing the 'Cafe Boy' the next night. They'd been telling Daryn how great it would be once he was the KOTU and could truly do whatever he wanted. He knew they all meant well but he just didn't feel like hating the other Rider and talking about the future right now. As he stared blankly at Sonny laughing with his date, he envied him. Not because Sonny didn't have to be the KOTU or have a controlling father, but because Sonny had risen from obscurity to become a Pike Rider. He had accomplished something against great odds and yet, he would most likely not return from the Run tomorrow. Sonny's greatest days were upon him. In spite of the whole Realm's eyes on him, and what may likely being the last night of his existence, Sonny was completely, thoroughly, most absolutely living in the moment. Savoring the greatness of... *now*.

Daryn nudged Bebe's foot under the table. She looked suspiciously at the vamps around the table over her wine glass. When she ended up staring at Daryn next to her, she lowered her glass and carefully licked the dripping blood from the corner of her mouth. Daryn grinned, leaned over, and kissed Bebe's thick red lips. He bit at her bottom lip as he slid his arm around her waist and pulled her onto his lap. Bebe flung her arms around his neck and kissed him wildly.

"Holy hell, get a room!" Erik Von Castlehuhn joked loudly as he set a tray of drinks on the table.

"Oh, we have one," Bebe growled as she slid off Daryn's lap.

"That, we do," Daryn smiled at the table and raised a fresh pint.

As his mates grabbed their glasses, dozens of patrons around the room raised or tipped their hands as well.

"I have to say," Erik said, in a rare moment void of sarcasm. "These vampires in the valley sure are a friendly lot."

"Indeed," Lucius said stoically at the edge of the booth.

"Hey, Dare, maybe you should relocate the KOTU's office down here!" Mills laughed.

"Oooo" the two female vampires on either side of him giggled excitedly.

Erik began quickly sermonizing, pleading an imaginary case to the imaginary High Council at their booth.

"Members of our distinguished Council, I would raise to the floor, the motion to discuss, the therapeutic value of having our KOTU spending his long nightly, duties in the comfort of the supple teat of the Valley!"

Erik nearly ran out of air and dramatically inhaled an enormous amount as the table erupted in laughter.

"Realizing the imposition that's placed on the remaining Council Members to fulfill the KOTU appearances and Kingly burdens, I shall bequeath my title to the trusted friend and ridiculously handsome servant of the Realm, Mister Erik Von Castlehuhn."

The table clapped politely and Erik bowed saying, "Thank you, thank you, thank you.'

Mills straightened up in his seat and leaned in toward Daryn.

"Seriously though, Dare, I bet you could mandate a Valley office for the KOTU."

Erik nodded his head thoughtfully, "I could look into it for you…"

"Eh!" Daryn laughed and drank. "No more talk of Council and KOTU. Let's just enjoy this moment. All of us, together… on the eve of the Ninth Pike's Run of the Realm."

As the glasses of their tables rose together, glasses were raised like a wave of water through the pub, until even the barkeep held his cup high. The whole room stood with their arms raised as Andi tapped Sonny's hand. He was in the middle of telling a story and was startled at the roomful of vampires apparently waiting for them to join. Sonny looked at Daryn's table. Bebe smiled widely and gently waved her free hand. Daryn's smug grin slowly relaxed and his eyes grew warm and kinder. He nodded his head respectfully at Sonny and held his pint even higher at him. Sonny grabbed Andi's hand across the table and they raised their glasses. Sonny smiled back and gave Daryn a similar, respectful tip of his head.

As the last vamp had lifted his glass in the Lumper's Head, Julian Evermore slowly yelled.

"RUN…"

The entire room helped him finish.

"FOR…"

"GLORY!!!"

The walls shook as the burly Valley vamps roared in unison and drank. Before the cheering could quiet, a steady foot stomp and hand clap had spread through the crowd. Within seconds every vampire on the floor had found the beat. A lanky vampire near the fire produced a flute and began blowing the familiar notes of the song most associated with the Pike—"Run for Glory." The crowd on the main floor gently parted to form a circle, still stomping and clapping to the beat. A stocky vampire with a deep scar along the side of his face stepped to the center of the room. He carried a walking stick that he marched with, striking it on the floor to time with the claps. He danced foolishly and the crowd hollered and howled at him.

When the flutist finished his fourth pass of the melody, he stopped and the scar-faced vampire sang to the beat.

Musical accompaniment for this scene:
"RUN FOR GLORY"
FROM THE ALBUM "RISE OF THE CAFE RACER"
DEANO JONES & THE SWEET DEATH SYMPHONY

Staring 'em down, our Riders are out.
We're grabbing a pint, they're out on the town.
Tellin' ya boys yer making us proud!
The whole room roared: *Run for glory!*
Another vampire jumped in to steal the scar-faced singer's spot light and yelled:

Rubber is down, toe is to toe.
This time tomorrow yer lettin' us know,
Who is the king and the best in the show
Run for glory!

Again, the crowd's roar shook the lanterns on the outside of the tavern as they joined in at the end of the verse. And again a new vampire took the spotlight to sing to the crowd. This time, a tough looking female vampire strutted out, waving her mug of blood and sang directly into the eyes of Sonny:

We're raising our glass and winking our eyes
To Riders that run in the dead of the night
Be glad that it's done by the first sign of light
Run for glory!

Another vamp ran to the center to sing a refrain that was peppered with *'Hey!'* from the crowd.

You never know what lies ahead
or how the Pike will play – HEY!
She tricky and she's treacherous and deadly as the Day.
Remember that tomorrow night, we don't forget to say – HEY!
A prayer for our boy who don't come home.
Hey! Hey! Hey! Run for Glory.

The song continued for many more rounds of verses, with as many new singers and variations on the words as could be improvised by the crowd.

It was at the mention of the Rider that 'won't come home' though, that Sonny shot a quick glance at Daryn, who similarly had just moved his eyes from the merriment in the center of the room to focus on Sonny. The two Riders of the Pike stared solemnly at one another, both with entirely different thoughts running through their minds.

Sonny had come to accept whatever happened tomorrow night as his destiny. He still intended to try like hell to beat Daryn, but after a few days of anger over the circumstances of Slim's plight in this Realm he was at peace with whatever fate lied before him. Watching Bebe next to Daryn clapping and radiantly happy, Sonny smiled at Daryn. After years of dreaming of Bebe, of thinking *if only* the right circumstances were in place, she might want a vamp like him. Sonny finally understood that he had always had his own Bebe, he just wasn't paying close enough attention. He turned and squeezed Andi's hand, thankful that he had realized, even if it may be a little too late to matter.

Daryn, however, looked at Sonny and felt ashamed. The whole Pike seemed like a ruse designed to publicly keep a ruling class in power while the whole Realm toasted the 'contest' and became drunk with national pride. At that moment Daryn was embarrassed of his privilege. He didn't want to be the King of the Undead if he couldn't earn it. *Where's the honor?*, he thought. "And for Hell's sake where's the GLORY in that?" he muttered to himself.

Daryn dragged Bebe by the arm as he pushed Lucius from the edge of the booth, so they could get out. Bebe knew that something was wrong, but made gratuitously frisky expressions to their friends so that they would all stay at the table. Daryn quietly stepped behind the circle and snuck outside unnoticed. Once outside he walked quickly toward the docks and coughed loudly. He kept coughing, adding an occasional, loud *'Ahhhhh'* at the end.

"What's the matter, Honey?" Bebe asked quietly from several few feet away, while Daryn stepped onto a boat dock.

Daryn heaved and flared his nostrils. He began to speak, but shook his head in desperation and looked at the river.

"Do you want me to have Lucius get the motorcar? Did you have too much to drink? "

Daryn looked back to Bebe and growled in a self-loathing tone, "Too much to drink?!" He had a wild stare in his eye. "I haven't had enough to drink." He spit in the river and bounced between angry and saddened expressions. "Because no matter how much wine and liquor I pour down my throat… I cannot silence the screaming in my ears that's telling me that this is a farce!" Daryn had a look of exhaustion and disgust on his face as he faced Bebe. "That I don't DESERVE to be the KOTU!"

Bebe looked down at the ground. She took a couple deep breaths and stared at her shoes. "You know, years ago." She cleared her throat. "When our fathers were getting into business together… My father had suggested that I should think about dating you."

Bebe was still looking down and began to smile. "He said you were good-looking and smart. But mostly that you were Vlad's son and they both liked the idea." She shook her head. "I never liked being told what to do." Bebe looked up at Daryn. "Even though you were really cute. So I continued dating whoever I wanted."

She laughed and held her hand over her mouth.

"I would *torture* those boys. I would tease them, lead them on, demand gifts." She shook her head pretending to be ashamed, but continued to laugh. "Poor Johnny Carlyle, he actually *ran away* on a date with me."

Musical accompaniment for this scene:

"WALK MY BEBE"

FROM THE ALBUM "RISE OF THE CAFE RACER"

DEANO JONES & THE SWEET DEATH SYMPHONY

Bebe looked to see that Daryn was still there, then back down again. She remembered that it had been at that time, during all her Johnny Carlyle type of dates, that she had first met Daryn.

"My father started chasing all these vamps off and we began being really at odds with each other. It got to the point that we weren't even speaking to each other and he took all treasure from me. I truly hated him for a little while."

Bebe looked up at Daryn seriously.

"But then you took me to Rezzies that first time. Do you remember?"

Daryn nodded and made a tiny smile. Bebe tried to swallow but her throat was choked up.

"And I realized right then, that I had been dead wrong about everything my father was trying to do. Because on that night... I knew for certain that you and I were meant to be together in this World. Fighting it had only delayed the inevitable."

Her lips quivered and she nodded her head. "And you are meant to be our KOTU. It's your destiny."

For the second time in two nights Bebe had stunned Daryn. He had always pretended to be so confident, but now it was Bebe that was so assuring. He stared in awe of how assuredly she believed in him, and in them being together.

Daryn finally began to breathe easier. He pushed his hair from his eyes and back over his head. As he stared straight up at the moon, after a moment his balance teetered, He clenched his teeth and grinned, realizing that she had been right yet again and he actually may have had a bit too much to drink. He walked off the dock and hugged Bebe.

"All that time you were tutored by Legatus you never thought he might be the one who would be KOTU."

Bebe held Daryn tightly and looked up at him, smiling. "Sonny is actually a really nice vamp. But he's no KOTU." She laid her head on his chest.

"Well, we will see. I intend to race him fair and square. Just me and my motorbike."

"Is there any other way?" Bebe pulled her head up.

Daryn sighed and thought of the Motor Hell additive he had cheated with at the Capital Run.

"There's always a way to hedge a bet. But this will be a real race. And may the best vamp win."

They walked back from the dock and toward the tavern. When Bebe began to walk back toward the door of the Lumper's Head, Daryn pulled at her to keep walking.

"I've had enough of the crowd for one night. Let's walk back."

Bebe hugged Daryn and they strolled back the softly lit streets to Castle Strigoi.

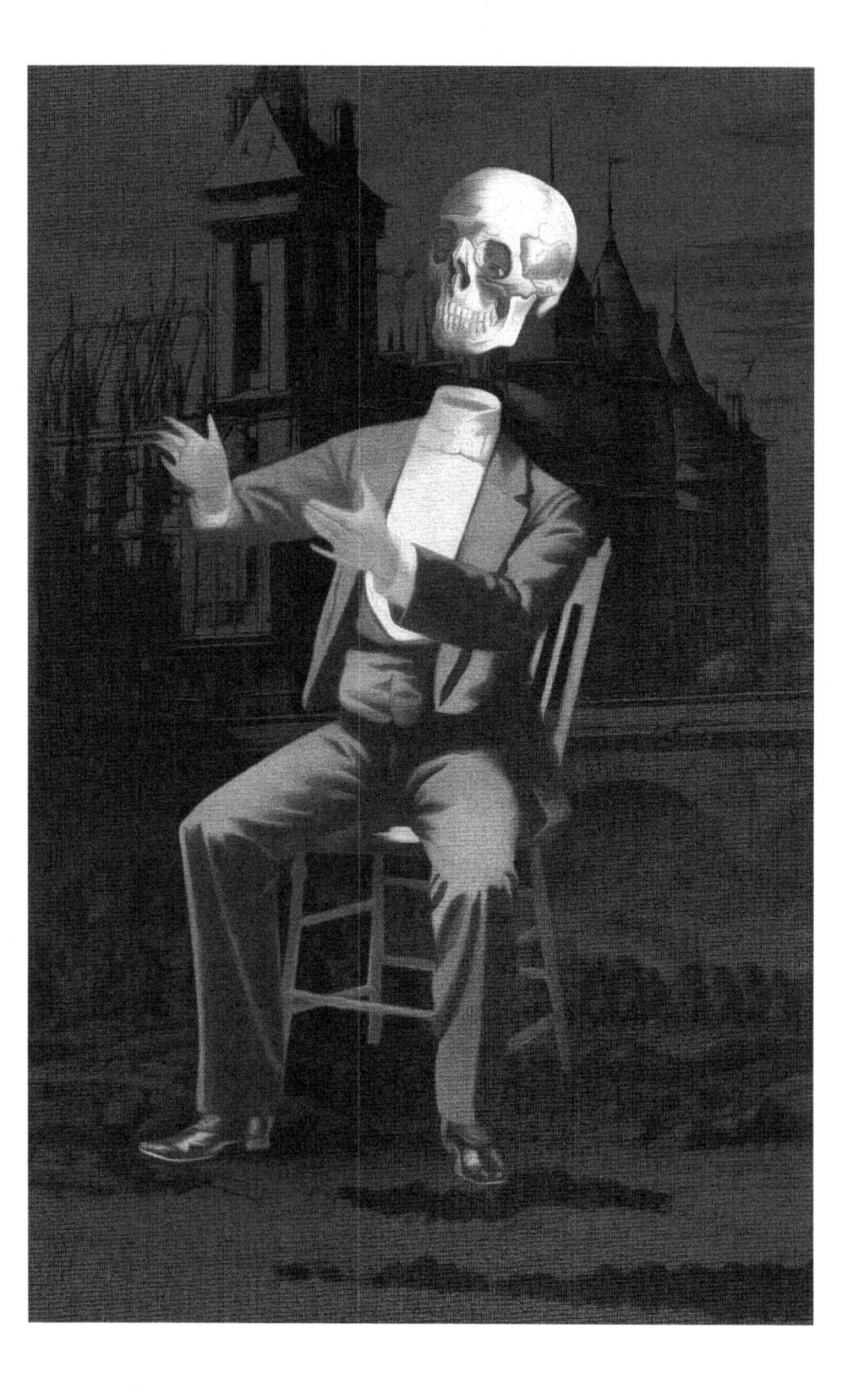

CHAPTER THIRTY FOUR: THE SHADOW

Hellamina's legs were stiff from sitting in the tiny dayhouse she had quickly assembled near the motorbikes at the Square. After shadowing the Riders last night at The Lumper's Head and seeing them both safely back to Castle Strigoi, she staked out the motorbikes' pit until First Dark.

The castle valet had brought her a piping hot cup of blood. She thanked him for the breakfast and for steering the Riders to the Lumper's Head the night before so she could keep an eye on them. Even when she shadowed Daryn back to the Castle she knew Sonny was in the capable hands of her old mate Julian's watchful eye. He was an Uprising Vamp who had known Slim and was all too happy to help her out.

There were only a couple hours until the start of the race, and Hellamina was happy everything had run smoothly. Even out of the cramped little day-house, she wanted to stay concealed. She found a dark corner at the edge of the bandstand that gave her a perfect view of the entire Square, including the bike pit and castle lobby.

It was still late Dusk and no vamps would chance walking about before proper Dark. Not that Dusk alone would cause a Hellfire, but more for fear of all the debilitating diseases that many vampires believed even low light could cause.

Her blood was almost cooled enough to sip and she wedged herself comfortably into the hay bales she sat on. She blew lightly at the edge of her blood and was about to try the tiniest sip when she noticed a shadow. It was just a blur of dark twenty yards away, near the trees that flanked one side of the motorbike pit, but she remained perfectly still and watched. It could be nothing she thought, but she would wait. It was two full minutes until again, a shadow moved, this time from one tree to another. Within a minute the shadow had slowly moved to a tree that stood against the fence that kept spectators from wandering into the motorbike pit.

She looked at her cup of hot blood painfully as she set it on the hay bale and stealthily circled away from the shadow. She carefully moved along the outward perimeter of the Square until the Ale Tent, erected at the back of the bike pit, had obscured her view of the last place she had seen the shadow. She then moved quickly and silently to close her distance from the pit, hidden from the view of anyone in the pit. Once there, she rolled under the heavy canvas at the back of the Ale Tent and moved carefully along its canvas wall.

At the open-ended front of the tent she had a clear view of both areas designated for the Riders. The Cafe Racer was closer to where she stood, and it was clear to her that the station had been disrupted. She couldn't place exactly how, but she had looked at this entire site the night before and knew that something was out of place. Then she noticed a small leather pouch of tools at the rear tire of the Cafe Racer. It didn't appear that there was anything, or anyone, in the pit area, but that pouch was saying otherwise. She moved instantly to a defensive stance and quickly found a soft focus ten feet in front of her. She suspected whoever brought those tools not only hadn't had enough time to use them, but knew she was there.

Hellamina stood on her toes, hands held vigilantly out like antennae. She waited, motionless. She thought of the possibility that she had scared the shadow away, but knew that was unlikely—any vampire keen enough to catch her sneaking up was a pro and no doubt had an agenda that didn't afford walking away from what ever he was up to in the Riders' pit.

Her hyper-sensitive soft focus had not yielded anything and she felt suddenly vulnerable. At that second, her eyes caught faint yellow blip to her left. She focused quickly and watched a yellow spot move slightly on the side of a keg of Hell Blood that sat in front of the Ale Tent. It was a reflection off the keg and in a fraction of a second she knew that yellow spot was behind her, at her eight o'clock.

She grabbed a pint glass from the stack near her right hand and spun at once, throwing it where she calculated the spot stood.

A heavy thudding impact was followed by a deep growling vampire rushing from the shadow of the tent, directly at her.

The vampire from the shadow ran his hand along another table of glasses that were inside the tent. This sent a stack of glass flying at the detective and effectively ruined her intention to use his momentum to try and flip him. As she swatted at glasses, the shadowy vampire landed a punch that sent Hellamina into the table behind her. Still standing and out from under the cover of the tent, Hellamina could see his face. It was the vampire she had seen two nights ago as she was leaving the KOTU's office! She knew she recognized him and now remembered his name was Ike Bludworth. She had questioned him a few years ago about a stolen crop of blood berry.

Hellamina reached behind her head and with lightning speed swung her arm back down. Her baton would have landed on his head if he hadn't raised his arm to take the hit. Again he growled. Hellamina yelled and raised her baton again.

"R.E.D! Stand down!"

After only one second of Ike Bludworth not moving toward the ground quick enough for the Agent, she swung the baton again. This time from the side, with a powerful blow landing hard on the side of his face.

Ike Bludworth rocked to the side and Hellamina was instantly lifting her arm again. He quickly held his palm out to her to submit but braced for another blow. When she didn't strike he looked hatefully at the Agent and continued holding his hand out for her to stop.

"I said DOWN!!" She yelled, rearing the baton again.

Ike took his right knee to the ground and continued to hold his left hand up at Hellamina. It looked as though she had broken his left arm. Since he was almost entirely on the ground and appeared to be submitting, Hellamina sheathed her baton on the back of her jacket.

No sooner had she brought her empty hand back to her side when Ike frantically pulled a long knife from his boot. In one fluid motion he leapt at her, thrusting the dagger like a spear.

Hellamina spun gracefully like an ancient matador, letting Ike's own momentum send him stumbling toward the middle of the pit. It was there, with the moonlight of First Dark setting in, that she could see the unmistakable glint of his silver-coated blade.

Her expression went cold. Fury rose in her eyes like fire swells in a fanned coal engine. It was bad enough that this vampire would feign submission, and then wield a blade on an Agent. But silver would destroy her, polluting a vampire beyond saving, with even the smallest wound. She was infuriated.

Hellamina stared angrily back at Ike. She slowly stepped to her side circling him while he sized her up.

"Go ahead, then." She quietly called at him, "Take your best shot."

After a second of staring at each other, Hellamina raised both arms, palms out. She was not only exposing her body but mocking him. Ike growled and launched at her. Hellamina immediately clenched hands and snapped both fists forward. This released the large, razor sharp talons from the sleeves of her leather jacket. The blades sprung quickly and extended past the top of her fists.

As Ike Bludworth followed through with his best stab at the R.E.D. Agent, she brought down both arms on either side of his neck, completely severing his head. The decapitated corpse dropped violently onto broken glass and the head rolled back into the Ale tent.

Hellamina stood there for a few moments, catching her breath and looking around. With all the broken glass, an overturned table and of course the headless vampire lying in the middle of the Rider's area, this was now not just a completely wrecked Pike's Run motorbike pit, but also a Rule Infraction Crime Scene.

At the front gate to the pit area she noticed a young vampire, undoubtedly one of the many hands that would be on-site early to help with the Pike's Run. He looked at her with wide eyes of amazement. Her R.E.D. uniform had at least removed much of his uncertainty of what he had just witnessed. The boy eventually called out in the meekest of voices.

"Is there anything I should do, Agent?"

He looked nervously at Hellamina who sighed irritatedly.

"Yes." She wiped Ike's spattered blood from her forehead.

"Get me a cup of piping hot blood now."

CHAPTER THIRTY FIVE:
I'M NOT AFRAID

Sonny had been awake for hours. He was too anxious to sleep and just wanted to just enjoy lying in bed before the night of the race. It had been a great night of merrymaking at the Lumper. Vanian Von Schleiben had shown up there with some more of the Sweet Death Sympathy musicians and they had made up songs on the spot with the local vamps and improvised instruments.

As it turned out, several members of the SDS had already been in attendance for the rousing version of 'Run for Glory.'

Sonny chuckled as he remembered leaving with Andi, while Vanian had tried to convince Julian to shutter the tavern so they could merry-make through the day.

In confidence, Vanian mentioned that the SDS were officially hired to play music on the bandstand for the Pike. Sonny had thought it was bizarre and couldn't figure why radicals would want to be a part of something like the Pike. Vanian only smiled like a madman and drunkenly raved, *'Because we are just the regular vamps sent here to entertain you for one night. Providing you with song and a glint of hope that Commoners could rise to become KOTUs!'*

Vanian chugged half a pint of rabbit blood and continued, *'So that you may go back to your lovely, repetitive Specialties until the next Pike in one hundred and twenty one years!'*

Sonny had found out that Vanian had been provided a room at the castle as well, and upon returning Sonny had sent a bellboy with the bundles of Slim's activist posters to Vanian's room. Sonny thought that Vanian would like them and thought what better home for Slim's activist art than with the SDS.

Sonny felt like he could lay in bed the whole night after all the excitement last evening. He turned and gently pet Andi's hair while she slept next to him. He was mostly happy about how they had ended up last night. He was still surprised at how everything had changed between them down there in the valley. It wasn't that she had dressed so differently, though that sure didn't hurt. In fact, he was still shocked at how he had never, ever looked at Andi and seen her in a sexual way until last night. But it was a lot more than that. Being far from home had allowed Sonny to not see her in the same light. Not the little girl he grew up with, but a mature and beautiful female vampire. The same way he had felt and saw things differently as he traveled the Realm for qualifying Runs, so had Andi, down in the magical Great Crimson river valley.

Andi stretched and opened her eyes. She blinked a few times and smiled when she saw Sonny. "So it wasn't just a dream," she purred and grabbed his arm.

"No, that would've been a very long and exhausting dream, I'm afraid."

Andi made a playful face.

"Well, you're the one who fed me rabbit juice all night! What did you expect?"

Andi pulled him and he let himself fall onto her, kissing her as he landed.

"What I expected," Sonny whispered, "Was nothing in comparison to how wonderful last night was."

Andi felt her toes curl up and crawled close to Sonny under the giant bedspread.

"I think I feel some of that rabbit juice gurgling in my belly."

"No, no, no, Miss Kepler," Sonny sprang from the bed laughing. "I need to save my strength to ride hundreds of miles tonight." He glanced at his watch. "I also have to get down to the pit and go through my checklist with your father."

Sonny quickly threw on his trousers and shirt while Andi smiled from under the covers at him. He pulled on his boots and quickly dipped his fingers in a can of pomade. As he ran a comb through his hair, slicking it back, exactly the way Slim had wore his hair, Andi sat up in bed and shook her head slowly.

"You know, with your hair like that… you really look an awful lot like Slim."

Sonny looked at the riding jacket draped on the desk by the window that Slim had given him. His chipper mood seemed to stall for a moment.

"Sonny, I'm sorry, I didn't mean to bring him up right now."

Sonny shook his head and smiled. "No, it's fine." He picked the jacket up and put it on confidently, almost ceremoniously.

"I don't mourn him."

Sonny pressed both open hands to the middle of his chest firmly and then stared intently at her. His nostrils flared as he spoke.

"I can feel him. He's with me. I know it sounds crazy, but I honestly feel him with me."

Sonny swallowed hard and shook his head side to side.

"And I'm not afraid."

Andi wished she could be fearless. She wanted more than anything to not think about the Run right then.

"You don't have to be, either," he smiled.

Sonny crossed the room toward the door, leaning over her as he passed. Andi raised her head and closed her eyes. Sonny waited, then kissed her on the forehead. She left her eyes closed and laughed, waiting for the grown up version.

"Oh. I guess it's better if we're just friends now, huh?" She laughed again. When she opened her eyes Sonny was gone.

CHAPTER THIRTY SIX:
READY RIDER CALL

Vladimir Von Firstenstein was talking to a group of wealthy older vampires on the street in front of Castle Strigoi when Daryn walked out from the castle lobby. The KOTU hastily excused himself and stepped fast to catch Daryn.

"Where have we been hiding, Son? I was beginning to think you might not show up." Vlad chuckled artificially and waved at some passersby.

Daryn kept walking and his father did too, thinking his son would answer him. After just a few seconds, Vlad growled boldly, "Stop, please!"

Daryn stopped and looked at his father. Vlad drew a deep breath and blinked his eyes very slowly. "Look, Son, I know you are probably still very angry about the announcement I made the other night," Vlad sighed, "It's the sort of thing that we will look back at in a hundred years and laugh."

Daryn stared expressionlessly at his father. Vlad knew there was no time for the sort of arguing they had been engaging in, so he moved on. "It's about an hour until we start the race. I have a lot to do before then, and I'm sure you'll be busy with your preparations." Vlad cleared his throat.

"It's unlikely that we will have any time before the Ready Rider Call, and I would just like to tell you… that I'm very proud of you. I know I've been…" The KOTU paused as he chose his words, "Demanding, at times. But I can assure you it is with your, as well as the entire Realm's, best interest that I have made such demands of you."

Vlad reached and put his hand on Daryn's shoulder.

"Soon, when you are King of the Undead, you will understand."

Daryn continued with an expressionless stare at his father. He was simply waiting out this pseudo-emotional exchange until he could continue walking.

"Oh, for Hell's sake, Daryn, can you at least say something?" The KOTU tilted his head slightly to the side, expecting an answer.

Daryn shrugged lightly. When he realized that his father was not going to allow him to carry on until his question was satisfied, Daryn answered calmly.

"I already understand, Sir. I know it's not about me." Daryn moved his hand at the crowds already assembled around the Square and the bandstand area. "It's about all this. It's about the spectacle." Daryn smiled artificially at the KOTU. "It's about keeping the line in place."

Vlad moved his head back to a fully upright position and smirked at his son's sarcasm and with his master-of-ceremony tone and persona he laughed loudly.

"Well, not entirely, but that's good enough for me today. Just do whatever it takes out there."

Vlad leaned in close to Daryn and spoke in a loud whisper, "Just survive out there, Son. There is only one Rider that will return tonight. Make damned sure that Rider is you."

Vlad leaned back and smiled as if he were already addressing the crowd. "And Run for Glory tonight, Son!" He added gratuitously for the crowd walking about in the street around them.

Daryn wanted this artificial conversation to end as soon as possible and happily played the part, answering his father loudly and shaking his hand. "That I will, Father! Whether I win or lose I will have the satisfaction of running an honest race."

Vlad looked puzzled at his son. That seemed like an odd choice of words, he thought. After a few moments Vlad simply smiled. "You'll have to excuse me, apparently there's been some sort of an incident at the pit."

"What do you mean?" Daryn looked to see a dozen R.E.D. around the motorcycle pit.

"Oh, probably just an over-anxious race fanatic. I've heard there was someone tampering with the equipment and he put up a struggle, so an Agent had to destroy him."

"Hmmm," Vlad looked up at the night sky with his eyes. "I don't recall assigning anyone to stake out the motorbike pit... but we can now rest assured that everything is in tact in the Riders' area."

The two separated with Daryn walking to the pit and Vlad heading for the bandstand where he would soon be addressing the crowd from its stage.

As the KOTU made his way through the crowd he waved at his wife Tessa in the boxed seating next to the podium. Andi and Anastasia Kepler were seated near her. Toland was just sitting down to join them. To Toland, it appeared that Vlad was waving at him. Toland halfheartedly waved back to Vlad before he realized the KOTU's wife was sitting near them. Both vampires sensed the awkwardness. Not wanting the situation to become any more uncomfortable, Vlad boldly stepped up to the podium and directly to Toland. Today nothing would interfere with the KOTU soaking in every last drop of performing his public title.

"Doctor, so nice to see you," Vlad beamed happily.

Toland returned a tightlipped smile and shook Vlad's extended hand, but said nothing. Undeterred, the KOTU continued on to Anastasia and Andi.

"Ladies, you're looking lovely tonight."

Vlad trailed off slightly as he looked at Andi. Her attire had startled him.

"Thank you, KOTU." Anastasia smiled politely.

Andi was less enthusiastic and could only think of the incredible grief the KOTU was causing her father by heading the unjustified investigation of K&S. She forced a quick nod and pursed her lips in recognition, then looked back ahead.

The KOTU was still staring at Andi's clothing. Her attire was outrageous and would have been just as suitable for an SDS event. She wore a deep cut, traditional blouse and leather corset with a mid length, bustled skirt. Her hands were in her lap with long gloves and held a bejeweled clutch, which of course was all very traditional clothing. But she had also mixed in modern items and added R.E.D. surplus motorbike riding boots with netted leggings. Her hair was traditional— up and stacked high - but with grey and black extensions held together by iron, hair sticks sculpted into serpents. Finally, a black iron spider hung from a chain around her neck.

The KOTU looked at her as she tried to ignore him. He knew that traditional clothing was worn to be rebellious and thought it inappropriate for the event.

"Is there a costume ball tonight, Miss?"

The KOTU was being exceptionally pleasant and wouldn't be ignored.

Andi smiled to herself as she looked ahead, then very quickly turned her head to the KOTU.

"Not that I'm aware of," She smiled charmingly.

She then acted as if she had just discovered that he had meant to comment on her choice of clothes and added with a bubbly, girly tone.

"Oh, why, I find that traditional attire seems the best way I can honor the Riders." She smiled again.

As if gambling in a game of cards, the KOTU saw her sarcasm and raised it.

"Oh… with serpents and spiders. Hmmm, that would be a first."

Andi looked at the KOTU with deadly aim and spoke with none of the playfulness from a few moments before.

"Well Sir, this may be one of many firsts at the Pike tonight."

Vlad's eyes tightened at her for a second. Anastasia lightly placed her hand on her daughter's wrist while looking straight ahead.

"Indeed," the KOTU nodded and stepped away from the Keplers, and toward his wife Tessa in the next row over.

Twenty yards away, Sonny had cut off the engine to the Cafe Racer in his section of the pit. He'd been testing the air intake Demon and everything seemed to be running perfectly. Toland had been helping Sonny in the pit up until a short while ago. In light of all the commotion, with the R.E.D. having to destroy an overly excited fan, Toland wanted to sit with his family in the stands and make sure they were safe. He wished Sonny the best of luck and made his way to the seats near the podium.

The crowds were huge by now and there were hundreds of Fledges and smaller vamps leaning against the fence on the motorbike pit. They were all anxiously trying to get either Rider's attention. On the occasion that either would wave, the fans would roar from that side.

"Can I get your autograph?" A voice behind Sonny begged.

Sonny sighed and slowly turned, but his eyes went wide when he discovered who it was.

"Viktor, how goes the night!"

Viktor Blackheart laughed "Very well, and I expect yours is uh…" He paused as a handful of very small fledges were repeating *'Viktor! How goes it!'*, mimicking Sonny's every word as if he were a God.

"Yeah, It's madness." Sonny shook his head and rolled his eyes lightheartedly.

Sonny pointed to the Ale Tent and they both stepped in, out of the view of the crowds.

"Hey, uh… I'm sorry to hear about Slim." Viktor's brow wrinkled.

"Oh, thanks." Sonny sucked air through his teeth and looked out at the Cafe Racer.

It would have been easy for Sonny to think longer about Slim. That he wasn't going to be there to wink and say *'Run for Glory, Sonny boy!'* But Sonny needed to stay excited.

"Oh hey! I think you might like this." Sonny stepped in close and lowered his voice. "The band, right over there," Sonny pointed at the bandstand across the Square. "The band that's going to play with the KOTU before the race and while we run the Pike…" Sonny looked around and leaned even closer to Viktor's ear. "It's the SDS."

Viktor pulled his head back in disbelief while Sonny nodded and grinned.

"What do you mean? They're performing as the Sweet Death Symphony?"

"No, no. But they somehow managed to get selected to perform at the Pike. I've even become friendly with them." Sonny shook his head. "And knowing their leader Vanian, I can't imagine that they don't have something unusual planned."

Viktor was wide eyed and excited. He wouldn't have thought Sonny would have remembered that they talked about the SDS back in Suntora. That race seemed like ages ago.

"I can introduce you if there's time." Sonny winked.

Viktor went a little limp and nodded his head in approval. But before he could even tell Sonny how wonderful that would be, the Seven Notes of the Pike played loudly from the bandstand. That signaled fifteen minutes until the start of the Pike's Run.

"THE SEVEN NOTES OF THE PIKE"
Musical accompaniment for this scene:
FROM THE ALBUM "RISE OF THE CAFE RACER"
DEANO JONES & THE SWEET DEATH SYMPHONY

Sonny sighed as the weight of the race finally started to settle in on his shoulders.

"You want me to push the Cafe Racer to the line for you?"

Sonny bowed his head slightly. "That would be a great help."

As they made their way to the opposite end of the pit they walked past Daryn's station. His mechanic, Lucius Creed, had already started wheeling the Gargoyle to the line. Daryn was pressing the gaps between his fingers, making his riding gloves snug.

"Sonny…" Daryn called and let his hands fall to his side.

Sonny stopped. Viktor paused also but Sonny gestured for him to go on ahead. He looked back and stepped to Daryn with an even, hard glare.

For a moment Daryn just looked at Sonny. He leaned somewhat to his side and nodded.

"You know… no matter what happens tonight… and even with all that's been said between us," Daryn paused and tried to make sure he found his most honest tone. Even the expression on his face became a bit humbled. "I'm proud to run the Pike with you." He held his hand out. "You deserve to be here."

Sonny looked at Daryn's hand. This behavior was suspect, and part of Sonny was ready for some foolish trick. After sixteen long weeks of constant harassment from Daryn, it seemed truly unbelievable that this could be happening. But finally Sonny grabbed Daryn's hand.

"Thanks," Sonny said slowly.

From the bandstand The KOTU was greeting the crowd and his voice sang loudly, "Welcome everyone and all, to the Pike Run Race Ready Rider Call!"

The crowds cheered and howled. The KOTU extended a hand toward the motorbike pit.

"Come and claim your entrance to the race that only happens here!"

Again, the crowds roared with excitement.

"Now, just when it's about to go…" Vlad paused dramatically and looked at the scarred small vamps in the front in of the podium. "I'll raise my hand, then ready, steady, go. This race that we've been waiting more than a century to see, begins in a few moments, while the Riders meet the referee."

Again the KOTU extended his hand toward the pit and offered the Riders instruction as to what they need to do.

"Riders on the ground, need to bring your bikes around as we inaugurate the sound of the Run. Do a gear check, then ready on your mark. There will be an inspection before the race will start."

There was more clapping and cheering. Vlad looked back at the huge crowd and waited for the applause to die down. He then gave an emotional finale to his performance.

"You're riding for the honor, and for all the Realm to see. Remember that you're brothers… and this Rider's not your enemy."

Musical accompaniment for this scene:
"READY RIDER CALL"
FROM THE ALBUM "RISE OF THE CAFE RACER"
DEANO JONES & THE SWEET DEATH SYMPHONY

The crowd adored his touch of sentiment and after a polite clap, roared with anticipation.

Vlad quickly made his way from the podium and down to the line. The Referee he spoke of was, of course, the Geezer at the line. Once again, Vlad meant to relieve the Geezer of his testing duties so that he may conduct the purification portion of the inspection himself. Even though Ike Bludworth had been destroyed tonight, Vlad knew that Ike had successfully delivered Motor Hell to Daryn back in the Capital. A Geezer would easily taste this modern anti-friction concoction in Daryn's engine oil.

But as he arrived at the line the KOTU was mortified to see the Geezer already at Daryn's bike. In fact, Daryn had asked the Geezer to start with his bike.

"Stop right there!" The KOTU bellowed as he sped to the line.

The referee looked quizzically at the KOTU.

"I should like to relieve you, Sir."

The Geezer placed a hand to his ear, but Daryn interjected.

"Nothing to worry about here, my KOTU, I have a fresh batch of Realm Motor Oil in my Gargoyle's belly." Daryn stared at his father. "Nothing but good, clean, motor oil, Sir!" Daryn reiterated.

Vlad glared at his son while Daryn smiled proudly with brows high.

The Geezer had already dipped one of the small wooden sticks from his hand into the engine by the time Vlad looked back at him. He licked at the brown syrupy oil that coated the end of the stick.

After a moment of light chewing motions the Geezer said loudly, "That's fresh oil alright!"

As the referee moved on toward Sonny's bike the KOTU looked at his son and sighed. "Do you think that was wise? Having Lucius change the oil tonight?" Vlad squinted to let his son know that he thought it was a mistake.

Daryn pressed his lips together firmly and rocked his head 'yes'.

"I hope you know what you're doing," Vlad muttered as he walked away.

As the referee had been testing Daryn's bike, Sonny spotted Andi at the edge of the crowd. She waved to him. As much as her heart was breaking at the thought of Sonny not returning from this race, she forced herself to be optimistic. She clapped excitedly as he lurched toward her in his head to toe riding leathers.

"I had to come wish you luck one more time," She smiled from ear to ear. Sonny stepped into the crowd and put his arms around her.

"It's as I've said, you've always been my good luck charm."

"Well, let's hope I work." She smiled again.

As much as she was trying to be strong, looking into his eyes she trembled with fear.

"I love you, Sonny."

"I'll see you in ten hours," he winked and kissed her deeply.

Andi quickly took two mice from her bejeweled clutch and stealthily zipped them into Sonny's left side pocket of his riding jacket. Doing so took a bit more time than she had planned so she ended up raising the temperature on their kiss in order to buy more time. The vamps around them started oooh-ing and ahhh-ing at the couple. Within seconds, heads were craning to see what was happening and a chant of 'Sonny' began swelling through the crowd.

By the time they stopped kissing, the chants were massive and felt like every voice in the Square was calling out Sonny's name. He stepped away from Andi and, not knowing what else to do, he waved at the masses of vampires.

The volume exploded. Sonny turned and stepped back to the line. The KOTU would eventually raise his hands to bring the noise down.

The inspections were completed and the Riders were on their marks. Vlad stood in front of both Riders and raised his hand again for the crowd to calm.

"And so it begins, in the year One Thousand Eighty Nine since the Day That Death Was Born, the Ninth Pike's Run of the Realm is to begin!"

The KOTU paused but no cheering followed. The crowd knew the race was about to start and remained quiet.

"Whosoever shall leave this line, following the course of the Run into the Forbidden Land, and return over this line first... shall be named King of the Undead of the Realm."

The KOTU walked ceremoniously to the podium. Both Riders mounted and started their motorbikes. Daryn revved his throttle and looked at Sonny. Sonny looked directly ahead. Any kind words they had exchanged previously were already distant memories. Sonny meant to win the Pike's Run or be destroyed trying.

Behind the Riders the KOTU raised both arms high. The crowd waited on baited breath for his signal. Like a conductor of the largest symphony in the world, he waved his hands to conduct.

"READY..."

"STEADY...."

"GO!!!"

The white lights on either side of the starting line went blue. The Cafe Racer and the Gold Winged Gargoyle screamed from the line, both front tires lifting off the ground.

The last Pike's Run that the Realm would ever see had begun.

CHAPTER THIRTY SEVEN: THE PIKE'S RUN

The Run's path at the top of the race would have Riders weaving through the streets of Strigoi. There were shorter routes out of town, but this way gave all the spectators a chance to see the Riders before they disappeared into the Realm's countryside.

Once out of Strigoi, the course ran through the lush farmland of the Crimson Valley. Vampires along the route were gathered intermittently along the designated course. Every mile had blue reflective signs posted, but it wasn't necessary. It was abundantly clear where the course ran. Even in the most scarcely populated sections of the Run there would still be handfuls of vamps from surrounding villages lining the sides of the Pike's Run.

The Riders had been running neck and neck through the city, but Daryn had pulled a small lead as they ran out into the surrounding farmland. It wasn't until after they had crossed the Kharis Archway that everything changed.

The Kharis was a beautiful suspension bridge that served as the largest artery for goods to travel from the port at Iron Gate to all points West of the Great Crimson River. The river was a half mile at its widest. Although there were several bridges along its path, none compared to the majesty of the Kharis. It was one of the crown jewels of vampire architecture with metal belfries atop the two hundred foot iron pillars that connected the woven iron cables. The road on the east side of the Archway also became very wide and straight, allowing for the Riders to open up their motorbikes and finally really start racing.

Sonny had waited until after he had traveled over the Kharis to turn on the air intake Demon. Daryn was probably a half-mile ahead when Sonny flipped on the Demon with his thumb. Within minutes Sonny closed that gap and slowly crept past Daryn. This would continue for forty more miles when Sonny reached the village of Narkissa, and the first official Pike's Run refueling station.

There were a couple hundred spectators who immediately began chanting

Sonny's name and cheering the moment he pulled in. He stretched his legs and quickly looked around as he fueled the tank of the Cafe Racer. Only the Rider could fuel his motorbike and spectators were kept at bay behind ropes.

"We love you, Sonny!" a fetching young female screamed from behind a roped-off area. After several shouts to '*Run for Glory!*' and a quick gulp of blood from an official, Sonny was back on the bike and kicking dust at the cheering towns people of Narkissa.

Ten minutes later Daryn came skidding into the same station. There was wild cheering but no chanting of his name. Though many of the young girls close to the station still called at him and waved. Daryn sipped a cup of blood as he filled his tank.

"How far ahead is the other Rider?" he yelled to the official.

"Nine minutes, Sir!" An older, rotund vampire called back.

Daryn threw his cup on the ground and cursed, which was met with an overwhelming swell of support, with dozens of vampires shouting for him to '*Give 'em Hell!*' and '*Run for Glory!*' Daryn waved and screamed away on his Gargoyle.

From Narkissa it was sixty miles to the city of Emeraldblood. Daryn didn't know if he would be able to close much of the gap before there, but was hoping the city streets of the quaint valley city would afford him another chance to regain some ground.

From there the Pike's Run would head southeast, toward the Gulf of Gehenna. There was another refueling station fifty miles south west of Emeraldblood in a town called Thana.

Sonny pushed the Cafe Racer hard and kept the Demon engaged until he reached Emeraldblood. There he flipped it off and allowed the bike to cool down as he navigated the narrow city streets at lower speeds.

Emeraldblood was similar to Strigoi and held tens of thousands of spectators. Vampires who would travel from the north would usually opt to watch the Pike from the streets of Emeraldblood, so there was clearly a different look to the spectators here. Dooners and Fomorians had the distinctly shorter stature with wider faces. Vampires from Tamerlane had a unique style too, with a much heartier, warrior accent to the way they dressed. Many of their older vamps still wore the popular two-piece suits, but many were tweeds and heavier trousers with suspenders. Most of the time their jackets would be off with vests, ties and various sorts of weapon garters harnessed over their button down shirts with sleeves rolled up. Tamerlans were some of the fiercest competitors and favored sports of combat. Whereas most of the Realm considered fencing their sport of choice, Tamerlans liked crossbow and sword competitions and absolutely loved bare knuckle boxing matches.

As Sonny leaned his way through the tight streets he was bombarded with howling from the crowds. Some of the faces looked fierce as they screamed for Sonny to *'Go all the way!'* and to *'Kill the bastard!'* It was a far cry from the even-tempered support he had seen so far. He didn't give it much thought though and tried to stay focused since he had no idea how far behind Daryn was. Sonny opened up his throttle as he left the city, while Daryn rolled into town behind him.

Daryn took the city corners at alarming speeds. The rowdy northerners in the crowds loved the display. Even if he may not be their favorite, they loved his spirit. And in spite of any heated support they had yelled at Sonny, none would think to shout anything but encouragement to the other Rider. Not only would it be bad form, it would undoubtedly warrant a baton strike to the head from an R.E.D. Agent or any local militia.

By the time Daryn had weaved his way through Emeraldblood, Sonny was already nearing the third refueling station at Thana. The course outside of Emeraldblood had followed the Emerald River for several miles but would head due west to the small village of Thana. The air was already balmier, with winds from the south blowing the humid Gulf air into the Valley.

Thana was a smaller and wilder version of Emeraldblood. There were only several dozen spectators but they were drinking and singing improvised versions of Run for Glory as Sonny blazed into the station. It seemed as though these vamps may have been waiting all year for a chance to sing for a Rider as several vamps all sang each section of the song together. They were merry-making and dancing harder than anything Sonny had seen at the wildest SDS event. Sonny smiled as he fueled and when prompted by a young traditionally dressed vamp to take a verse, he simply raised his fist and yelled 'Run for Glory!' The vamps were beside themselves with excitement. Even the Pike officials and local R.E.D. howled along with the crowd.

Before he had started back onto the Run, a burly older vampire stepped near the front of the roped off area and growled loudly, "The Dead Hills sa-

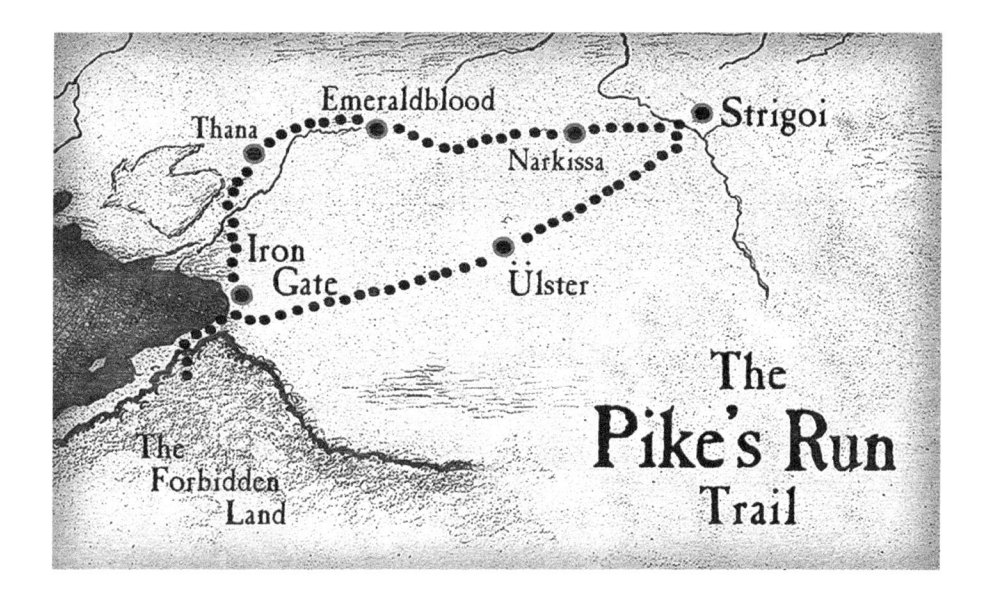

lute the spirit of Slim Jimmy Nightshade!"

The Pike official grew wide-eyed and looked at the R.E.D. Agents at his sides. The burly vamp howled alone while all others were silent with fear. Sonny too had frozen in his tracks at the mention of Slim's last name. He knew what it meant to utter a name that had been ruled an Unspeakable. Those R.E.D. Agents could have destroyed this vampire on site and face no disciplinary action whatsoever. The Agents looked at each other for only a few moments and finally raised their batons high in the air and cheered right along with the burly vamp. When finally the Pike official joined in cheering as well, Sonny felt an overwhelming sense of confidence. His chest was tight with pride. He was the son of James Nightshade and he knew he would win this race! For a moment it felt like the superstitious rumors that Slim had left himself out in the light so he may become a spirit guardian to Sonny were true. Sonny revved the Cafe Racer loudly and shot like an arrow out of the station.

At that time Daryn was only a few minutes out of Emeraldblood and digging in as hard as he could, but he was now a solid forty miles behind Sonny. He knew that after Thana the Run went south and into marshier lowlands. Near the Suicide Plots, the Run would go southwest and toward the port city of Iron Gate. There they would fuel for the last time before riding into the Forbidden Land. Daryn wondered if he might have been mistaken to not use the Motor Hell supplement.

As Sonny headed south from Thana it grew wetter and quieter. For the first time since the Pike's Run began, there were no spectators lining the course. Apparently no one wanted to stand anywhere near the haunted ground near the Suicide Plots. Even vampires from Grindylow would hug the land along the coast to get to Iron Gate rather than be anywhere near the Plots. It was commonly accepted that there was a great, ancient evil that surrounded the Suicide Plots.

Back in the first century, in the early years After Death Was Born, famine and sickness prevailed in the Realm. Thought vampires were learning to satisfy their blood lust with animals, it was a slow learning process and caused great physical and mental sickness in the population. Nearly a hundred thousand vampires would commit suicide in the years before blood berries were synthesized using cranberries and animal tissue. Even then Blood Bog Fever was striking all over the Realm, and some still chose suicide over the slow pain-

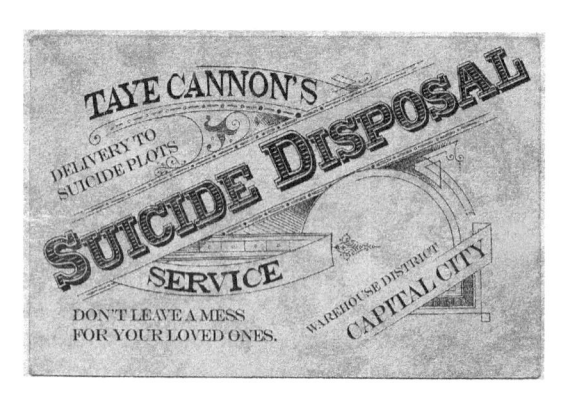

ful demise of the Bog. The most common method of suicide was to plunge a silver dagger into your heart. Staying out in the Day was a slow and painful process, since it could take hours to catch fire. Ones who tried would usually give up and be scarred and burned as well as sick from the light.

In spite of the popularity suicide gained as a relief from the terrible suffering in that first century, killing off your own existence had always been a shameful sin. It was also believed to guarantee rejection from admission into the Kingdom of the Dead. So horrible was this act that the remains of a suicide victim couldn't be committed to the ground near other vampires who had expired in other, natural ways. The High Council had designated an area specifically for all these corpses. Before the suicides stopped, there was an entire industry in the Realm to deal with transporting and burying remains in the soft ground north of the Gulf of Gehenna.

It is better for you that one of the parts of your body perish than for your whole body to go into Gehenna

On a couple occasions, heavy rains had washed bodies into the Gulf and started the rumors of those waters being haunted or cursed. So much so that the Council began warning vampires not to go in the Gulf of Gehenna. You could still see signs near and around the Gulf that said "It is better for you that one of the parts of your body perish than for your whole body to go into Gehenna."

During that portion of the Pike, Sonny remembered these historical facts and many other stories he had heard as a child about the haunted land of the Suicide Plots. The difference now was that he was unafraid of anything that could harm him in this world. Losing Slim had made him start to believe that it was less important how long he stayed in this world but what he made of his time while he was here.

Speeding down the road near the Plots, Sonny imagined what the Realm might look like with him as the KOTU. In the middle of nowhere, alone in the swampy flatlands, he laughed out loud at himself. He knew the very idea of himself as the KOTU was ridiculous, the Realm just didn't work that way. Still, he thought of the message of the SDS, and how freeing it felt to live in the moment. Sonny pictured how a KOTU might implement those ideas into the lives of vampires. That instead of always planning for and living in the future, vampires could savor their time in the moment. This made him think of Andi. In those last couple days together they had been closer than they had been in the fifty-odd years of their friendship. The idea of making it back to Strigoi and being with her was strong in his heart.

Shortly thereafter, Sonny crossed the Emerald River again and he began seeing spectators lining the road. The small villages before Port Iron Gate brought back some friendly faces that cheered the Riders on. There would be only thirty or so miles to the Port city, where Sonny would fuel up before riding south and up the cliffs of the coast, into the Forbidden Land.

Behind him, Daryn had pulled into the fueling station in the lively town of Thana. The mob was still merrymaking and cheered with all their hearts for the Rider of the Pike. As Daryn filled his tank, the official walked over with a cup of blood in one hand and a small box in the other. Daryn sipped the blood as the official told him that the KOTU had instructed him to hand deliver this to Daryn.

Inside the box was a pocket flask with the Von Firstenstein name on it. The official smiled in spite of Daryn's obvious bewilderment and told him that his father *'must be confident enough of your winning that he's already sent your victory drink'*.

Daryn thanked the official and opened the flask to sneak a sip for the road. It smelled horrible and after a second Daryn poured some of the brown syrupy liquid on his finger. It was Motor Hell. Daryn made a disgusted face. *My own Father doesn't think I can win the Pike,* he yelled in his mind. As he stood there in Thana, probably forty-five miles behind Sonny, he looked again at the flask his father had sent. He remembered of Bebe's story the night before and thought maybe his own father had simply tried to save him from himself. He knelt down and examined his motorbike as he feigned drinking from the flask. He casually unscrewed the oil cap and poured the contents of the pocket flask into the motorbikes engine.

A minute later, the Gargoyle already sounded different when Daryn started it up. It pulled like a dragon from the station and he was instantly satisfied with his decision to add the anti-friction lubricant. Now it seemed like the Gargoyle had been crawling since Strigoi, and Daryn wondered if he would be able to overtake Sonny before Port Iron Gate. He knew that every KOTU in history had been in the lead as the Riders rode into the Forbidden Land, and he hoped he too could be ahead by then.

Sonny was drawing closer to the final fueling station and there was now a steady stream of onlookers along the roadside. They waved and cheered as the Cafe Racer screamed past them. He had never been to the port at Iron Gate and the city lit up the sky in the distance with warm yellow light.

Soon after Sonny rode past the city limits sign he saw the lights of the fueling station. Rolling up to the pump the crowd roared with confetti and flower petals blowing through the air. Again, Run for Glory broke out, this time with what sounded like a full band with instruments spread throughout the crowd. As Sonny fueled he felt strange. Since before Narkissa, hours ago, he hadn't seen Daryn and it seemed as if he were racing himself at that point.

The Pike official approached with a tray of small cups of blood. He told Sonny the ones on the left were Hell Blood. Sonny capped his fuel tank, looked around at the crowd, smiled widely then grabbed a cup with fermented blood. He raised it high and the crowd exploded with cheers. He downed the cup in one large swallow and started the bike up. With flower petals under the tires he tore out of the station.

By that moment Daryn had already ridden past the Suicide Plots and crossed back over the Emerald River. He too had started to notice the repopulated sidelines to their race. He pushed the Gargoyle hard as the road straightened out for many miles.

Sonny weaved through the port city streets quickly. He had flipped off the air intake Demon but he too was not taking anything for granted and pushed himself hard. Near the south section of the city, the streets became cobblestoned and at times he needed to slow to a crawl on tight corners. Through this section spectators would lean into the street and wish him well.

At the opposite end of the city Daryn was screaming to a stop at the fueling

station. He scrambled quickly to refuel and asked the official how far out the other Rider was. 'Eleven minutes!' the official yelled. Daryn howled and capped the tank. Leaving the station the Gargoyle went up on its back wheel and Daryn rode thirty feet before his front tire fell back onto the road. The crowd loved it and called his name after him.

On the south side of the city, Sonny was passing under the enormous iron arch that spanned above the Run. It had intricate latticework with a huge motorbike tire sculpted from iron in the center. Hundreds of lights and flowers decorated the arch and it was the final sendoff from the port city to the Riders, as they headed south into the Forbidden Land.

Daryn raced through the streets of Iron Gate. After overshooting his corners a couple times he realized he would have to hold back his speed. There simply was only so fast he could navigate this portion of the Run.

Once Sonny cleared the city limits he flipped on the Demon and tucked in tight to the Cafe racer. Within a couple miles the elevation began rising and sheer cliffs appeared on his right side.

Daryn slid wildly on the final corner of the cobblestone street and accelerated through the iron arch at the south end of the city.

The temperature was already cooler as Sonny rose along the cliffs of Gehenna. There were still the blue reflectors every mile along the road, but little else.

Daryn opened the Gold Winged Gargoyle up completely and began flying up the cliffs along the Gulf.

Sonny leaned as the road bore left toward the darkness of the forest. Within a minute the moonlight was slowly choked from the sky as he became swallowed in the Forest of the South. The air smelled heavier and the woods hung like velvet curtains on either side of the much narrower road.

After a minute Sonny noticed a faint glimmer of light on the knuckle of his leather riding glove. He quickly looked over his shoulder and recognized the unmistakable glare of a motorbike's headlamp in the far distance.

When he turned around he slowed for a moment to read a sign that hung from a tree next to the forest road. At first he thought it may be the name of a town or property in this unfamiliar land. But a knot formed in his throat as he read:

ABANDON ALL HOPE, YE WHO ENTER HERE.

Sonny dug in his heels and screamed defiantly at the forest ahead.

CHAPTER THIRTY EIGHT:
INCIDENT REPORT

After the Riders had ridden out of the Square at Strigoi, the crowd had broken into an informal version of Run for Glory. The KOTU had made his way from the podium, slowly through the crowd, and toward the motorbike pit. He had successfully avoided Detective Muntz prior to the race but he knew he would have to get a briefing on the Incident.

Hellamina had been watching the KOTU from the pit. She had always been a bit suspicious of the KOTU, but this latest incident seemed particularly unusual. She was curious what business the KOTU had with this vamp who, only a couple days later, she would destroy as he tried to tamper with a Pike's Run motorbike.

Vlad was shaking hands and laughing with vamps along the walk from the podium. At one point, while chatting with some wealthy vampires seated near the starting line, he glanced at Hellamina. He was mid-sentence and didn't break dialog but nodded at the Detective that he was on his way. She simply stared back at him with no expression.

The KOTU patted the shoulder of the R.E.D. Agent at the gate of the pit as he walked in.

"Ah, Detective, so sorry to have kept you waiting," Vlad smiled. He quickly sighed and put his hands on his hips. Vlad looked around, shaking his head and grimacing. "It's just such a shame that even during an event like this, we can't let our guard down."

Vlad looked at Hellamina and squinted. "The Agents said you decapitated this scoundrel." He slowly grinned. "Great work. Swift justice is the best justice I always say—"

"Sir," Hellamina interrupted, "This vamp, this… perpetrator that I had to destroy..." She folded her arms. "As I left our last meeting, I passed him as he was going into your office building."

The KOTU made a puzzled look.

"Really? That seems odd." Vlad looked gratuitously at the night sky. "I wonder what that vamp was up to?" Vlad pretended to search for motives. "You don't suppose this was part of a larger plan to sabotage the Pike's Run, do you?"

Hellemina adjusted her folded arms and leaned slightly to the side.

"I don't know Sir, I was hoping you might tell me."

"Excuse me?" Vlad said instantly.

Hellamina bent down and opened a leather-padded coroner's bag. She slid it with her foot toward the KOTU. Inside was the severed head of Ike Bludworth. Vlad looked at it and suddenly covered his mouth. He then glared angrily at Hellamina.

"Detective, what in the daylights is the meaning of this?!"

"This isn't your business associate that met you after our meeting two days ago?"

"You have absolutely no right to startle me with this. Not everyone is so comfortable with blood and gore, Detective!" Vlad shook his head.

"No, that's why some of us have others do our dirty business for us." She stared coldly at the KOTU.

Vladamir raised his head back and looked viciously at Hellamina. "I don't know what you *think* you're doing here, Detective, but you have overstepped your authority."

"I am the lead R.E.D. Detective investigating an incident regarding a vampire's demise, as well as tampering with a Pike's Run motorbike." Hellamina unfolded her arms and leaned at the KOTU, "I am well within my authority, sir!"

Vlad stared disgustedly at Hellamina and eventually began lightly laughing at her.

"I believe the loss of your friend last week may have clouded your judgment and made you delusional, Detective. I'm going to see to it that you are re-evaluated and reassigned." Vlad laughed louder. "Somewhere that your foolish notions won't bother anyone. Hmmm... " Vlad made an obligatory expression as if thinking deeply. "Ah, yes, I believe there's a need for an outpost Ranger in the Black Deth Mountains. Consider yourself reassigned."

"That's strange, I didn't get the paperwork." Hellamina looked at her watch. "And seeing how you will only be KOTU for another six or seven hours, I'll just start ignoring you now."

Hellamina closed the coroner's bag and tucked it back behind the roped off section in the pit that pertained to the incident.

Vlad quickly shed his anger and adjusted his tie. He made a fake smile at Hellamina. "I may not be the King of the Undead at the end of this night. But my son will be, and I'll see to it that you pay dearly for your ridiculous accusations."

Hellamina was not intimidated and fired back sarcastically, "You seem so certain about the outcome of the Pike's Run, so confident that your Son will be the winner."

Vlad grinned. Fire and corruption burned in his eyes.

"Absolutely... *positive*."

Nuemania

The Order of Na' Dir

CHAPTER THIRTY NINE:
THE BARON OF NÜEMANIA

Sonny stood in front of massive iron doors. They were set in the side of a mountain of stone with sheer walls. They were twenty feet wide at the bottom, rose straight for ten feet, then arched to meet with a point nearly fifteen feet high. There were no handles or knockers, not even an imprint where a doorkeeper may slide them open and ask you your business. Just flat iron halves of an arch that spanned the width of the road.

The forest road Sonny had been speeding down, with Daryn Von Firsten-stein not far behind, had simply come to an abrupt halt. To the sides of those doors the trees thinned and the imposing stone wall stretching into darkness.

As the headlamp of Daryn's motorbike closed in, Sonny quickly tried to determine if this might be some sort of combat portion of the Pike. He wondered if he was meant to fight Daryn for this title. He frantically scanned the ground around him. It was meticulously clean, too clean for a forest floor. Sonny only had seconds before Daryn would be at these doors. He considered whether he should take Daryn by surprise and attack him at once, but then remembered Slim's advice about confrontations. Sonny would remain calm, even in the face of such great uncertainty. Maybe this was a test of sorts, to try his resolve or evaluate him in some way. As Daryn's bike slowed down Sonny wondered if they were being observed and slightly worked his eyes around their perimeter.

Daryn stopped and cut his motor. He rapidly dismounted and pulled the goggles from his eyes. He looked at Sonny, then quickly at their surroundings. Sonny stood silently poised as Daryn inspected the doors then the wall, just as Sonny had done in the minute before Daryn had arrived.

Daryn walked cautiously back toward Sonny and their bikes. They looked at each other suspiciously, both with arms floating at their sides as if ready to begin fighting at any moment. Daryn glanced curiously back in the direction they had come. He wondered if maybe they were to simply turn around and race back. Then he, too, noticed the unusually clean ground around them. He felt as if they were being watched and began to guess that this may be an arena of sorts.

"Seems a bit odd that we would arrive here with no mention." Daryn began ever so slowly circling Sonny.

"Maybe these doors open and we are to race through the Forbidden Land." Sonny began countering Daryn's movement, slowly stepping to keep his eye on him.

"Or… maybe one destroys the other and returns victorious." Daryn huffed lightly, not entirely believing what he had just said.

Sonny nodded but squinted as if he too thought that was hard to believe. "Maybe. But it seems like quite a waste of time with all this motorbiking, then. Why not just have a bare knuckle match out in Tamerlane for the title of

KOTU and be done?"

Sounding very much like his father, Daryn quipped back, "Ah, for the spectacle, of course. For the distraction!"

Sonny nodded and smiled, realizing Daryn may be right. The qualifying runs of the Pike had amounted to a speaking tour of the Realm for the KOTU. The Pike meant huge rallies and crowds, perfect for re-indoctrinating vampires with the virtues of the High Council.

"Still, I just can't believe that it's to end here, like this. What a sad and dismal finish to a glorious Pike." Sonny shook his head but stared intently back at Daryn.

"Hmmm," Daryn laughed with his lips tightly together. "I guess even during our quite civilized spectacle… it is *still* just the brute who seizes power."

"Power?" Sonny laughed too. "Is that why you're running the Pike? For the power?"

For a moment Daryn thought Sonny was joking. "And you don't ride to take First Prize and be the King of the Undead?"

Sonny blinked slowly and shook his head.

"If I were to win and be awarded title of KOTU, I would give it back to the vampires of the Realm."

The two Riders had been slowly pacing each other in a circle. At these words Daryn stopped and stared at Sonny, confused at what he had said. He let some air from his inflated chest out and relaxed his stance a bit.

"Give it back? What does that even mean?"

Again Sonny mirrored Daryn and stopped pacing. "Just like I said. I would give it to the people of the Realm." Sonny shrugged.

"How would they rule?" Daryn was intrigued at the idea and unbuckled his helmet.

"They would rule themselves." Sonny relaxed his aggressive posture. "They'd quit worrying about Specialties and mandates and Rules. There's no reason for all that anyway." Sonny paused and took a deep breath. "They'd just *live*."

Something about the way Sonny was talking made Daryn feel like the giant hands that gripped him, constantly squeezing him into the perfectly molded image that his father pictured him as, had relaxed their grip. For a moment Daryn didn't feel the urgency of the Pike.

"But they'd never let you do that. They'd destroy you."

"Who would destroy me? If the title is won, then it's the winner's to give freely. If the people were the KOTU, then that power would be dismantled. There would be no need for a High Council."

Daryn looked away at the doors as he thought about that concept. It seemed unimaginable to give away something as valuable as the title of King of the Undead of the Realm. *But what if somebody actually did*, he thought. Daryn turned and leered at Sonny. The entire idea was the opposite of what any logical, reasonable vampire would ever think.

"It's unheard of to even speak words like this."

Sonny coughed a small laugh. "So was my Father's name until a week ago." Sonny shook his head smiling. "I don't fear the future. I would simply do the right thing in that moment and deal with whatever consequences follow."

Daryn felt as he had in the tavern the night before. He looked at his gold winged Gargoyle and had shame for cheating with the Motor Hell again. The entire contest seemed foolish, with all its talk of glory and honor for a race that was designed to award a position of status. A position that bred corruption and promoted obedience to the High Council.

Daryn gently nodded his head as he thought about everything Sonny had just said. He slowly stepped to Sonny.

"Let's ride back to Strigoi, brother, so you may give the title of KOTU to the vampires of the Realm."

Daryn held his hand out. Sonny grabbed it firmly and smiled.

"Hear, hear."

At that exact moment, the noise of iron latches being moved filled the dead air around the Riders. In another moment the hinges cried as the doors began to swing open.

Sonny and Daryn stood frozen and couldn't even dream of what may be on the other side. After the doors had separated completely, nothing but total darkness hung behind them. The Riders glared intently at the void until eventually a shadow moved from the emptiness and toward them. As it came closer they could see that it appeared to be a vampire. It looked similar to them but with ghoulish features. Its skin was pale and grayish. It grasped a staff in its one hand, its bones showed like a skeleton with wet linen for skin draped over them. The creature's clothing was more similar to the traditional vamps of the

Lowlands, but there were peculiar, intricate patterns and designs on the fabric. Much of the clothing seemed to hang on him rather than a tailored fitted. It stood almost a foot taller than either Riders and at fifteen feet from them, it stopped.

The pale creature examined each vampire slowly before finally resting both hands on the top of its staff. It grinded its jaw for a moment, as if pondering the words it would use.

Both Sonny and Daryn wondered if this creature would even speak in their language. Before either could guess how to communicate with it, the pale creature opened its mouth.

"I have seen Riders turn and try to leave. I have seen them strike at the doors. I have even seen them attack each other. But I have never seen them agree to give away their title."

His voice was bizarre and almost hypnotic. It sounded similar to the older vampires in the Realm, but there was a creaking tone at the bottom of its voice. It was similar to the sound a tree makes as it bends in heavy wind or the sound leather boots make as they're stretched over feet. His voice didn't just sound like he was from this forest, it sounded like he was the forest.

Both Riders were fascinated and fairly afraid at what was happening— not because this was a larger creature than them; it wasn't a physical threat he posed as much as that there was something otherworldly about this creature. This was clearly not a vampire of the Realm.

"You," the creature pointed at Sonny. "You arrived here in the lead. Are you the Von Firstenstein?"

Sonny very slowly shook his head.

"Hmm. Oh, well… it's no bother." The creature looked then at Daryn. "Just curious, really."

He then straightened up and cleared his throat.

"I suppose you are both wondering who I am. Maybe even *what* I am. My name is Nosfarious Pike, Baron of Nüemania. Or, as your kind call it, the Forbidden Land."

"Are you… a vampire?" Sonny swallowed hard.

"Ah, yes. Yes indeed." Nosfarius sighed. "I am of the ancient order of the Undead. The *real* vampires of your lore."

The Riders looked at each other in total confusion. Instinctively they pulled closer to each other.

Nosfarious remained icy calm; he had seen this look several times in Pike's Run Riders. He gestured with his hand that he would explain.

"Dear Riders, you are both here to honor the age old tradition of The Pact. The one thousand and eighty-nine year-old agreement between our kinds to stop massacring one another, and exist in peace."

Nosfarious raised his brows.

"You see, my young Riders of the Realm... you are Humans. The Sons of Man. As part of The Pact, your kind were given the gift of immortality. In exchange, we vampires were taught to satisfy our bloodlust with animals. And of course, left alone to exist without the constant threat of extinction by all of Man's hunting and killing machines."

"We... hunted *you*?" Sonny pointed slowly at himself then at Nosfarious.

Nosfarious nodded at them.

"Yes, in your fear of us, the undead, you had all but destroyed our race. To you, we were a plague—just another of the many diseases that were spreading uncontrollably in your rapidly sinking world. So we made a pact, a Blood Oath actually, to stop all the senseless killing."

Nosfarious paused long enough for them to process what he was saying, then squinted at them.

"We offered you the one thing that Man has always sought—particularly as your world was falling apart in front of you. Life everlasting."

Daryn quietly straighten his posture. "Actually, Sir, we only usually exist about eight or nine hundred years. We're not really immortal."

"Yes, well, I suppose there were a few flies in the ointment with that. This was an experiment, after all, that had never been done. But your souls, they belong of The Order, they will endure. Your bodies... well, they can't seem to heal themselves the way ours do. It is no doubt because you were not committed to the Na' Dir, without actually dying and coming back from the dead. You're merely Half-lings, with your original ancestors choosing only to drink vampire blood for six days straight to achieve the gift of life everlasting."

"So we are not dead?" Sonny seemed to be understanding Nosfarious and was surprised by this.

"No. You are still barely alive. Your hearts still beat, even if it is only roughly once per year. And your veins are still filled mostly with human blood. It is the power of the Na' Dir, the ancient Vampires, that sustain your lives."

Sonny and Daryn looked at each other with troubled expressions. They both understood what Nosfarious was saying, but did not want to believe him. It made everything back in the Realm seem like a bad joke. A whole world balancing on a notion that wasn't even true.

"As completely... insane and, almost unbelievable as this all sounds. I think I understand what you are saying." Sonny had been looking up and taking deep breaths. "But if all of what you say is true, why are we here? I mean, what purpose do we have in all this?"

"Yes, and will everything continue to stay the same?" Daryn too understood, but it was overwhelming and he wished he hadn't ever known any of this.

"Excellent." For the first time since he began speaking his tone changed and Nosfarious was pleased. On him that look resembled a bloated reptile that had just swallowed an animal whole. "Usually it takes much longer to get you Half-lings to understand what exactly our situation is."

Nosfarious paused, took a deep breath and looked around. It seemed as though he was finally able to take a moment to taste the air of the Realm. Just as the Riders had noticed a stale, metallic bite to the draft that crept out from behind the doors, it seemed Nosfarious was savoring the smell of pine tar and autumn leaves of the Lowland forest.

"The Pact is renewed every one hundred and twenty-one years. At that time the night sky is in the same position as it was when the first Pact was agreed upon. It's then that I pass this information on to the next of your KO-TUs, firsthand. This way it will be believed and not thought some trickery of your fellow man. It's important that you, and only you, will know of the pact. The problem with your kind is that you like war. If the common man knew that there were ancient vampires to the south, inevitably we would all be back to where we were before The Pact—hunting and killing each other."

Nosfarious looked at Daryn as he spoke.

"It is a hardship to carry this knowledge. The Rules and mandates of your Realm are designed to uphold The Pact and maintain its secrecy. The KOTU before you will guide you and mentor your time, until the next in line comes to these gates."

All at once Daryn was flooded with a wave of realization of his father's burden. Suddenly so much of the hard line that his father had taken over the years made Daryn recognize that he may have been wrong.

"So it's never been a contest," Sonny interrupted, "Why doesn't the ruling family just come for a holiday down here in beautiful Nüemania and you could do this over dinner? Why the whole business of the Pike's Run?"

Nosfarious sighed and turned his attention to Sonny.

"In part, for the spectacle. But also to justify two of your kind coming South into forbidden land."

Both Riders stood quite and waited. They knew there was still the other Rider's fate that had yet to be explained.

Nosfarious waited too. He stared at Sonny for a few moments before creaking slowly, "The other Rider... is sent to honor the second half of The Pact. That Rider, in this case you, will stay here in Nüemania. Your blood will serve to honor our blood lust and guarantee my line authority in our land. You see as ancient, real, if you will, Vampires, human blood affords us power. When I, and my descendants, consume your blood we will be restored to the majestic versions of our kind. We are made more powerful and remain the leaders of Nuemania. And Vampires, like Men, need to be led."

Both Riders were shocked, but Sonny held his palm out at Nosfarious. "Wait, what are you saying? You're going to suck my blood?"

The Baron of Nüemania gently blinked. "No, of course not. Sucking blood is wasteful, not to mention painful. You will endure no pain. You will fall gently to sleep, after which every drop of your blood will be drained and ceremoniously shared with the Order members of Nuemania. You are the Initium, your blood maintains the symmetry in our world. "

Sonny was numb with shock. "I guess... I don't have a choice in this matter."

"This is as it has always been done. This is The Pact between our kind and the reason we live in peace with each other."

Daryn was affected as well, but quickly felt compelled to try and bargain for Sonny's life.

"What if I sent another in his place?"

The Baron sighed.

"Let me guess. You'll offer to return to your Realm and send a criminal, or maybe a lesser of your kind. Someone you feel deserves such a fate. But how then do you get them here without being detected? And who brings the replacement, you? You forget this is the Forbidden Land."

Daryn sighed and looked down at the ground.

"You see, it is done this way because this is what works. Besides… " Nosfarious stared at Sonny, "This is the highest honor with both of our kind. The Initium is our holiest of sacraments. It breaths the very essence of Na' Dir back into our world and keeps order in place. And in your Realm you live on in legend, as a hero—The Rider of the Pike. They sing songs and build statues to your memory. What better way to honor yourself and your people."

Nosfarious turned to Daryn.

"You'd have some random person taken in his stead? A condemned Man?" He shook his head. "Just as it is your destiny to return to your Realm as the King of the Undead," Nosfarious looked at Sonny. "It is your to stay and serve as Initium for Nuemania"

Daryn coughed and began to speak but Sonny held his hand up.

"He's right. This is bigger than us, Daryn. We knew when we began this race that it would end like this. We just didn't know all these other details."

Daryn looked at Sonny with total bewilderment. He respected it but couldn't understand how Sonny could so willingly accept this fate.

As Daryn turned to face Nosfarious, he felt the ancient vampire was ready for this meeting to end. They had been standing in the forest talking for thirty minutes. There weren't tables and chairs there. The Baron wasn't asking how they felt about all of this. And it certainly didn't seem like there was going to be a discussion about if all of this was going to happen.

Daryn looked back at Sonny with a heavy heart. It felt tragic to leave him there. "I'm so sorry, Sonny. I don't know what to say."

After a moment Sonny raised his head up and smiled. "Yeah you do. You tell them I was one Hell of a Rider."

Daryn winced and looked down.

"You tell them that I ran for the honor and the glory of the Realm." Sonny held out his hand. "And you tell Bebe every day that you love her."

Daryn nodded and managed a weary smile back. "I can do that."

Daryn pulled Sonny in and patted his back with his other hand. At that point Sonny looked behind Nosfarious and saw three more of his kind standing with him. To the sides of the road were large shadows with glowing eyes.

Sonny knew instantly that they were HellHounds. After Daryn stepped back, both Riders watched as several more Hellhounds lined the side of the forest road.

Only minutes before Sonny had wondered what exactly was stopping him from simply speeding back toward Iron Gate city. A sad resolve set in at the site of all the Hounds. It seemed to validate everything Nosfarious had said.

Everyone stood silently as Daryn buckled his helmet and straightened his goggles. After he started the Gargoyle up he looked at Sonny one last time and gave a heavy nod. Sonny raised his fist and tried to smile.

Daryn opened up the Gargoyle and was out of site within seconds.

Nosfarious stretched his arm out and waited for Sonny to walk toward him.

"Come, Sonny. The Feast of the Initium starts, and we honor you as a savior."

CHAPTER FORTY:
KING OF THE UNDEAD

The scene in the City Square at Strigoi was festive and loud throughout the night. Vladimir had remained on site for the duration. He was savoring every last morsel of his term as KOTU. He would take the stage several times introducing the various acrobats and jugglers as well as the "Pike's Run Players" that served as musical accompaniment. More than once Vlad had thought the vampire fronting the group had a peculiar style of addressing the crowd. Vanian would wrap his arms around his head, contort himself around the microphone stand and ask the crowd questions with subtle sarcasm and rolling his R's.

'Do you want to Rrrrun for Glory?'

Most people were oblivious or cheered regardless, but as the night wore on, the KOTU began to notice Vanian more and more.

As Vlad sat in the special seating with Tessa and Bebe next to him, he muttered, "There's something so strange about that one."

Bebe looked at the KOTU and then in the direction of where he was staring. Andi sat with Evanna in the next row and in the path of the stage. Bebe assumed the KOTU was talking about Andi smiled.

"Oh, she's actually not a bad girl." Bebe paused and looked at Andi's outrageous outfit. "I mean, she's a little obsessed with weird stuff like human blood and ancient lore, but you know…"

"Excuse me?" The KOTU turned around in his seat and pointed at Andi, who was oblivious to their attention. "That vampire right there? Doctor Kepler's daughter?"

Bebe was surprised at the KOTU's intensity and simply nodded yes back at him.

"What exactly do you mean 'obsessed' with human blood?"

Bebe shrugged and wished she hadn't said a word. "Sonny said that she has, like… made it. From an old recipe or something."

Vlad's eyes narrowed and he turned back to watch Andi. "Is that so."

Bebe swallowed and cleared her throat. She felt as though she had created needless suspicion over something completely impossible.

"But that's ridiculous, right?"

The KOTU kept staring, as if deep in thought. Finally he snapped back from his introspection and grinned.

"Of course, it's nonsense. But these are the sorts of things we need to always be vigilant about. You know, the Bog was created by some young vamps playing around with these absurd notions in a laboratory."

As the hours passed, the crowds had thinned in the Square. There was still merrymaking happening all over the city but it had spilled into the taverns and restaurants of Strigoi. As the clock crept up near four Ante Meridiem and closer to Dawn, the crowds returned to the Square to greet the first Rider.

Hellamina had remained a fixture at the perimeter of the Square but had kept a helmet on and visor down. Many of the R.E.D. would wear their visors since it generated more fear but she also wanted to remain unrecognizable to the members of the SDS that were remaining in the Square that night.

Vlad checked his watch and wondered why they hadn't seen a Rider yet. It had been well over an hour since the first Rider usually returns. He dreaded the thought of anything going wrong in the Forbidden Land.

What Vlad didn't know was that Daryn had a tire go flat on his motorbike, just outside of Ülster, a town about halfway between Port Iron Gate and Strigoi. As he waited while vamps found and replaced his tire, Daryn considered not even coming back to Strigoi and finishing the race. He thought how happy his father would be to inherit another term, and he to wander the Realm. As the local vamps rushed to accommodate him, Daryn realized there could never be an anonymous life as a traveler for him. It was just as The Baron of Nüemania had said, his destiny waited in Strigoi. Daryn made his way back, but he took his time, enjoying the last couple hours of freedom.

When the light of his motorbike had been spotted arriving at the far end of town, the word spread through signals from rooftops like lightning dancing across the sky of Strigoi. The KOTU took the stage and raise his arms. Slowly the crowd hushed to a whisper.

"Within minutes the first Rider will return from the Ninth Pike's Run!"

The crowd cheered then, in a surprisingly orderly fashion, returned to a quite whisper to hear the KOTU speak. Toland and Anastasia had returned to the boxed seating area to sit with Andi and Evanna. The KOTU continued from the stage.

"No matter which Rider it is, we will honor both as heroes of the Realm and celebrate our new King of the Undead!"

Andi squeezed Evanna's hand and the spectators cheered. Two R.E.D. Agents walked out and placed the First Prize trophy on a stand on the stage. Vlad picked it up and held it in his hands for the last time as KOTU. He took a deep breath then shook it at the crowd and yelled.

"Who will take First Prize!?"

The crowd roared with excitement. Bebe and her parents sat with Tessa Von Firstenstein. As the crowd yelled, Andi stole a glance at Bebe behind her. Bebe was smiling nervously and already looking at her. The two girls just stared at each other as they hoped it was their own vampire was on his way into the finish line.

At the edge of the Square a Vamp waved a torch high in the air. The crowd instinctively parted, exposing a straight path from Vlad to the torch. The crowd quieted as the sound of a motorbike screaming toward them filled the Square. Within a minute Daryn launched into view at the edge of the Square.

The Gold Winged Gargoyle screamed through the hushed crowd of the Square and flew across the finish line, skidding dramatically to a stop. Daryn dismounted aggressively and threw his helmet to the crowd. They loved it and exploded with cheers. He waved with his empty hands and the spectators chanted "KOTU! KOTU!"

Bebe ran from the seating area and into his arms. Daryn was surprised how happy he was to see Bebe and all but forgot about the crowd as he kissed her.

Standing behind the new KOTU and Lady KOTU, Vladimir smiled with his arms open as if encouraging the crowd to cheer even more. Vlad grabbed First Prize from the platform and pushed it into Daryn's hand. Daryn looked at his father and nodded. It seemed like an entirely different world from the beginning of that night and Daryn felt differently about his father now. So many of the times his father seemed like a tyrant now seemed to make sense. Daryn still didn't want the job but had a new found respect for the vampire who carried the burden of The Pact.

Vlad just smiled and slowly blinked his eyes at his son. He understood the feeling. Two hundred and twenty years ago he had hated his own father the same way and felt a fool as he stood in the very spot his son was standing at.

"We will talk later," Vlad said quietly. "Now, speak to the Realm as their KOTU."

Daryn paused and looked out at the crowd. He eventually smiled and held First Prize high. After some cheering he bowed his head at them.

"I am humbled by your grace and committed to serving the Realm."

The crowd yelled and cheered. Vlad smiled artificially and leaned in to Daryn's ear. "Only servants are humble, and serving is for a tavern waiter, Son. For the daylights, act like a KING!"

Daryn could hear the anger in his father's voice but Vlad smiled as if he had just given his son a new motorcar. Vlad's words had cut any enthusiasm Daryn had mustered, so the ex-KOTU grabbed the reins.

"All hail the King of the Undead!"

A loud chorus of 'Hip, hip, hooray!' rang through the Square.

Daryn raised his hands to quiet the crowd.

"I would also like to ask that you remember in your hearts and honor the Pike Rider Sonny Legatus. For he left this world in the Forbidden Land."

The crowd sighed collectively. Soon small pockets of the spectators were chanting 'Sonny, Sonny'. Daryn looked sadly at Andi. Her chest heaved and her lips quivered. She felt like her pain was made even worse by the huge mass of vampires chanting her vampire's name.

The KOTU was furious at what was happening in the Square and waved at Vanian to begin a song.

Vanian had been watching with a disgusted look on his face. When the KOTU waved to him he made a farcical bow like a court jester to the King. He looked around cautiously at the other members of the SDS on stage with him and counted off a beat.

The drums pounded and strings joined in before the loud chorus of voices rang out in the opening section of "Light of the Moon."

At once the KOTU, the High Council members and most of the crowd stared in bewilderment at the stage. Although there hadn't been any radical words spoken yet, the sheer nature of this music was not of the Realm folk song variety.

At the same moment Vanian began singing the verse of the song, vampires in traditional clothing walked out from the sides of the stage with banners on sticks. Some of them were Slim's old Anti-Uprising posters and others were newer, much more confrontational messaging—things like 'Reject the Council' and 'Live For The Moment.'

It was shocking to all who watched, but it wasn't until the song reached its chorus and Vanian improvised new lyrics for the occasion that all Hell broke loose.

They say don't look into the light of the Moon.
All our lives they've told us lies,
The Council takes you for fools!

Vlad stood and yelled at the top of his lungs at the R.E.D. Agents all around the Square.

"Take that stage and charge them with blasphemy!"

Immediately R.E.D. Agents began pouring in from every direction to the stage. All of them were in helmets with their visors down. They quickly lined

each side of the stage. They were all fierce and clad in riot gear.

For a moment, not of the Agents did anything. Then the Agent directly in front of Vanian lifted her visor. It was Hellamina. Prior to that, Vanian had been running around prompting his bandmates to dig in and keep playing on in spite of the mounting threat from the Agents. But when he saw Hellamina's face appear from behind that visor his heart sunk and he went limp. He froze with shock and then bewilderment as he tried to quickly imagine why she had worked so hard at getting the SDS to come down and play at the Pike's Run. Vanian was overwhelmed with a feeling of wasted effort and foolishness.

Hellamina looked expressionlessly at Vanian and reached behind her head. She called out to the other Agents.

"BATONS!"

All of the other twelve Agents reached for and drew batons. Vanian was still frozen, but now with the sting of betrayal. Hellamina winked at Vanian and yelled to the Agents, "About face and hold strong!"

With that, every R.E.D. Agent turned and faced out from the musicians, creating a vampire shield of defense for the performers and their sign holding supporters.

Vanian sighed and hung his head. Within a second he was laughing devilishly and then launched into the next verse as if completely mad. Hellamina
stood crouched in front of him and stared at Vlad hatefully, almost challenging
the ex-KOTU to try and stop what was happening.

Vladimir cursed at Hellamina and screamed at the Strigoi militia Captain
to take that stage. The older, local Rule Enforcement officer captain was trying
unsuccessfully to reason with Vlad, but he eventually ran off toward the motorbike pit and then to a small office on the Square.

During that time, younger vampires had emerged from the back of the
stage with even more handmade posters. Viktor Blackheart was among these
vamps and proudly wore his number from his qualifying race at Suntora on
his riding jacket.

Just as the band had begun playing the song all over again, several dozen
uniformed Strigoi militia and volunteers had made their way to the stage. The
Captain walked boldly to Hellamina and told her to stand down. Hellamina
had simply smiled and slowly raised her baton up to tap her visor down. Immediately the Strigoi militia began charging the R.E.D. at the stage.

Batons swinging, kicking and punching, it was a bizarre spectacle of vampires sworn to protect the Realm, fighting tooth and nail against vampires
sworn to protect the Realm. The locals were dropping quickly and none had
gotten past a single Agent. It was brutal to witness and the crowd was soon
begging for the new KOTU to stop it. Vampires were pulling their young away
from view of the stage. Vlad was screaming for more militia or volunteers to
join the fight and Daryn had simply sat down in total despair.

It was then that the same vampire with the torch at the edge of the Square
began waving his fiery beacon wildly. At first, no one even noticed. It was, after all, in the opposite direction of all the action on the stage. But soon a few
vamps at the back noticed and would elbow the vamp next to themselves, and
so on. Talk began to spread like a ripple on water. The wave moved through
the crowd and when it reached the stage, slowly the local militia began standing down. Soon everyone in the Square was watching intently at the far end of
the Square, wondering exactly what was coming. Within a few more moments
the unmistakable sound of a motorbike's engine was bouncing off the iron
structures surrounding the Square and spectators were looking at each other

and chattering.

Andi broke free from the arm her father had placed around her and her mother when the fighting broke out. She ran to the finish line with wide eyes and hands over her mouth with fear.

The noise had brought total silence to the Square by the time the Cafe Racer came barreling through the opening at the far edge of Strigoi's City Square. The motorbike tore over the finish line and rolled widely around the crowd. The spectators continued to step aside as the motorbike waded back into the crowd, toward the middle of the Square.

When the engine was finally cut off, the Rider calmly stepped off the bike and looked around. Mud and dirt were caked on his face and helmet. He began walking slowly through the crowd toward the stage. The crowd was still very quiet but gradually began to slowly chant his name with a whisper. Daryn walked out to intercept the Rider before he could climb onto the stage. Vlad stood behind his son with utter disbelief.

At first Daryn was smiling as he met the muddied Rider on the Square. But quickly his expression became confused when the Rider simply stood there, silently.

"Sonny, is that you?" Daryn looked sideways at the filthy Rider.

Vlad came quickly from behind his son and squinted his eyes. "Is this the Rider Sonny Legatus?" Vlad yelled.

The Rider unbuckled his helmet. He paused and then ripped the helmet and goggles from his head in one fell swoop. He spit and shook his head before looking at intently back at Vladimir Von Firstenstein.

"Yes. I'm the Rider who left here tonight... " Sonny smiled at the crowd.

"But my name is Sebastian Nightshade."

END OF BOOK ONE.

GLOSSARY

Able-All: An old battle cry of the Realm's KOTU or similarly official militias. It was issued at time of crisis and meant that all able-bodied vampires were needed to serve and/or protect the Realm's interests. When an Able-All is issued, no one can refuse.

Agent Tarc: A HellHound that works with the R.E.D., in particular with Agent Hellamina Muntz.

Agricultural Agenda: The department in charge of issuing policy for growers and blood marketers. Overseen by the High Council.

Anastasia Kepler (Ana): Toland's wife, Andromeda's mother. Owner of Gallery Ophelia.

Andromeda Kepler (Andi): Born 1035 ADWB. 54 years old. Lives in Bridgeway district with her parents, Toland and Anastasia Kepler.

Briana Bellmore (Bebe): Born 1033 ADWB. 56 years old. Lives with her parents, Alexander and Tessa Bellmore, in the Bridgeway district of the Capital.

Blood Berries: A hybrid fruit made from synthesizing animal flesh and cranberries and grown in the Lowlands. First synthesized by scientist Leximanus Kepler.

Blood Bog Fever: An infection vampires can contract from improperly filtered blood berries.

Blood Oath: In an agreement between Vampires, a blood oath is taken to request that the supernatural powers that be will intervene and destroy any vampire that breaks their end of the agreement. In reality, and under Realm Rule, this would allow any vampire to swiftly and without any repercussion, execute a vampire who violated such an oath. It is an oath so powerful it is thought to have implications on one's afterlife if one was to dishonor it.

Blood Wagons: Street vendors push or drive these carts, selling blood products.

Borgo Aref: The Bellmores' valet.

Cheshko Billings: KOTU Von Firstenstein's driver/chauffeur.

Common Bats: Slang to describe Vampires of lesser means. Usually used by Upperlanders to describe Lowlanders or any rural vampire.

Daryn Von Firstenstein: Born 1032 ADWB. 57 years old. Son of Vladimir Von Firstenstein, the sitting King of the Undead of the Realm.

Day that Death Was Born: The first day of measured time in the Realm, after the last human was killed.

Dayhouse: A structure that shields vampires from the sunlight. They come in all shapes and sizes, though dayhouse usually refers to the large and extra-large versions. Most every town or city has public dayhouses, some that could even cover a small town, and contain homes and merchants' stores. It's not uncommon to find smaller dayhouses scattered around the countryside as a refuge for travelers. No one is ever denied entrance to a dayhouse; it's a Rule of the Realm. However, in more remote towns it's common for some dayhouses to be frequented by groups of vampires who ultimately claim them as their own, making it uncomfortable for outsiders.

Demon: Or "Little Demon." Nickname of the air intake device Andi Kepler designed for use on the Cafe Racer. The device is built onto the engine and uses exhaust to force more air back into the engine, creating a more powerful explosion and a greater output of power.

Dooners: Slang for Baldooners, vampires from the northernmost territory and or city of Baldoon.

Dorrenesh Dupree: Assistant scientist at K&S.

Erik Von Castlekuhn: Son of a High Council Member with a presumed Specialty of Realm Rule.

Evanna Legatus: Sonny's mother. As a young girl, she worked as a teacher and tutor before choosing her Specialty in Administration at Bellmore Industries.

First Prize: The trophy awarded to the winner of the Pike's Run. It was rumored to be the skull of the last human killed before the Day that Death was Born. It has a dagger with a bat handle plunged into the skull and mounted on a black rock base.

Fledgling: A male or female vampire in their early years of existence. Usually refers to their first 60 years.

Focus Interviews: Officially called "Focus on your Future" interviews, they were conducted on young vampires as they neared the end of their Fledgling years, usually around fifty-five to sixty years of age, to determine what career path is best suited for them.

Geezers: Nickname of the officials who, among other things, taste the motorbike fluids at the Pike's Runs. These elder judges are also in charge of inspecting motorbikes for additives and use of superstitious trinkets or imagery. The Run at Suntora Flats is the first of the qualifying runs where these Elders start inspecting motorbikes.

Healthy Blood: A triple filtered, purified version of blood berry juice, marketed by Raymond Kepler—Toland's father and Andi's grandfather.

Hell Blood: Fermented Healthy Blood, the triple-filtered blood berry drink.

Hellamina Muntz: Born 795 ADWB. 294 years old. Detective in the R.E.D. Also the one and only female to ever ride in qualifying runs of the Pike. In the Fourth Pike, 847 ADWB, she made it all the way to the Top Eight in Black Lake before losing a Run.

Hellfire Incident: When a vampire is out in the light too long, catches fire, and is destroyed. Almost always these occur from being intoxicated and passing out somewhere exposed.

HellHounds: Ancient order of canines found mostly in or near forests of the Realm. They communicate with each other through speech ("Hündesh"). Very few vampires can understand their tongue. Theoretically they served vampires as daytime sentinels but the HellHounds of the Realm have grown continually distant over time. The Hell-Hounds of the northern forests have remained friendly toward people in their area, largely due to the Tamerlane people's effort to work with them (they call them "Hel-lunds"). The HellHounds that work with farmers in parts of the Lowlands and on the southern plains, however, are less cooperative and much more reclusive—even hostile toward vampires.

Houses of the Holy Union: Vampire wedding.

Hündesh: The language of the HellHounds, sounding similar to other canine barking but with 'kha' and 'esh' noises. Almost no vampires can speak or understand Hündesh. The expression "Speaking Hündesh" is commonly used when someone didn't understand something but could also refer to being very intoxicated.

Incubator: A heated appliance used for keeping blood and blood-related products warm.

Julian Evermore: Bartender at the Lumper's Head in Strigoi.

Kharis Archway: A suspension bridge that crosses the Great Crimson River outside of Strigoi. The Kharis is an innovation in Vampire architecture and joins the East and West regions of the Realm.

King of the Undead: "KOTU." A title bestowed upon the winner of the Pike's Run motorbike race. Though not an actual ruling position, it does carry much prestige and duties include officiating the Realm's most important functions. The KOTU can also carry weight on policy decisions in the Realm and is in many ways the mouthpiece of the High Council.

Knuckles Bonnelli: Bartender at the Owl in the Grenish district of the Capital.

Leshka Reese: Keplers' housekeeper. Originally from the Baldoon region in the north.

Leximanus Kepler: Born 2041 AD- Demise 566 ADWB. 625 years old at time of passing. Andis Kepler's grandfather and Toland Kepler's father. Creator of Blood Berries.

Light of the Moon: The signature song by the Sweet Death Symphony that challenges the conventional notions of the older vampires by suggesting to defiantly look into the light of the moon. The folklore associated with staring into the moonlight is that even though it is indirect sunlight, it is harmful. Symbolic of doing the 'wrong thing.'

Lowlanders: Vampires living in the southern plains and western region of the Realm.

Lucious Creed: Daryn Von Firstenstein's head mechanic.

Lumpers: Vampires who did the tedious work of off-loading cargo from ships in Iron Gate as they arrived from the northern ports.

Marius Mockba: Capital resident and Rider of the Pike that ranked in the Top Four. Son of a High Council Member.

Millington Brimstone: Son of a High Council Member and Rider in the qualifying Pike Runs.

Motor Hell: Official project name: Molecular Hydrocarbon Latency Laboratory. An industrial lubricant that greatly reduces the friction and chemical breakdown that petroleum based oils succumb to. Synthesized by Toland Kepler at Kepler & Sons.

Penny Whistle: Cheap pig blood liquor.

Pig Ale: Cheap and crudely fermented pig blood.

Raymond Kepler: Toland Kepler's father and creator of the Healthy Blood product, a triple-filtered blood berry drink.

Realm Rule: The Rules that govern vampires' conduct.

River Rasputin: Flows from the peaks of the Capital City mountains and through the west sections of the city.

Rule Enforcement Division (R.E.D.): Protection officers with Realm-wide jurisdiction that enforce the Rules of the High Council.

Seven Notes of the Pike: A short musical scale, usually played on a horn, at the assembly of any of the Pike's Runs. It's meant to call all Riders to the line to prepare for a race start.

Slim Jim: "Slim." Born 698 ADWB. 391 years old. Jack-of-all-trades vampire who lives in the garage near the edge of Legatuses' property. Atypical for a middle-aged vampire, he had traveled the Realm and did not keep a particular Specialty. At one time he had the iron ore mining Specialty, but gave it up after the uprising of 767 ADWB.

Sonny Legatus: Sebastian "Sonny" Mach Legatus. Born 1035 ADWB. 54 yrs old. Lives in Brimberg district of Capital with his mother, Evanna Legatus.

Specialty: Field of employment or career in the Realm.

Sturmer Von Schlieben: Large doorkeeper and brother of Vanian Von Schlieben.

Suicide Plots: The land in the far east region of the Lowlands, designated specifically for the burials of vampires who committed suicide. Because suicide is an immortal sin, it is said to deny the soul entry into the Kingdom of the Dead. The land where a suicide is consecrated is considered cursed.

Sweet Death Symphony (SDS): A group of musicians who get together and play rebellious songs in and around the Capital City. Most of their messaging encourages Fledgling-aged vampires to ignore choosing a Specialty or planning for the future, and instead encourages living in "the moment."

Teddy Krauss: Junior doctor and assistant scientist at K&S.

The Begrafen: The prayer spoken at a Hellfire Incident, usually by the King of the Undead, but in his absence the oldest vampire present is required to recite the words: "Our fallen Brother (or Sister) has left this world to join the souls of our ancestors, and to begin everlasting life in the Kingdom of the Dead. May the keepers of the kingdom let this soul pass."

The High Council: A collection of affluent vampires whose exact numbers and identities aren't common knowledge. They make all policy in the Realm.

The Pike's Run: A motorcycle race that occurs every one hundred and twenty-one years. It is open to any male vampire between the ages of 50 and 250 years. The winner is titled the King of the Undead of the Realm. There are a total of eight qualifying races that produce the two Riders who compete in the final Pike's Run race. The final race leaves the city of Strigoi and heads west past Emeraldblood, then southwest toward Thana and the Suicide Plots, then south through Port Iron City and then south into the Forbidden Land. In the history of the Pike only one Rider returns from the Forbidden Land, rides across the plains and back to Strigoi to be the new King of the Undead (KOTU).

Toland Kepler: Scientist at Kepler & Sons. Andromeda's father. Grandson of Leximanus Kepler, creator of Blood Berries.

Unspeakable: Any event or settlement ruled an "Unspeakable" by the High Council cannot be mentioned publicly or privately. It's not often that an Unspeakable is issued, but when done it most certainly must be adhered to by all.

Upperlanders: Vampires living in the mountainous, mid-country region of the Realm. Generally considered anything north of Strigoi and south of the Forest of the North.

Uprising of 767 ADWB: A conflict that broke out between the Iron Ore and Coal Miners at work on Mount Cain in the Fall of 767 resulting in dozens of vampires being destroyed. In an effort to put pressure on the coal miners to increase coal production, the iron ore mining company began terrorizing coal miners and their families in and around the site. The iron ore organization leaders were convinced the low coal production was a deliberate act by the coal leaders to drive the price up and couldn't be reasoned with. The R.E.D. was called in to settle the conflict, but the small number of Agents sent were ineffective, and they became stranded in the mountains for the winter. It resembled a war with R.E.D. Agents and coal miners defending themselves from the mobs of iron ore workers. Iron worker Slim Jim defected and joined the R.E.D. Agents and coal miners, and played a instrumental role as an activist, by convincing vampires to "volunteer" to fight with the coal miners' cause. The sitting KOTU, Dracov Von Firstenstein was also a silent partner of the iron ore mining company. Although he publicly sent the R.E.D. to dissolve the uprising, he had a vested interest in the iron ore miners successfully leveraging the coal miners to release more coal. Because of his activism, the weight of Dracov's resentment for the iron ore workers' lack of success fell squarely on Slim Jim.

Valentino Vossen: From Enoch, near the Dead Hills. One of the Top Four Riders in the Pike's Run. At the qualifying run in Hunedora, he let out a chilling screech in the home stretch that effectively shocked his competitor enough to allow Valentino to barely win and rank Fourth, advancing to the Top Four Run in the Capital.

Valkries Market: Small specialty store in the Market district of Capital City.

Vanian Von Schlieben: Originally from Hunedora. An artist and musician who lives in the Grenish district of Capital City. Has a brother, Stürmer.

Viktor Blackheart: From Port Iron Gate. Pike Rider that didn't make it past the first Suntora Flats qualifying run.

Vladimir Von Firstenstein: Born 703 ADWB. 386 years old. Son of Dracov Von Firstenstein. A two-term KOTU (847-1089).

Wolfgang Snagov: One of the Final Two Riders in the Fourth Pike's Run. Coined the popular phrase "Run for Glory."

Year that Death was Born: The First year of measured time in the Realm, after the last human was killed in the year of Man 2067 AD.

ABOUT THE AUTHOR

Deano Jones is a musician, graphic designer, improvisor, actor and comedian.

Living in New York City during the 90's Deano fronted the theatrical punk band Clowns for Progress.

Since moving to Austin in 2005, Deano has recorded music as a solo artist and is a regular performer in Austin's thriving improv comedy scene.

He runs a graphic design company and has a small army of French and American Bulldogs at his castle in Austin, Texas.

Made in the USA
Las Vegas, NV
09 March 2022

45300445R00213